ISBN: 978-1-7386194-2-9

A BOND IN FLAMES

SHERILEE GRAY

Author Note

I can't believe we've reached the end of The Thornheart Trials Series! A Bond in Flames is my fortieth published book and one that I'm super proud of! I love this vast, dark and twisty world, and I hope you do too, because I have so many stories I want to write in and around Roxburgh... and in case you missed it, the hounds are coming next and Relic is up first!

As for Zinnia and Death's story... let's just say they led the way and I followed. Like all my stories in this world there are dark vibes and themes, and I also play fast and loose with Greek and Latin mythology—in that, I take little bits of what I want, leave the rest, and twist it to suit my characters and stories—and A Bond in Flames is no different.

But most importantly, I want to thank you so much for coming along on this journey with me! I've been writing and publishing for over ten years, and I appreciate every single reader who has taken a chance on one of my books. It honestly means everything to me. I wouldn't still be here without you!

Yes, this is the last book in The Thornheart Trial Series, but it isn't the end, there is so much more to come!

Playlist

- Bring me to life - Evanescence
- My Immortal - Evanescence
- The Kill - Thirty Seconds to Mars
- Crawling - Linkin Park
- Down in a Hole - Alice In Chains
- Can We Kiss Forever? – Kina
- Hurt - Nine Inch Nails
- Fade Into you - Mazzy Star
- Nothing Compares 2 U - Chris Cornell

Prologue

Zinnia

ROSE LOOKED INTO THE MORTAR. "Will there be enough?"

"That's just for you." I took the blade from my pack, sliced both palms, and smeared blood all over my naked body.

My sweet cousin's eyes widened. "What will that do?"

I flashed her a grin, refusing to let her see my fear. "Boost the hell out of my power... and make me look badass. I'm coming face-to-face with Death. I plan on making a memorable first impression."

She stared at me in disbelief. "But your soul... you need the oil."

"My soul is going to be just fine. It's going to be okay, Roe, I promise," I lied. This was far from fine, but there was no other choice, not for me, not anymore.

Rose quickly finished covering her body with the oily potion, and I took her hand.

The pile of stones rumbled behind us, and we spun around as the ground shook, the earth rolling beneath our feet as if it were trying to force Rose to let me go. Her hand slipped in my blood-covered one, but we linked fingers, holding tight.

The stones rolled, reforming, revealing skulls, as if the bones had been fossilized in each one, empty eye sockets and jaws hanging wide. When they stopped, we were staring into a gateway —right into Limbo.

It was dark on the other side, shadowed, cold. A thumping sound echoed in the distance, rolling through the portal. It was a slow, steady beat, growing in volume until I felt the thump in my bones.

Death.

Rose trembled.

He was coming for her.

She squeezed my hand. "What should I say?"

The wind became violent, her blonde hair whipping around her lovely face. I squeezed her hand in return. "Let me do the talking," I called over the raging storm.

The rumbling sound was constant now, the icy blast making it hard to draw breath.

Then I saw him.

A shroud of moving shadows. He kept coming until he stood on the other side of the gate, so tall, he towered over us. I watched, unable to breathe as he lifted the twisted wooden staff in his hand, glowing with power, and thumped it one last time against the ground.

The wind stopped in an instant, the world seeming to still around us.

I gasped for breath, and I felt Rose's fear spike higher. I tightened my hand on hers. I'd seen Death once before, when he came to me in a nightmare and turned my world upside down. He had to be close to seven feet tall and was completely concealed, except for a thin, tattooed hand gripping his wooden staff and blue eyes that glowed from beneath his hood.

We waited as that frigid glare moved between us.

"I told you to come alone," he said to Rose.

The deep way his voice resonated, arctic and terrible, washed over me, invoking a multitude of emotions—grief and heartbreak, loneliness and despair, but worse, oh goddess, the pure, raw horror. It took everything in me not to fall to the ground, shaking and sobbing.

I had to be strong, though, for Rose, for my entire family. "I'm afraid you can't have her," I said and hoped like hell he didn't hear the waver in my voice.

Rose moved closer to me, and I held on to her tight.

Death studied me for several long seconds. "And you think you can stop me from taking what I'm owed?"

"If you take Rose's soul, you'll be interfering with a bargain between Lucifer and her sister's mate. Lucifer granted immortality to the Thornheart sisters if they mated. Rose is mated. She can't die."

Rose spun to me, shocked.

Death grew larger before my eyes, his grip on the staff so tight, the wood creaked.

I pushed on, refusing to back down. I couldn't. "If you make an enemy of Lucifer, there'll be a war. You'll disturb the balance between the four realms."

Death made an inhuman sound that sent spikes of terror through me. "She doesn't need to die to enter my world, witch. I can take her as she is. Her soul will still be mine."

"Rose's brother-in-law is Lucifer's alpha hellhound, a male he considers a friend. Do you think Lucifer will let that stand?" I said, trying to sound as strong as I could in the face of his immense power.

"The bargain grants her immortality, not where she'll live out eternity. Lucifer will have no grounds to start a war."

His voice made me want to cover my ears and scream.

"Come here, Rose," he said to my cousin.

She turned to me, shaking, teeth chattering. "It's okay."

Death held out his hand.

I held on to her tighter.

"It's okay," she said again, taking a step forward.

I pulled her back. It was time.

"You did all you could, but you can't stop this. No one can," Rose said.

Gritting my teeth, I turned from her and back to Death, my heart beating fast. I wanted to run the fuck away from here so badly; instead, I stared into his cold gaze. "It's not Rose you want. It's me."

Rose spun to face me. "What?"

Death stilled.

"You've been searching for me for a long time, but I made sure you couldn't find me. I hid, using this." I lifted my arm, showing him the tattoo. "I'm the one you want, the one you've been waiting for." Releasing Rose's hand, I stepped forward. "You came to me in my dreams when I was fifteen years old. You told me who I was, what you wanted from me, and I ran. Do you remember?"

Death said nothing, his tall frame stilling under his cloak.

"I woke up after that first visit from you, and I refused to go back to sleep until I found a way to keep you out of my head. It cost me, but I did it."

Death leaned forward, still in his realm, but right at the edge. "Who are you?" he demanded.

Scooping up my blade from the ground, I pressed it to my forearm and, with a cry, sliced the small tattoo from my arm, removing the mark I'd worn on my skin for the last thirteen years. "Your birthright. I was born to be your consort, Mors," I said, using Death's true name.

He jerked back, then flew forward again, hand outstretched, but unable to reach me.

"Zinnia, no," Rose cried.

I turned to her, holding my cousin's horrified stare. "I've been running from this for a long time. He was drawn to your soul because of me. I need to make this right, to protect our family and our coven."

"Don't do this," she choked.

"You were willing to sacrifice yourself for your coven, Roe. And so am I. It's the only way."

"Come to me, consort," Death said, so deep and menacing, it chilled me to my core.

I straightened my spine and turned to him. "Your consort must enter Limbo willingly, and I will go with you, but I have a condition."

"Name it," he said.

All his focus was on me now, as if Rose no longer existed.

"Zinnia, don't do this. There has to be another way," she said.

"I have a sister who needs me, and I won't abandon her. I'll come with you, but only if I'm free to move between realms."

"No."

"That's my condition."

He was silent for several long moments. "Each time you visit, you must remain with me for at least one lunar month before returning to your realm."

"Then I want a lunar month here as well."

Death made a sound raw and violent. "I will agree, but only until your sister's eighteenth birthday. After that, you will remain here with me."

"Her twenty-first birthday," I countered.

He shook his head, about to argue.

"If you agree, I'll leave with you now," I said.

He was quiet for a moment, then finally inclined his head. "But know this, consort, if you fail to return to me, the bargain is void. I will come for you, and when I have you back, I'll never let you leave."

"Understood," I said. "And if you refuse to let me leave, same deal, the bargain is void. And I promise you, I'll find a way to escape, and you'll never see me again."

"Don't do this," Rose sobbed beside me.

I closed the space between us and pulled her into a tight hug. "I knew this day would come, Roe. I can't hide anymore. It's done." I looked into her eyes. "Take care of Jazzy for me, and Hemlock. It's only four weeks, and then I'll be back."

"Thank you," Rose choked out.

I tucked her hair behind her ear. "I want a party when I get home, okay? Something to look forward to."

"You've got it," she whispered.

"Consort," Death said, making me jolt.

I stepped away from my cousin, grabbed my clothes, shoved them in my pack, and turned to Death. He held out his hand as I strode up to him. "Pass on the hand holding. I'm not a fan of PDA," I said, then turned back to my sweet cousin, blew her a kiss, and walked through the archway and into Limbo.

The gate closed immediately, locking me in.

I was naked and covered in my own blood. A moment ago, I'd felt powerful—not now. Now I felt vulnerable and alone, but there was no way in hell I was showing the god staring down at me that. Death stood tall on the path of skulls, a path that disappeared into the dark forest surrounding us. He was concealed by his cloak that moved around his body like a living shadow.

Dropping my pack, I quickly pulled on my clothes and shoved my feet in my boots, then looked up at him. "Well?" I said, when he said nothing. "I assume we follow the path?"

"Do not veer off it."

At the sound of his voice, my knees almost buckled under me. Somehow, I locked them before I fell to the ground and screamed. "Awesome. Let's get going, then." I strode ahead and immediately wished I hadn't as creatures I couldn't make out darted along beside us, disappearing into the forest. Branches cracked as if something large was moving through the trees close by. Shrieks and strange mournful howls from animals I did not recognize echoed around us. And Death himself, right behind me. Goddess, I felt him there every step of the way.

I didn't think it actually took that long, but with Death looming behind me, it felt like an eternity before we rounded a bend and a huge black stone castle came into view. It jutted up from the ground, imposing and dreadful, and it took everything inside me not to just *run*. Even though there was nowhere for me to go, the urge to run was almost impossible to resist.

We walked up its wide steps, to the massive arched doors, and they instantly swung open. A horned demon stood there. His skin was leathery and mottled green. His eyes were scarlet, and he had pointed, shiny black horns. I grabbed my knife.

"No," Death rumbled behind me.

My knife was snatched from my hand.

"Egon is my servant. You will not harm him."

Egon backed away, staring at me in an odd way, a look in his eyes that I couldn't read. Death kept coming, still close behind me, directing me to a wide black staircase without a word.

My stomach was in barbed knots when we reached the second floor. I was his wife for all intents and purposes, and I'd made a deal to be with him. Nausea churned in my stomach.

You can survive this. Whatever happens next, you have to survive this. Jasmine needs you.

Wall sconces lit the way, making the stone hall gleam, and macabre shadows danced along the walls. Something scurried in the dark, and I had to bite back my shriek.

Death stepped in front of me, forcing me to stop suddenly. I stared up at him, fear in my throat so thick, it damn near choked me. Those glowing blue eyes watched me from under his hood as he reached out and shoved the door open beside me.

"Your quarters," he said, and with every word, his voice vibrated with a rage that I didn't understand. "This is where you will sleep. You may move freely throughout the castle. If you go outside, always stick to the path." The words he said didn't match the fury in his voice, which rolled off him in heavy waves. "There is no escape and nowhere to hide. Running is pointless. I will always find you." Then he turned and walked away.

Chapter One

Zinnia

Eighteen months later

A ROAR ECHOED down the hall, and I shot up in bed. It was deep and filled with agony and sent ice shooting down my spine. Hemlock scurried onto my lap; my familiar was the fiercest little rat in existence, but even he found those roars of pain unsettling. I ran my hand down his back to soothe us both.

The sound of Death's bedroom door opening was closely followed by the heavy thud of his boots as he strode past my room and down to his brother.

Somnus, his twin and the personification of sleep, lived in the castle as well. I'd yet to see him awake, though, and sometimes, like tonight, he roared and made awful noises for hours, as if the god were being flayed alive in his dreams.

He was also how Death first visited me when I was just a teenager, so it was a good thing he stayed asleep because the god was not one of my favorite people.

Hemy ran up my arm and tucked himself against my neck.

There'd be no sleep tonight for anyone, not with Somnus having one of his episodes.

Sliding my hand under the pillow, I grabbed my knife, scooped up Hemlock, and slipped out of bed. Easing the door open, I checked that the way was clear, then rushed down the hall.

Somnus's door was ajar, and I could hear Death's voice rumbling low from inside. Just hearing him talk used to make me tremble in fear and horror. Yes, there was still some fear, and on occasion, I was overcome by the volatile emotions that he was able to evoke in me, but I'd been coming and going from this place long enough now that I'd managed to gain some control over my responses to him. Well, I had until I arrived back a week ago. I'd gone to the library to let him know I'd returned as instructed and found Death *without* his cloak. I'd never seen him without it before and it wasn't something I'd ever forget.

"You came," he said, his voice rolling over me like thunder.

Words he said every single time. It took me several attempts to reply. I was having trouble catching my breath. "L-like I had a choice," I said, like I always did, but this time, my voice shook.

He carefully placed his glass on the mantel and turned to me, firelight dancing across his features.

I took an abrupt step back. Mors was... terrifying, his features etched by violence and carved by death, and so utterly beautiful, it was hard to look at him.

His face was free of ink, and he had a prominent nose, high cheekbones, a strong jaw, and sensual dark crimson lips.

"Your robe?" I rasped.

"I no longer require it."

He'd said it in that deep, terror-evoking voice, shaking me to the depths of my core, and offered nothing more. After eighteen months of not knowing what he looked like beneath that dark shroud that covered him from head to foot, it had been a major shock, and it was still taking some getting used to.

Before the cloak came off, all I knew was the brutal intensity and raw power that poured off him. I hadn't been able to see the way he watched me or, goddess, feel the lightning strike when his glacial gaze pierced right through me. Every time that stare locked on mine, it caused shards of ice to shoot through my chest and down to my gut, and since finding him like that, I'd felt as off-balance as I had the first time I'd come here.

The god was inscrutable, watchful, stubborn, infuriating, and confusing as hell, and I didn't know him any better now than I did that first cold, wintry night he'd brought me to his castle. In fact, somehow, I knew him even less.

Doing my best to ignore the constantly moving shadows and the weight of a multitude of invisible eyes watching me, I darted into the library, shut the door, and climbed into the massive leather chair that sat in front of the always-blazing fire. Curling up, I dragged the fur that Egon left draped over the wide arm for me across my lap while Hemy scurried down from his spot tucked against my neck, settling in under it as well. I didn't know what it was about this room, but spending time in here was the closest thing to peace I'd found inside this castle. Maybe it was all the books, the smell of leather, that reminded me of home, of the library in Aunt Daisy's house or the rows of spell and recipe books in Aunt Else's workroom.

The book I'd been reading was still in its spot, on the deep mahogany table beside the chair, and I picked it up—

Somnus roared again, so loud that the windows rattled. Hemlock trembled, and a cold chill skated down my spine.

I covered Hemy's back with my hand to calm him. I hadn't known if it was safe for him here in Limbo the first time I came, so I'd left my tiny familiar at home. It'd been extremely hard on both of us.

But this was my life now.

Even though my family at home in Roxburgh was still desperately trying to find a way to get me out of this bargain, I knew there was no escape.

And deep down, I thought they did too. Jazzy's twenty-first birthday would be here before we knew it, and my visits home would end. I'd be trapped here in Limbo with Death, in this castle, for the rest of my life.

I ran my fingers over the scar on my forearm, where I'd cut out the markings given to me by a demon—a different bargain that had kept me hidden from Death for thirteen years until I couldn't hide anymore. The price I'd paid for it was immense, but even then, deep down, I'd known my reprieve was only temporary.

In the end, it had all been my choice—protecting my cousin, my coven; leaving my sister; and coming here. Yes, an impossible one, but a choice all the same, and one I'd make again and again.

That meant I had to make my peace with it, with saying goodbye for good, with never seeing my family or Jasmine ever again.

I woke to the clink of ice against crystal.

Blinking the sleepiness away, I lifted my head from the arm of the chair, and my heart immediately leaped into my throat before I snatched up my knife.

Death stood in front of the fire, a drink in hand—watching me.

I sat up straighter. My body had instantly sensed the threat and reacted before my mind fully had a chance to engage. His gaze dipped to the knife now gripped in my hand, his brow lifting. I shrugged. What did he expect?

He was shirtless, as he often was now, in only a pair of black trousers that sat low on his hips. I tried not to stare at the shadows the fire created on his skin or the way they danced over the taut ridges of his muscled chest, but it was hard. That smooth, hairless, inked body was as beautiful and terrifying as the rest of him. The very thought of touching him was so utterly absurd and wrong and frightening, it was laughable. It'd be like petting a beast capable of eating you whole or swimming in lava or touching the sun—unthinkable.

He took a sip of his drink and ran a hand over his tattooed skull.

I waited for him to say something; he didn't.

Death looked tired.

The room was still dimly lit, but it was morning. There was no sun here in Limbo; there was the illusion of one, though, and light filtered through the arched windows.

"A little early for that, isn't it?" I said, eyeing the amber liquid in his glass instead of looking directly at him. I couldn't take the silence any longer, not with all that turbulent energy radiating from him.

"You didn't sleep in your bed," he said, ignoring my comment.

"What gave it away?"

He ignored my sarcasm. "Why?"

"Because I didn't want to." Hemlock poked his head out from under the fur. He'd become bolder around Death lately, and I'd noticed a look in his cute, beady eyes that was beginning to look alarmingly a lot like worship when he gazed at our jailer.

"Somnus kept you awake?" he asked.

"He kept the whole castle awake." If it wasn't Somnus screaming in his sleep, it was Death playing his piano—dark and mournful songs that I'd never heard before and made you want to curl in a ball and sob. I shoved the fur aside and stood, holding Hemy to me. "I need a shower."

"You will eat first. Meet me in the dining room in fifteen minutes."

I paused, fighting down my natural instinct to tell him to go fuck himself and his orders, but I'd been there and done that, and it'd gotten me nowhere, so I bit back what I wanted to say and carried on toward the door.

Are you just going to roll over and stop fighting?

No, I wasn't. I would never stop. If I wanted a goddamn shower first, I'd have one. I turned back to tell him so and froze.

Death had his back to me, facing the fire. He held the fur I'd been wrapped in all night in his hand—and it was pressed to his face.

I spun and darted off on silent feet. Death hadn't touched me, not in all the months I'd been coming here, even though he called me his consort. After that first night when nothing happened, I'd been relieved. Then, as the months drew on and still he didn't demand more from me, I'd actually started to feel... even more off-balance. Yes, I was thankful, but if not that, what did Death want from me? Why was I here?

Then he'd gone and taken off the cloak, after all this time, and I had no idea why or what it meant, but it had to mean something, right? And now he was smelling the fur I'd slept with?

I rubbed my arms, now covered in gooseflesh, and rushed into my room, shutting myself in.

The room he'd given me was large and filled with antiques and trinkets. It was like someone had just gotten up and walked out, leaving everything behind. It also had its own sitting area, but I didn't use it. I wasn't sure why, only that I got this odd, queasy feeling when I did and an ache in my chest that I didn't understand, which was why I preferred the library.

I sat Hemy on the bed that was shoved in the corner like an afterthought, snatched up some clothes, and quickly showered. I may be his prisoner, but I wasn't going to just give up and obey every one of his unreasonable demands. Still, I didn't linger. I needed to make a stand, but I didn't want to make him angry either.

Death was already sitting at the massive black lacquer table when I walked in.

He eyed me over his mug, gaze sliding from head to foot and back. "You ignored my order."

"Are you surprised?" I said and sat, smiling at Egon when he put a cup of tea in front of me, just the way I liked it, smelling of the fragrant herbs I'd grown.

I'd planted the herbs I needed in the kitchen garden. I was a witch—being without my herbs wasn't something I could tolerate. Death hadn't said anything when I'd brought a bagful of seedlings my third month coming here and made room for myself in his grounds. It was bad enough my medium powers were greatly hindered here, which was not surprising. I was in Limbo, after all. There was no need for souls to communicate with me; I didn't even know where the hell they were. Honestly, I had no idea how this realm worked. Thankfully, my magic was still okay.

"No," he said, his long, thick, tattooed fingers curling tighter around his mug. "I'd be more surprised if you actually did as I asked of you, consort."

"You don't ask—you demand. In case you haven't worked it out yet, I don't like orders." I smiled at Lyle, Egon's adult son, when he placed my overnight oats beside my tea. "Thanks, Lyle." He gave me a quick grin and hustled back to the kitchen.

"Eventually, you will learn my way is best," Death said. "In all things."

"Well, that's not going to happen," I said, scooping up a spoonful of oats and shoving it in my mouth. Something moved through his eyes; they kind of brightened, or maybe I was imagining it.

"Since we missed our evening drink, we'll make up for it now. I'll go first," he said.

Dammit, I'd hoped he'd forgotten. I shook my head. "You went first last time."

Death had pulled on a shirt—it was black—but he'd only done up a couple of buttons, so most of his chest was visible. It was as if he didn't like wearing clothes or could barely tolerate them. I wanted a better look at his tattoos, but I didn't want to stare. I'd caught glimpses of them but not a good look—again, because staring was not something I wanted him to catch me doing. The only one that was easy to see was the star that covered most of his chest. The center of it was decorated in swirls that created the appearance of shadows and light.

He sat back in his seat. "Your answer the night before was unsatisfactory. So I'll go first."

"And you gave me the same answer you do every time," I fired back.

"Because, so far, that has been the only answer required."

Our nightly drink took place in the library and consisted of us each asking the other a question. I'd refused when he'd first proposed it. The last thing I'd wanted was to spend any more alone time with Death. When I'd denied him, he'd raged for hours, throwing an epic tantrum. Then, when my cousin Magnolia had inadvertently pissed him off during her trial, I'd been forced to barter with him. The only way to save her from his wrath was to let him have his way. So I'd reluctantly agreed to question time.

From the moment I first came here, he'd been angry and intense and volatile. He still was, but since I returned a week ago, the anger wasn't rolling off him in hot waves like it had, and the volatile energy had calmed as well. It was still there but not as bad as before. Again, I wasn't sure why. This Death was different from the one I left the month before, and I wasn't quite sure how to deal with him.

I defied him—something I'd done since I first came here—but the Death sitting across from me now wasn't furious because I was bickering with him. He seemed almost... intrigued.

There had been questions I'd wanted to ask him but hadn't dared. I'd kept them simple for a reason. But without all the unhinged rage, I decided to try my luck. "Fine. I'll let you go first, but I get two questions."

He sat his mug down and rested his lightly clasped hands on the table. "Very well."

I was taken aback by his easy acquiescence.

The blue of his eyes grew darker and then stormy, the calm I stupidly thought I saw vanishing before my eyes. "Tell me, wife, how many males have you fucked?"

Inside, I flinched; outwardly, I showed nothing, or at least I hoped I hadn't. This was a turn I hadn't anticipated—not at all. I shrugged. "Does it really matter?"

"Yes."

"I'd have to count."

"I'll wait." He stared me down.

I tried not to squirm. What the fuck was this? Was this some kind of trap? Was he hoping for a virgin bride? I had no reason to lie, and I wouldn't, but this could be a good way to test this newish version of Death. I sat back and pretended I was having a hard time remembering, counting on my fingers. Was it stupid to rile Death? Absolutely. Had I been doing it anyway since I came here? Definitely. Finally, I sat forward and winked. "Less than ten."

"I want a number."

"More than five. I will say, my number would be a lot higher if I hadn't been so busy looking after my sister and working all the time. I've had more offers than I can count."

He set his mug down slowly. "Are you mocking me?"

"Of course not." I scooped another spoonful of oats. "Seven," I said, giving him his answer and shoving the oats in my mouth.

Fury etched his terrifyingly beautiful face, turning it utterly sinister. He didn't like that.

I gripped the edge of the table so he didn't see my hands tremble and forced a smirk. "Am I too much of a whore to be your consort now? By all means, send me back and forget I exist."

Darkness began to swirl around him. His cloak was made of moving shadows. Right now, they were barely there, but I saw them. His cloak gave away his moods—the more volatile he was feeling, the darker it became, wrapping around him. "Ask your questions," he said, voice filled with quiet menace.

I refused to be intimidated, even if I was trembling inside. "From what I understand, your mother created you and your brother rather than birthing you, turning you both into gods. Is that true?" My question obviously took him aback as well. He was used to my simple, no-stress questions. Nox, his and Somnus's mother, was the personification of night. I had yet to meet her, and from what little information I'd been able to find about her, that was a good thing.

"Yes," he said.

The passage I'd read said she'd created him and Somnus from light, that he'd existed before his godly status. "What were you before she made you a god?"

He went utterly still, studying me so closely, I had to fight not to whimper.

"A star," he finally said and stood.

I stared at him, unable to hide my surprise. "Like you were part of the universe?"

"Yes," he said. "I have something I need to attend to, if you'll excuse me," he said, then strode away, the dark shadows of his cloak flowing heavily around him as he left the room.

Chapter Two

Zinnia

I PLUCKED a sprig of rosemary from my hair while I smeared on lip balm. I'd been outside all day working in my garden. The seasons here... well, there weren't any—not here at the castle, anyway. It was different every day. Today the air had been dry with an icy bite to it, and my lips felt windblown and swollen.

The light was gone outside now, and I preferred to be indoors when that happened. Too many noises I did not like came from the woods around the grounds when night fell. I glanced at the silver clock on the wall; it was intricately tooled, delicate birds and foliage all over it. It was one of my favorite pieces in my room—it was also time to get a hustle on.

Scooping up Hemy, who'd been watching me from the top of my dresser, I put him on my shoulder. He pressed his little body against my neck as we walked out. "Let's go face the music."

If I'd known Death would force me to make up for our missed question time this morning, I would have hunted him down last night and forced him to do it when we were scheduled to, because twice in one day was not something I ever wanted to contend with again.

As always, the shadows and harsh whispers followed me as I rushed by. They were souls, or at least some kind of reflection of them from around Limbo, their voices echoing down the hall, their emotions like a heavy cloud. They haunted the halls, and I'd tried many times, but I couldn't reach them, couldn't communicate with them—with any souls at all when I was here. I was more than a little curious about the souls here and how this realm worked, but no one had offered to share.

Death's voice rolled from the library, followed by Egon's far gentler one, answering.

Death had made himself scarce since we ate this morning, when things took a weird turn with the whole what's-your-number question. He'd been pissed when he left. I really hoped he was in a better mood tonight, because I was tired, I missed my sister and my cousins and aunts, and the thought of sparring with him this evening had me feeling weary to the bone. It was all we did, but no matter how tired I was, I would meet him barb for barb. You gave Death an inch? Well, I didn't want to know what him taking a mile entailed.

Taking a fortifying breath, I knocked on the door. Death's gaze slid to me when I walked in, and I felt it like a lick of fire up my spine.

"I'll stay with him, my lord," Egon said, dipping his head and rushing from the room.

Death turned to the sideboard, and the *tink* of crystal came next.

He was pouring our drinks, which was all part of the ritual, I guess. I wasn't sure why he'd wanted this so badly.

I sneaked a glance over at him. His black shirt clung to his massive upper body, open to just below his pecs, giving a flash of the star tattooed on his chest. On closer inspection, I realized there were two more inside it—one slightly smaller, the same shape exactly, and another, much smaller one among the intricate swirls in the center. Small but bright. He lifted his gaze, and I quickly looked away.

"You smell like your garden," he said when he closed the space between us and held out my drink.

Oh, cool. He was smelling me again. That wasn't unsettling at all. "No flies on you tonight, my dark, malevolent one," I said with a smirk, trying to hide my discomfort, but couldn't meet his eyes.

This was the part I dreaded the most during our usual question time, taking the glass from him without our fingers touching. I usually just grabbed it on the top and bottom, avoiding where his hand wrapped around it. I wasn't sure why, but I couldn't do it. Touch Death? Not fucking likely, but tonight, he stood beside me, facing the fire as well, and instead of turning to face me when I did, he stayed where he was. His hand engulfed the glass, and his pinky was tucked under it. There was no taking the glass from him without my fingers touching his.

"You think me malevolent?" he asked, still holding out the glass.

Goddammit, I had no choice but to take it, or I'd draw attention to the fact that I was quietly freaking out at the prospect of my fingers touching his. "Aren't you?" *Three, two, one.* I grabbed it, and my breath was slammed from my lungs when his rough, warm skin seared mine. His gaze sliced to me, and the one-two smack of power had me staggering back.

"Sit down," he said without concern or explanation.

I all but fell back onto the leather chair. "You did that on purpose," I bit out.

He sipped his drink. "Did what?"

"Forced me to touch you. Gave me a bump of your power." Why lie? It was obvious at this point, and my avoidance of touching him couldn't have been lost on him.

He studied me. "You're stronger than I expected."

"You were testing me? Why?" He didn't answer, just stared at me. I refused to squirm as the silence stretched out. "You won't tell me?"

"It's time for us to begin," he said. "I believe it's my turn to go first."

No, he wasn't going to tell me; in fact, he was going to ignore what I'd asked completely. "You know I'll only ask you when it's my turn."

"You will not," he said. "You will ask something else."

I stared at him, and it was so incredibly hard, but I didn't look away. "Then I'd strongly suggest you don't ever do that again. I agreed to come here, but I didn't agree to be your entertainment or whatever the hell that was."

"The males you fucked, consort, were you in love with any of them?" he asked, as if I hadn't spoken at all, jumping into what was obviously his question for the night.

What the actual hell was this? Death seemed to be in the midst of some fucked-up metamorphosis, from a cloak-wearing, staff-thumping, rage-fueled monster to what stood before me now. He was all god, there was no mistaking it, but at times like this, there was a humanness to him that took me off guard. I sipped my drink, trying to decide how to answer. "I've believed myself in love many times."

He stilled, then placed his glass on the mantel above the fire. One moment he was there; the next, he was looming over me, his massive, tattooed hands on either side of me, gripping the arms of the chair. "Did you give your heart to any of the seven males you lay with, wife?"

"You're really hooked on that number, huh?" I said absolutely unwisely and despite my pounding heart, but I wasn't the kind of female to let a male walk all over me, not even Death himself, it seemed—not without a little fight, anyway. His scent filled the space between us, and it was like nothing I'd ever experienced before—dark, rich, and smooth, heady in a way that made you want more. It was too much, like everything else about him. Having him this close was like facing off against a fire-breathing dragon, and I tried so hard, but there was no controlling my body's deep trembles.

"Breathe," he said roughly.

That's when I realized my lungs were screaming for oxygen, and I gasped in a much-needed breath.

"Now, give me my answer," he said, studying me.

I was all but panting. "No, I have never truly given my heart to any male," I choked out. "And I never will," I added for reasons unknown.

His gaze slid over my face, and I felt it like the lick of the dragon's tongue. His eyes did that thing they had at breakfast earlier, almost brightening. "I believe you."

Then slowly, too slowly, he straightened, reclaimed his drink, and looked back into the fire as if none of that had just happened, while I sat there panting and trembling and trying to get my shit together. I wanted to make him squirm. I wanted to throw him off-balance like he seemed to be enjoying doing to me today.

Hemy gave me a little nudge, then pressed against me, sensing my unease and trying to soothe me. I drew strength from him. He may be tiny, but his love for me, his loyalty, was mighty. I licked my windburned lips and looked up... and caught Death looking at my mouth. I cleared my throat, and his gaze slowly slid up, locking on mine. It would be so easy to look away, to lose the battle of wills between us. He may be stronger, his battle plan more forceful, his arsenal far better equipped, but I was just as relentless. My attack was more subtle, yes, but I had no intention of waving the white flag anytime soon, no matter how exhausting this fight was.

"Tell me, my lord, am I the only consort you've had?" Someone had used that room before me, a female, and I'd wondered....

His glass paused on the way to his mouth, and he stared into it. His jaw tightened slightly. "No."

I stilled. "How many? I want a number," I said, throwing his words back at him from earlier that day.

"More than one and less than ten," he said, doing the same as I had.

What the hell did that mean? And where were his other consorts now? "What happened to them?"

"You asked your question, and I gave you your answer," he said.

"That was a non-answer—"

A roar of agony rattled the castle walls. Death slammed his glass on the mantel, spun, and strode from the room. I didn't know what possessed me, but I shoved off the chair and rushed after him. This was different. Somnus's roars of pain sounded different—goddess, horrifying and more... desperate.

Death shoved open the door to his brother's bedroom. Egon was at Somnus's bedside, using a cloth to wipe his face. Blood slid from the sleeping god's eyes, nose, and ears, dripping onto the white linen pillow beneath him, staining it scarlet.

"He's gone too long," Egon said, his hand trembling as he tried to swipe away more of the blood.

Death moved closer and cupped his brother's face. He said something low and guttural in a language I'd never heard before. Somnus's eyes snapped open suddenly, and I gasped. They were black and glossy with distant stars, like staring into the night sky.

"*Frater*," Death said, accent thick and in that same guttural voice. Somnus stared blindly ahead, and then his eyes closed again. Cursing, Death looked up at Egon. "Prepare my things. It's time."

I looked between them. "What's going on? Time for what?"

Death turned to me. "You'll need to pack for at least a week, but pack light."

"Pack?"

"We leave in the morning," Death said and strode from the room.

~

There was a soft knock on my door.

I opened it, and Egon walked in carrying a set of leathers—body armor—black with deep burgundy patches at random spots.

"The master wanted me to give you these," Egon said and placed them on the chest at the end of the bed.

"He wants me to wear those when we leave tomorrow?"

"Yes, my lady." He dipped his head and turned to leave.

I got in his way. "Why do I need to wear body armor, Egon?"

He shook his head, his glossy horns shining in the lamplight. "It is not my place to say, my lady."

I'd told him to call me Zinnia more times than I could count, but he refused. "Wherever we're going, it's dangerous?"

He wouldn't meet my eyes. "It will be a... a difficult journey, yes."

"Egon—"

"I must finish packing for my lord," he said and rushed out the door.

If Death was going on some dangerous quest, why take me along? To him, I was just some weak mortal. A witch, yes, but mortal all the same. He was a god; I'd just slow him down. I rubbed my arms. He'd been playing his piano earlier, and the song had been so achingly sad, I still felt unsettled from listening to it. When he played, it was as if the whole castle stopped, as if everyone was caught up in his song, pulling emotions from those who listened and breaking their hearts into a million pieces.

It was agony.

Shaking out my hands, I tried to let go of it—the feelings his song had stirred in me along with the concern over this trip he was forcing me to take with him—and paced the room. I strode to the window and looked out at Death's night sky. Stars twinkled down as if I were back home, but I wasn't staring up at the same sky as Jasmine; no, Death had created it when he created this realm.

Movement caught my eye in the garden below.

I stepped closer to the window. He was down there. His chest was bare, and his smooth skin glowed while deep shadows high-lighted every ridge and muscle. His head was tilted back, his gaze aimed to the heavens, while his lips moved.

Was he praying?

I moved closer to the window to get a better look and gasped. The shadows covering his body moved, reforming his appearance. They transformed him, his face reshaped by darkness into a skull, his chest and arms, a skeleton, and his eyes were black, as if reflecting the night sky, just like Somnus's had looked earlier.

He jolted suddenly, and his eyes cleared, the shadows moving and reshaping, his face and body returning to what they were before. I quickly stepped back, my heart beating hard in my chest.

Whatever I'd just witnessed, I got the feeling it was a sign of things to come.

I needed to be ready for anything.

Chapter Three

Zinnia

THE LEATHERS WERE sturdy but well-worn. Whoever owned them before me had obviously kicked ass because they were scarred and patched in a bunch of places. From the inside, you could see most of the damage was from clean slices, most likely knives or swords. If I was wearing what amounted to armor, then there was a chance I'd be fighting, so I'd strapped several throwing knives to my waist and my larger knife to my thigh. I also had a few of Magnolia's nasty potions with me—one that was straight to the point and melted the face off a creature in seconds, and another that caused temporary confusion, hallucinations, and blindness.

I walked out of the castle and had to fight not to suck in a sharp breath.

Death stood at the foot of the stairs, wearing heavy boots and worn leather like me. It molded to his tall frame, and dressed like that, goddess, the already large male was massive and even more imposing. I thought about the way he'd looked in the garden—

utterly transformed, his features skeletal, his eyes aimed at the sky while his lips moved rapidly, speaking to... only he knew who—and shivered. He'd never looked more like the God of Death than he had last night. My gaze trailed over him now; yeah, there was no mistaking who he was right now either. His shoulders looked even broader this morning, his long, lean body hugged to perfection in all that black. His muscle wasn't bulky. If I had to describe Death, I'd say he had the body of an extremely tall Olympic swimmer: long muscles, agile, fast. His movements would be smooth in a fight, gliding from one move to the next—

"Ready?" he asked.

I jumped, not prepared for that voice. I never was.

"As I'll ever be." I carefully lifted the strap of the small bag I'd borrowed from Egon over my head as I descended the wide stairs. The bag was small and made of a soft but thick felt, perfect for Hemlock to stay warm in. I carried my pack in my hand. Hopefully, I had everything I'd need since I'd packed light as instructed. "So who did the leathers belong to?" I asked him.

His gaze swept over me, from the boots to my wavy red hair that I'd braided down my back to keep out of the way. "A warrior," he said.

"A friend of yours?"

Something moved through those crystal clear, glacial eyes. "No."

"Lover?" My belly twisted in an uncomfortable way for some reason.

He didn't answer, which was answer enough, wasn't it? I was wearing his ex-lover's armor. Realization struck. "She was your consort?"

"Yes."

What did it matter to me? Still, I felt kind of weird wearing something that had belonged to a female he once... cared about? Loved? Then again, who's to say he loved her? I was his consort, and we sure as hell weren't in love. "Where is she now?"

"Dead."

He was doing that thing he often did, watching me in a way I didn't understand. The way he replied, leaving things unsaid, as if he was waiting for me to figure out the punch line on my own when there was no way I could. "How did she die?"

"Gruesomely."

I couldn't read him at all, which was nothing new. "You don't seem very upset about it. Was she consort number one or number ten?"

He said nothing.

I jerked back. "Do all your consorts die gruesomely?"

"Not all." He held my gaze. "Some a little more peacefully."

Well now, wasn't this a new and horrifying discovery. "And how long do you expect me to last?"

"That is entirely up to you, consort," he said, then held his fingers to his lips and whistled.

He'd actually answered several questions without asking for anything in return. A crashing sound came from deep in the forest. "What the hell is that?"

"Our transportation."

The trees at the edge of the forest, several yards away, shuddered, followed by the sound of several large branches cracking; then two giant monsters burst through.

"Holy fuck." I stumbled back, but Death grabbed me, his fingers curling around my wrist and holding firm, and then he tugged me forward. I jolted as electricity bolted through me. Still, it was less shocking than it had been in the library. I could breathe at least. He called out to the beasts in that same language, in that same low, guttural voice he'd used with Somnus.

They slowed, stopping in front of us.

Their skin was thick like a rhino's but mottled black and gray. They had long, thin, muscular legs and claws like razors. Their heads were elongated, birdlike, with lower jaws that jutted forward and mouths that were full of sharp teeth and fangs like a wildcat.

Death said something to one of them, again in that language I didn't understand, before he turned to me. "She won't hurt you unless you mistreat her. She understands verbal cues." He still held my wrist, and even through the leather, I felt his touch pulsing through my arm.

I tried to pull away, but he turned to me, and his other hand came up fast, wrapping around my throat in a firm hold. I gasped and grabbed his wrist, trying to get him off, to pull away, but there was no dislodging him.

Was this how I died? Death having some random psychotic break and choking me to death?

"They only understand one language," he said, voice low as he held me, gasping and thrashing, immobile in his grip. "Stop fighting me."

I realized when I gasped in a desperate breath that I could breathe. At least he wasn't trying to cut off my airway. Warmth filled my throat, and little sparks danced down to my chest.

He dipped his face close to mine. "Now when you speak to her, she'll understand you." He was right there, closer than he'd ever been to me before. Goddess, I'd actually felt his warm breath against my lips.

Blinking, I tried to fight the pull, but I was sucked into his gaze, like a black hole dragging my soul from my body. He didn't need to cut off my breathing; I was holding my breath all on my own.

He released my throat suddenly, and I gasped in another lungful of air, but the reprieve was short-lived because he gripped my waist before I knew what he was about to do and hoisted me onto one of the beasts.

What I wanted to do was jump right the hell back off. I was disoriented and freaking the fuck out, but I had to get it together. No, I wasn't a warrior, but I was no slouch either. So instead of letting him see how rattled I was, I scooted forward on the beast to the only place I could sit comfortably, where there was a natural groove behind her shoulders. Death wrapped a girth belt around her belly, just behind me, and strapped on my pack, then slid on leather bridle-like headgear over her beaky jaw, secured it, and handed me the reins.

I gripped them while Death ran his hand down her long nose. "Thank you, Zuri, for your service to my consort and me. I know being away from your loved ones will be painful, but you and your family will be rewarded for your sacrifice."

I heard the words as he said them in another language, but this time, I understood them. "That's her name? Zuri?"

"Yes." He ran his hand along the larger beast on the other side of him. "And this is her mate, Raze," he said as he secured Raze's girth strap, then tied his wooden staff to it. He slid the bridle on before swinging himself up onto the beast's back. "Let's go," he said, and Raze started walking.

Zuri instantly followed her mate, moving up beside him, so close that my leg kept brushing Death's. I tried to steer her away, to put more distance between us, but she wasn't having it. *Awesome.*

Death rode toward an opening in the forest.

"So where are we going?" I asked, because the silence was making me jumpy. I glanced at his staff. "And why do you need that?"

"My staff has many purposes, including a weapon."

"You're Death, what do you need with weapons?"

"I'm never without my staff. We're also going to the Outer Realm, beyond Limbo, beyond everything, and I need a weapon because my powers will be significantly weakened there," he said.

Fear coiled deep inside me. "Going there kind of sounds like a seriously dumb thing to do, then."

"Perhaps, but it is necessary."

"Why?"

He stared straight ahead, and his strong jaw tightened, the muscle there pulsing several times as if he was grinding his teeth. I didn't think he'd answer, but then he glanced my way. "Because

Somnus has been asleep too long. It's why he suffers, why he's in pain. He's fighting it. If I don't wake him, he'll fall into an eternal slumber, never to return."

Obviously not good for Somnus or Death. "Why won't he wake?"

Death looked away from me again. "Because time moves differently in the dream realm, and his task there is of the greatest importance. He can only leave for a short time before he must return, but he must leave. He must wake occasionally, or he never will again."

This journey was obviously dangerous, so what the hell did he think I could do? Why was he making me go with him? "And there's something in the Outer Realm that can wake him?"

"No. What we need is in the Night Realm."

His mother's realm. "So we're going there as well?"

"Yes."

"How long will it take to get there?"

"It will take two days and nights to pass through Limbo's forests and reach the gateway to the Outer Realm. How long it takes to reach our destination after that will depend on what is waiting for us on the other side."

"We could die?" I said, filling in the blanks.

"You could. I can't die—I'm a God—but I could be seriously injured and out of commission for a very long time."

Fuck. "I'd rather not die, if it's all the same."

"If you do as I say, you'll be fine. Now hold on tight," Death said, then patted Raze. "Run, my friend."

The beast took off, and Zuri bounded forward. I jerked back, almost coming off, and yanked on the reins to right myself, then hung on like hell. They were massive and ungainly, but they could move.

Death kept that pace for the rest of the day, and by the time we stopped for the night, I was exhausted. My thigh muscles ached and cramped, my back hurt, and my fingers were stiff from gripping the leather reins so tight.

Death jumped down as if we'd been riding for minutes, not hours, and removed Raze's girth strap and bridle. I groaned, dragging my leg over Zuri's back, and kind of slid to the ground. My legs buckled under me, but before I could hit the dirt, Death was there, his arm hooked around my waist, stopping me from falling.

"You need to work on your stamina," he said roughly.

The coarseness to his voice lifted goose bumps all over me. I quickly pulled away, clinging to Zuri's girth strap while the blood pumped back through my muscles. "I'm not used to riding all day, that's all. I'm not weak."

He stepped away from me. "If you say so."

I gritted my teeth and barely resisted picking up a rock and tossing it at his head. I removed Zuri's girth strap and bridle and hung them over a branch, watching as she and Raze trotted off into the forest to eat and rest.

Wordlessly, Death led me to the mouth of a cave that cut into stone at the base of a tall cliff. It was getting dark, but there was still enough light that when I looked up, I could tell it was hundreds of yards high.

"What is this place?" I asked as we walked in. I stopped in my tracks. "Whoa." There were candles already going, and an ornate fireplace was carved into one of the rock walls. A small kitchen was on the opposite side, a wooden table and four chairs beside it, and a large bed on a four-poster iron frame sat back, recessed in the stone. Dark fabric hung down the sides, tied back by leather cords, and the bed was draped in black velvet. Everything smelled clean and fresh, as if someone still lived here and had just done a spring clean.

"This was my home when I first created this realm," Death said, surprising me.

I spun to him. "You lived here? How long for?"

He shrugged a broad shoulder. "I can't recall. A long time." He opened his jacket hurriedly, sliding it off, and instantly rolled his shoulders as if he had been desperate to remove it. He turned to the entrance as he tugged off the shirt he wore underneath, visibly relaxing. The entrance vanished, just from a look, and now stone covered it—trapping us in. His gaze slid to the fire next, and flames immediately ignited in the hearth. "Sit. We'll eat."

I looked around again, for a door, for an escape, if I needed one, but there wasn't one. I was trapped in a cave with Death.

"Consort," he said, jolting me. I tried not to look panicked as I turned back to him. "Sit. Eat."

When I turned back, the table was set, plates piled with food at either end. "Neat trick," I said and managed to walk to the table without collapsing again. Sitting at the table, I took Hemy from his bag and set him on the table beside me. He blinked up at me, still drowsy. He'd slept all day. "You hungry?" I looked down at my plate. All my favorites were there. Slow-roasted beef, gravy, crispy potatoes, green beans, and glazed carrots. I put a couple carrots and a potato in front of Hemy and poured some water into a saucer.

Death's boots thumped against the stone floor, echoing through the room, and somehow, I managed not to jump, but my nerves zipped across my belly as he drew closer, then pulled out the chair opposite. I glanced up as he sat. His plate looked the same as mine, but he had twice the amount of beef. There was a pitcher with water and a mug, and a glass of wine as well. I took a fortifying sip. It hadn't escaped me that there was only one bed, and the idea of lying on it next to Death was more than I could even contemplate.

"Stop staring at your food and eat it," he said, voice low. "You'll need to keep up your strength."

I picked up my cutlery and sliced off a succulent piece of beef. "For all the fighting I'll be doing?"

His gaze dipped to my mouth, watching as I slid the fork past my lips. "I don't know what awaits us. We need to be prepared for anything." He shoved food in his mouth, his biceps flexing, then took a gulp of wine. "Where we're going, demons are rampant, but you're a warrior. I've seen you fight. It's nothing you can't handle."

I lowered my knife and fork. "You think I'm a warrior?"

"I know you are. My consort wouldn't be anything else," he said as if it were obvious, a fact, then lowered his gaze back to his food.

I sat there, kind of frozen, surprised he saw me that way and, yeah, pleased that he recognized my abilities and didn't see me as some weak female. "So all your consorts were warriors?"

"Not all warriors wield a sword."

This was true.

"Eat, Zinnia," he rumbled, not looking up, and the oxygen was punched from my lungs.

I quickly shoved a piece of carrot in my mouth so he didn't feel the need to look up again, but my heart was pounding wildly in my chest. He never called me by my name. Ever. It was always *consort* or occasionally *wife*. I took another sip of my wine and tried to get it the hell together while he ate across from me.

Finally, he wiped his mouth on a napkin and sat back. "Do you have a question for me tonight?"

I nodded, swallowing my last mouthful. I'd asked him multiple questions today, and he'd answered most of them. I didn't remind him of that, though.

"Good, but I have one for you first," he said.

I rolled my eyes. "Fine. I'm too tired to fight with you about it tonight."

"Why would you fight with me? It's my turn," he said, and his eyes glittered in the candlelight.

"Sure it is, Mors," I said, firing his name at him. If he was doing it, then so was I.

He stilled, unnaturally so, his eyes darkening. "I told you what would happen if you spoke my name again," he said. "Did you forget?"

Fuck. I had. I was full and warm from the fire and the wine and growing sleepier by the minute, which was why I was more relaxed than I'd ever been around him before. "I guess I did."

"You realize you must do whatever it is I ask? You vowed, and a vow cannot be broken."

In other words, I'd fucked up big-time. "What do you want?"

"I'll tell you when the time comes," he said.

Awesome, that didn't sound ominous at all. "Fine, not much I can do about it now, right?" I was doing my best not to let him see how freaked out I truly was. How the hell could I forget? He was watching me closely. Maybe he was waiting for the freak-out? Well, I wouldn't give him the satisfaction. "So what's your question? I'm as ready as I'll ever be."

His massive, scarred hand curled around his glass, and he took another sip of his wine, dragging it out, trying to torture me with suspense. "If you had the means, would you kill me?"

Okay, I hadn't expected that one. Was that Death's way of asking if I liked him? Yes, I'd kill you, equals no? No, I wouldn't kill you, equals yes? Despite everything, I didn't hate him. I wasn't naïve enough not to understand that there were bigger things at play here. He hadn't chosen me to be his consort any more than I'd chosen him, and going by his actions since we made our deal, I wasn't so sure he even wanted me here. It felt more like he needed me than wanted me. So no, I didn't hate him. "No, I wouldn't kill you."

He abruptly sat forward in his seat. "Why?"

I automatically jerked back; the intensity flowing from him had skyrocketed. "You get one question, remember?" Again, I was struck by how different he was. He was more... animated, and he seemed to possess more than one emotion. He wasn't just angry all the time like he had been before.

He ground his teeth, then visibly forced himself to relax, his big shoulders losing their rigidity. "I remember. Ask your question."

After all that had happened at this dinner alone, I should go for an easy one, but I couldn't stop the question that was forming in my head from coming out of my mouth. "Do you miss them, grieve them... your past consorts?"

No, he didn't like that question, not at all. His face had turned to stone. He didn't want to answer it, but we'd made a deal, and he had to. A low, rumbling growl came from him, and I barely managed to hold my ground and not jump from my seat and find a hole to shove myself into.

"If I allowed myself to truly feel the weight of their loss, I would never sleep come sunset, and I would never leave my bed come sunrise." Then he stood suddenly and strode to the hearth, giving me his back.

Shock had me glued to my seat. Again, Death had surprised me. He'd cared for them, and he'd lost them, all of them.

"You should get some sleep. Take the bed," he said without looking at me.

I jolted from my chair, scooped up Hemy, and did what he said without a word.

We'd done more than enough talking for tonight.

Chapter Four

Death

THE CANDLELIGHT and shadows made her red hair look like dimming embers. Her face was to the side, her thick lashes resting against her cheeks. My consort was just as fiery in temperament, possessed a warrior's heart, and had the kind of beauty that could bring the strongest of gods to their knees.

But I would not fall.

I would not let sadistic hope infiltrate my heart. I knew better. Still, I approached the bed to get a closer look, drawn by a higher power, by a force I had no control over. Resisting her wouldn't be easy, but if I let myself fall again, Nox would only take pleasure in my inevitable destruction; it was all she had left.

I'd bartered for our nightly question time because not only did I want an excuse to learn all there was to know about her life, but I craved her nearness and the sound of her voice. I thought I might actually be addicted to her sexy husky laugh, when she had occasion to, though that only usually happened when she was with Egon or Lyle.

And though I knew I shouldn't, that it was dangerous beyond measure, I climbed in beside the female sleeping soundly in my bed. I may not have hope, but this little witch was still my guiding star, and not getting closer to her was like asking the wind not to blow or the snow not to fall.

Just tonight.

I'd sleep beside her only tonight.

~

Zinnia

Wrapping the fur around her shoulders, she walked to the hearth. The fire crackled, light dancing on the stone walls. Anticipation moved through her while she waited for him to come home. She missed him when he left and counted the hours until he returned.

But tiredness eventually won out, and she got into bed.

She woke as his palm drifted up her thigh. Shivering, she covered it and brought his big, tattooed hand to her lips, kissing his scarred fingers. "I missed you, my love."

I woke with a jolt, gasping in a breath. It was dark, only a small candle glowing from somewhere deep in the room. My eyes were desperately trying to adjust while my heart still raced, and my belly, it felt... strange.

That's when I became aware of the massive male lying under me. I was draped over a wide chest, my hand resting on ridged abdominal muscles, skin molten and smooth. Death's intoxicating scent filled my lungs, and my body buzzed with electricity.

I broke out in a sweat.

I was lying on him, draped over his body like I had a right to be here. I was frozen in place, wanting to pull away but too scared to move in case I woke him. My nerve endings itched, and my belly squirmed. I couldn't take it; I scrambled back, but I shouldn't have been worried about waking him. His eyes glittered in the candle-light, not blue but black, the night sky in their depths, and they weren't cold; they were hot, smoldering.

"What... what are you doing?" I choked out.

"I was sleeping."

"You can't just get in here with me," I fired at him, freaking out so bad, I was breathing hard.

His lips peeled back. "That's where you're wrong, wife."

Oh goddess. "You look... as if you want to...."

"How do I look, little witch? Tell me." His voice was nothing but gravel, resonating through me, over me.

"Like you want to ..." Punish me. Hurt me.

Suddenly, shadows swirled around him, thick and heavy, and the room filled with a deep and horrible dread. Darkness moved around his face, reshaping it, gathering at his eyes and cheeks, his nose, transforming his face into a skull, into Death. His hand shot out, and I scrambled out of his reach.

It paused midair.

"Mors?" I said. Yes, it was stupid to say his name again, but something was wrong, and I needed to get through to him somehow.

Rage blasted from him, like a furious storm, and I wrapped my arms around myself.

"I will not harm you," he roared, his words and his tone a total contradiction. It wasn't the first time he'd done it, and it was unsettling as hell.

Then he climbed out of bed, and his cloak settled around him as he stormed across the cave. A door appeared, swinging open, and he strode out before it slammed behind him.

I stood there frozen, staring after him for several seconds. At least until the adrenaline drained from me and that awful heaviness left the room with him. My legs shook, and I flopped back on the bed. What the hell was that? And not just the weird way Death was behaving.

That hadn't just been a dream; it was more... an apparition, a manifestation? Maybe my medium powers weren't totally smothered here? What I'd seen, it was like one of the visions I had when I communed with a spirit, when they wanted to pass on a message, and the vision I'd just received was here in this cave. Did one of his consorts die here? Is that who I saw? I only saw it for a moment, but that had been Death's hand she'd kissed. No one else had hands like he did.

I tried to go back to sleep, but I lay awake for hours; my mind wouldn't shut the hell up. I had too many unanswered questions. Who was that with him in the dream? Why was she reaching out to me now? If she was one of Death's consorts, how did she die?

Somehow, I'd managed to drift back to sleep, because when I woke again, it was to the smell of bacon and coffee.

Shoving back the covers, I scooped up Hemy and got out of bed. Death was sitting at the table, facing the hearth. He was leaning forward, his elbows resting on his knees, a mug of coffee in his hands, and he was staring into the unlit fire.

I stood there, not sure what to say.

"Come and eat," he said, not looking my way. "We need to leave soon."

Cautiously, I walked over. I wasn't sure what to expect. I could say nothing about what happened last night and pretend he hadn't done what he had, but I wasn't going to do that, not anymore. I'd been coming here, to Limbo, for a long time, putting up with his mood swings, and if what he said was true, and he had no reason to lie, all his consorts died, which meant I might not have all that much time left. So what the hell did I have to lose? Yes, he scared the hell out of me at times, but again, dead girl walking over here.

"You want to tell me what happened last night?" I asked as I pulled out one of the chairs and sat. I put Hemlock on my lap.

"'Cause I have to tell you, it was fucking weird." There was a mug of hot coffee in front of me, and I sipped it as he straightened and turned in his seat to face me. And go me! When his blue eyes collided with mine, and there was a good amount of fury in them, I didn't shudder *or* pee myself. "Don't look at me like that. I've put up with your mood swings for eighteen months. I'm not going to cower before you anymore," I said and snatched up a slice of bacon, broke off a small piece, and gave it to Hemy. My hand was hardly even trembling when I shoved the rest in my mouth. Again, go me!

"I don't recall one instance of you cowering before me, consort. You have snarked and battled your way through every one of our conversations. You have conveyed your disdain for me with every encounter. You leave my castle with glee when every cycle of the moon has passed and return with a thundercloud over that head of fiery red hair when your time with your family has ended." He shook his head, and his lips actually twitched. "But cower? No, there has been no cowering, little witch."

I was momentarily stunned, and I shoved another piece of bacon into my mouth while I rallied. "Will I live long enough, do you think, to truly know you? I can't help but wonder, because you are not the male I first met. You're constantly changing."

He quirked a brow, and the blue of his eyes deepened, darkness swirling from within. "How so?"

He knew exactly *how so*, but he was trying to intimidate me, daring me to say it out loud... testing me. "Your moods, for one," I said, taking some toast and smearing it with butter, then spooning scrambled eggs on top. "You raged all the time when I first came here."

"Did I now?" he said.

A little shiver slid through me, but I ignored it and pushed on. "You also hid under your cloak, skulking around the castle like a pissed off, moody shadow." I bit my toast and chewed, looking across at him. "It was like you were trying to scare me off, which was kind of surprising considering how desperate you were to get me here. Why is that?"

He just stared at me.

"Your intimidation tactics won't work on me, not anymore. The way I see it, my days are numbered. The worst is already coming, probably sooner than I'd like." I shrugged, even as the thought of never seeing my family again twisted brutally in my gut. "There's nothing you can do or say now to scare me, so why don't you just answer the damn question?"

He ran his hand over his tattooed skull, making his biceps bulge, then sat forward in a deceptively relaxed pose. Like we were just two normal people shooting the shit over breakfast. "What did you expect me to do?" he asked instead of answering.

I noted, with not a little unhappiness, that he hadn't contradicted my premonition of my own rapidly approaching demise. "Honestly? I thought you were going to force me into your bed and make me your sex slave. I am your wife, right? Essentially. I thought you'd want to consummate this unholy union, then try and breed me until I eventually died a shriveled, used-up old crone." I scooped another forkful of eggs into my mouth and watched with satisfaction as his expression, always so stoic—except when he was raging, that was—shifted into genuine surprise. I mean, I was exaggerating. I hadn't expected him to attempt to breed me until I died or make me his sex slave, but I hadn't really known either. I had, at the very least, assumed he'd force me into his bed, and I was more than thankful he hadn't.

Then he'd gotten into bed with me last night and looked at me like he wanted to make a meal of me. In that moment, terrifyingly, I knew he'd wanted me, and that seemed to just piss him off more.

His fingers tightened around his mug. "You thought I would repeatedly rape you and force you to bear my offspring?"

I shrugged and sipped my drink. "Yeah, kind of."

He shot to his feet, the chair crashing to the floor, making me jump, and then he paced from one side of the room to the other.

He turned back to me now with those shadows swirling around him, his eyes darkening, his face transforming.

I opened my mouth to say something. I wasn't quite sure what, but I needed to defuse the situation somehow because what was coming off him wasn't... good.

But before I could, he spun away and stormed out of the cave.

Well, shit, perhaps I'd pushed him too far? The god's moods swung on a dime. You never knew what you were going to get. What I wanted to do was stay right the hell here, but I didn't think it was wise to make him wait, not now. So I quickly finished my coffee, put Hemy in his bag with some breakfast, and headed outside.

Death stood with our beasts. He'd already put on their girth straps and bridles and was tying a water bladder to Zuri.

I was stuck with him, with no escape for at least a week. I needed to rein it the hell in or this trip would be unbearable. Biting my lip, I walked over to him, fighting my nerves. I was going to have to apologize, wasn't I? Goddammit. "I'm sorry," I muttered. "I thought you were—"

"The kind of male who would force himself on a female?" he snarled low, still with his back to me.

"I'm sorry," I said again. "But in my defense, you are a god. Some of you guys have a pretty bad rep, even you have to admit that."

He turned to me, his eyes so bright a blue, I startled. "You're right—we're all sick, evil monsters," he said, and there was definitely sarcasm in his voice.

That was also new. Right, time to change the subject. "So how far are we riding today?"

He closed the space between us, so close now, I had to tilt my head all the way back. "About the same as yesterday," he said, then curled his fingers around my waist.

My breath punched from my lungs, and then I was in the air, tossed up onto Zuri's back, and he was already walking away before I realized what had happened. I let out a shaky breath and tried to get my shit together while he swung up onto Raze.

He glanced my way. "Try and keep up." Then he told Raze to run.

Zuri took off instantly without me having to tell her to, and I held on for dear life as we bounded through the forest at full speed.

Toward what? I had no idea, but I got the feeling wherever we were going—whatever came next—would change me in ways I couldn't even imagine.

Chapter Five

Zinnia

WE STOPPED FOR A QUICK LUNCH, but other than that, we'd ridden hard all day. Night was falling, and the air had chilled. I rubbed my arms as Zuri slowed, following her mate's cues, then stopped in a clearing in the middle of nowhere. Howls and cries echoed in the distance, lifting the hair on the back of my neck. I slid down off Zuri, managing to stay upright all on my own this time, and pulled my knife free as I scanned our surroundings.

"We're getting close to the gateway," Death said.

"Are those sounds coming from the Outer Realm?"

He shook his head. "Occasionally, creatures—demons—get through."

"Is that how Egon came to be here?"

"Yes. There's no real way to stop them. Egon regularly takes out a hunting party and culls the more dangerous breeds."

"Do I need to be worried? Will they hunt us?" Our little cave last night had been like a five-star accommodation, because, looking around now, there was nothing here, no cave, no cabin, no place to hide.

"It depends on the creature. While some will sense me and stay away, others will see me being here as a challenge."

"Why the hell would they think that?"

"They are Nox's followers. She won't want me in her realm, and she'll try and prevent it."

I turned fully to face him. "Your mother doesn't like you?"

"Nox hates me and my brother," he said and pressed his hand to one of the largest trees near us, looking up.

"Why?"

He tilted his head back, and his eyes rolled back as he muttered under his breath. A ladder rolled down from nowhere. "Up you go. I'll take care of Zuri and Raze," he said and waited for me to jump to it.

"I don't need you to protect me, you know? I'm not the kind of witch to hide while danger lurks beneath me—" He hooked a strong arm around my waist and all but tossed me halfway up the rope ladder. "What the hell are you doing?"

"Saving time," he said and turned away to take care of our mounts.

So goddamn arrogant. I spun away and climbed up the rest of the way. It was a tree house, kind of like the one Magnolia lived in with her crow-shifter mate, Bram, but not as big. The room was a large circle, with soft clay-colored walls and an open fire in the middle, already going, the flue disappearing up through the peaked roof. A bed was to one side, shaped to fit the wall, and there was a low table on the other side with cushions around it and more along the wall to sit on. Everything was bright jewel colors, and the place had a warm and cozy feel.

I found it hard to believe Death just came up with this out of thin air.

He popped up through the floor, pulled the ladder up after

him, and the hole in the floor vanished, sealing us in. "No escape, huh?"

"No way for a demon to get in while we sleep," he said.

"And what if I need to pee?"

He motioned to a doorway with a colorful piece of fabric hanging over it.

Awesome, he'd be able to hear me. "The demons can't actually hurt you, though, right?"

"The closer we get to the gateway, the more I can feel my powers weakening." He turned to the low table, and this time, he needed more than a look to make food appear; he closed his eyes and held his hand above it.

His mother wanted him powerless when he was in her realm or close to it. Didn't she sound just lovely.

We sat on the ground on cushions, and I loaded up my plate with rice and beans and lamb. I took a sip of my wine. "This looks amazing. If you can do this, why have Egon cook?"

"He likes to do it."

"Take care of you?"

"Yes."

Death cared about Egon, considered his feelings, wanted him to be happy. "He's your friend."

He grunted and stabbed a piece of meat and put it in his mouth, and as soon as he'd swallowed it, his gaze came back to me. "Why wouldn't you kill me if you had the means?" he asked, picking up the same line of questioning from the night before.

I'd really been hoping he'd forget about that, but the male had the memory of an elephant. There was no reason to lie. "I don't hate you. I never really did. When I was younger, I was scared, so I hid from you. But I figure, you didn't specifically *choose me* to be your consort, and this whole... thing, whatever *this* is"—I glanced between us—"was out of your control as well. So how can I hate you for it?"

The muscle in his jaw jumped, but he said nothing.

I took another sip of my wine. "My turn." I could ask what exactly *this thing* was. He demanded I be here in Limbo with him, but I had no idea why. I didn't think asking that right now was a great idea, though. "What's with this place?" I asked instead, deciding to appease my curiosity.

"What do you mean?"

"I live in your castle. This place is the complete opposite of that. This is not you."

"No, it's not me, but it was the first thing that came to mind, so I recreated it."

"Recreated? Who lived here before?"

"You asked your question, and I answered it," he said and carried on eating.

I studied him. "It belonged to one of your consorts, didn't it?"

He said nothing.

Which meant, why yes, yes, it did. "So what was this place? Did she build it here in Limbo? Or was it something she lived in before she became your consort, and if so, how do you know what it looked like?"

Still, he said nothing, and then a thought occurred to me: was this where they spent quiet time together? Like a night away from the castle, just the two of them... the Limbo equivalent of a dirty weekend?

A weird feeling swirled in my belly, and without my say-so, my eyes slid to the opulent bed, big and draped in soft, richly colored fabrics. I swallowed audibly in the utter silence that had engulfed the room. I was right. Somehow, I knew I was right. I mean, the bathroom didn't even have a proper door. This place was for people who had no boundaries, no inhibitions, and were completely at ease around each other.

I turned back to Death and noticed he was watching me closely.

Clearing my throat, because it felt impossibly tight all of a sudden, I carried on eating, but Death didn't look away from me, not once. If anything, he grew more intense, and the energy he was throwing off was filling the room. Goddess, goose bumps had lifted all over me. I licked my lips nervously.

Death made a low sound that shot right through me, and I took a swig of my wine.

"So what time will we reach the gate tomorrow?" I said because the silence, the tension, felt like a rope pulled taut and about to break at any moment.

He snapped out of whatever this was and unfroze, the tension dialing *way* down. "If we leave early, we should be there before midday."

I nodded. "I'll need to prepare before we leave. If there's a chance I'll be fighting, I need my magic at full power, and an extra boost would be a good idea as well. I'm not ready to die quite yet."

"You can have as much time as you need," he said. "Do you need to perform a spell or some kind of ritual?"

Whenever he talked to me like this, no deals or bartering or demands, like he could be anyone, just your average Joe asking questions—well, except for that voice—I was always taken aback, but I knew better than to let my guard down. Not with how fast his moods shifted. "Yeah, a simple ritual. I'll use blood to increase my power."

"Do you want me to kill something for you?" he asked in his destroyer's voice, but somehow, it came out like crushed velvet.

It slid over my skin, and I barely suppressed my shiver. Jesus, the way he said it, so intimate, as if he were whispering dirty things in the dark.

This was a different version of Death, again. This transformation hadn't been slow and steady; no, he just seemed to have suddenly changed when I came back, and every day that passed, this new side of him was making an appearance more and more. He was giving me more "human" vibes and less of the vengeful God of Death. Though that was still there as well, it just wasn't all he was now. He was... more.

I cleared my throat again. "Ah... no, thank you. That won't be necessary. I'll use my own blood."

His gaze shot up from his food. "No," he said so loud, I jumped.

I frowned at him. "I'm a blood witch, you must know that?" I held up my hand and showed him my scarred palm. "How do you think I got this? I mean, when I first came here, I was covered in my own blood, so this can't be a surprise to you."

"You are not to cut yourself, not anymore," he said, his eyes darkening, burning into me.

I stared at him, not backing down despite the tremble in my belly and the way the hair on the back of my neck stood up. "Cutting and magic go hand in hand in my coven. It gives us strength and increases our power. It's what we do, and it's who we are," I fired back at him.

His fingers curled into a tight fist. "You test me, consort. You push me at every turn, but I will not concede to you on this. You will not win."

What I wanted to do was scream in his face, just release all the rage and fear I was feeling in that moment, but somehow, I knew that would be the absolute wrong thing to do. Instead, I forced it down, and then I reached out and covered his clenched fist with my hand. It was rough, his skin scarred and hot. Power sparked from him to me, and it was hard to keep holding on, to keep my breathing even, but I didn't let go and made myself look deep into his eyes so he'd see the truth of my words as I said them. "If you take this from me, you may as well kill me now. This is not a battle for you to win or lose. Without my magic, I am nothing. I don't exist. I won't be Zinnia Thornheart anymore. Without my magic, I won't be me, and that's not something I ever want to face." I shook my head. "I'm here, and I'm not going anywhere. I've accepted that this is my life now—what's left of it, anyway— but you have already ripped me from the people I love most in this world, and you need to know that I won't let you take this from me. Whatever the cost, I won't let you take this from me as well."

The hand under mine was pulled away, and then it shot out, curling around the side of my throat, not tight, similar to the way he'd held it outside the castle before we left. Then his hand slid higher, his long, thick fingers sinking into my hair, shocking me. "Always so fucking stubborn," he rasped.

I stayed completely still, breathless, as his thumb touched my chin. His gaze dipped; he was no longer looking into my eyes but watching what he was doing as he slowly slid his thumb higher, his rough skin scraping mine, until the very tip brushed the bottom of my lower lip. His gaze was focused on that connection and nothing else.

A shaky breath punched out of me at the look on his face while he touched me.

He blinked, as if knocked from wherever he'd just gone, and looked up at me. "You may practice your magic then. Stubborn little witch." Then he finally released me.

I sank back in my seat as if I'd been unplugged from an electrical socket, my body still buzzing and my heart pounding.

Death strode across the room. The trapdoor reappeared, and he kicked the ladder back down and jumped to the ground after it.

I took another shaky breath and tried to get my heart back under control.

She turned in strong arms, sliding her hands over wide shoulders.

"Do you want me to fuck you, Aster?"

"Yes," she whispered.

Firelight danced over his bare skin, making the tattoos on his flesh come alive. She trailed her hands up his stomach and over his chest. They were slender, beautiful hands. He rolled her to her back, his long, thick fingers curling around her throat. "My precious Stella."

She wrapped her legs around him, and he slammed inside her—

My eyes flew open, my body hot and coated in a fine layer of sweat. The room was warm, too warm, and I blinked up at the ceiling. A vision, not a dream.

Aster.

She'd been with Death in this tree house, and she may or may not be the female I'd dreamed about the previous night. Why were they showing me these things? If I could use my medium power to its full potential here, I could call them to me and ask what they wanted.

Was it a warning of some kind? Had Death killed them? Was that what they were trying to tell me? Not to get close to him, not to let him in, or I'd end up the same?

It was still night; I could tell by the sounds the insects made outside. Pushing myself up, I shoved back the covers, then bit my lip. Death had come back sometime while I'd been asleep. He'd arranged himself on the larger cushions. His upper body was kind of propped up; one hand was behind his head, and the other, resting on his abs. With his arm back like that, I could see the tattoo that ran all the way down the back of it more clearly. He had two of them, another identical one on the other arm. Inverted torches. The death of the flesh, and the eternal life of the soul— that's what they meant. The one I could see was beautiful, flames licking down his forearm to his wrist.

It looked so real, like if you reached out and touched it, you'd feel cold steel or the heat of the flames.

My gaze slid over the rest of him. He looked the same as he did in my vision: his skin, golden in the firelight, the dancing flames moving over the dips and valleys of his muscled body, the way his tattoos almost looked alive in the dim light.

He was devastatingly beautiful.

Something in my lower belly tightened, and I bit my lip again.

I didn't want to be attracted to him, especially now, when I thought about what those visions could mean, but I guessed it was inevitable, right? He was essentially my mate; an attraction; whether you wanted there to be one or not, was part and parcel with that whole thing. A higher power had brought us together; fate had chosen me for him, and him for me. The only difference here was, Death could have more than one consort in his lifetime.

What happened if I didn't die an untimely death? Would the consorts keep coming? Would I end up the head sister wife of Death's polygamist family? His hand slid lower, and he groaned in his sleep. I slammed my legs together when unwanted lust, caused by that sound, zipped right through my belly and landed between my legs. *Shit.*

My gaze trailed back up his body, over his square jaw and that strong nose, to his dark lashes resting on his cheeks. The male had perfect bone structure, but then he was a god, so what did I expect—

His eyes opened, locking on mine.

My heart thumped against my ribs. "I just... I woke, and you... you were snoring," I blurted, lying through my teeth while my face went up in flames. "Keep it down," I snapped and rolled over so I was facing the wall and could hide my humiliation.

Silence rang out for several stunned seconds, and then I thought—though I had to be wrong—I heard a low laugh before the room went silent again.

Chapter Six

Death

SHE'D BEEN in a trancelike state for the past ten minutes. She sat with her hands pressed to the forest floor, eyes closed, lips moving rapidly, spelling. The knife was on the ground beside her, and I had to grip Raze's girth strap to hold myself back when she finally opened her eyes, picked it up, and sliced her forearm. The scent of her blood hit me instantly, and the darkness rushed forward, confused, enraged, the shadows afraid we were losing her.

That she was being taken away from us already.

The shadows fed off my emotions, and I couldn't fight down all that was warring inside me, couldn't hold them back. The weight of my cloak fell around me, and the world turned gray and misty as the shadows gathered at my eyes, transforming the rest of my face.

Her blood dripped down her arm and pooled on the ground, absorbed into the earth, becoming part of my world, part of me. I'd never felt anything like it; heat trickled over my shoulders and back, sliding around my hips and down my cock. My eyes rolled back in my head.

What the fuck is happening?

She did it again, slicing the other arm, then closed her eyes and tilted her head back, muttering her spell over and over. I could *feel* the power move through her, because it was moving through me now as well. More blood hit the ground, sinking into the dirt, and I gritted my teeth so I didn't groan when the warmth washed over me again, down my chest, my stomach—

Fuck.

I fought not to go to her, gripping the leather strap tighter.

"Are you okay?" Her voice drifted over to me, and the shadows instantly receded, her voice soothing them, reassuring them. She was alive. She was okay.

I wasn't. I was far from fucking okay.

"Yes," I bit out and somehow managed to stay where the hell I was.

She nodded, watching me closely, but I could tell she didn't believe me. It seemed I was incapable of hiding anything from her. Taking out a small pot from her bag, she scooped out some of its contents and smoothed it over her cuts, then bound them with linen and slid her jacket back on. "All done."

Zuri bumped Zinnia with her snout when she reached her, and my consort ran her hands down the beast's neck. "I'm okay, sweetheart," she said. "I promise."

The gentle voice she used didn't help the way I was feeling right then, so I closed the space between us and tossed her up onto Zuri's back. She made a sound of surprise, then scowled at me. "We need to leave."

"Well, I'm ready when you are."

I swung up onto Raze, and we headed off. I tried to focus, to prepare for what was to come, but all morning, visions of her lying in bed in that tree house, looking at me from across the room, kept infiltrating my mind. The way she'd been looking at me, there was lust in her eyes. I could barely resist her as it was. If she ever decided to act on those feelings, I was fucked, because there was no resisting her. What she didn't know was that I was hers to command.

She was my queen, and I existed to bow at her feet.

To worship only her.

~

Zinnia

The gateway's power was like a giant magnet—the closer we got to it, the stronger its pull.

Zuri was restless beneath me, jumpy and nervous. I ran my hand down her neck. "It's okay, sweet girl," I said. "You can go home soon."

We wouldn't be riding them past the gate. We'd be traveling on foot once we entered the Outer Realm.

The forest grew darker the closer we got to it. I shivered. It felt as if night was falling when it was barely after midday. I studied Death; his wide back was rigid as he searched our surroundings.

How the hell had we gotten here? The first time he'd come to me, I'd been fifteen, and he'd terrified me—so much so, I'd refused to sleep until I was sure he wouldn't invade my dreams again. How did we go from that night to now? To me traveling through realms with him on the back of a beast.

The memory of that night rushed forward unbidden.

A voice whispered through my head, then another.

I felt awake, but I wasn't.

"There she is, brother. I found her for you."

The owner of that voice was nowhere to be seen. I was in a forest, dark and dense. I spun around, searching the trees. "Who's there?"

Electricity clawed over my skin, like tiny talons clinging to my flesh. Dread sliced down my spine, and the veins on either side of my throat felt as if they were struggling to pump blood fast enough. I felt dizzy and out of breath.

Shadows moved among the trees, and I tried to step back, but I couldn't move. My feet were locked in place, thick roots twisted around them, holding me fast. I shook my head furiously. Why wasn't I waking up? I needed to wake up.

The shadows swirled more furiously, twisting closer.

No, not shadows.

Oh goddess, it was a massive black robe, the hood up, concealing the being underneath. It moved as if it was alive. It came closer, and I fought harder, but there was no escape.

"Do not fight." A voice drenched in sorrow and agony and rumbling with earth-shattering rage rolled over me.

I froze, terror locking every muscle in my body.

Death.

Somehow, I knew who he was.

He stopped in front of me, bright blue eyes piercing me from beneath his hood. "You belong to me," he said in that horrifying voice. "On your eighteenth birthday, I will come for you, consort."

I stared at him in terror.

"You will belong to me, serve me... love me."

I wanted to scream, to cover my ears and curl up on the ground. The dread and despair that filled me made me want to die. If I had a knife, I would've slit my own throat then and there. I'd never felt this way, this hopeless, this depth of emptiness. Oh goddess, it hurt.

I tried to shake my head, to say no, but my body was locked solid, utterly immobile. I felt a hot tear streak down my ice-cold cheek while my mind screamed, the sound trapped inside me, unable to leave my mouth.

His arm lifted, a bony hand about to cup my face—

I jolted awake.

Jasmine stood over me, her face wet with tears. "You were scream-ing. I thought you were dying," she sobbed.

I pulled my baby sister into my arms as Hemlock scurried up my arm and curled around my neck, hissing in my ear, letting me know he was scared as well, looking for the danger. "I'm okay." I shoved back the covers. "Go back to bed, Jazzy. I just had a bad dream, that's all," I lied.

She nodded, her eyes wide and filled with fear. "Something's wrong."

I wrapped my arm around her narrow shoulders. "I promise I'm okay. I just... I remembered I had a paper due tomorrow. I dreamed Mr. Anders was chasing me with a knife, demanding I give it to him. Go back to bed. I'm gonna make some coffee and get it done." I couldn't go back to sleep, not when Death might be there waiting for me.

She nodded and yawned. "Don't ever scream like that again," she muttered and headed to the door.

"I won't," I said, which was useless since I had no idea I'd been doing it.

Jasmine wandered out, and I snatched up my phone and searched the word consort.

A wife, husband, or companion.

I shot to my feet. No. Never. I would never be his.

Zuri stumbled, jolting me back to the here and now, and I ran my hand down her neck to soothe her.

In the end, the fates had gotten their way, like they always did. There'd be no escaping my destiny, and there never had been. When I thought of the price I'd paid to conceal myself from him—I shuddered. I hadn't known. Even after what was stolen from me was gone, I still hadn't understood the magnitude of it.

I shook off the memories, not wanting to go back there, to what happened three days later in that grimy little house, or think about those dead yellow eyes that haunted me still on my darkest days.

Zuri tilted her head to the side, and I felt the tension in her body as unease built behind my chest; something was seriously off. We were still in Limbo, but I felt it—the Outer Realm was seeping through the gateway and polluting this part of the forest. What the hell would it be like on the other side?

Death continued to scan the area around us. He felt it as well. "We're close, aren't we?"

With a growl, several demons burst from the trees and attacked Zuri. She shrieked in pain, and Raze spun around, roaring. I jumped from her back, before she bucked me off, and went after the demons biting and slicing her with their claws. I pulled out my knife and stabbed the one closest in the eye, about to spin him around and stab him in the throat—but then Death was there. He still had powers, even if they were diminished, but instead of making them go *poof*, he grabbed the one I'd stabbed. His hand and forearm turned black—something I'd never seen before—and as soon as he touched the demon, blood spilled from the creature's mouth. Death gripped him under the chin and wrenched his head back, tearing it clean off with a snarl.

Another came at me, and he slashed its throat with his staff, kicked it in the sternum, and went down with it. He pulled a knife from his boot, and gripping the demon's face with that black hand, holding him down, blood oozing from between his fingers, he hacked its head off, and it turned to ash.

Death finished off the rest before I could even get to them. The touch of Death was real, and I'd just seen it in action.

When the last demon disintegrated at his feet, he strode to me, his gaze slicing over my body. "Are you injured?"

"No, I'm fine." I quickly checked on Hemy. He was curled up, trembling, and I held him in his bag close to me. "I'm so sorry, baby," I whispered.

Death closed in. "It's only going to get worse. Let me send him back. Egon will look after him."

I hated being parted from Hemlock—he was my familiar, and it physically hurt to be away from him—but I would never forgive myself if something happened to him. He was terrified, and it broke my heart to see him like this. I nodded and scooped him up.

"Egon is going to take good care of you until I get back, okay? You know he loves to give you treats." Hemy squeaked, then gave me a little hiss, not happy, not wanting to be away from me either. "Do you have enough power this close to the gateway?"

Death nodded.

I kissed Hemlock on his fuzzy little head and handed him over.

Death gently took him, cradling him in his big, tattooed hands. Hemlock looked up at him wide-eyed as Death closed his eyes, head tilted back.

One moment, Hemlock was there; the next, he was gone. When Death opened his eyes again, they were bright, glowing. "Egon has him. He knows what to do."

Zuri whimpered. She was bleeding badly, and Raze was pressed to her side. "Is she going to be okay?"

"As long as they leave now so Raze can tend to her wounds— his saliva has powerful healing properties," he said and strode over to them. "You may go now, my friends. I'm sorry your mate was injured, Raze. When she has recovered, come to the castle, and I'll make sure you have all the food you need and clean wool and cotton for your nest."

Raze made a low sound and leaned into Death when he ran his hands down the beast's side. We quickly got our bags, removed their bridles and girth straps; then Raze nudged his mate, and they loped off into the forest.

"We need to keep moving." Death scanned the trees surrounding us. "There could be more demons close by."

Slipping on my pack, I tightened the leather straps, then secured my hunting knife to my thigh and motioned ahead. "Lead the way."

We walked quickly and quietly through the dense forest, and every now and then I heard the crack of a branch or a distant howl. "They're stalking us."

He glanced down at me and nodded. "We'll be harder to detect once we pass through the gate with my power so diminished. We should hopefully get a head start before they work out we're there."

"So what are we doing when we get through? Is there something we need to collect, something that will wake your brother?"

Death continued to look ahead. "His physical body is in my castle, but his dream-self is in our mother's realm. It's the only way he's safe from her there. We need to go to the location his dream-self resides and call for him to wake." He tilted his head to the side, listening, and I did the same, but then he carried on.

"Why is his... dream-self there in the first place?"

"He guards something there that only he has the ability to protect."

"What's he guarding?"

He paused, just for a moment. "Something precious."

That pause was enough of a tell that I knew he wasn't going to share more than that—not yet, anyway—but there were also a whole bunch of holes in that story, not just what this "precious thing" was.

We carried on without too much trouble after that. At one point, Death spun around with a snarl, pounding his staff on the ground, and whatever had been following us changed their mind and stayed back.

The trees were dense here, and when we broke through to the other side, I saw it. The gateway. It was stone, similar to the gate out of Limbo, but this was made of glossy onyx, flecked with silver, like tiny stars.

Coldness, dread, evil seeped through the gateway as I stared at it. "I can hold my own, but I'd be lying if I said I wasn't afraid."

"I won't let you die," Death said, his voice resonating through me.

I swallowed, my throat impossibly dry all of a sudden. "Promise?" I smirked up at him, as if I could hide just how scared I was.

"You have my word."

Then Death took my hand, and we stepped through.

Chapter Seven

Zinnia

WE ENTERED INTO DARKNESS.

"This way," Death said, voice low, tugging my hand and leading me into a forest of jagged obsidian. Lightning flashed through the night sky while thunder rolled repeatedly in the distance.

Hisses and growls came from somewhere behind us.

Death spun around and cursed. "Run."

He didn't need to tell me twice. "Go, I can keep up." He was fast, really fast, veering left and right through towering rocks. Pumping my arms, I shadowed his every move, afraid I'd fall and impale myself on one of the vicious-looking rocks poking out of the ground like giant stalagmites. The growls grew louder. "They're gaining on us," I called.

Death spun around suddenly, hooked me around the waist, flung me over his shoulder, and took off, just as a horde of something loud and angry exploded around the edge of a wide rock behind us. I hung on to him as he sprinted over boulders and tore around the jagged towers of stone that seemed to have burst through the ground.

Lightning flashed bright, turning night into day, giving me a good look at what was chasing us.

Holy fuck.

Their mouths were hanging open, drool streaming behind them as they chased us, moving faster than should be possible on all fours. Death's powers were all but smothered here, but my magic still burned bright inside me. I couldn't call on nature, to shake the ground beneath our feet or call on the wind, because we weren't in the Earth Realm anymore; we were somewhere else, somewhere Mother Nature wasn't.

So instead, I sent my power at them with a roar from deep in my gut, blasting them with a wall of magic. It had strengthened after cutting, after spilling blood, and several of the creatures flew back, smashing into the sharp rocks, but there were more coming. I called on the fire inside me, and it manifested, flames dancing above my palms. With another cry, I fired it at them—not easy while I was bouncing on Death's shoulder and close to throwing the hell up. Several were tossed aside, engulfed in flames and screaming, but there were still more.

I had hoped to save Magnolia's potions, but now seemed like a good time to use one. I shoved my hand in the side pocket of my pack. There were several different vials, all different shapes. I finally found the one I was looking for—the long, thin one. I tapped Death's back. "Let them get closer," I yelled.

"You better have a good plan," he yelled back but instantly did as I said and slowed.

If I weren't facing a horde of bloodthirsty monsters, I'd probably wonder why he so easily did what I asked, without question, but I was, so instead, I egged them on. "Come on, you ugly fucks," I yelled. "Catch me."

One of them roared, spittle flying everywhere and flashing

their long, piranha-like teeth. They bounded toward us at full speed, and my heart pounded in my ears as the huge demonic creatures got closer. It roared again, so close to us now that I got a clear view of its tonsils. There were five of them left, and their eyes were wild and filled with hunger. *Just a little closer.*

The one at the front leaped, snapping its teeth barely a yard from us. The rocks had become less crowded. I needed to do it now, before the creatures had a chance to spread out. They snapped and bounded closer—

I tossed the vial hard, smashing it against the rocks beneath their feet. It shattered, the potion and its toxic fumes covering them. Their roars turned to shrieks as their flesh melted, dissolving, leaving only bone as they all but turned into piles of goo behind us.

Death spun around. "Fuck," he said roughly, lifting goose bumps all over me. "That'll do it, little witch."

Silence surrounded us. We'd gotten them all—at least, the ones chasing us.

"So, um... you wanna put me down now?" I said from my position still dangling over his wide shoulder.

His hand pressed against the backs of my thighs and applied pressure as his other hand went to my back, and he carefully eased me down. He did it slowly, too slowly, and my front dragged all the way down his chest.

We were close, too goddamn close.

"Nice work," he said, looking down at me.

I cleared my throat. "I'm glad you approve. My cousin's potions are vicious." I stepped back, and his hand, still resting on my back, slipped away.

He seemed to lean forward, his eyes darkening.

"So now what?"

His chest expanded sharply. "Now we walk. Stay close."

I had to power walk to keep up with him, and every now and then, he'd tilt his head and listen for anything else following us. The terrain changed as we went, the rocks becoming even more sparse now, and I'd spotted the odd vine of an ivy-like plant curling around boulders and crawling along the ground.

Lightning flashed over us, forking through the dark sky, followed closely by ground-shaking thunder that felt as if it rolled right through me. "Is it always dark here?"

"It never used to be, but it is now."

"Because of your mother?"

"Yes."

"When will we reach her realm?"

"In a few days," he said, scanning our surroundings.

"Will we see her while we're there?"

"Not if I can help it." When he spoke about her, the shadows instantly gathered around him.

Ahead were trees; they were sparse, but as we got closer, I could see they shimmered, like they'd been sprinkled with fairy dust. "It's beautiful."

"Don't touch anything unless I do, and definitely don't eat anything," Death said.

Awesome. The vines I'd seen were thicker here, and some had grown up the tree trunks. I rushed to keep up with Death, who hadn't stopped. As we traveled deeper, I realized the vines had flowers, and they unfurled, opening and closing as we got close, like stars blinking in the sky. "What are these?"

"They're deadly," Death said, "like most things here. The Outer Realm should be more of a no-man's-land, relatively safe to move through and ruled by no god, but over centuries, Nox has been slowly claiming it for herself. Now it's like an extension of the Night Realm—always dark, the lightning, the plants and trees, and now crawling with her demons and other creatures. It used to be all rocks here, like the ones we ran through, but my mother is greedy, and she knows taking the only buffer that exists between us will anger me."

Based on the way Death had described his mother, it seemed

Nox had created a world as toxic as she was. "She sounds bored. Time to get a life."

Death's gaze sliced to me, and his eyes did that brightening thing they did sometimes. "Yes, it is."

We carried on walking, and the trees went from sparse to a dense forest. I stayed close to Death. It was impossible to avoid everything with how thick the forest had become, and my leathers were the only thing protecting me from the noxious plants around us.

A weird hooting sound came from above, and Death stilled immediately. One moment, I was beside him; the next, he'd pulled me in close to him, and we were surrounded by darkness, by shadows. His cloak had settled around us.

"Be still," he rasped.

I blinked up at him, trying to breathe with his arms around me again, with him so impossibly close, and with those blue eyes glowing down at me in a face that now looked like a skull. The shadows hadn't just covered us; they'd gathered around his face, turning him into the god he was. Again, I tried to breathe, but being this close to him while he looked like that? Yeah, I was having some trouble.

The hooting came again, closer this time.

One of his large, tattooed hands came up, and he took hold of my jaw. He dipped closer, his face only a couple of inches from mine, and shook his head, telling me to be quiet. My heart smacked against my ribs with force. I opened my mouth, but I couldn't drag in the oxygen I needed. What I felt coming off him… it was nothing like I'd ever experienced—the darkness, the anguish, the rage, and all that banked power, locked down against his will, unable to be accessed. It wasn't gone, though. No, it was still very much there, writhing under the surface.

And alarmingly, it wasn't just fear I was feeling all of a sudden. My nipples tightened, and a pulse throbbed between my thighs.

The hoot came a third time, but it was in the distance now.

"Breathe," he said huskily.

Finally, I was able to drag in a ragged breath.

"And again."

I stared at him, unable to look away from those glowing eyes and that shadowed face as I drew in oxygen like I'd never breathed before. My head spun, and my body was still thrumming. Goddess, I was so hot and achy.

"What was that?" I whispered to break the unbearable tension.

"An owllike creature that can tear a face off with one swipe of his talons. He's Nox's pet, and she can see through his eyes."

"That doesn't sound good," I said, still whispering. "Do you think she knows we're here?"

"Possibly."

I licked my lips as nerves coiled impossibly tight in my belly. "Your cloak... I thought your powers didn't really work here."

His glowing gaze studied me closely. "My cloak isn't a power," he said, still perilously close. "It's part of me. We are one and the same."

The mournful hooting sound came again, and it was far in the distance now. Still, he didn't take the cloak away, keeping us ensconced in his camouflage, turning us into shadows.

His breathing grew rougher, and he wasn't moving away. His arms were still around me, and his hands were hot against my back.

"Who's Aster?" I blurted. Ever since I dreamed about her last night, I'd been wanting to ask.

He flinched.

"One of your consorts?"

"How do you know that name?"

The roughness to his voice tore a shiver from me. "She came to me while I slept. She showed herself, offering me a vision of her... and, ah, you while we were in the tree house."

"What do you mean showed herself?" he bit out.

"I'm a medium, communing with the dead is what I do. I

didn't think those powers worked in Limbo, but somehow, she showed me a... a memory of the two of you."

"What were we doing?" His eyes bored into me.

I wished I'd kept my damn mouth shut, but he wasn't going to let it go, not until I shared what I saw, because he never let anything go. The fact we were so close, still under his cloak, and he looked like... *that* while my traitorous body burned for the terrifying god holding me made it all the more humiliating. "You were... making love."

His nostrils flared, and a growl rolled from his chest.

I didn't dare tell him it wasn't the first one that I'd seen or that I'd started to wonder if the consorts that came before me were trying to warn me of something. "She showed me. I didn't ask for it. She—"

"Stop," he growled out, so much banked rage in that one word.

I swallowed convulsively, my mouth impossibly dry. He'd loved her. He'd loved Aster, and he'd lost her, like the rest. "I'm sorry. I didn't mean to cause you pain."

He released me suddenly, and the cloak vanished, the shadows going with it. "We need to keep moving."

I nodded and followed as he strode off, wondering what the hell just happened. I felt that way a lot when I was with Death.

We didn't speak much after that, and in the darkness, I lost track of time and place. I had no idea how long we walked for—long enough my feet ached, anyway. Finally, we broke through the trees, and the landscape changed again. The only constant here was the thunder and lightning, and when the next flash forked through the sky, it gave me a better look at what was ahead. It was wild and vast; there was rugged coastline and the sound of a turbulent sea along with the squawk of birds, or at least birdlike creatures, echoing in the distance.

"We'll rest for the night," Death said.

"This place is way too exposed. We should keep walking," I said, even as my feet screamed in protest.

Death lifted his staff, pointing to something in the distance as more lightning flashed.

There was a glossy black tower, thin and tall. A beacon of pale light glowed from the top, aimed out to the furious black ocean, like a demonic lighthouse. "Does anyone live there?"

"Yes."

"Will we be welcome?"

"No, but they will let us in," he said and started for the tower.

Chapter Eight

Zinnia

Death banged on the black wooden door.

This place seriously gave me the creeps.

Heavy footsteps, slow and ominous, came from behind it, and I had visions of Frankenstein's monster standing on the other side. I wasn't ashamed to say that when the door slowly creaked its way open, I stepped a little behind Death.

A short male with long, wispy gray hair that reached his waist and gray skin only a shade darker stood there, scowling at us. "My lord," he said with distaste.

"We require a room for the night, Horace."

His beady red gaze sliced to me, then back to Death. "But of course." Then he disappeared back inside, and we followed.

Horace wasn't a breed of demon I'd ever seen, but every instinct in me said that's what he was. His feet were disproportionately large to his body. His legs were strong and muscled, but his body was wiry and misshapen. His features were somewhat humanoid but bulbous and exaggerated in a way that gave him away, and of course, there were those red eyes.

"He doesn't seem happy to see you," I said to Death under my breath. "Will he rat us out?"

"He can't, at least in theory. This tower is supposed to be a sanctuary, a safe place for travelers to rest before sailing the Night Sea."

I spun to Death as Horace stepped behind a small reception desk and grabbed a key from the wall. He handed it over. "Do you require a repast, my lord?"

"We do," he said.

No, thanks. Whatever this guy was serving, I wasn't eating. Of course, with Death's powers basically out of commission, there would be no pulling a five-star meal out of thin air.

"I'd also like to hire a ship for our passage tomorrow," Death said.

"We're going in that ocean?" I asked, unable to bite back my horror.

"Yes." He pulled two gold coins from his pocket and handed them to Horace. "I want your best." He took out another coin and held it up. "And I want provisions, enough for two days, and the ship better be seaworthy, and the crew trustworthy, demon, or I will come back here, no matter how long it takes me, and I will torture you, flay the skin from your flesh and the meat from your bones, and I won't stop until you are ash. Do you understand?" Horace grabbed for the coin, and Death pulled it out of reach. "Do you understand?" he said again, his earth-shattering voice making Horace wince.

"Of course, my lord."

"Do not *of course* me. I know your tricks. I've been on the receiving end of them more than once, and I know that despite your post here, you are my mother's lapdog. That will not save you if you fuck with me or my consort." Then Death tossed the extra coin at the demon, snatched the key from the desk, and strode toward the stairs.

Horace's red gaze was burning with fury when it slid to me. I quickly spun away and rushed after Death.

He took the stairs two at a time, obviously angry as hell.

"You've had some issues with Horace before, then?"

His lips curled back. "You could say that."

"What kind of issues? Not like ship stuff, right?"

"Yes, ship stuff. It ended up at the bottom of the ocean."

Fuck.

"Well, after the warning you gave him, I don't think you'll have any trouble this time." I freaking hoped not, anyway.

Death grunted. Not reassuring at all.

"By the way, when were you going to tell me about this little sea voyage? 'Cause I have to tell you, I'm not much of a fan of boats and wide-open ocean... like at all."

"I know," he said, "but you'll be fine."

"You know? How?" I said when he finally stopped outside one of the rooms and slid in the key.

His hand stilled, just for a split second, but then he turned the key and shoved open the door. "I know a lot of things."

Great, another room with one bed. Like seriously? "Can we get another room?" I eyed the huge bed. On second thought, he could have it. It looked like it was made out of charred bones from creatures of unidentifiable origin, if the skull in the center of the headboard was anything to go by. At least there was a fire going against the wall, because it was cold and miserable.

"No. We stay together, especially here." He hurriedly undid his jacket and slid the heavy leather off, tossing it on the back of a chair. He wore nothing underneath it, and this time, his back was to me, so when he rolled his broad shoulders and flexed his arms, I watched the way the muscles bunched, making the inverted torch tattooed down the backs of both his arms move and the flames dance.

Seeing him like this was so... weird. He was the God of Death, and I was forced to spend time with him in a way only—well, possibly ten—other consorts had. He'd obviously had intimate relationships with the others, at least some of them. The very idea of taking things there with him was... not something I could even truly contemplate.

Not only was it way too intimidating, but that didn't seem to be what he wanted from me, and I certainly didn't want that from him.

Then I thought about the way my body had reacted while we hid under his cloak, and I inwardly winced. I had no control over my reaction; it didn't mean I wanted to go there with him. Maybe that's why the others had died. The kiss of Death. Once you let him into your pants, you'd signed your own death warrant. "You don't like wearing a shirt or a jacket, why?" I asked.

He turned to me. "I've spent very long periods of time in only my cloak, so it takes time to get used to clothing again."

That made sense since, up until a week or so ago, I'd never seen him in anything but his cloak.

There was a knock at the door, and Death strode over, opening it. Horace rushed in, pushing a trolley. There was food crammed on top of it, and surprisingly, it didn't smell terrible. The demon left it by the fire, then hurried off without a word.

I eyed it. I'd planned to give the meal a miss, but I was starving now, and I needed to keep up my strength. "Is there anything here that you need to warn me about?"

"It's safe," he said, picking up what looked like a turkey leg and biting off a hunk of meat.

"Safe isn't what I asked." I picked up an orange and started peeling it. "I'm more concerned with what that is," I said, motioning to the leg he was tearing into.

"A bird. Not one you would know, but still a bird. It tastes like chicken."

Okay. It wasn't an orange I was peeling, but it had a deep red flesh and looked super juicy. "I'll take your word for it." I took a bite. *Nope.* Grabbing my napkin, I spat out the offending piece of fruit. "What the hell is that?"

Death's lips actually curved up on one side, and the effect was, well, nothing short of devastating. "A centeen egg."

"A what?"

"It's a kind of giant insect. Their eggs are enjoyed like caviar here."

I gagged and scrubbed the napkin over my tongue. "Jesus, that's disgusting."

A low sound rumbled from him. My gaze shot up. He was—holy shit, he was laughing. If I thought the grin was devastating, then Death laughing was... life-altering.

I tried not to stare, stunned, as he took a loaf of bread and tore it in half, then used a knife to scrape out some flesh from the centeen egg and spread it across the bread. "If you eat it the right way, it's quite delicious."

"Like hell it is." I grabbed my wine, which was thankfully good, and swilled it around my mouth. "I'll be tasting that until the day I die, and thankfully, according to what you've told me, I don't have long to wait." I smirked and grabbed a piece of bread without bug eggs on it. "How will you remember me? The most annoying consort you've ever had—"

"Don't." He slammed his hand on the table.

I jumped, tossing the piece of bread in my hand in the air, my heart flying into my throat. He was breathing hard, his nostrils flared, his hand curled into a tight fist.

"Don't," he said again, with less force but with a whole lot more feeling.

His blue eyes were burning into me, conveying a lot of things that I didn't know what to do with. I didn't know what to say, where the hell to look. "I'm sorry," I rasped, finding it hard to find my voice. "I... I didn't mean to upset you."

He was breathing hard, that fist still clenched tight.

"I was just joking around, okay? I do that when I'm freaked about something. It annoys my sister as well."

Still, he said nothing. What the hell was his problem, anyway?

"You really are pissed off?" Now I was getting pissed. "Well, that's kind of selfish of you, honestly. It's my head on the chopping block. I think I have a right to deal with it however I like."

He stood with a snarl. "Do you want to die, is that it? Do you have a fucking death wish, consort?"

"No, but I am one of a *long* line of consorts, and you told me yourself that most have died pretty fucking gruesomely, so forgive me, but something like that is kind of hard to forget."

He leaned forward, planting his hands on the trolley between us. "Then don't fucking die."

I stared up at him. "I'm definitely going to try not to, Mors, but my odds don't sound that good," I fired back at him.

"All you have to do is stay close to me, and you'll live. It's not hard."

"You make it sound so easy, but obviously, it's not, or consort number one would still be here with you, right? Or is that not how it works? 'Cause you sure as hell haven't tried to help me understand."

He ground his teeth. "There are things I can't tell you, things I want to tell you... so..." he growled. "So fucking badly. But I can't, so your only hope is to trust me."

I scoffed. "Right? Easy. Trust the guy who obviously does not trust me in the slightest. You make deals and barter with me because you don't trust I'll keep my word, yet you want me to just give you blind trust without even attempting to earn it?"

He straightened and paced away, his hand running over his tattooed skull. His back moved with the way his chest heaved. Where the fuck had this come from?

"If you want me to trust you, why don't you tell me what the hell is going on?" I said. "Why are you so pissed off right now? It can't just be about what I said."

He spun around. "You saw me in your vision, in your dream, with... with her. Tell me, Zinnia, what you saw."

I'd seen him with possibly more than one "her" but I knew the one he was talking about—the one he'd called Aster. I swallowed, my throat dry. "You were..."

"'Making love' were the words you used. Try having that, *feeling that*... then reaching for it over and over again and having it taken from you. You dying, little witch, isn't something I want to even fucking think about." Then he snatched up his bag, turned, and strode into the bathroom, slamming the door after him.

Leaving me sitting there utterly stunned and, again, seriously confused.

I lost my appetite after that, and when he finally came out of the bathroom, subdued and smelling like soap, I grabbed my own bag and locked myself in the bathroom as well. I took my time, having a long, hot shower. My muscles ached, and I didn't smell the freshest after days of riding and walking.

As I dressed, pulling on a pair of shorts and a soft T-shirt, I thought about Hemlock. Egon would look after him, but I missed him so damn much. Where would he sleep tonight? Shaking it off, I forced myself to open the door and walk back out into the room. The only light was coming from the fire. Death was in bed, one arm behind his head, his eyes closed. The chair would have to do. I started toward it.

"Get in the bed, Zinnia."

He'd said my name again. "I'll just take the chair."

"You've called me by my name three times now."

I spun to face him. "Seriously?"

"Seriously," he said, his eyes still closed. "I'm calling the first one in."

"You're going to make me sleep with you?"

"I'm going to make you sleep in a comfortable bed and get a decent night's rest before we face the Night Sea tomorrow, and I know you're too stubborn to do anything I ask, so I'll make you do it."

I huffed out a breath. "Why are you like this?"

"Get in the bed."

"You're an asshole, you know that?" I was pretty sure I saw his lips curl up again.

"Shhh now, I'm trying to sleep," he said.

I stared across the room at the hideous bed made of bones and the god lying in it and tried to freaking breathe.

"If you're not in this bed in five seconds, I'm coming to get you."

That spurred me into action. "Fine," I muttered and rushed across the room, because again, Death always meant what he said.

Shoving back the covers, I climbed up, staying as far over on my side as I could without falling out, then dragged the heavy comforter up to my chin.

There was no way I was going to fall asleep. No way.

Chapter Nine

Zinnia

SHE KISSED her way across Death's stomach, grinning at him. "You're beautiful, you know that?"

"The only thing beautiful in this room is you, my precious Stella."

A growl came from outside the tower, and she shivered. "I don't like this place."

His fingers delved into her hair, and he tilted her head back. "As long as you stay close to me, you'll be safe."

She smiled again. "I know, and I insist on repaying you for your protection."

Death flashed his teeth. "And how will you do that?"

"Watch," she said and kissed his chest again.

I blinked into the darkness, my skin tight, my belly swirly. I was hot; my skin was burning up, probably because I was draped over Death... again. This time, with the way my lips tingled, I had the horrifying feeling that, like the female in my vision, I'd been kissing his chest—

Long fingers delved in my hair, fisting, tilting my head back. *Oh fuck.*

My gaze sliced up to Death, and he stared at me in the shadows, his blue eyes glittering. "I tried to wake you," he rasped.

It felt like I'd only closed my eyes for a moment, but I'd been asleep for hours. It was early morning. I licked my lips nervously, trapped, locked in place by that gaze. A part of me was still in my head, feeling what she had, as if this weren't real.

"Were you having a vision?" he asked.

His deep otherworldly voice moved through me, making me tremble, and I became more aware of where I was, and how incredibly hot and smooth his skin was. How hard his body was beneath mine. He was wearing pants, but I felt his solid thighs flex beneath me.

The female, he'd called her only Stella this time, was right—he was beautiful. The God of Death was awe-inspiring in every way, and she'd gotten to touch him, to kiss him.

You're touching him, and I'm pretty sure you kissed him as well —his chest, anyway.

He massaged my head gently, and I almost freaking purred.

"Zinnia?"

Goddess, the way he said my name. I shivered again. I felt mesmerized, like he was the witch and not me, and I was fully under his spell. "Yes?"

"Were you having another vision?"

I nodded, and my chin grazed his chest. My nipples hardened immediately. "Um... yeah."

Why aren't you moving? Move.

He continued to massage my scalp, and I was trapped by his sorcery, frozen in place.

"What did you see?"

I didn't know what these visions meant, but there was no use hiding this one, I'm sure he'd figured out what it was about for himself. Was the female I saw in bed with him here in the tower the same one I'd seen in the tree house? Did he call all his consorts Stella? "You were with a female." It came out a whisper. "She was on top of you."

"Like you are now?" he asked in a velvety tone.

"Yes."

The space between us felt electric, the room closing in, as if the world around us had vanished and he and I were the only two beings who existed.

"What else?"

"She was kissing your chest, and you were fisting her hair."

His fingers twisted, then curled, tugging lightly, and humiliatingly, a moan slipped past my lips. "Then what happened?"

Get off him. Move. "She was... being playful and offered payment for your protection."

His nostrils flared. "How?"

"She, um... she kissed your chest again..." His eyes narrowed, and he licked his perfectly formed lower lip. "And then I... I woke up."

A heaviness fell between us, and the tension grew, kept growing until I had to fight not to squirm on top of him. His gaze was on me, moving over my face, and the urge to lift higher, to slide up his body and suck that lower lip into my mouth was almost overwhelming.

His chest was rising and falling faster while he watched me, waiting. He knew what I was thinking, and he was waiting for me to make the first move.

Don't. Don't do it. Kiss of Death, remember?

I shouldn't, but still, I pressed my hand into the mattress, about to slide up his body, to risk everything to get to that mouth—

A loud knock had me jolting and shoving away from him.

Death's lips peeled back with a low snarl before he shoved back the covers and strode to the door. The muscles in his back shifted, flexing, his biceps bulging when he clenched his fists before yanking the door open.

Horace stood there, and his eyes widened when he looked up at Death.

"What?" Death snarled.

"Your ship is ready and equipped with enough provisions for your journey," Horace said, a slight tremble to his voice. The demon definitely wasn't as brave this morning in the face of Death's fury.

"We'll be down when we're ready."

Horace bowed as he backed up. "Of course, my lord."

Death slammed the door and turned back to me as I slid out of bed.

"Get back in the bed, wife," he said, his tone fierce.

Goddess, I felt that in my belly and lower. I was about to laugh at his arrogance, but the hunger in his eyes, the power of a god demanding he be obeyed, gave me pause. My go-to of escaping awkward situations with humor or being a straight up smart-ass definitely wasn't the way to go in this instance.

Easing away from the bed, I shook my head. "No, I won't be doing that."

His head tilted to the side, his glittering blue gaze tracking me. "What did you say?"

Death was like two different beings—the new, more human side of him had been dominating, but then the other, the scarier version of Death, would make a surprise reappearance, like now. This was the Death I'd met when I first entered Limbo. The rage-filled, demanding god.

"Take a breath," I said, probably unwisely. "Think about what you're saying."

"You called me by my name, consort, three times—"

"And what? Now you're going to use one of those times to force me to fuck you?" I fired at him, all thoughts of trying not to piss him off further flying out the door. "You'd really want that? For the first time we have sex to be because you forced me?"

He blinked, his heaving chest stilling for several beats, and then he shook his head, like he was trying to shake something from his mind. "I would never force myself on you," he said, the shadows starting to swirl around him. "You are my consort. I protect you. I'll never harm you." His nostrils flared as he dragged in another breath.

"Glad to hear it. Whatever that was that just happened a moment ago, you need to rein it in. I'm here with you because I have no choice, but I'm not powerless. You said it yourself, I'm a warrior, and I will fight to protect myself, even against you, and even if that means it kills me." Which it would; there was no beating Death.

The shadows swirled more fiercely, and one side of his face had transformed, now a skull, with the other side unchanged; he had one glowing blue eye, but the other was a black void. He took a stilted step forward, and it took everything in me not to stumble back, but somehow, I held my ground as he strode across the room.

I tilted my head back when he stopped in front of me. I tried to say something, but my voice wouldn't work as his hand came up. Still, I flinched.

He made a rough, wounded sound, and then gently, so gently, his fingers brushed under my chin, across my cheek. "Forgive me, Zinnia," he said, the power of his voice making my knees weak. "I would never harm you. I am... not myself here."

I locked my damn knees and searched his pained expression. He was sorry, tormented by what just happened, and I couldn't bring myself to punish him more when he was obviously punishing himself. "I forgive you." I shoved my hands into my pockets. "And I believe you."

He nodded, obvious relief in that one blue eye; then the

shadows swirled again, dissipating, and he dropped his hand. "Gather your things. We need to leave."

The dinghy creaked as Death rowed us away from the shore and toward the black ship anchored and waiting in the Night Sea. Horace sat behind me, not saying a word.

The water was as black as the ship, the only contrast from the white foam when the waves broke.

"How long will it take to reach the Night Realm?"

Death pulled the oars through the water, the veins in his biceps popping. "Tomorrow night, when we reach land."

The ship was getting closer, and I could see the crew watching from the deck. "How dangerous is it?"

"You will be safe as long as you stay close to me," he said, the same thing he'd said to me before, and the same thing he'd said to the Stella I'd seen in last night's vision.

We reached the ship, and a rope ladder was tossed down. Death held it and motioned me forward. I climbed it quickly, and the demons on board stood back, keeping a respectable distance when I reached the top, but all of them were looking at me as if their last meal had just boarded the ship. No way was I turning my back on them, and it was hard not to pull my knife free under the weight of all those hungry eyes.

The rope ladder creaked, and the sound of the oars knocking the side of the boat reached me. I refused to turn and look, but I knew Horace was rowing away, leaving us here. The thump of Death's boots hitting the deck echoed behind me, and the demons quickly dropped their gazes.

Death handed our bags to one of them and turned to another. "Anchor up," he said to who I assumed was the captain of this ship —a ship that looked as if it would be more at home at the bottom of the ocean. The demon called the order, and the rattle of a heavy chain came as the anchor came up and a massive black sail dropped. The old ship groaned as wind filled the tattered sail, and we started moving.

The demons rushed off to do whatever it was they needed to do, and I turned and gripped the railing, watching as the land grew more and more distant. I had no idea what was coming, but dread filled me, growing deeper the farther from shore we got. The demon captain called orders, Death now at his side, and his crew called back, their collective voices filling me with more dread.

I wanted the hell off this ship already, but I didn't want to reach land either. The gods only knew what Nox had in store for us.

Chapter Ten

Zinnia

THE SHIP SEEMED to lift completely out of the water before crashing back down. Rain and wind battered us as the ocean churned, throwing the ship around like it was a rubber ducky in a hot tub.

We went up again, and my stomach dropped as we slammed back down. My feet slipped from under me as water washed onto the deck. I grabbed for the railing as a strong arm locked around my middle, and I was hauled off the deck and dragged back under the small eave above the door that led down below. The door swung open behind us, and Death reached back and yanked it shut.

"Thanks," I said and tried to move out of Death's hold.

He tightened his grip. "You're not going anywhere, little witch," he said close to my ear, making me shiver. "No fucking way I'm letting you get swept overboard."

"I'm fine. I'm just more of a land lover," I called over the wind.

"In case you hadn't figured it out." I'd spent the first couple hours throwing up over the side, much to the amusement of the crew.

"Yeah, I got that," he said, still way too freaking close.

The way his voice affected me made my face heat. Thankfully, in this position, with him behind me, he couldn't see his "warrior consort" blushing like a besotted teenager. I didn't want to want him, but with every day that passed, lying to myself got harder—because I was definitely feeling things, or my body was, anyway.

The ship rolled again, and I managed to bite back my scream, just. "Can this thing capsize?"

"It's just a storm. It'll pass."

"That didn't answer my—" Something moved in the darkness, rising out of the sea, then diving back down, something huge. I grabbed Death's forearm locked around my waist. "There's something in the water."

"Where?" he yelled over the furious wind.

I pointed just as it rose out again and gnashed long, sharp teeth, then dove back down. The ship jolted sharply, but this time, it wasn't the storm. "Oh fuck."

Death brought my hand to one of the beams beside us before releasing me. "Don't let go," he said as he took off his jacket. "Knife," he said to me.

"What?"

"I need to slow it down, or he'll put a hole in the hull," he yelled.

And we'd sink. "What are you going to do?"

"If he's bleeding, he'll be more concerned with other predators on his tail than sinking us." He slid the knife from the sheath strapped to my thigh, then pulled his own from the side of his boot.

"What the hell are you doing?"

He signaled something to the demon captain. "I won't be long," he said to me. Gripping both knives tighter, he ran to the ship's railing, jumped up onto it, then dove into the sea.

I rushed to the edge just as he surfaced, then dove back down. "Holy shit." I searched the water, waiting, but he didn't surface again. Clinging to the railing, I ran around the edge of the ship as it jerked and lilted to the side, groaning and crashing down against the waves throwing us about. Death was immortal, but even he couldn't survive the jaws of a monster like that.

It was so dark, the ocean nothing but swirling obsidian, and I couldn't see anythi—

The monster rose with a roar, then dove back down—then nothing.

I ran around the ship again, hanging over the edge, desperately searching for Death. A hand landed on my shoulder, and I was shoved back from the edge. I spun as one of the demons pulled me toward the door that led below the ship, the bastard's yellowed teeth sharp and its bullish face curled in a sick grin. "No, Death can't die, but coming back after being minced up by that monster out there will take months, maybe even years. He'll have forgotten all about you by then."

Another demon joined him. "I got her first. You owe me," he said to his buddy.

This wasn't happening. No fucking way. Death had my big knife, but my small one was just as lethal. Twisting from his hold, I pulled it from my boot as I spun around and slashed. He grabbed his throat, roaring as blood sprayed from the severed artery. Spinning back, I kicked his leg out from under him, and he hit the deck. More demons gathered around to watch as I smashed my boot down on his ribs, cracking several of them, then pulled his own knife from the sheath at his hip, a nice big one, and used it to saw off his head, tossing it overboard before it had a chance to turn to ash.

Another came at me, the crew laughing and egging him on. Thank fuck Hemy wasn't with me right now. If these demons had hurt him... just the thought fueled my rage. The demon lunged at me, and I ducked, spun, and shoved the knife into his side. He screeched as I wrenched it up, then back down, spilling his guts all over the deck. I shoved my elbow into his throat, spinning back to slash it open. The blade's serrated edge was so sharp and brutal, it half decapitated him with one swipe. I yanked his head back and hacked through his spinal cord and vertebrae, severing his head, and he turned to ash as well.

The next demon stepped forward. "She's mine," he spat.

I was conserving my magic. If I had to take them all out one by one, I would, but I wasn't using my powers until I absolutely had to. I wouldn't risk draining myself too soon. I lifted the knife—

Death bounded over the railing. He was covered in blood, deep gouges across his chest, and the fury on his face when he took in what was happening would have given me pause if I wasn't so fucking relieved to see him. "No, demon, she's mine," Death roared, so fiercely, I stumbled back.

He strode forward, grabbed the demon in front of me by the throat, and tore his head from his body with his bare hands. The demons around us dropped to their knees, their heads bowed, their fear obvious. Death spun to the captain, who was on his knees as well. He grabbed him by the throat as well and lifted him, shoving him against the mast. "You allowed your crew to attack my consort," he said in a voice that had more than one demon pissing themselves and several more openly weeping.

It was full of all the things that the God of Death could deliver —horror, pain, terror.

"Has it been so long since I entered the Outer Realm that you forget who I am, demon?" he roared. "Have you forgotten what I'm capable of?"

"No, m-my lord," the demon stammered.

Death's hatred swirled around him, the shadows transforming him into the vision of his name, his face a skull, his cloak whipping about. He moved fast, slamming his fist into the demon's chest. His hand had turned black when he pulled out his beating heart and shoved it in the screaming demon's mouth before he tore him open, emptying his insides out all over the deck to slide around in the ash already there from the two demons I'd just killed. Death got in his face. Holding the demon's gaze and ignoring his muffled screams, Death gripped his throat tighter.

The demon shook his head frantically, his eyes pleading for mercy, but Death had no mercy to give and tore his head from his body, tossing it on the ground before he turned to ash as well.

Finally, he turned slowly, his cloak whipping around him in the storm. "If any of you look at my consort, I will kill you," he said, and then he pointed to one of the demons standing out of the circle—the only demon who hadn't been cheering when they'd all surrounded me. "You're the captain now. Keep your crew in line."

Then he took my hand, shoved the door open, and led me below deck.

Death shoved the door open to one of the rooms and pulled me in.

"Stay here," he said and disappeared.

Mounted lanterns flickered against the walls. There was a table against one side of the small room, an old steel tub down from that, and a bed on the opposite side. I flicked back the covers and inspected the worn cotton sheets. They looked clean. Risking it, I leaned in and sniffed. They smelled clean. I assumed we had Horace to thank for that. Though I wasn't sure I'd get much sleep tonight, not when the entire crew was after my blood—or something even worse.

The door opened again, and Death strode back in, a demon rushing in behind him carrying two buckets of steaming hot water. He dumped them into the tub and rushed off again while Death unloaded his armful of food on the table. Bread, cheese, and a bottle of wine.

I said nothing and neither did he as the demon returned and dumped more water in the tub, another demon behind him with his own buckets. They came and went until it was three-quarters full, and then Death told them not to come back and slammed the door and locked it.

"Those scratches on your chest, they look really bad," I said and closed the space between us. I lifted my hand, and he stepped back.

"They're full of poison," he said. "I need to soak the wounds in hot water now, or they won't heal properly."

"Could the poison actually kill you?"

He shook his head. "It could make me sick, though."

"Well, get in the tub. What are you waiting for?"

His gaze swept over me. "Are you hurt? Did they hurt you, Zinnia?"

He was using my name more and more, and it was an assault to every one of my senses each time he uttered it. "I'm fine. I should've expected it. I'm the idiot who dropped her guard."

He did another sweep of my body. "You're not an idiot." Then again, from head to toe. Finally satisfied I was okay, he nodded and sat on one of the chairs.

"It's kind of you to say, but we both know that's a lie."

He made a rough sound and pulled off his boots, kicking them aside. Then he stood again, his hands dropping to the buttons of his pants, and he undid them—and shoved them down.

Holy shit.

He didn't turn away. He stood there in all his slick, hairless, naked glory. I tried not to look; I really did. My mouth went dry. "Looks like I can cross shy off the list," I said and tried not to sound as breathless as I felt. Goddess, I knew he was beautiful, but I was seriously struggling to breathe. He was just all finely sculpted muscle and tattoos. No female could look at him and not be... affected. *You're still staring.* Yes, yes, I was. I pulled out one of the chairs and sat at the table as he stood by the tub. His hand changed color—pale gray, then deepening until it was black again. He held it above his chest, and the slashes oozed, a black substance bubbling to the surface. He swiped his hand down, and the poison splattered on the wooden floor before evaporating.

"So the hand of death does more than just straight up murder, then?" I said as he climbed into the tub.

"It does."

The polite thing to do would be to sit with my back to him, but I refused to show weakness. He knew what he was doing, and I wouldn't give him the satisfaction of letting him see he'd gotten to me, and I would not freaking blush. It's not like his was the first cock I'd seen. Was it the most perfect? Yes. The biggest? Hell, yes. But I was no shy little virgin, and I refused to act like one. It didn't matter who he was.

Breaking off a piece of bread, I topped it with cheese, then poured us both a glass of wine. "How long do you have to soak those wounds?" I asked and glanced up again. He was sitting in the tub, facing me, of course. He'd want to see if he'd gotten to me. The tub was pretty big, but his knees were forced to bend a little and spread wide.

He had his head tilted back, resting on the edge. "Until I feel all the poison's gone. I should have gotten most of it, but with my weakened powers..." He shrugged. "Could take a few minutes, could be an hour—depends how deep its claws went."

"So what else does the hand of death do?"

"Besides what you just saw? Not much. Mainly just the whole straight up murder thing."

"Nice," I said, ignoring the stupid flutters in my belly at the way he was looking at me. "You want some food?"

His head lifted, and those mesmerizing blue eyes locked on me. "Please."

I made him a cheese sandwich and grabbed his wine. He tracked me as I walked over to him, and I did my best not to ogle him as I handed him his wine. He drank it and gave me the glass, then took the sandwich.

"Thank you," he said. "You can go first tonight."

Of course he hadn't forgotten. No matter the circumstances, the evenings were question time. I took my seat again and popped a piece of cheese in my mouth while I contemplated my question. One kept circling my mind. It was a dangerous question and probably not the one I should ask considering our circumstances, but I wasn't sure I could help myself. "I should get two questions tonight. Your crew just tried to make me their sex slave, so you owe me."

His hand exploded out of the water and gripped the edge of the tub like he was about to bound over the side. "Do not remind me of that. We still need to make it to land, and if you talk about what they were going to do to you, Zinnia, I will get out of this tub and slaughter the entire crew. Do you know how to sail a ship? Because I can't do it alone."

He meant it. Vengeance burned in his eyes. He was fighting it, the need to slaughter every one of them. "I won't mention it again, promise." I pretended to zip my lips. "So that's a yes on the two questions?"

"Yes, but I get two as well."

I guess he had jumped into the ocean during a storm to fight a giant sea creature, so it'd be rude not to agree. "Fine."

He smirked.

Goddess, that smirk was dangerous. I tapped my lips and mulled over the best way to ask my question while he waited patiently. I cleared my throat. "How many times have you made this trip with one of your consorts?"

His nostrils flared. "Twice."

"Twice? You've had an unverified number of consorts. How could it only be twice?"

"Is that your second question?"

Was it? "I don't know."

"Well, while you decide, I'll ask you one. During the times you've been away from me, have you fucked anyone else?"

The vein pulsed at the side of my throat. He was obsessed with my sex life, and the way he'd been looking at me when he asked that... goddammit, I was having trouble breathing again. "*Anyone else* implies that we're already fucking," I said, for reasons unknown.

He bared his teeth in a way that should be terrifying but didn't scare me anymore. "Answer the question, wife," he said, using my title as if it held all the weight in the world.

As if that title actually meant something. As if me being with another male would actually be a betrayal. "Would you truly be angry if I had?"

The steel tub bent under his hand. I'd take that as a yes.

"Answer the question, Zinnia," he growled.

"No, I haven't been with anyone since I revealed who I was to you."

He visibly relaxed.

"Why do you care?" I said before I could stop myself. "You don't love me. You didn't choose me. I was chosen for you, just one of, well, possibly ten random other females to darken your castle steps. I don't get it."

His jaw tightened. "That's obvious, but what you need to understand is, you are mine, Zinnia. You are everything I want, all I want. I have no use for any other female, no desire to be with anyone but you. You don't need to *get it*. That's just the way it is."

I stared at him, stunned, for several seconds. "So what you feel, it's like a mate bond?"

"Yes, it's a lot like that. Which is why being parted from you is... hard." The tub buckled further under his hand. "And why the thought of you with someone else..." His lips peeled back. "I don't like it."

I was stunned. I had no idea. He'd never shown it—well, not until the last week or so. Until he'd just spelled it out, I'd had no idea what he was thinking or feeling. "I feel sorry for you then," I said into the silence. "This must truly suck. I don't know why your consorts keep... dying or why fate has an endless supply of us lined up for you, but it has to be painful to feel a connection like that to someone, then have them taken away over and over again."

Something shifted through his eyes that I couldn't read, and then his head tilted to the side. "You feel sorry for me? You think you're going to die in the near future, but it's me you're concerned about?"

I shrugged. "Don't get me wrong, I don't want to die, not yet. But I have family waiting for me. Loved ones who will welcome me with open arms when that time comes. This... it's endless for you."

"Don't," he said roughly. "Do not accept death as the outcome. Do as I say, and you will live."

He was delusional. The odds were not in my favor. The way he was looking at me, the pain and desperation, the need for me to believe it, to be the exception, was hard to look at. I was a realist, though. Whatever the fates had in store for me was what would be. No, I wouldn't go down easily, but I needed to come to terms with the possibility of my reality.

"Right, next question," I said, not wanting to talk about my death anymore. "Did you sleep with all your consorts? You're old as hell. You wanted my number, but I'm assuming yours is pretty freaking high." Where the hell had that come from? I was trying to lighten the heavy mood that had fallen over the room, but now it sparked with electricity.

His chest rose and fell as if he was trying to steady his breathing. "Not quite as old as Hell."

"Answer the question."

"No."

"Because you didn't want to, or because they didn't live long enough?"

He said nothing.

Nope, not feeling overly reassured by the whole *don't accept death as the outcome* thing. My gaze dipped to his chest. "The poison out yet?"

"Yes." His gaze darkened, the shadows beginning to swirl around him. "My turn."

My stomach squirmed, and that look in his eyes, I felt it. Goddess, did I feel it. "Shoot."

"Do you want me to fuck you, Zinnia?"

My body instantly responded. A pulse throbbed deep inside me. So many things were flying through my head right then. He was beautiful; he wanted me and only me. I was his consort and I would be until my last breath, and if things went the way they usually did for Death, that would be coming sooner rather than later. I'd lived my life to the fullest, as best as I could, anyway, with the responsibility I'd had. And I realized, looking over at him, I wasn't about to stop now. "Did your consorts die because they kissed you? Slept with you?"

"No," he said.

He could be lying, but I didn't think so. His pain was too real. He didn't want to lose me; I saw it, felt it. "You're overwhelming, Mors, in so many ways. The idea of surrendering to you, of letting you have me in that way, it's too much. So no, I don't want you to fuck me, not yet."

He flinched, but besides that, he didn't move, every muscle in his body rock solid. "I understand—"

"I haven't finished," I said and took a steadying breath while my heart tried to leave my body. Apparently, I was a masochist, and I'd decided to give in to it completely. "No, because the first time we do sleep together... I'll be the one fucking you."

Chapter Eleven

Zinnia

Death rose from the water.

Every muscle on his lean body was taut, his veins popping from his smooth, inked skin. He was breathing heavily, and the shadows around him swirled faster. "Come here, Zinnia."

His voice rolled through the room like thunder, and my knees almost gave out. I shook my head. "If you want me, it has to be on my terms."

With each of his exhales, a growl rattled his chest. His stomach was roped with muscle, his thighs bulged, and his cock jutted from his body, hard and thick and long and, goddess, intimidating.

Death looked every bit the god he was, and he was looking at me as if he was on the verge of insanity from his hunger—*for me*. I wanted him so badly, I trembled all over. But this was Death. I was no coward, but he was, shit, too much... of *everything*. "I have to call the shots this time... and you have to let me call you Mors without holding it against me. I'm not calling you Death while we're in bed."

"I agree to your terms," he said. "Take your clothes off."

An unexpected laugh burst from me. "You've waited this long, so how about you find a little patience?"

"Impossible." He stepped out of the bath, water dripping from his body. "Tell me what you want, and I'll give it to you. Anything your heart desires—it's yours."

This was another new side of Death. Yes, he'd been giving me glimpses, but this was next-level, and the more he showed me, the less afraid I became. I reached up and undid the top button of my jacket, working the rest until the heavy leather slipped from my shoulders and hit the floor.

Death watched my every move like a predator waiting to pounce on prey.

I dropped my hands to the buttons of my pants; he took a step forward. I stepped back, lifting my hands. "No."

He snarled.

"I come to you."

His fingers curled, clenching and unclenching at his sides as he watched me shove down my pants. "Is the water safe? Is there poison in it?"

"You don't need to wash," he said, baring his teeth. "I like you like this."

"Covered in sea salt, sweat, and demon blood?"

"Yes."

"Is the water safe?" I asked again, even as my belly went wild with nerves and excitement.

"The poison evaporates when it leaves the body. It's safe."

"Good." I dragged off my shirt and then removed my underwear. "Step back," I said. "At least four paces."

He growled low but reluctantly did as I said, tracking me as I walked to the bath and got in. He was barely holding himself back;

I could see it in the way his muscles twitched and his breathing grew heavier with every passing second.

"Your body is perfection," he said. "Fuck, female, I want to lick every inch of you."

I lifted my gaze, letting it move over him as I slid the soap over my skin. "I like the way you look as well." Understatement of the century.

He stood straighter, a pleased light flashing through his eyes. "Cup your breasts for me. Play with your nipples. Do it," he said.

This was going to be a challenge; gods didn't like to be told what to do, but that was the only way this was happening. Still, I did as he asked, cupping my heavy and achy breasts. "I'm only doing it because I want to and not because you told me to. I'm in charge here, remember?"

"Will you ride my face, little witch?" he said, his hands still fisted at his sides. "I'll fucking beg you for it, if you like? I'm desperate for a taste of you, Zinnia. You have no idea how much."

Death had a dirty mouth, and yeah, it was working for me— big-time. "Are you in pain?"

"Yes."

"You can stroke your cock if you like." A vision of Death stroking himself filled my head, and my inner muscles clenched.

"If I touch my cock now, I'll come, and the next time will be inside my wife's sweet little cunt."

I flushed hot all over, so turned on, my next breath shook out of me. "Go to the bed and lie on it," I said.

He gave me another flash of his teeth, a look that said he was frustrated and entertained by my demands all at the same time. He strode to the bed and sat. His head dipped so his eyes were shadowed by his brow. "You need to know that after you fuck me, Zinnia, I will have you my way. I'll claim you so often and so deep that even when I'm not inside you, you'll feel me there. Every single day."

I was trembling now from how much I wanted him. It was

getting seriously hard to hold my composure. Every word he said was stripping away my armor. This was probably a terrible mistake, but if my mortal life was reaching its end, I was making the most of every moment, even if it scared me. I knew what was about to happen between us—for me, at least—would be life-altering, soul-searing, earth-shattering, and I'd be a fool to pass that up.

"Lie back," I said and mentally gave myself a pat on the back when my voice didn't tremble like every other part of me was.

He lay back, his abs tightening as he did, then slid his hands behind his head. His gaze slid over my chest—what he could see of it above the water, anyway. "Now what, wife?"

Jesus, now he was being cocky? Or, at least, he was trying to be. He was still trying to maintain some kind of control. I got the feeling he hadn't been in this position, letting someone else lead, many times in his long life. He'd called me wife sparingly in the past, choosing consort more frequently, probably because wife seemed more intimate, more claiming, and considering when he chose to use it, he felt the same. I licked my lips because they were dry as hell. Had there ever been anything in existence as utterly beautiful, as awe-inspiring, as Death, hard and naked, lying on his back and waiting for me to have my way with him?

I rose from the water, and the cocky look on his face vanished. He ate up the sight of me, his cock jerking against his flat stomach. I grabbed the clean towel draped over the back of a chair, and slowly, carefully, dried myself off. "That feels better," I said and dropped it.

"When was the last time you were fucked, little witch?"

"It's not question time right now, Mors."

His nostrils flared. "When we're together like this, you can call me by my name, and I can ask you as many questions as I like."

Fair enough, I guessed, but talking about me sleeping with other males wasn't really something I wanted to get into right now. "Do you really want to know the answer to that?"

"Yes. Tell me."

I moved closer, standing at the end of the bed. "A couple years ago, I guess." I shrugged. "I've been busy."

"Who were you with?"

"No one special, just some guy I met while I was on the road. It used to get lonely, and he was nice. We had fun," I said, trying to get across how little the encounter meant.

His eyes darkened, the blue swirling with black. "I want to tear his limbs from his body."

Well, shit. I needed to turn this back on him and make him see how hypocritical he was being. I could guarantee he hadn't had any dry spells. "What about you?" I asked, taking a deep, steadying breath and climbing onto the bed. He tracked me as I crawled up beside him, his hands slipping from beneath his head.

"Keep your hands where they are," I said, and he growled again. "Answer the question. When was the last time you had sex?"

"A very long time ago, with my consort, before she was taken from me," he said, then, ignoring my order, reached out and slid his fingers down my cheek. "I've been waiting a very long time for you, Zinnia."

He was telling the truth; there was no doubting what I saw in his eyes and on his face. "Why?" I whispered, my throat tight with an emotion that surprised me.

"Because I didn't want anyone else."

None of this made sense. Could he only be with females destined to be his? Or was he just that into monogamy? There was so much I didn't know and desperately wanted to, but now was not the time to ask. Now, I was going to be the first for Death after what could be hundreds of years of celibacy. Curling my fingers around his wrist, I took his hand from my face, put it back behind his head, then grinned at him. "Well then, my lord, I'm about to rock your world."

A grin broke out across his face, and it was like it had the force of a thousand stars behind it, its impact like a sucker punch to the sternum. "Show me what you've got," he said, and there was no missing the teasing note to his voice.

My heart crashed into my ribs like a car in a head-on collision. "Well now, that sounds like a challenge."

His grin slipped. "Now, Zinnia—"

"Did I tell you I liked to take things slow?"

He growled. "We'll go slow next time."

I tutted and cupped his square jaw as zaps of electricity shot through me, making me squirm. Kissing Death had been on my mind a lot. At first, it had been unimaginable, but now? Goddess, he had those utterly perfect lips and the thought of it, the temptation, had become too much to ignore. "Making out really gets me in the mood." I was about to make out with a god. I'd laugh and scream—both at the same time—but I was too turned on in that moment to do anything but try to remember to do the whole oxygen thing.

"You're already in the mood. I can smell it. Your cunt is hot and slick and more than ready for me," he said through clenched teeth. "Kiss me, but do it while you fuck me."

The please went unsaid, but it hung between us. Death didn't beg, despite what he said earlier, and he'd get no mercy here, not tonight. For the first time since I started coming to Limbo, I was the one with all the power, and in this, I needed it.

Sliding closer, I lay beside him and pressed my naked body to his. I was trembling, but there was nothing I could do about that. "Don't move," I rasped as I leaned in and pressed a kiss to his jaw. "Stay right where you are."

He hissed. "Do you enjoy torturing me, little witch?"

"Doesn't this feel good? Having me pressed against you?"

"You know it does." He was panting now.

"Then stop complaining and let me kiss you." I lifted up to my elbows, so I was looking down at him, and studied his handsome face. "You have perfect lips. I've thought about kissing them a lot."

"Zinnia," he said, his voice full of raw hunger.

I dragged my nose along his throat and kissed the corner of his mouth. "You smell really good, like dark spices." He was shaking as well. Goddess, he was perfection. I pressed my mouth to his, and he groaned against my lips, then jolted as if he was about to pounce, but I reached back and grabbed his wrists, reminding him to keep them where they were.

Slowly, I ran my lips over his, reveling in their firm warmth, then dragged my tongue along his lower lip, desperate to taste him. My body was on fire, my nipples impossibly hard against his chest, and the pulse between my thighs was so damn deep, I couldn't stop myself from sliding on top of him, from straddling his hard body as I opened my mouth to slide my tongue deep into his mouth. He groaned again as his tongue slid against mine.

My hips rocked all on their own, working my pussy against his hard stomach, while I made out with Death like it was the end of the world, and I guess it kind of was—my world, anyway.

His skin was scalding hot against mine, and there was no way he couldn't feel how wet I was now. Kissing him was addictive. I could stay where I was all day and just kiss while rubbing up against him, but my body was screaming for more.

"Up," Death growled against my lips. "Sit on my face. Let me taste you."

I lifted my head a little and stared into his otherworldly eyes. "That sounded like an order."

His gaze seared mine. "Please."

His plea rolled through me, making me shudder, and my pussy clenched hard with need. Death never begged for anything, but he was, for me. How could I deny him? Why would I want to? Licking my lips, I slid higher.

"Yes," he said. "That's it."

I kept going until I was sitting on his chest.

"I'll need to hold you steady," he said.

His hand was out from under his head and wrapped around my waist before I could tell him no. He lifted me like I weighed nothing, putting me where he wanted me, and all thoughts of stopping him from touching me flew from my mind when he opened his mouth over my pussy and dragged his tongue through my center.

His deep moan was so incredibly sexy, my hips rolled on their own. He gripped me tighter, holding me down on his face with more force, and my head dropped back as he used that tongue with the kind of skill only a male who'd been alive since almost the dawn of time could have. I was shuddering and sweating, crying out with every skilled swipe of his tongue and every suck of those perfect lips.

I tried to hold back, to make it last, but I couldn't; I came with a scream. Death locked his arms around my hips, holding me down on his mouth, sucking and feasting on my pussy as I came against his lips.

When I collapsed, he dragged me down his body, thrust his long, thick fingers in my hair, and took my mouth in a claiming kiss that had my world spinning. I'd had every intention of being the one in control, but I didn't try to stop him when he worked his legs between mine and forced me to spread wide with his bent knees, or when he hooked me around the waist, just above my ass, and lined the head of his hard cock up with my opening.

I expected him to slam inside me, but he didn't; his entire body trembled, but somehow, he held back. "You need to control how much of me you take. I don't want to hurt you, but after seeing you fight those demons, after almost losing you, after how long I've waited for you, the force of the hunger I'm feeling is dangerous, and I would rather die before hurting you... so please, my perfect, feisty, beautiful little witch, put me out of my misery and fuck me the way we both need it."

Chapter Twelve

Death

Zɪɴɴɪᴀ ᴡʀɪɢɢʟᴇᴅ ʜᴇʀ ʜɪᴘs, her hot, slick pussy scalding the head of my cock. My arm banded around her tighter, and she whimpered. "You're going to break my spine, Mors, and then no one will be fucking anyone," she said, panting.

I quickly let up my grip, which felt impossible in that moment, but somehow, I did it. I wrapped her wild red hair around my fist and sucked and kissed the skin along her throat, her shoulder. Gods, I wanted to take a fucking bite out of her, that's how deep my hunger went. I wanted to suck and bite and crush her to me. None of it was enough; nothing would bring her close enough to me.

Throughout my life, I'd been tipped into madness of the darkest and most twisted kind, but nothing had ever made me feel as out of control as this moment. I'd waited for her for so long, so long I'd been without my consort, and now I would finally claim her. Gods help anyone who tried to take her from me. Not this time. This time, I would keep her; this time, she would stay.

She squirmed against me, her hips wriggling, working the head of my cock inside her. I gritted my teeth, breathing hard, trying to stop my heart from exploding out of my chest and my hips from slamming up. "That's it, nice and easy," I said, the opposite of everything I was feeling. But my precious consort came first, in everything. My wants and needs, my desires, they all came second to hers. She thought I was the one in control, that I controlled her, but nothing could be further from the truth—I was her servant.

She was my queen, and I would worship at her feet until the end of time. All she had to do was trust me.

Believe in me.

Stay with me.

Want me.

She whimpered again, but this time because she pushed down, taking more of me inside her.

"*Oh fuck*," she gasped and rocked her hips, the wet sound of her cunt making me insane as she worked the inch of my cock she'd managed to take, letting it stretch her before taking more. "You're too big," she moaned, then took more, sinking her teeth into my shoulder.

I almost fucking came. Gripping her ass, I barely held on to my sanity. "You were made for me, Zinnia. The fates chose you for me," I growled out. "We will fit together, I promise you." Her pussy, tight and scalding, swallowed more, and I locked my muscles so I didn't thrust upward. "Feel good, little witch?"

She rolled her hips again and took more. "I-I think I'm losing my... my mind," she said with another roll, right there with me. "Oh goddess, you're... it's..." She shuddered. "Fuck," she hissed and started rocking on top of me. Each time she took more, her needy sounds grew, until she had every hard inch buried inside her. "Mors," she groaned my name like a cry for help.

"It's okay, Zinnia. Relax..." She moaned against my throat as she carefully rocked her hips. *Fucking hell.* My eyes rolled back. "That's it. Now show me how good it feels. Show me," I said, gripping her hips and encouraging her to move again.

She wrapped her arms around my head, and then her mouth came down on mine, feeding me her needy kisses and panted breaths while she started to move. "Yes," she whimpered against my mouth. "So good."

I let the reins slip, just a little, and lifted my hips, desperate to get closer.

"Oh fuck," she said; then my little consort completely lost control. My sweet, feisty witch moved faster, giving me everything she had until she was begging me for more.

Gripping her hips, I gave it to her. I pulled her down as I thrust up, filling her deep. The feel of her wrapped around me, of her holding me so tight, of her wanting me, was so sublime, she had me spinning. Gods, I was back in the night sky because my precious consort had me seeing the stars.

"Mors," she moaned.

My name on her lips had my hips snapping up, meeting hers with force, making her cry out. I'd be worried I'd hurt her, but she was so wet that I was gliding in and out of her with ease, and her moans hadn't stopped and were full of pleasure, not pain.

Then Zinnia sucked my lips one last time and sat up, planted her hands on my chest—right over the stars tattooed there—and swiveled her hips. No, she definitely wasn't in any pain. Her head fell back as she took from me exactly what she needed.

I watched her in awe. "Take what you need," I growled. My wild, willful consort. My beautiful warrior. A female of power and intelligence, of beauty and warmth.

She was everything.

She was mine.

And I would not lose her. I wouldn't survive it, not this time.

She was fierce, lost to her pleasure now, and the sounds she made as she gave in to it sent shivers all through me. She cried out

—a raw, wild sound that I would never ever forget—as her pussy clamped down hard on my cock. I had to hold on to her hips as she bucked and cried out, falling against my chest while she rocked mindlessly, lost in her pleasure. Wrapping my arms around her—one arm over her back, and the other on her ass—I locked her to me, and then I fucked her, thrusting my hips up hard to meet hers again, while she trembled and cried out, still coming for me.

There was no more holding back. "Yes, that's it, my precious Stella," I groaned and came hard inside my beautiful little wife, my Stella, my everything.

I thrust into her until I was spent, until we both lay there panting. I gently fisted her soft, warm hair and lifted her head, in need of her kisses badly, but she turned away, then tried to slide off me. I tightened my hold on her.

"Let me go, Death," she said, no longer using my name and making it clear she was not just pulling away physically. She was going to distance herself from me again.

No fucking way. Not after that. She couldn't pretend she didn't feel for me some of what I did for her, not after what we just shared. "Look at me," I growled.

She turned toward me but averted her eyes.

"You're angry with me. Did I hurt you? Did I—"

"I get it, you've had a lot of consorts, and I'm most likely heading toward total annihilation in the very near future. This is... whatever the hell it is, but would it hurt you to get my fucking name right while you're inside me? This Stella, she was obviously your favorite or whatever, but even the dude I had a one-night stand with remembered my fucking name."

I froze. I had said that, hadn't I? *Idiot.* "I've never had a consort named Stella."

She rolled her eyes. "I literally heard you say it in my visions twice."

I swallowed, my mouth dry, hating that I'd hurt her. "Stella means star," I rushed out. "When I say my Stella, I'm saying my star."

Her gaze dropped to my chest, to the intricate stars tattooed there, then back up. "So you what? Call us all the same term of endearment so you don't fuck up?"

"No. You are my consort, my guide, my light, my sun. That's just what you are. You are my little witch, but you are also my Stella," I said, trying to make her understand. I wanted to explain, to tell her everything, but I couldn't; doing so would mean losing her for certain. So I waited and hoped like hell she accepted my explanation.

She chewed her lip. "So this is another one of those bigger-than-me, dawn-of-time things that I'm never going to understand? Gotcha. Fine, whatever, but I've had visions of you with one, possibly two other females, so I know this isn't some grand love, and we're just fucking to kill time, but in all those visions, you called her... or them Stella, so I'd rather you didn't call me that again, thanks."

We weren't fucking to kill time, and even she couldn't believe that bullshit. And as for grand love? She had no fucking idea, but she would. "I'll try my very best not to call you that again," I said.

She eyed me for a moment, then finally, thank the gods, relaxed back against me. Her warmth instantly put me at ease. I slid my hand down her back, and she shivered. Yes, I liked that.

"You need to do better than try, my guy," she said. "Because if it happens again, it doesn't matter if I'm riding you like a rodeo bull, if you call me that name again, there will be no happy ending for you. I'll leave you to buck it out all on your own."

I stilled. "A rodeo bull?"

"You heard me," she said and wriggled against my side, getting comfortable.

A grin spread across my face, so wide, my cheeks hurt.

She paused in her wriggling and lifted her head. Her breath burst from her lungs. "What the hell are you grinning about?"

"You entertain me, little witch. I haven't been this entertained in a very long time."

"I'm glad I amuse you," she said, trying to be sarcastic, but her lips were twitching.

"I'll be your rodeo bull anytime, by the way."

She snorted. "Like there was ever any doubt."

The laugh burst from me before I knew it was coming. Zinnia startled, and I laughed harder, wrapping my arms around her and holding her to me.

Zinnia

Gripping my sword, I slashed at the bloated, foul-smelling demon swiping red-tipped claws at me. I shifted my body to protect my back; my leather armor creaked as I slashed again.

They kept coming. I was on my own. There were too many. I stumbled back, closer to the rocky cliff. Oh gods, there was no way out of this.

The demons closed in, one grabbing me by the throat while another snatched something from my back, something I needed to protect, something precious. The demon released my throat, then slammed a fist into my stomach.

I stumbled back, and then I was falling, falling toward the sea and jagged rocks. My screams turned into a roar of fury. This did not end here. They would pay for this—

With a gasp, my eyes flew open a moment before I hit the rocks.

My heart pounded in my chest, the familiar ache more intense than ever before, because instead of making me watch the scene unfold, whoever that was, she'd put me in her shoes. It was as if that were happening to me. Something tickled my cheek, and I reached up to brush it off, my fingers coming away damp. I realized tears were pouring down my face, likely from the lingering feeling of my entire world being ripped from me in that vision. Goddess, it was suffocating. Death was still beside me, breathing slow and steady. I needed air; I needed to shake the vision. I had no idea what his past consorts were trying to tell me, but the more they showed me, the more real they felt.

Easing out of bed, I quickly dressed, grabbed my knife from where Death had put it earlier, and slipped from the room. I wasn't worried about the crew attacking me, not now that Death was here, and even if one of them did, they were lacking in skill and, as I'd proved earlier, not overly hard to kill.

Rushing up the steep stairs and onto the landing, I shoved the door open and stepped out onto the deck. I dragged in a desperate breath, letting the sea air fill my lungs, before I strode to the railing, sucking in another frantic breath.

Her pain, whoever she was, had been like nothing I'd ever experienced. She'd been filled with so much fear and heartbreak and rage. Her world had been snatched from her along with the people she loved with a fierceness that I felt to my soul, that I understood.

The revenge in her heart had been white-hot.

Was that what she wanted, what they all wanted? Revenge?

Against who? At first, I thought they were warning me about Death, but I didn't believe that now. The female in that vision had loved him. Had all of them felt that way?

The thought had me gripping the railing tighter. Had they all fallen in love with him?

Did I truly think I would be the exception? That I'd somehow resist him? I wrapped my arms around myself. Did I really think I could outsmart the fates? That I could prove them wrong? I wasn't better or smarter or stronger or in possession of greater self-restraint than the females who came before me. I knew I wasn't. Death was a god, and I was a mere mortal; there was no resisting this pull I felt between us, not when it grew in strength every day.

Goddess, the way he'd touched me, held me, the things he'd

said, the way he'd wanted me—I'd never experienced anything like that in my life.

His laugh when he'd wrapped his arms around me, holding me tight to him, had been heart-stopping—

A rough hand clamped hard over my mouth, and an oddly shaped body slammed into me from behind. I tried to fight, but there was no getting out of the demon's hold. He pulled his hand away, but only long enough to stuff a dirty rag in my mouth.

"Over you go," he said against my ear, then tossed me over the side.

I flailed, bracing, preparing to hit the water.

Instead, I was snatched from the air and shoved into the bottom of a dinghy. The demon who'd tossed me over the side quickly made his way down the rope ladder and got in as well. I didn't recognize either of them; they weren't crew. Someone else had sent them.

One of them started rowing while the other secured my wrists and ankles and tied a gag around my head, trapping the rag in my mouth. I couldn't spell, and I couldn't reach for my blade; I was fucking helpless.

The demon rowed for a while, and I wondered where they were taking me. We were too far from shore, but then I saw it, another ship, black and huge, camouflaged in the darkness.

Someone moved around on the deck, another demon, their misshapen shadow striding to the railing and watching us approach. They kicked down the ladder and stepped back.

Whatever this was, it was bad.

The eerie *coo* of an owl echoed overhead.

Really fucking bad.

Chapter Thirteen

Death

I JOLTED AWAKE.

It was quiet—too quiet.

My arm shot out across the mattress. Nothing. It was empty.

No Zinnia.

Only cool sheets. She'd been gone a while. Bounding out of bed, I stormed out of the room, not giving a fuck that I was naked, and leaped up the stairs and onto the deck. "Zinnia!" My roar echoed through the night, causing the demons asleep up here to startle awake. "My consort! Where the fuck is she?" I demanded.

"I haven't seen her," one of the demons said as he scrambled from his pallet.

Rushing him, I grabbed him by the throat and shoved him against the mast. "Where the fuck is she?"

He shook his head, trembling, the smell of piss reaching me. "I-I promise. I haven't seen her. I didn't do anything."

Shoving him away, I strode back the way I'd come, jumped

down the stairs, and kicked every cabin door open, yanking back covers and flipping beds. She wasn't here. I knew it deep down; I felt her absence like a festering wound in the center of my chest. The same as when she left me, when she left Limbo to go back to her family for a month, and I was left counting down the fucking weeks, days, hours, minutes until she returned.

She was gone, but she hadn't left me. Someone had taken her, and when I caught up with them, I would tear them to pieces, until they were nothing but bloody chunks of meat wriggling on the ground.

"Everyone, up!" I bellowed. "Get me to the docks, now."

~

Zinnia

The captain of the *Fetid Slug*, Sig—I mean, it was as if the ship had been named especially for him—sidled up to me again, like he had been with increasing frequency since I got here, and pressed his face to my throat, sniffing deeply. He made a weird, excited little noise.

"Does she still smell like his lordship, Sig?" one of the other demons asked excitedly.

"Oh yesssss, and her cunny is still ripe from his tupping. His seed marks her," the captain said.

It took everything in me not to gag. That this creep was smelling me and, by the looks of it, getting off on it was more than I could stomach. "Bring your nose anywhere near me again, and as soon as I get the chance, I'll slice the fucker off." They'd at least removed the gag. They seemed to be amused by my threats. Little did they know, they weren't just threats. I would deliver every one of them, slowly. Unfortunately, there was some kind of ward on the ship, and my magic was bound tight.

Another demon dropped to his knees and crawled closer.

"Back the fuck up," I snarled.

He ignored me and kept coming. If my legs weren't tied to the chair, I'd kick the ugly fuck in the face. I jerked and fought, but it was hopeless, and he dragged his bulbous oily nose along the leather of my pants all the way up, until he was pressed between my thighs, and dragged in a deep breath.

"Oh yes," he said and laughed excitedly. "His lordship has used her. The scent of his seed is strong. She is the right female. The mistress will reward us."

They all giggled their weird fucking giggles, eyes flashing with glee.

"When I tell *his lordship* what you just did, asshole, he'll tear your face off and feed it to the fishes," I snarled. "That is, if there's anything left of it when I'm through slicing your ugly fucking face to ribbons."

They laughed again, uproariously.

Sig picked up a piece of my hair and pressed it to his nose, breathing deeply again. "You are a weak female. Your words are stupid. Your threats are false and make us laugh."

"And your breath smells like shit and makes me want to puke," I said, probably foolishly, but I didn't give a fuck at this point. I was usually good at controlling my temper, my emotions. I'd had to be with a mother like mine, and with my line of work, you learned to lock it all down. So when I did lose it, when I let that side of myself take hold, it was hard to get control back, and these ugly pervs had pushed me so far past my control, there was no coming back.

Sig's face darkened with rage a moment before he balled up his sledgehammer-sized fist and slammed it into the side of my head.

When I regained consciousness, I was being jostled, carried unceremoniously by the demon who'd sniffed my crotch and one of his buddies. It was dark, and I blinked, trying to clear my fuzzy vision. He'd hit me hard, and the side of my head still throbbed.

We were off the boat and moving across rocks and stones toward a massive temple surrounded by forest—the same kind of forest as the one we'd walked through in the Outer Realm. The towers on either side of the temple looked like the demon lighthouse we'd stayed in.

It wasn't hard to guess who was so desperate to meet me that she'd had me abducted off our ship.

I tried to fight, but it was no use; I was still trussed up and gagged again.

The massive stone doors swung open as I was carried toward them. The demons strode inside and continued on through an enormous entranceway. The tile floor was black obsidian with flecks of opal. Everything else was dark and cold. The only light was coming from a giant chandelier made of bone and huge charred antlers from some kind of otherworldly creature.

Another set of double doors opened as we approached, and I was carried into a room full of demons, and other creatures I'd never seen before in my life. They all went silent as I was brought in and dumped on the floor. The crotch sniffer undid the ropes around my wrists and ankles and tugged off the gag as the crowd gathered around, looking at me as if I was the oddity in the room. I tried to flex my magic, but the temple had the same ward, binding my powers here.

My hands and feet throbbed as blood rushed back, and it was hard, but I dragged myself to my feet. I was more than outnumbered, but that didn't mean I'd give up. No, I'd make as many of them bleed as I could before they took me down. I slid my blade free, gripping it tight, and turned in a slow circle, waiting to see who struck first.

Several of the demons laughed, one of them jerking forward, trying to scare me. I slashed fast with my knife, surprising him, and sliced through the side of his face, splitting it open. He shrieked and bared his bloody teeth, about to lunge.

"Enough!"

A voice echoed through the room, and it had the same kind of resonance as Death's. I locked my knees and turned to face Nox as the crowd parted to let her through.

"What do you want?" I said through gritted teeth, bracing for anything. I couldn't win, but that didn't mean I'd just lie down and die.

There were hisses and gasps around me at my question. Perhaps addressing a goddess the way I had was considered rude, but so was being kidnapped and knocked out.

"Forgive her. She is a witch and ignorant. She means no offense, I'm sure," Nox said as she finally emerged from the parting crowd.

She was tall and willowy, her skin like mother-of-pearl, her hair a glossy black waterfall down her back. She wore a long, flowing black gown in a sheer fabric, and her hands were folded in front of her, tipped with long, pointed black nails.

She blinked, staring at me with large black eyes, no white to be seen. It was the same way Death's and Somnus's eyes looked when they changed, looking like the sky on a starry night. On Death, it could be unsettling; on Nox, it was terrifying.

"I honestly don't care if you're offended," I said. There was no surviving this. If Nox wanted me dead, I was sure she could click her fingers, and I'd be splattered all over the marble floor. I wasn't going to bow down to her.

"I can hear your weak little mortal heart pounding in your chest, witch. Best you speak to me with respect, or I will rip it from your chest and crush it in my fist." She smiled, revealing bright white teeth. "But none of us want that now, do we, Zinnia?"

"I have no idea what you want."

Her eyes narrowed, but she smiled wider. "Oh, you are delightful, so full of fire, even when it can be so easily extinguished."

"The fact you can easily kill me isn't lost on me. You're a goddess, and as you pointed out, I'm a witch, one who has her powers currently bound by you. I know I can't win here, but if you think that scares me, you're wrong. I've faced fiercer monsters than you before, and if I die today, I will do it fighting."

Nox blinked at me, then threw her head back and laughed. The peanut gallery joined in, laughing with her uproariously. When her chuckles finally died down, she wiped away an invisible tear. "My dear, I only wanted to meet my son's consort. He can be..." She waved an elegant hand through the air. "... so possessive of his things."

"I'm not a thing."

"Of course you aren't, dear." She smiled wide again. "I want to get to know you, that's all. You've arrived just in time for dinner, so we can sit and talk." Her gaze slid over me, her mouth twisting with distaste. "We dress for dinner here," she said, then waved her hand toward me, and my leathers were replaced by a long black gown, my weapons vanishing. I looked down at myself. The dress brushed the floor, and the lace was like a delicate black spiderweb that covered nothing. My naked body was totally visible beneath. The gown was old, extremely fragile, and smelled slightly musty.

I ran my hands carefully over my hips, and a strange feeling filled me—a weird kind of excitement, a rush of happiness. I was getting something off it, vibrations from the past, from the female that had worn this before me; there was no other way to explain what I was feeling.

"Something wrong, dear?" Nox asked.

I looked up. "Give me back my things."

She ignored me and glided forward, toward a massive table. "Sit, Zinnia, it's time to eat." I had no choice but to follow. She sat, and a demon rushed ahead and pulled out a chair. I reluctantly took my place beside her. Was she going to kill me by poisoning my food? Poison could be nice and fast or slow and drawn out. Nox wouldn't enjoy clean or fast. She'd want to take her time; she'd enjoy my screams of pain. I grabbed the steak knife beside my plate and gripped it tight.

Nox glanced my way and shook her head with a tittering laugh. "Are you going to stab me with that, witch?"

She said *witch* with mockery in her voice, as if I were so insignificant, it was hilarious, and I supposed I was to her, but the demons still gathered around, sizing me up, were another story. "If any of your friends come any closer, they'll be losing an eye."

She chuckled again, then clapped her hands, and the food was brought out.

"Are you planning on poisoning me, goddess?"

She gave me a sidelong glance. "Poison? How very boring. No, my dear, the food is quite safe."

"You would say that."

She shrugged one elegant shoulder. "Suit yourself. Go hungry if you must."

I would be. No, I didn't really think deadly wolfsbane in the soup or hemlock baked into the bread was her style, but I wasn't going to take her word for it.

"So how have you been getting along with my son?" she asked after swallowing a spoonful of wolfsbane soup.

"Why don't you ask him that yourself when he gets here?" I said, because Death would be coming, and he would be furious when he arrived. "I'm sure he's worked out who snatched me off our ship."

Her smile turned indulgent. "Mors can be rather possessive, can he not? An independent female such as yourself must be finding it hard to adjust." She broke off a small piece of hemlock bread and popped it in her mouth. Then she held out the basket. "Are you sure you won't have some? It's very good."

"I'm sure, thank you."

"Did you know there were others before you?" she asked, turning on her seat to face me.

Bitch. "I did, yes."

She did her tittering laugh. "Of course you did. Do you think you're different? That you'll be the exception, Zinnia?"

"Why not?" I said, because I knew it would annoy her. She liked to be the most arrogant monster in the room, but I could be arrogant as well. If nothing else, it'd amuse me to piss her off. "I'm no goddess, but I am a powerful witch, and your son likes me very much. He doesn't seem that fond of you, though, for some reason. Why is that?"

The amusement in her eyes vanished, quickly replaced by vicious glee. "Do you want children, Zinnia?" she asked, ignoring my question.

Every part of me stilled. She knew. She knew my deepest, darkest secret. "I'm not sure. I haven't really thought about it."

"You probably should. My son has always wanted a child—a lot of them."

Nausea swirled in my belly. "We haven't talked about it," I said, trying to stop my hands from shaking.

Her black eyes bored into me, sinking deep. "Perhaps you should, dear." Then she turned, her gaze sliding to the main doors a moment before they flew apart, the wood splintering into shrapnel.

Demons ducked for cover a moment before Death strode in, expression like thunder. He was shirtless, his leather pants straining over his thighs. His stomach was taut, and the fist of one hand was clenched around his staff as shadows swirled, gathering around him, turning into his cloak. My heart thundered in my chest at the sight of him. His face was transformed, the shadows turning it into a skull, but instead of dark eye sockets, his blue gaze glowed out from under the hood of his cloak. "Zinnia!" he roared.

Nox waved her demons forward, and they instantly and stupidly ran at him.

"It's better if he blows off some steam before we converse," Nox said to me, completely unaffected. "He seems agitated."

He looked ready to tear the temple down around us. The

demons ran at him, and he smashed his fist into the first one's head, crushing his skull. He spun his staff, slamming into them as they attacked, slicing and hacking them to pieces, but they kept coming, essentially committing suicide, one after the other, blindly doing as Nox bid them.

Death was smeared with demon blood and ash, veins bulging, jaw clenched, rage rolling off him. It didn't seem as if mutilating a roomful of demons and other creatures was helping calm him down; in fact, it seemed the opposite to me.

I stood so he'd see me over the chaos, and his gaze sliced to me instantly. He strode toward me, swiping demons out of his way with one brutal swing of his staff after another, until he reached me. He didn't spare his mother a glance; he hooked his arm around my waist and hoisted me up so I was partially over his shoulder.

"So sensitive," Nox said with a sigh. "You always were my sensitive boy."

Death's grip on me was bruising and kind of humiliating, but I didn't say a word or try to get down, not when fury sparked off him like a live wire ready to set everything in his path on fire.

"You know why we're here, and if you try to stop us, if you come near my consort again or have your demons follow us, I will slaughter every demon in your realm. You know I can, and you know I will."

Her lips pursed, and the look in her eyes turned nasty. "You're wasting your time with this one—you know as well as I do. She's not fit to rule beside you, my son. She's as weak as the others." She tilted her head, a look of fake sympathy rearranging her features. "Maybe next time?" She stood and lifted her hands palm up, and shadows began to swirl above them, so thick and dark, it was like she held the night in her hands. Power snapped from her, making the hair on the back of my neck stand up. "Let me end this for you now. Let me end this before you grow attached to her and you're hurt when this ends as badly as the rest."

"No," Death roared as he slammed his staff onto the floor. The marble cracked, a fault line snaking across the entire room and out of sight. "You are not the only god in this room. You may have limited my powers here, but I am not powerless. Attempt to take her from me and see what happens. You're not as strong as you once were, whereas I grow stronger with every passing day. Make a move to hurt her, and I will destroy you."

Malice lit her face, but she dropped her hands. "It was only a suggestion. I care about you, you must see that?"

"Do not follow us," he snarled, ignoring her bullshit, and pointed a thick, tattooed finger at her. "I'm warning you now, and I won't do it again—I will strike you down." He strode from the room into the massive entrance hall, then out the doors.

As soon as we were outside, he lowered me to my feet. "Are you injured?" His eyes narrowed. "Your face. They hit you?"

"I'm fine."

His fury ratcheted back up. "I told you, more than once, do not leave my side."

He was roaring again. "Stop yelling at me," I bit out.

"It seems it's the only way to get you to listen to me. 'Do not leave my side' means exactly that, or are you hard of hearing?"

I scowled. "If I wasn't before, I am now. Lower your damned voice. If you said, 'stay by my side because my megalomaniac mother will send crotch-sniffing demons to abduct you,' then I would have stayed in bed and ignored my need for fresh air."

"What? They did what?" he roared again, then spun back to the temple doors, about to storm back inside.

I grabbed his arm. "I'm fine. And I'm pretty sure you decapitated the offending demons back there already, so punishment has been meted out."

Death's gaze sliced down my body and back, and a strange stillness moved over him. His brows lowered. "Take that off."

"What?"

"The gown, take it off." He didn't yell this time; no, his voice was low, tight.

There was a note to his voice I'd never heard before. "My clothes are back in the temple."

"Take it off, Zinnia, now." Then he grabbed the front of the dress, holding the delicate fabric in his hands... and tore it off my body.

"What the hell are you doing?" I tried to cover my nakedness as he stared down at me, nostrils flared, panting like a furious bull.

His hand shot out, and using his weakened powers, he summoned my leathers and knives from inside. They appeared in his hands. "Cover yourself."

If I weren't cold, I'd ignore him and stay naked just to piss him off. "What the hell is your problem?"

"Put them on," he growled.

"You're an asshole, you know that?" I said as I snatched my clothes from his hands and quickly pulled them on.

Death watched me the entire time, his gaze sliding over my bare skin until I was finally covered. Then he tilted his head back and made a strange throaty sound. A moment later, a creature appeared at the edge of the forest in the distance and headed straight for us.

It was similar to Zuri and Raze but also not. It was stockier, its legs thicker. It trotted over and stopped beside Death.

He ran his hand down its side. "Thank you for your service," he said, then grabbed me around the waist and tossed me up before he swung up behind me as well.

Then the beast took off.

Chapter Fourteen

Zinnia

WE RODE FOR SEVERAL HOURS, picking our way through the forest before, finally, we came to a small clearing. A stone building sat in the middle, not huge, but still a decent size. It was made of glittering steel-colored marble with vines wrapped around the columns on either side of the entrance and partially over the roof.

Death jumped down from the beast, grabbed me around the waist, and hauled me off after him. He'd been quiet the entire ride, barely saying more than a few words.

At first, I thought it was about his mother and what just happened and the fact he thought I'd disobeyed him, but now, I wasn't so sure. The rage that had radiated from him had receded, and something else had replaced it. Something that felt a lot like melancholy.

"What is this place?" I asked, standing beside him.

"Somnus and I spent most of our time here as children. I created it when I was very young. It was safe, warded, impenetrable

126

by anyone but him and me and those we chose to grant admittance."

I studied his profile. The night sky swirled in his eyes, but again, there was no anger. They were wide, as if he was about to face something that frightened him. "Not even Nox?"

"Not even her."

So even as children, they'd avoided their twisted mother. "You created it? When you were just a child?"

"Yes."

He said no more and seemed to go somewhere else for a moment. I touched his arm. "Why are we here?"

"This is where Somnus is. His dream-self, anyway."

"Why would he come here, back to this realm, so close to Nox, even while he's asleep?"

"I'll show you," Death said and took my hand, leading me to the tall main doors.

They were damaged, the marble chipped and gouged. "Someone's been trying to get in."

Death's eyes swirled, and I felt his fury return. "Yes, but breaching them is impossible."

Whatever was in here had to be something important or powerful for Nox to be so desperate to get in. "That must piss Nox off."

"It does, but still she tries, and the fact Somnus and I have a temple in her realm and still she's denied admittance infuriates her."

Death slid my knife from the sheath strapped to my thigh, then sliced his forearm. He handed the knife back to me, then, dipping his finger in the blood dripping from the wound, drew a symbol on the door. The door rumbled, and a moment later, it swung open.

Taking my hand again, he led me through the massive doors, and I saw that the slice on Death's arm had already healed. The doors closed behind us, and I took in the room. Inside was vastly different than outside. Everything was pristine, lush couches and cozy blankets, vibrant colors.

"Did you and Somnus choose the furniture?"

"Yes, when we were very young. This was a refuge from our mother, so we made it as comfortable as we could. We created every piece in this temple," he said absently.

"You were powerful even as a small boy." Something was seriously wrong with Death; he didn't just give away information like that.

His hands hung loose at his sides, but they curled, his fists tight. "When you're a terrified child, it's amazing what you can accomplish."

My heart broke for him and Somnus. "You were here a lot?"

"Sometimes, we were in here for months, and sometimes, years at a time."

"Years?" I choked out.

The veins bulged in his forearms. "Nox created us because she was lonely. She wanted to know what it was like to love someone besides herself, but after we were born, she quickly returned to her default of using everything and everyone for her own gain. She sold Somnus regularly, bartered her small son in exchange for power." His lips curled in disgust, his eyes bright with fury. "She let other gods sleep beside him, let them piggyback off his power. He didn't have full control over it yet, so he didn't know how to distance himself from it. He was forced to see the twisted shit they did in the Dream Realm to others, and sometimes, they turned their twisted shit on him." His nostrils flared. "I made it so she couldn't get near him anymore, and as punishment, she stifled my powers in her realm so she'd always be stronger."

I felt sick to my stomach. How could she do that to her own children? "I'm so sorry. She really is a monster."

The muscle at the side of his jaw tightened. "More than you know."

He carried on through the main room and down a short hallway. Right at the end was another closed door. Death pressed his hand to it and whispered words I couldn't hear.

The door swung open, and he stepped inside.

I followed but abruptly stopped, definitely not prepared for what was in there. I expected an altar dedicated to Somnus or something like that, some artifact that we could take back to the castle to wake his brother in Limbo; instead, there was a little girl.

Death walked to her side, staring down at her. He kept his features hard, but again, somehow, I felt his emotions and just how wild they were in that moment.

She was very young, maybe two or three years old. "You have a sister?" I whispered and joined him. My breath caught. She was utterly beautiful. Her hair was long and glossy black like Nox's, her skin the same shimmery mother-of-pearl. "Why is she here? Why isn't she with her mother?"

"Her mother doesn't know she exists, and that's the way it must be for now," he said, voice low.

"Doesn't know she exists? How? And if Nox doesn't know she exists, then why is she trying to break into the temple?" I glanced up at him.

He ran the backs of his fingers down the child's round cheek. "It's complicated."

"How long has she been here? How old is she?"

"She's been here in stasis for a very long time. In human years, she is but three years old."

"Why is she like this? Why is she being kept asleep like this?"

"This was a punishment, part of a curse, and there is only one way for it to be broken. Until that happens, she must stay here, and Somnus stays with her in the dream world, protecting her, taking care of her so she is not alone or afraid, until she can finally wake again."

"A curse? So there's no way we can take her from this temple?"

"No, not without breaking it first."

He didn't elaborate, which meant he couldn't tell me.

I couldn't take my eyes off the child lying there. "Are you able to talk to her through Somnus like you did me? In the dream realm?"

"No, she is blocked from me in every way. Only Somnus can reach her."

I didn't think I could despise Nox more. I was wrong. "What will happen to her when we wake him? Who will protect her in the dream realm?"

His jaw tightened again, and his hand actually shook as it hovered over the little girl's cheek. "There are places she can hide. Somnus will ensure she's hidden before he rises from his slumber. It will be only a few days, and then he can return to her."

"She must be so scared," I choked out, thinking of Jasmine when she was that little and my responsibility, and of baby Violet. I don't know what came over me, but I reached out and cupped her tiny, little face, leaning in close and smoothing my hand over her hair. "It will be okay, little one," I whispered. "Your brothers will keep you safe." My heart squeezed. "What's her name?"

"Marigold."

I glanced at him, but he wasn't looking at me or his tiny sister; he had moved to a small statue beside her bed. "Your knife," he said and held out his hand.

I took it from its sheath again and handed it to him. This time, he sliced through his palm and squeezed his fingers into a tight fist, letting his blood drip down the small statue while muttering words in a different language.

Death's head was back, his eyes closed, and power rolled through the room, shaking the ground. I grabbed onto the side of the bed so I didn't fall.

Finally, he opened his eyes, swiped his thumb through the blood pooled in his palm, and pressed it to Marigold's forehead.

"While you walk the Dream Realm alone, let my blood be your protection, let it shelter you, guide you, comfort you," he said in a low, raspy voice.

Then he stepped back, and the power pulsing through the room dropped, returning to how it was when we walked in. "You still have power in here?"

"Enough."

"Now what?" I asked when Death said nothing more.

"Now we go home. Somnus will wake in the next few days, and I'd like to be there to greet him." His gaze slid to me, and his eyes were back to black, flecked with distant stars.

He studied me in a way that made me uneasy. I glanced at Marigold, then back at him. "Is there something else you need?"

He shook his head. "Wait for me in the great room. I'll be out in a moment."

I nodded and hustled out of there, but I couldn't help but glance back before the room was out of sight. Death had dropped to his knees beside the bed, the child's hand held in his massive, tattooed, and scarred ones, and his head was bowed. He was talking, but there was no way I could hear what he was saying. I quickly turned away, feeling guilty for watching such a private and obviously painful moment, and did what he said.

When I walked back into the great room, I spotted a set of wooden animals. They lay on a small table by one of the couches, and I imagined two little boys in this place, playing with toys, sheltered within these walls. They'd been here sometimes years at a time. Were they always alone? What the hell was wrong with Nox that she didn't care for them or protect them? They were gods, yes, and I had no idea how children with that kind of power were raised, but this was wrong any way you looked at it.

After meeting Nox and seeing the way Death loathed her, I doubted she'd ever cared for them the way a mother should.

When Death walked into the room, he was back to being somber and contemplative. Leaving Marigold behind had to be incredibly difficult.

We walked back through the massive doors and outside. "How long has it been since you've been with Somnus awake?" I asked to try and take his mind off his pain, to remind him that he had something to look forward to.

He lifted me onto the beast, then swung up behind me. "Thirteen years."

Thirteen years ago, I'd been just fifteen years old. "When Somnus found me? Is that the last time you talked?"

"Yes."

His arm wrapped around me, and he fisted the beast's knotted mane. "Sleep if you need to. We're not stopping until we're back at the ship."

Then the beast lowered its head, and we took off, galloping back toward the Night Sea.

The closer we got to the ship, the more Death's mood deteriorated. He wasn't speaking, and the shadows swirled around him constantly now. A profound sadness and that anger, so much anger, burned from his chest behind me and went right through me, settling in my gut. I found myself wrapping my hands around his forearm, my thumbs sliding back and forth in an attempt to soothe whatever was going on with him.

When we reached the ship, Death ushered me down to the cabin, then headed back up, and I heard one demon scream followed by Death roaring threats. I waited for him to come down after that, but he didn't.

A demon knocked on the door an hour later carrying buckets of water. He filled the tub, then left. I quickly washed and changed into a pair of tights and a T-shirt, but despite Death telling me to sleep, I couldn't; it was impossible when all those volatile emotions inside him were so raw and real to me.

I lay in bed, stared at the dark and moody sky through the small round window in the opposite wall, and pressed both hands to my chest to try and ease the ache. Goddess, I had this hollow feeling inside me. I didn't know what was causing it, but I needed it to stop.

It wasn't because of Death; it was something else. Though, I kind of felt like he was avoiding me. I shouldn't care, but I did. So many things had happened during this trip that could have him feeling the way he did, but it felt as if he was directing the force of his emotions at me when we'd ridden—that he was angry at me. But why? Yes, I went up to the deck without telling him and got myself kidnapped, but that didn't warrant that kind of fury. It had to be something else.

I was still mulling all this over hours later, when the door opened and closed. Death walked to the tub, stripped off, and climbed in, barely looking my way, but when he did, his nostrils flared and he ground his teeth.

Any doubt I had about my hypothesis vanished. He was most definitely pissed at me.

Words flew around my head as I tried to think of what to say. Despite how long I'd been coming to Limbo and how things had changed between us this last week, I didn't know him, not really. How could I? He was as old as time, a complex god, and he told me nothing.

He also didn't owe me his trust, and I hadn't earned the right to hear his deepest and darkest secrets, like he hadn't earned that from me. Which meant there was only one thing I could do. Shoving back the covers, I got out of bed and walked over, stopping at the foot of the bath.

"Go back to bed," he said, his gaze locked on the edge of the tub.

"Look at me."

His lips peeled back, but he did as I asked. His eyes were still black as night, like his mother's eyes, not a bit of white showing. "It's my turn," I said.

"Not tonight, witch."

Not consort or wife, not little witch, just witch, as if he was trying to put distance between us.

"Yes, tonight. We made a deal. This is what you demanded, so we'll do it."

His eyes flashed. "No, we will not. Now go back to bed."

He stood abruptly and snatched the towel, roughly drying himself off, then slung it around his waist.

"You're angry with me, why?"

He growled.

"Mors—"

His growl exploded in volume. "Do not... call me that. We are not in bed, witch, so you do not call me by my name."

For some reason, that hurt a lot. It was almost as if... as if he hated me in that moment. "Why are you angry at me?" I asked again. He turned away, and I grabbed his arm.

He swung back, pulling from my hold. "I told you to go back to bed."

"Since when have I done anything you've told me?" I fired back.

"Never, not one fucking time." He ground his teeth again. "You did this, you caused this..." He stopped himself.

"Tell me what I did." He was breathing hard. "Death, tell me what the hell is up your ass, because I've got to tell you, this tantrum of yours is starting to piss me off."

"Is that right?"

"You're not just angry, are you? You're angry at me?"

His face contorted. "Yes," he yelled.

"Why?"

He shook his head, his fingers in brutal fists, the veins in his arms and neck popping. "That is something you have to figure out for yourself."

"You can't just tell me?"

"No."

"And what if I can't figure it out?" I asked. All that volatile emotion pouring off him was too heavy a burden to carry.

He took two steps toward me, closing the space between us, and grabbed my arms. "You have to, do you hear me? You have to because I can't do this anymore. I can't fucking do this again."

I stared up at him. "Do what? I don't understand."

He cursed so loud and full of anguish, I flinched. When he saw me do it, another growl rumbled from him, and he hauled me off my feet. "You're not afraid of me, little witch."

It wasn't a question; it was a demand.

"No," I said and hooked my arms around his neck, pressing my body close. "I'm not."

"Fuck, you piss me off," he snarled, then twisted my hair in his fist and slammed his mouth down on mine.

Our mouths weren't in a dance, moving together; no, they were dueling. "You piss me off more," I said, digging my nails into his shoulders hard enough to draw blood.

He growled. "You disobey me again, and I will lock you in my bedroom and never let you out." He shoved me against the wall. "No, I think I'll do it, anyway."

I hissed, "No, you fucking won't."

My shirt was yanked off over my head and tossed away. "You think you can stop me?"

I bit down on his lip and tasted blood. "I can try, and I think you know me well enough now to know I won't stop until I win."

He swiped his tongue over his lip, coating it in blood, then yanked my head back and thrust it in my mouth, kissing me hard. "I have nothing but time, female," he said against my lips.

My legs were around his hips, fighting to get him closer while making him work for it at the same time. "You're a confusing, arrogant pain in the ass."

He shoved his hand down the front of my tights, into my underwear. "Turns out confusing, arrogant pains in the ass make your cunt wet as fuck."

"And it turns out infuriating, disobedient witches make you hard as hell." I yanked the towel away, and the long, hard ridge of his cock dug into my stomach.

The sound of fabric ripping came next. "They were my favorite tights, asshole."

"I'm about to stuff your pussy full of your favorite cock, so I think you'll get over it," he said, maneuvering me like a rag doll, then shoved my panties aside.

"How do you know yours is my favorite?" I fired back, even though we both knew I'd never had better, that no one had ever made me feel the way he had in this cabin.

He laughed, and it was dark and arrogant; then, he slammed inside me.

I cried out, the invasion too much but exactly what I needed. *"Oh fuck."*

The smile dropped from his face as he slid out, then thrust back in. "When I'm finished with you, I will be the only lover you remember. The rest will cease to exist. How long did you feel me after, little witch, when I fucked you the first time?"

I hadn't stopped. I'd still felt him before he filled me a moment ago. "G-goddamn... ah, arrogant."

He pressed his forehead against mine and thrust inside me again, then held there. "You were made for me, inside and out, and the first time I claimed you, I ruined you for every other male for the rest of your life."

The rest of my life could be only a matter of hours or days, so I guess he was right. I didn't say that, though. When I talked about that, it angered him, and I currently had as much angry Death as I could handle. "You... th-think so?" He still hadn't slid back out; he was still deep inside me, doing this subtle swivel of his hips, and goddess, it felt so fucking good. I was close to coming from just that. My pussy started clutching at him desperately.

"I know so, and if another male comes near you, I will tear him into tiny pieces, but not before I've made him scream for mercy."

I couldn't hold back; my pussy clamped down on him, and I cried out, coming for him and moaning his name.

"That's it, wife, moan for me." Then he lifted me away from the wall, pulled out, spun me to my front, shoved me down on the bed, and, dragging my ass in the air, slammed back inside me. His hand went between my thighs, and one of those long, scarred fingers slid over my clit while he pounded into me from behind. I came again, screaming this time, mindlessly clawing at the sheets.

His big body covered me, one hand curling around my throat, his mouth coming to my ear as he fucked me hard and fast. "You are mine, Zinnia, and I won't fucking lose you, do you hear me? I won't," he said the last part in a way that resonated though the room like an oath.

All I could do was make an incoherent sound as the God of Death claimed me in the most primal of ways over and over again.

Chapter Fifteen

Zinnia

WE WERE FINALLY on the last leg of the journey, and I gripped Zuri's reins as she galloped through the forest. She'd healed while we were gone, but Raze had been sticking close to his mate since Death called for them after we walked through the gateway back into Limbo.

He nudged her every now and again, making her move where he wanted her, to keep her from edging too far ahead or putting any kind of distance between them at all. Zuri would make this high noise and shake her head in frustration, overwhelmed by his dominance. I got how she was feeling; the last few days, Death hadn't left my side.

I glanced over at him. He'd invaded my life at fifteen years old, and had been completely unaware of how terrified I'd been of him or that the way he went about it had sent me down a dark path, driving me to go to extreme lengths to avoid him. I'd lost something precious as a consequence, far more than was fair, and that was before I'd been forced to leave my family and come here. After all of that, after all I'd lost, I never dreamed I'd actually like him. That I might actually enjoy his company—but I did.

The castle finally came into view, and Death galloped up to the stairs, his anticipation at seeing his brother awake for the first time in so many years palpable. He swung off Raze, and I eased off Zuri, stretching my aching body. Death had made good on his promise; he'd taken me at any opportunity, deeply and thoroughly, and there wasn't a moment, not since the first time we were together, that I hadn't felt him with me, inside me.

And I wanted him. Goddess, I wanted him all the damn time.

Shivering, I focused on taking off Zuri's girth strap and glanced up when the doors swung open and Somnus strode out. He should be frail from never moving, never eating, only sleeping, but he wasn't. He looked every bit the god he was.

Death grinned wide, taking the steps two at a time to greet him. I couldn't take my eyes off them as they embraced, as Death said something to him low. Their connection was obvious, the love between them unmissable.

When they released each other, Somnus looked over at me. I lifted a hand in greeting, feeling awkward, not wanting to intrude on their reunion, but I also kind of knew him as well. He'd been here the entire time I had, even if he'd been asleep. He smiled, but it was strained.

Death strode back to me. "Come and join us."

I shook my head. "You two have a lot to catch up on, right? Like thirteen years' worth of gossip to share. I'm going to take a bath, snuggle with Hemy, and have a nap. I'll join you afterward." Death had regained his control somewhat since losing it completely on the ship, but I could tell it was a battle. He didn't want to be angry, but it was still there.

"Okay, but don't stay away too long," he said and pressed a sweet kiss to my lips before he strode back to his brother, and they disappeared inside.

I'd said thanks to Zuri, and she and Raze had just trotted off when Egon hustled out, his horns glinting in the light. Hemlock was on his shoulder, and he squeaked, making excited noises when he saw me. I scooped him up and held him close. "I've missed you, my sweet baby." He wriggled and squeaked some more, trying to get as close as he could to me, and I giggled when he tickled my neck.

"Thank you for taking such good care of Hemy. He's happy, so I'm happy."

"No thanks necessary, I assure you." Egon took my bag. "I thought you might like a bath, my lady."

"Are you saying I stink, Egon?"

His lips twitched. "Never."

"Well, I do, and I'd love one."

"Good, because I've drawn one for you," he said.

We headed inside. "Have I ever told you that I love you?" I said and hooked my arm through his. "Because I do."

He didn't profess his love back to me, but I did see the corners of his lips curl up, and he patted my hand. "I am exceedingly glad you're home safe."

"You and me both. Were you bored without me?"

He made a rough sound that was absolutely a laugh. "Oh, most assuredly. The castle was a sad and lonely place without you stomping around and bickering with his lordship."

"Stomping? I do not stomp."

His lips twitched again. "Of course not."

"Or bicker."

"Never."

"Smart-ass."

"Possibly."

I laughed then, and it felt really good. "Just so you know, you're my favorite."

"Second favorite, surely," he said.

"Maybe."

The slight lip curl became a full, fang-flashing grin. The demon had not missed that something had changed between Death and me.

"Shut up," I said, then couldn't hold back my own grin, because I wasn't... unhappy. For the first time in all the months I'd been coming here, I wasn't desperately missing home. Yes, I was confused and scared of the things I was starting to feel, plus a whole lot of other things, but I wasn't unhappy. I thought I might actually be the opposite, which just made me all the more terrified.

We walked into my room, and Egon put my bag on the trunk at the end of the bed.

"Lyle made you a mug of your favorite tea. It's waiting for you by the tub. Would you like a light repast brought up?"

"No. Thanks, though, Egon. I'll wait for dinner. And I deeply appreciate the tea."

He smiled and dipped his head, then walked out, closing the door behind him. I sat on the edge of my bed, pulled off my boots with a sigh, and wiggled my toes while Hemy had the zoomies on the mattress around me. I undid my leather jacket and let it slide off my shoulders. Next, I shucked off the pants and let out another sigh of relief. Striding to the dresser, I pulled out some clean clothes, and my gaze caught on the knickknacks sitting on top.

I picked up a silver thimble; it was worn inside, with tiny dents from needles pressing against the tip. Someone had used it regularly. Without realizing I was doing it, my hand went to the center of my chest, rubbing at the ache that came out of nowhere. That seemed to be happening a lot. Some of the pieces on the dresser and around the room had to be ancient, and some were probably just a century or two old. There were things all over this room, little oddities, keepsakes—a random book still open face down on the table by the chair next to the window, a delicate bedside clock inlaid with jewels, small dried-up pots of paints, and several paintings of the view from the window or the garden that were executed with passion and pleasure, but even I could see they were by someone who only painted as a hobby.

Only now, right in this moment, did I realize what they were.

They were small pieces of the females who had come before me. Each of Death's consorts had left something of themselves in this bedroom.

One day soon, would all that remained of me in this castle be some trinket left behind?

More than likely.

No, I wasn't going to just give up. I wasn't going to let someone end my life, or whatever had happened to the females before me, without a fight, but I had accepted that death could be the eventual outcome of this journey fate had sent me on, whether I liked it or not.

"How are you enjoying Limbo?" Somnus asked as he tore another strip of meat from the bone he was holding.

Somnus had been quiet, distracted, and his leg jiggled almost nonstop. He hadn't said much since I sat, instead choosing to devour everything on the table like a man who hadn't taken a bite in thirteen years.

"Does anyone really enjoy Limbo?" I said, grinning as I cut off a small piece of carrot and handed it to Hemy, who was perched on my shoulder.

Somnus glanced at Death, not looking amused by my little joke in the slightest. "A person can enjoy any location as long as they are in close proximity to those they love."

He was also protective of his brother.

"Yes, that's true. It's hard being away from my family a month at a time. I have a younger sister—"

"Who is newly mated, yes? She does not need you to be there for her like she used to," Somnus said. "I understand the hardship of being absent from the lives of my family, of being parted from them, but sometimes, we need to do what's best for ourselves as well as others."

I stared at him, surprised that when he did finally choose to speak, it was to essentially scold me for not being excited enough about being here with his brother. "That's true. When did you last do something for yourself, Somnus? As I understand it, you've spent centuries— longer?—trapped in the Dream Realm to protect your sister. No, I still don't fully understand all the ins and outs of your situation…" I glanced at Death. "Because no one will tell me, but you're not really practicing what you preach." Was that a dickish thing to say? Probably, but I wasn't a fan of being judged by someone who knew nothing about me.

He blinked over at me several times. "I am immortal. I have been alive since almost the dawn of time and will continue to live when we reach the end. I have many lifetimes ahead of me. My time with Marigold in the Dream Realm is but a blip in my lifetime. Best you consider the situation you find yourself in closely, or you will end up—"

"Somnus," Death growled.

He froze, then blew out a breath and slumped back in his seat. "Apologies, both of you. I'm not… I'm not myself. I'm anxious to get back to Marigold."

"It must be hard being away from her," I said.

"It is. Thankfully, I have a… a friend, Pascal, who can check in on her from time to time." His gaze went to Death. "I trust him with my life," he added, reassuring his brother.

"Are you sure, Som?" Death asked, looking tense.

"I've never been more sure of anything."

Death held his brother's stare, then nodded.

I took a sip of my wine. "So, how do you know so much about me and my sister?" I asked Somnus.

He looked up from loading his plate with more mashed potatoes. "I have access to every living being in every realm in existence.

Dreams, nightmares—they come to everyone. I was searching for you, and then one night, there you were."

I turned to Death. "How does it work? How did you reach me in my dream that first time?"

Hemy pushed closer to me when he sensed my emotions shift, my little familiar trying to comfort me. That time of my life was not something I liked to look back on. Death was studying me in that way of his, like he could sense it as well and was trying to reach inside me and learn my secrets.

He had his elbows on the table, his hands linked together in front of him. Darkness swirled in his eyes. "If I sleep beside Som, as long as we're touching, I can tap into his powers, and he can point me in the right direction."

I looked away, down at my food, when Somnus asked him a question, changing the subject. But I couldn't shake the memories of that time, of what happened next. The night the God of Death came to me—a terrified kid, only fifteen years old—in my dreams and told me I belonged to him.

How I'd struggled to stay awake afterward so he couldn't reach me again. I'd taken potions to keep myself awake until I was delirious and desperate. Until I'd finally learned of a demon who could help me. Then I'd made a choice in fear and delirium that ended in me losing something precious, something that I could never get back and could never be undone.

I stumbled to the demon's door and knocked.

His name was Fluke, and it had taken me three days to find him. Three days of drinking coffee, of using forbidden potions and elixirs to fight off sleep. If my family knew I'd come here, they'd be furious, but this demon was my only chance. "You said on the phone you can help me?"

The demon's muddy yellow eyes looked me up and down. "You are Death's consort?"

"That's what he says." The demon was old, powerful. He'd been around so long, his skin looked thin and almost translucent. His eyes

were cloudy, and the fangs that curved around his chin had blackened. If I weren't so exhausted and scared, I would've probably peed myself. But what waited for me in my dreams, my future, if the demon couldn't help me was far worse.

"What's your fee?" I asked, my words sounding slurred from exhaustion and the potions still in my system.

He opened his door wider. "Come in and we can make a deal."

I needed to get this done quickly. Mom was gone again, and Jaz had been staying with a friend. I hated being away from her for more than a couple of days. I followed him in, and he led me to a tall bench, motioning to it. I sat, and he walked to a shelf and pulled down a small bottle. The liquid inside was black or maybe deep red, it was hard to tell in the shadowed room.

"This is the blood of the goddess Nox. She is the night and Death's mother. This cost me deeply to acquire, and if you want my help, you must be prepared to pay a great price."

"Whatever it is, I'll pay it."

"Then lie on the bench and lift up your shirt," he said as he closed the space between us, excitement dancing in his eyes.

"What are you going to do?"

"Take something you do not need. Now do it, or leave and await your fate."

I would never leave Jazzy. She needed me. And I would never belong to Death, and I sure as hell would never love that monster. I had no choice but to do as the demon asked. I lay on the bench and lifted my shirt. He stalked over and kneeled on the floor beside me.

"Once I take payment, I will mark you with the blood of Nox. Only her blood has the power to conceal you, and the only way for Death to find you will be if you cut the markings from your skin, do you understand?"

I nodded, my heart racing wildly in my chest.

Pulling up his sleeves, he rubbed his hands together, his translucent skin glowing the faster he rubbed. Then he pressed one to my bare stomach, pushing and grinding his palm. I screamed and *thrashed, but leather binds snapped up like snakes and wrapped around my arms and legs, holding me down. White-hot agony burned through me as his hand pushed through, disappearing inside me. Shadows danced at the edges of my vision—and then the pain was too much. Everything went dark.*

When I woke again, only a few candles flickered around the room. I looked down at myself. My stomach looked as if nothing had happened, as if the demon hadn't shoved his hand through my skin and into my body. My forearm stung, and I lifted it. There was a small tattoo-like marking there.

"You're awake finally," the demon said, and I quickly sat up, almost unbalancing and falling.

I looked back down at the tattoo. "What did you do?"

"The deal is done. You are now concealed from Death for all eternity."

I struggled to my feet. My stomach ached, and I felt weird. "What did you take from me?"

He motioned to a jar on a table beside me. Something fleshy floated in pink-tinged liquid. "I've given you your life back. That is a powerful thing and requires something equally as powerful as payment. I restored your life, and now you will never be able to create it. I took your womb, child."

"Zinnia?"

Death's voice pulled me from the horror of that memory, one I chose not to revisit, ever, but tonight, for some reason, I hadn't been able to shake it off.

"Where did you go just now?" he asked, studying me closely.

I forced a smile. "Sorry, I must've zoned out. Tired, I guess. I didn't sleep earlier like I'd planned to." I was trying to hide how that memory affected me, but Hemlock was totally giving me away. He was pressed into me, nuzzling my jaw, pouring as much love and comfort into me as his little soul had to give.

"Egon," Somnus called. "Bring the ambrosia, my man. My brother and I have much to discuss."

I smiled at him. "Looks like you're in for a big night. I'm going to head up to bed." I stood, but Death grabbed my hand, stopping me from walking past.

"Are you well?" His gaze moved over my face again. "You seem unsettled."

"I'm fine," I lied. "I just need a good night's sleep, that's all."

"And you'll be in my bed while you do it. Tonight and every night from now on. When I come up later, that's where I expect to find you."

"How very presumptuous of you," I said, raising a brow.

"This was inevitable. If you try to defy me, I will come for you and put you where you belong," he said, and darkness flashed through his eyes again.

This side of him hadn't been present as much, not after we left the ship and headed for home. I recognized it for what it was now —fear that I would reject him, deny him. He chose force, to bend me to his will, rather than ask and risk me saying no. That was something we were going to have to talk about, but I was too tired right then, and we had an audience.

So instead of giving him the attitude he expected before he inevitably made me do what he wanted, I decided to skip that part and, instead, cupped the side of his face, then leaned in close. His eyes widened, and I relished his surprise. It wasn't often I got one over on this powerful male. "All you had to do was ask, my lord," I said and pressed a soft kiss to his perfectly formed lips.

He made a delicious gruff sound as I straightened and walked away.

"Night, Somnus," I called.

"Good night, Zinnia," he called back, sounding a lot cheerier than before.

Chapter Sixteen

Zinnia

It FELT weird being in Death's huge bed on my own. It felt weird being in his room, period.

The fire crackled against the opposite wall, and that at least gave the place a bit of warmth, but here now, on my own, I was feeling out of place—insignificant.

I stroked Hemy, who had curled up beside my pillow, and that helped. But there was this niggling feeling inside me that wouldn't go away, that I didn't like much at all.

I'd never had low self-esteem or let insecurities get the better of me. I'd always been confident in who I was, how I looked, my place in the world. I'd basically raised my sister on my own since our mother was more absent than not. I'd protected Jasmine, taken over her care full time when Mom left to travel the world and barely looked back.

So I knew who I was. I was Zinnia Thornheart, Jasmine's big sister, and a powerful witch and medium. I'd liked being her—

loved it, in fact. Being a god's consort? One of possibly ten other females? Nope, that had never been on the cards. So no, I'd never had low self-esteem, but I needed to know where I fit into all of this. With him? I'd definitely never be his one and only love; he'd possibly loved them all. I wasn't the jealous type, but it was an odd feeling being one of so many and possibly not his last consort either—there would be more after me, possibly many more. I guess that was no different than meeting someone and knowing they had a bunch of exes. It was normal, right?

Again, I wasn't the jealous type, but something was developing between us, something wild and huge and unstoppable, and I couldn't help but wonder if this was what it was like for him with all of them.

"I'm being an idiot," I said to Hemy. He hissed his disagreement. "You're just saying that because you love me." He squeaked, and I scratched his tiny chin. "Thank the goddess I have you, my sweetheart." Because now that we were back in the castle, I was feeling off-kilter. I wasn't sure what my role was anymore, what I was supposed to do.

Death was into me, that much was clear, and I was seriously struggling to come to terms with the fact that after eighteen months of coming here, I was now suddenly into him as well, like in a seriously big way.

The door opened, and he strode in.

His gaze sliced to the bed as soon as he walked in, and when he saw me, he grinned.

Not his normal grin. I'd never seen this grin; it lit up his entire face. "You're pretty drunk, huh?" I said, sitting up and leaning against the headboard.

"Not at all," he said, and the way he said it made it obvious that he was totally drunk.

"How much ambrosia did you and Somnus drink?"

He sauntered over, kicked off his boots, and then reached back, pulling off his shirt before tossing it aside. He stared down at me, eyes glinting. "I like seeing you in my bed, little witch, very much."

I laughed softly. "I can see that."

He flopped down on the bed beside me, then scooted over and wrapped his arms around my waist. "Fuck, I love the way you laugh. It's husky and so incredibly bewitching." I was still sitting, but now, with his big body wrapped around me and his head in my lap, I was stuck out of the covers.

I looked at the huge, tattooed god in my lap, his face relaxed in a way I'd never seen before, and my chest warmed. When was the last time he'd allowed himself to be this vulnerable?

"I like your laugh as well." I ran my hand along his shoulder, massaging.

He groaned, then dragged the sheet under him back and curled his hand around my bare thigh. "And I love your smooth skin." He pressed his nose to it. "And the way you smell, like honey and your garden and the night sky."

Now my belly was all swirly. "What does the night sky smell like?"

"Clean and crisp... overwhelming, breathtaking," he muttered. "What do I smell like?"

I blinked at his question, not expecting it at all. "Well—"

"And if you say death or some variation of it, like decay or rot, I'll tan your lovely ass."

Another laugh burst from me. "That does sound like something I'd say."

"Because I know you, my sweet Stella. I know all of you," he said, and there was a little more slur to his words.

Stella. Yes, it meant star, but I still didn't want him calling me that, especially when I'd had visions of him using that name affectionately with other consorts. There was no point calling him out on it while he was like this, though, and I didn't want to argue with him either, so I answered his question because despite him using that name, I was enjoying seeing Death like this—relaxed.

Open. "Right now, you smell like leather and ambrosia and power," I said, giving him his answer.

"How does power smell?" he asked, turning my question back on me.

"Like endless shadows, vast and wild." I traced his lower lip. "Overwhelming, breathtaking."

He grinned. "Copycat."

"It's the truth."

He made a sound of agreement. "You always tell the truth, don't you, love?"

My heart kind of paused when he called me that, then exploded back to life. "I try to."

"Will you leave me?"

I was stunned silent for a moment, then quickly rallied. "I can't. We have a deal, remember?"

"But if you could, would you leave?"

I stared down at his profile. "If you'd asked me a couple of weeks ago, I would have said, yes, I would leave. Now... I'm not so sure."

He smiled, but his eyes stayed closed. "You're falling in love with me."

I had another of those heart explosions. "Again, you are being presumptuous. You're the most annoying male I've ever encountered. How could I ever fall in love with you?"

He chuckled at my sarcasm. "I have no idea, but you will."

"And will you fall in love with me?" I asked, while my heart tried to crawl into my throat.

He laughed again and shook his head against my lap as he held me tighter, as if I'd said something absurd, and I hated that sharp and unexpected disappointment filled me.

"I'm already in love with you," he murmured.

I froze.

His fingers dug deeper into my thigh, massaging, marking my

skin with his long, scarred fingers. "That's why you can't leave me. I won't recover if you do, not this time."

He'd lost everyone, and in a couple of days, Somnus would be gone again as well. "Mors—"

His eyes opened, and he rolled to his back, looking up at me, holding me captive with that bright blue gaze swirling with shadows. "If you leave me, if you go and never return to me, there will be no coming back from the cloak. I'll let it consume me. I will retreat into it, and I'll never see you again."

He'd revert to the Death he was when I first came here, when he first came to me. The way he was looking at me, what he'd just said, it was too intense... too much. "I bet you say that to all your consorts," I said, trying to lighten the heaviness that had fallen over us.

His gaze searched mine, the darkness overtaking the bright blue, and all traces of humor, of softness, left his face. The shadows thickened around him.

My mouth went dry. What he wanted, what he was asking of me, was too much, too soon. "Death?"

He sat up suddenly and got off the bed.

"Death—"

"Rest. I have some things I need to do," he said, and then he walked out.

I stared after him, confused. He was angry with me again; I could feel it. What the hell did he expect? So much was changing so fast. Did he expect to profess his love for me and I'd fall at his feet? That I'd say it back? I wasn't ready to do that, and who knew if I ever would be? I was still trying to get my head around this whole thing—the parts I understood, anyway.

I wasn't where he was—I just wasn't. And honestly, I didn't think he was truly there either. He didn't love me, not yet. It was too soon. This was the fate thing making him think he felt that way. I cared about him. Goddess, I wanted him, but love? No, because falling in love with him, careening toward a fate that would more than likely see me losing him anyway, was the most terrifying thing I could imagine right now.

Sliding back down the mattress, I tugged up the covers. Hemlock snuggled in against me and instantly fell asleep. I, on the other hand, lay there for hours listening for Death's footfalls in the hallway, wondering where he was and just how hurt and angry he was with me.

~

Death lay on his back, one hand behind his head, the other resting on his stomach. He was asleep, so still and so utterly gorgeous. I glanced over at Hemlock; he'd gotten sick of my wriggling during the night and was on the chair across the room by the fire, fast asleep.

I turned back to the male beside me. I wasn't sure what time he came in. I hadn't heard him, but he must have been gone several hours at least because I'd been awake that long.

My body was pressed to his side, and I wasn't sure if I'd sought him out while I'd slept, restless from more visions of the females of his past streaming through me, sending me a message that I hadn't yet figured out, or if he'd pulled me against him when he'd returned.

Considering how we left things last night, I was assuming it was the former.

I appreciated his attempt at honesty last night. Even if he'd been drunk when he said all those things and even if I didn't believe he truly felt that way, I hated that I'd hurt him. Death had suffered a lot in his long life, and I didn't want to be another wound on his soul. He didn't deserve that. But he was expecting too much from me way too soon.

That didn't stop me from feeling guilty, though. Leaning deeper into him, I rested my hand on his stomach and kissed his chest. His skin was so smooth—no hair, just taut, smooth skin over lean, hard muscle. I slid my hand down his hairless stomach, wrapped my hand around his hard, smooth length, and stroked slowly.

Death made a rough sound before his eyes blinked open. He sucked in a breath. "Fuck," he said when he released it.

"You were just so tempting lying there, I had to touch," I said, kissing his stomach. "How are you feeling this morning?"

His fingers delved into my hair. "Like I want to wake with you pressed against me every morning," he growled.

I shifted, moving down his body, and his legs parted, giving me room to slide between them. "I've been wanting to do this for a while."

He shoved his pillow higher behind his head and looked down, watching me. "You going to suck me, wife?"

The way he said that, dear goddess, my pussy clenched. "That was the plan."

"Then don't let me stop you. I've stroked myself to visions of this, of you right there, licking those perfect, full lips, with eyes eager and hungry."

I squeezed my thighs together. "You have?"

"The things I've imagined, Zinnia—the rough, the slow and intense, the raw and fucking dirty—it's kept me sane and driven me to madness all at the same time."

The web of veins from his lower stomach down to his cock stood out in relief, his cock hard and thick against his flat stomach. I licked my lips. "I've had a few thoughts myself."

He reached down and cupped my face, sliding his thumb over my chin, across my lower lip. Hungry but okay to wait for me to do as I pleased. "I'm sorry I walked out last night," he said. "Sometimes, the way I feel... the things I want to tell you..." He shook his head. "I get... frustrated."

"I noticed." Like on the ship, how angry he was that I didn't know whatever it was he was so desperate for me to figure out.

"Are you sure you can't just tell me whatever it is you want me to know?"

"Yes," he said, then fisted my hair, finally losing patience. "Suck me, my consort, before I lose my sanity."

"Your wish, my lord, is my command." Then I wrapped my mouth around the head of his cock and sucked him down as deep as I could, which wasn't far. His groan sent tingles of pleasure through me, and my inner muscles clamped down again.

Taking the base of his cock, I stroked as I sucked and kissed, as I teased him with my tongue, until he was panting hard, and then I took his smooth balls in my hand and massaged.

Death did an ab curl, hooked me under the arms, lifted me, spun me around, and planted me back on top of him so I was facing away. Then he gripped my hips and dragged me back until I was straddling his face. His tongue lashed my pussy, and I cried out, rocking against his mouth as I reached for his cock again and sucked him into my mouth. I could only just reach now with the height difference, and I could only suck the head into my mouth, so I used both hands to stroke the rest of his length while I sucked him as best as I could.

His tongue was relentless, working me the way he knew would get me off fast. I sucked him harder, rocking and moaning around his cock. Then he shoved two fingers inside me and sucked my clit, and I groaned, sucking him harder while I came against his mouth. His cock pulsed hard, and his hips lifted, thrusting deeper into my mouth as he came for me.

I collapsed on top of him, and he lifted me again, turning me back around like a rag doll and curling me into his side.

"Rest, love," he said, his lips against my hair. "When you wake, I'll fuck you and worship you until you pass out again."

"Sounds good," I said, wrapping my arm around his middle.

I drifted off to Death's chuckles.

Chapter Seventeen

Death

"So how does Limbo work?" Zinnia asked while she braided her hair.

I hadn't taken my eyes off her once. Everything about her fascinated me. Everything she did, everything she said. My obsession with her somehow grew with each passing day, despite trying to keep control of my feelings, despite knowing how dangerous it was. Now wasn't the time to fall, but it was too late—I already had. Thanks to Somnus and his ambrosia, I'd told her as much.

Nothing I'd said to her had been false, I just wished I hadn't said it, not yet. She wasn't ready to hear it, that much had been obvious, and again, thanks to the ambrosia, I hadn't been able to school my emotions when her avoidance of my declaration inevitably came.

I hadn't mentioned my feelings for her since, and neither had she. The last two nights we'd fucked in my bed and laughed and talked about things that were light and amusing, not only avoiding what I'd said to her, but also the things she wanted to know that I couldn't tell her.

Right now, she was trying to distract me from my pain. Somnus had returned to Marigold and the Dream Realm last night, and there was no telling how long it would be before I spoke to him again.

No, that depended wholly on the female watching me expectantly now. She had no idea just how much rested on her shoulders. If she did, if she knew the truth, she would probably run like hell from me, and I'd never see her again—or worse.

"What do you want to know?" I asked and stroked my hand down Hemlock's back. I watched the play of emotions moving across Zinnia's face and the way she chewed her pretty lower lip. It was still puffy from my kisses earlier.

If I lost her now...

Her familiar nudged my hand for another pat, stopping me from falling into that dark, hopeless pit, and I brutally shoved those thoughts aside.

"Where is everyone? Like, this place is full of spirits, and I know when a soul comes here, they're assigned their own kind of... personal Limbo, right? But where are they?"

I scooped Hemlock up and held out my hand. "How about I show you?"

She put down her brush and strode over, taking my hand with a grin. "Are we going on a field trip?"

I chuckled; I'd been doing that a lot lately. I'd forgotten what it was like until I found her and she'd pulled me from the cloak slowly but surely, without even knowing she was doing it. It had been so long since I'd had occasion to laugh, to feel happiness, to feel anything but rage. I didn't think it was going to happen, that again, it wouldn't happen, but it had. Zinnia had brought me back.

"Yes, a field trip." I loved the feel of her hand in mine; it was small and smooth and warm.

All she had to do was hold it back and not let go, and we would make it.

Just trust me, and finally, we'd make it to the other side.

Zinnia

Death led me from the castle and along the skull path, the one I followed when I came and went from Limbo. We walked until we reached the edge of the forest. Hemlock had stayed perched on Death's shoulder the entire time, which amazed me, honestly.

I gave his head a little scratch, and he squeaked, letting me know how happy he was, so I left him where he was.

"Which way?" If we took the path that went to the left, it would lead us to the gateway to my home, but there was a path that went right as well. I'd never explored it. It was less trodden, narrow, the skulls not as compacted down, leading into the thickest part of the forest.

"Right," he said, and since this path was only wide enough for one person, he pulled me forward so I was in front of him.

"This is where my reapers bring the souls," he said as he walked.

It was cooler in here, under the thick canopy of the trees, the scent of loam much heavier. Finally, we reached a clearing and stopped. "Now where do we go?

"Nowhere. We're here. This is where they are," he said.

"What do you mean, here? All of them? How?"

He lifted a hand, and his cloak appeared, shrouding him as he waved his palm in front of me.

The clearing transformed to a cottage with a woman sitting on the porch singing while she knitted. He waved his hand again. A man busking on a city street. *Again.* A woman on a beach walking her dog. *Again.* A wolf shifter howling mournfully in a dark forest. *Again*. A man playing violin in a concert hall.

I heard them all, felt them; the souls were bright and so incredibly vibrant.

Again and again and again, Death waved his hand, showing me the souls locked in Limbo, in the place they'd most wanted to be for eternity.

Finally, he lowered his hand, and his cloak vanished.

"That was…" Shockingly, I felt tears gather in my eyes. "I felt them," I whispered. "My ability to communicate with the dead, it's… bound here, well, except for the visions I've been getting, but I haven't been communicating with them. It's all one-sided." Having his past consorts trying to tell me something that I didn't understand was so goddamn frustrating. "But just now, I felt those souls. When you showed them to me, I felt each and every one… I heard them."

He cupped my face, brushing the tears from my cheeks. "It hurts you not to use your power?"

"It's a huge part of who I am, you know?" I shook my head. "It's what I do, how I help people. When I'm here, I feel… like I have no purpose, like I've lost a part of myself."

He swiped his thumb over my cheek again. "I'm sorry, Zinnia, I truly am. It won't… it won't always be this way…" The muscle at the side of his jaw pulsed. "If you… things won't be…" He cursed.

"What? Tell me."

He drew in a breath as if he was trying to regain control. "I can't."

"Or you won't?" I stared up at him.

"This is one of those things that you have to figure out for yourself."

Frustration filled me. "How the hell am I supposed to do that? You've given me nothing, no clues, no hints. Not one damn thing."

"That is where you're wrong," he said roughly.

I growled in frustration. "So what happens if I do figure everything out? What happens then?"

"Good things, little witch, really fucking good things."

I dropped my head so it rested against his chest. "So no pressure then?"

He chuckled low, his fingers sliding into my hair and massaging my scalp. "I believe in you," he said and kissed the top of my head.

His attempt at trying to keep things light, to pretend he wasn't tense, failed, because like I had been for a while now, I felt it. He was more than tense. There was this deep hollow feeling inside him, a feeling of total hopelessness. It was cold and lonely and desperate. No one deserved that. I hated that Death lived with it. Goddess, it must be torturous.

Lifting my head, I held his magnetic gaze. "I promise you, Mors, I will do everything in my power to do what it is you need me to." I didn't know if we would stay together, if I'd grow to love him the way he said he loved me, or if this thing between us would last—if I'd even survive it—but he didn't deserve to live a life missing a part of himself, and that's what this was, what I was feeling. It was like Death was missing a part of his soul, and I wouldn't stop until I helped him get that back. I thought about what he said to me after he'd been drinking ambrosia, about what would happen if I left him, and my heart squeezed tight. I pressed my hand to his chest and smiled up at him.

"I know you will, love," he said, not holding back, not asking for more from me, but not hiding the way he felt about me either.

He believed me, but he was afraid to believe *in me*. I felt that as well. "What you need to know about me is, when you become my friend, I will fight for you with everything I have."

"And am I your friend, Zinnia?" His eyes glinted, but he wasn't making fun of me; he truly wanted to know.

"You are most definitely my friend." Which astounded me after all we'd been through, but it was the truth.

He tucked my hair behind my ear. "I don't know what I did to deserve that honor, but I am privileged beyond measure."

He was serious. There was no sarcasm in his voice, no rancor or doubt. He truly felt that way, and it broke my heart to know that Death had been so lonely for so long. Taking his hand, I started back toward the castle. "You know what?"

"What?"

"I'm going to cook your dinner tonight. Do you like dumplings?" I glanced at him.

A smile curled his lips, and my heart did a dramatic flutter. "I'm not sure."

"Do you want to find out?" I asked.

"I'd love to."

Death wiped his mouth with the napkin and sat back. "That was exceptional."

"Well, there's more where that came from because I looked after Jazzy on my own most of the time, and we ate a lot of bland food, cheap and easy, so when we went to stay with our aunts in Roxburgh, I asked Else to teach me to cook. We spent a lot of time in the school holidays cooking for the family. I loved it, which is another reason I love a big garden."

"Where is your mother now?" Death asked, and there was a coldness to his voice that had me straightening in my seat.

"Last I heard, she was in Paris, but she could have moved on by now," I said. "It's fine. She does her thing, and we do ours."

"She abandoned you when you were children," he said, his voice deepening.

"She was around when we were young, just not when I was old enough to be responsible for Jazzy. She does love us, but having kids just wasn't her thing."

His gaze slid to the stairs and up, to where Somnus slumbered.

"Don't even think about it."

"About what?" he asked, all innocence.

"About sleeping in your brother's room tonight and paying my mother a visit in her dreams."

His jaw tightened. "I just want to talk to her."

"No," I said, "you will not."

He shrugged. "Fine, if you're so against it."

"I am."

He inclined his head.

"So how about dessert?"

His gaze darkened. "I know what I'd like for dessert."

My body heated instantly. "Well, you can hold that thought, because first we're having chocolate mousse."

"Sounds almost as delicious as what I had in mind—"

The door from the kitchens opened, and Egon rushed out. "Excuse me, my lord, but I must speak with you."

Death stood. "What is it?"

"Something that requires your immediate attention," Egon said, giving him a look.

"I'll be back as soon as I can. Stay here," Death said to me and rushed from the room.

He'd been gone for hours.

Egon said he had something important to deal with but wasn't saying what. He'd also looked kind of freaked out.

They may want to hide whatever this was from me, but I could still feel Death. His concern, his frustration, his pain and anger were being broadcast to me like I was tuned into his frequency. It was as if he was calling to me or reaching for me, and I couldn't just wait there for him when I was positive he needed me somehow.

Quickly dressing in my leathers, I strapped my knife to my

thigh and ordered Hemy to stay in the room, then rushed down-stairs. Once I was sure the coast was clear, I slipped out of the castle. Egon would try to stop me, but I would not be stopped.

Pressing my fingers to my lips, I called for Zuri. She trotted out of the forest a few minutes later on her own. I expected to see Raze right behind her, but he wasn't there. When she stopped in front of me, I ran my hand down her long nose. "Is Death with Raze?"

She jerked her head.

And they'd made her stay behind as well. "Can you take me to him, sweet girl?" I didn't have a bridle, but I didn't think I'd need one; she'd be able to track her mate without my guidance.

She bent her front leg, lifting it, and jerked her head again, offering me a boost up. I quickly hoisted myself up, then held on tight, wrapping my arms around her neck. "Take me to them, Zuri."

She took off at speed, the cool wind stinging my face and whip-ping through my hair. Nerves filled me; something wasn't right. No, something was terribly wrong. Zuri burst through the tree line and into the forest, and darkness closed in instantly. We rode at breakneck speed, dodging trees and jumping over fallen logs. My fight-or-flight instincts grew more desperate the deeper we went and as we got closer to wherever it was Zuri was taking me.

A drawn-out cry echoed through the forest, eerie and mourn-ful, like a banshee's wail. It was the sound of someone lost, hope-lessly searching for something. Zuri slowed to a trot, tilting her head to the side, listening. I searched the shadowed forest around us—

Something rushed at us, and Zuri reared, throwing me from her back. I hit the ground hard and, gasping, quickly rolled to my feet. I pulled my knife from its sheath and frantically searched the area around us.

Another cry filled the night, louder, closer. I stood beside Zuri. "It's all right," I said, and she snorted and stomped restlessly. I turned to hoist myself back up when something flew toward me, digging long nails or claws into my side, cutting into my flesh as they passed. Then they were gone, too fast for me to see what or who it was.

I hissed, covering the wound. I pressed my back to Zuri and held my knife out in front of me.

They flew at me once more with another swipe of their claws, tearing into my thigh this time, and then they were gone again. "Show yourself," I called. I tapped Zuri's front leg. "Let me back up, Zuri."

A strange, repetitive, high-pitched sound came from the shadows to my right, and I spun back.

"Come out and let me talk to you. I won't hurt you," I said, which was laughable. The only one getting hurt right now was me.

The sound came again, lifting the hair on the back of my neck.

They sped across the clearing again, and this time, the claws sliced across my cheek. "Fuck." I needed to get back on Zuri and get the hell out of here, but she was nervous, dancing away, torn between running and her instinct to stay and protect me. I tapped her front leg. "Let me up, Zuri," I said again. "Come on, sweet girl."

Her eyes were huge, but this time, she lifted her leg, and I gripped on to hoist myself back up—

Something slammed into me, knocking me back to the ground. "Fuck." I quickly rolled to my feet again. "Fucking show yourself, asshole," I called, in pain, scared, and pissed the hell off.

A branch cracked to my left, and I twisted toward it. Something moved in the shadows, slow now and in an odd, stilted way. My instincts took over all else, telling me to run, but there was no outrunning whatever this was.

They stepped closer, closer still, then finally into the clearing.

Zuri shrieked and reared.

Holy fuck. This was no demon or other creature, and it wasn't a lost soul either.

What stood before me had to have been brought to life using

the foulest of magic or the kind of power I quaked at the thought of. A female walked awkwardly toward me. Dirt stained her rotting, tattered clothes, skin hung from bone, and her long blonde hair was stringy around her skeletal face.

One moment, she was two yards away, walking as if her bones were about to snap, and the next, she was in front of me, her skeletal hand wrapped around my throat, gnashing her blunt teeth. I shoved my forearm against her bony throat, the smell of rot stinging my nose.

"G-give... it to me," she said disjointedly.

"What do you want?" I growled out.

"Give it to... me."

"Back the fuck up, and I'll give you whatever the hell you want."

She jerked forward more viciously, and I strained to push her back, then slammed my palm against her skull and fired my magic into her. She flew backward, slamming into a tree, but was back on her feet, and in a blink, she was in front of me, snapping her teeth. I did it again and again, hitting her hard with my magic, but she got back up every single time. I gave her more and more, until I felt my powers begin to weaken; she was draining me. *Fuck.*

She rushed back, and I shoved my arm against her throat again and smashed my fist into her jaw repeatedly to try and dislocate it. If she couldn't bite me, I only had the long, sharp nails to contend with. She shrieked, her head jerking forward, jaw snapping at speed. I punched her again, and one side of her jaw drooped, only a piece of rotting flesh holding it in place.

"Alga, stop!"

Death's voice echoed through the forest around us. She froze instantly, forgetting about me completely, and turned.

"That's it," he said roughly. "Come to me." She was at his side a second later. He wrapped his arms around her. "You shouldn't be wandering," he said.

"N-no... D-Death," she said. It was garbled, disjointed.

"It's okay now. It'll be okay."

"H-help... Alga," she said.

"I will," he rasped as he held her face in his hands and looked down at her. He smiled, kindness shining in his eyes—but then he tore her skull from her shoulders, and her body collapsed, falling in a heap at his feet. He dropped her skull with the rest of her bones, breathing hard.

"Mors—"

"I told you to stay at the castle. She could have killed you," he said.

"Who is she?"

He looked up at me. "Go back to the castle, Zinnia."

"I'm going to need you to explain what the fuck just happened here."

He held my gaze. "Now." His voice was filled with fury. He was not going to tell me anything, not one damn thing.

Movement on the ground caught my eye. The bones, they were reforming, the head rolling back to the neck, the jaw clicking back in place. "What the fuck is she?"

He strode to me, grabbed my hips, and tossed me onto Zuri's back; then he took her face in his hands. "Take her to the castle, and do not stop. Do you understand, Zuri?"

She shrieked the affirmative, then took off through the forest, flying back toward the castle.

I turned back in time to see Death shove Alga's reforming bones into a sack and carry her away.

Chapter Eighteen

Zinnia

I WOKE IN BED ALONE, the sound of the piano drifting up from downstairs. He was back. Blinking up at the ceiling, I fought down the dread inside me. I'd lain awake for hours, waiting for Death to come back, to explain what the hell happened in those woods, to tell me who Alga was and what she was searching for.

Pushing back the covers carefully so I wouldn't wake Hemlock, I got out of bed and walked out into the hall. Would he even talk to me? I had to try, because right now, my brain was struggling to understand what I saw out there or what any of it meant. I rushed along the hall, the shadows dancing along the walls as if they were swaying to the music. The song was achingly sad; goddess, it was heartbreakingly beautiful.

My footfalls were silent as I made my way down the stairs and across the main hall.

The room beyond it was dark still—only light from an artificial moon filtered in through the tall windows.

Then I saw him.

His bare, tattooed back, head dipped while his strong hands moved over the keys.

Emotion poured from him, so enormous that despite everything, it pierced my soul. I stayed where I was, listening as he played his mournful song, watching as he felt every note. When the song finished, he sat there, utterly still.

"Come here," he finally said, voice low.

He'd clocked me as soon as I came down the stairs; of course he had. I felt his words in the pit of my stomach, his deep voice rolling through me, pulsing inside me. As soon as the command left his lips, I was moving across the marble floor.

I stopped beside him, and he turned to me, waiting for me to say whatever it was I was going to say, and I could see in his eyes that he wasn't going to give me the answers I wanted. "One of those things I need to learn on my own?" I said instead of all the things I wanted to say.

He shook his head. "One of the things you never need to know."

I had no idea who Alga was, but he'd been gentle with her—at least until he tore off her head. He was the God of Death, and she'd most certainly been dead. "She wasn't a soul. She was... something else."

"She was," he said.

"Is she part of some fucked-up skeletal army? I've seen the way you look when your cloak is called forth, when the shadows cover you. You change—you are Death. Somehow, she's part of that, isn't she?"

"There are a lot of things you don't know about me, about my world, and a lot you will learn over time. There are other things, though, little witch, I pray you never have reason to learn." Taking my hand, he tugged me closer and cupped my cheek over the slices I'd cleaned and dressed when I got back. He stood, crowding me. "Where else are you injured?"

"My side and my thigh. I washed and dressed where she clawed me. I have my healing balm with me. It's fine."

"Are you in pain?"

"They're not that bad now. I have a potion that helps with pain, and it kicked in a while ago."

He studied me, trying to see if I was telling the truth. "You could have been killed," he rasped.

"I wouldn't have gone down easy," I said, now sounding breathless.

He gripped my hips, avoiding the slices on my side, and lifted me, planting my ass on the piano. His hand went to my throat, not gripping it, his open palm pressed to the base, and then he slid it lower, as low as he could go without his skin leaving mine.

I was in a pair of shorts and an old, stretched-out T-shirt, and the neck hung low. His palm sat directly over my heart. "You're so warm," he said roughly. "Your heart, it's beating almost frantically."

"You tend to have that effect on me." I lifted my hand, pressing it to his bare chest, right over his heart and the stars tattooed there. It was pounding, hard and fast.

"You have the same effect on me, love." His other hand gripped my uninjured thigh tight. "You always have."

"Even when you were stalking around, cloaked and full of rage?"

He licked those gorgeous lips. "Yes."

Hot, rough-skinned fingers slid up my thigh, then over my hip before gripping the worn fabric of my shirt tight. He dragged it up, forcing me to lift my arms. He dropped it on top of the piano beside me, and my nipples puckered as soon as the cool air hit them. Without taking his eyes off me, Death lifted a hand, aiming it at the door behind him, and invisible hands swung it shut with a loud click.

Then his hands were back on me, gliding, massaging, moving

over my bare skin. He watched where they traveled, as if what he was doing was the most enthralling thing he'd ever seen.

"I don't think you realize how important you are to me, Zinnia. You don't get it, and that's not your fault. But believe me when I say, if something had happened to you today…" He looked up, darkness swirling. "I would have torn it all down. I would have burned so hot in my fury and grief that there would have been nothing left but stardust."

I swallowed, trying to process what he was saying. I couldn't. "You can't say things like that… you can't—"

"It's the truth. Do you want me to lie to you?"

I was struggling to take it all in, to focus, because his hands were still moving over my body, making my skin warm and tingly, making my breasts ache and causing a deep throb between my thighs. He carefully but forcefully pushed me back so I was lying on the piano's cool surface. His hands slid down my belly, and then he tugged my shorts and underwear down my body and tossed them onto the piano with my shirt.

"Spread your legs for me," he demanded softly.

I did as he said, instantly obeying. I should stop this after what he'd just said, after that declaration, but I couldn't bring myself to do it. I wanted whatever he was offering with an intensity that made me quiver. Resting his hand low on my belly, he dragged his thumb through my slick pussy, sliding it up and back. I was fully exposed, naked, and sprawled out in front of him. Death seemed content to take his time touching me.

"You can't imagine how good it feels buried deep inside you," he said and pushed the tip of his thumb inside me. "You don't know this, my precious consort, but I am your humble servant. Anything you desire, all you need to do is ask, and I will bend and twist, I will contort my world to make it yours as well."

My hips rolled. "Mors…" I said, even though I had no idea what to say next. What could you say to that? I had a god in the palm of my hand, but not even he could save me from fate, from death, if that's what was destined for me—just like the rest of them. But while I had him, while he was mine, he would worship me, and I would worship him.

If anyone deserved happiness, it was the male watching me like I was the brightest star in the sky.

"But it seems no matter what I say, you refuse to allow me to protect you." He slid his thumb the rest of the way inside me and kissed the inside of my thigh. "Outside this castle, if you are not with me, if you are off the path that I already told you not to wander from, you are at risk... yet you left the safety of these walls and ventured into the forest." He grazed his teeth along my skin, then nipped me. It wasn't hard, not enough to really hurt, but I gasped. "How many times do I have to say it? How many times do I have to ask you to remain at my side or in the safety of these grounds?" He looked up at me. "Do I need to punish you to make you do as I say, is that it?"

I moaned as he slid his thumb from me and replaced it with two fingers. "Y-you needed me," I said, quickly losing the ability to think or speak logically.

"Did I now? How do you know that, little witch?"

"B-because..." My hips rocked against his hand, trying to take more, to take those long, rough fingers deeper. "Because... I felt you. Your pain, your anger. I felt it here." I pressed my hand to my chest. "I just... I just knew, and I had to find you."

He stilled for a second, and I whimpered in protest. He started moving again, fucking me with his fingers, as shadows swirled around him, as his cloak manifested. "Then let me make some-thing clear." He leaned forward. "Unless I ask you to come with me, you will remain here." Half of his face transformed, turning it into half a shadowed skull, half the male I was growing to care for more than I knew how to understand or process. "If you risk your safety again, your punishment will be a lot worse than the one I'm about to give you."

"What are you...?"

He lifted me, flipping me over. The stool scraped against the floor as Death planted my knees on it, and then he grabbed the back of my neck and forced my upper body down. My hands slammed down against the keys, making a chaotic, tuneless sound. He shoved the stool farther in and changed my position so my forearms were on top of the glossy black grand piano.

Then, leaning over me, he pressed his bare chest against my back, his arms bracketing me. His cloak brushed against my bare skin, and the power flowing through it lifted sparks all over me. I was in sensation overload.

One of his hands left my view, and a moment later, it was on my ass, squeezing. "Are you ready?"

"W-what are you…?"

His hand came down, hard.

I cried out and tried to bolt upright, but he held me down. "Mors—"

"You refuse to listen to me, so now I have to punish you," he said roughly, then spanked me again.

Humiliation burned my cheeks. "Don't you dare do it aga—" *He did it again.* I hissed, outraged, as his hand came down on the other cheek.

"You will learn, and you will obey me," he said against my ear as he massaged where he'd no doubt just left a massive handprint.

The burn sank in deep, and I squirmed.

"Hmmm, I'm not sure you've quite learned your lesson yet."

"Don't," I said, but my protest was weak because, goddess, it felt… I squirmed again, and my inner muscles throbbed, clamping down. It felt good.

He shoved my thighs wider. "One more," he growled.

This time, when he spanked me, his hand was low, slapping my pussy, but instead of crying out, I groaned, dropping my head to my forearms. Death covered my body, and having his skin against me, the feel of his hard body pressed to mine, was like having a craving I hadn't even known I'd had satisfied. He was hard; I could feel his cock through his pants pressed against my tender flesh.

"I need you," I gasped. "Please."

He dragged his nose up my throat. "Fucking you is a reward, love, and you haven't earned one, not yet." His staff appeared in his hand beside me.

"You want me," I managed, pushing back against his hardness.

"More than you will ever comprehend, but I've also had thousands of years to master my control, and if making you understand the severity of your actions means I walk around hard as fuck for a day or two, then that's what will happen." His cloak surrounded us, like a dark, warm cocoon. "I'm not a sadist, though," he said as he dragged his hand down my bare back, his roughened skin lifting goose bumps all over me. "I will deny you of me, but I also won't leave you wanting. Your needs are paramount always."

I pressed back against him more firmly. "Then don't deny me," I said, so hot and wet and achy, I was close to begging.

He kissed my shoulder. "I'll make you come, love, and it will feel earth-shattering." He pressed his mouth to my ear. "But nowhere near as good as when your male, the god who owns you, who is the master of your cunt and the owner of your heart, is buried deep inside you." He nipped my shoulder. "But that's the point. How will you learn without consequences?"

"Arrogant asshole..." The insult died on my lips as he kissed his way down my spine.

"I have reason to be arrogant, and you know it."

Something warm and smooth slid along my pussy, gliding over my opening, then up to my clit. "What... what is that?" I groaned.

"Did you know my staff is part of me?" His mouth came back to my ear. "I feel what it feels. It's alive in my hands, like another arm or leg or..." He pushed the tip of his staff inside me, the smooth wood hot, yes, as if it was alive.

"Oh gods," I breathed, dropping my head to my forearms, panting, desperate for more.

He pushed it deeper, and I felt every knot and twist of the gnarled, worn wood as it filled me. "If the conditions are just so, I can come just stroking it," he said, panting against my throat. "You feel... so good. So fucking good, Zinnia."

He slid it out, then back in, and I cried out.

"I'm going to make you come now, love, so hard that you'll make a mess all over my piano stool. Are you ready?"

I was only capable of making sounds—desperate, needy sounds, like an animal, a creature that only existed for Death and the pleasure he chose to give me.

He fucked me with his staff faster. His front was still pressed to my back, his cloak surrounding us. I knew his face was at least half his skull mask, and the thought only turned me on more. He was breathing heavily in my ear as he slid his hand down my stomach and started circling my clit just the way I liked it. Simultaneously, his staff hit me at the exact spot that had me quickly spinning out of control.

"Mors... *Oh fuck...*"

"You're dripping, love. Your juices are sliding down my staff, soaking into the wood, filling every divot and channel, marking it with your hunger, giving me a part of you for eternity." He groaned. "I feel you too now, love. I can feel how badly you need to come, how good you feel right now. How much you want your god inside you."

I sobbed. "Yes, please. Mors... please."

His hand left my clit, then came down on my ass, hard, before it was back at my clit, spanking me there as well. I screamed and came, spasming around his staff while he soothed my clit with firm pressure, circling, rubbing, prolonging my orgasm.

"I won't give in." He pressed his hard cock against my bare ass, the fabric of his trousers rough against my tender flesh. "Because I won't lose you. And until you prove to me that you won't put your life at risk, I won't fuck you. Understand?"

I collapsed against the cool surface of the piano, breathing hard, and shuddered as he slid his staff from my body. It vanished, and he scooped me up in his arms. His cloak was still draped over him, and it hid his eyes. His face was all skull mask now, all Death. I snuggled closer, sliding my hand over his chest, and stared up at him, into the shadows of his hood, where not even the blue of his eyes glowed anymore. He meant what he said. He would deny us both until I proved myself the obedient little consort and did as he said.

"I get you're worried, I do." How could he not be after what he'd been through? "I promise I won't take any more risks, okay? But you can't expect me to stay locked up here when you're away from the castle."

"I expect you to stay here where it's safe unless I'm with you," he said.

"That's what I just said."

"No, it's not. I won't ever lock you up."

"What you're suggesting sounds pretty confining if you ask me."

"Which means the punishment stands." He held me closer. "It pains me as much as it does you to do this. Denying you goes against every part of me."

I flashed him a grin. "Oh, it pains you much more, my lord, and if you think I'm going down without a fight, you are sorely mistaken."

Chapter Nineteen

Death

GROWLING, I rushed down the stairs, across the wide entrance hall, and into the kitchen. "Where is she?" I barked at Egon. I felt her close, but she wasn't inside the castle.

He looked up from chopping vegetables and pointed his knife toward the door that led to the back garden. Of course that was where she was. My heart thumped wildly in my chest. She spent hours out there every week, tending her herbs; I should have known that was where she'd be. Still, my heart refused to slow until I saw her for myself.

Shoving the door open, I strode out to the gardens. The oxygen was punched from my lungs the moment I saw her.

She was on her hands and knees, her wild red hair tied back in a messy knot on top of her head. She was singing low, something I'd never heard before. The kind of music they probably listened to at the hellhounds' compound or the wolf shifter keep or while she was with those twisted fucking crows. Where all those males no doubt watched her, wanting her.

My fingers curled into tight fists just thinking about their eyes on her.

Hemlock poked his head up from behind one of the bushy herbs, and Zinnia chuckled, making my heart fucking squeeze.

The last few nights had been unbearable. I told her I was punishing her for her carelessness over her safety, and I was, but it was me who was suffering. Especially since she was taking every opportunity to tempt me.

I rubbed at the ache in my chest. The thought of her leaving me in a week's time for another month twisted my insides. Every time she came back, the month passed by faster than the last.

It always caused me pain when she left, but this time, above all others, felt the worst. So much had changed between us this last month, and I'd actually contemplated breaking our deal and forcing her to stay, but I never broke my word; it was part of the foundation of who I was. Not to mention, forcing her to stay would not only push her farther away from me, it would be breaking her trust, and she'd never forgive me.

I also could never hurt her in that way.

Biting back a groan, I took her in. My body had reacted to the sight of her instantly. Gods, I wanted to lift her from the garden, pull her into the small orchard behind it, and claim her all over again, but I couldn't, not yet, not until she understood how important her safety was. She'd teased me about it again while we'd eaten dinner last night, making light of it. I didn't know why she insisted on testing me, but if she made light of something so important, how could I trust her to heed my warnings?

She glanced up then, spotting me, and stood.

I strode toward her. She was irresistibly beautiful, and her soul, it shone through her eyes, so bright and warm. It was all I needed —those eyes on me, that glimpse of her soul—and I was home.

I was no longer alone.

I missed you. The words lingered on my tongue, but I didn't speak them. I'd seen her less than an hour ago, but the way I felt about her, it surpassed love or any descriptive word for the emotion. What I felt for her surpassed explanation. "Your garden looks healthy," I said instead of all the other things flying around my head and filling my heart.

"Checking up on me?" she said, dusting her hands off on her jeans.

Yes. "No. I was simply passing by and saw you." She was looking at me as if she didn't believe me. I brushed my hand over a particularly bushy plant. "So what's this one for?" I asked, trying to change the subject.

No other being made me feel this mortal, or what I assumed it felt like to be mortal, than the female staring up at me, her lips quirked up on one side. The last three weeks, the shadows had receded more and more. It'd been so long, so long in the darkness, consumed by rage, I'd forgotten who I was. Until Zinnia. Until she drew me from the cloak and touched my soul.

"Do you really want to know? Or are you just trying to cover up that you were, in fact, checking up on me?"

She was making fun of me again, and I liked it. I was also interested. I was interested in every part of her. "I want to know." Hemlock poked his head up again, squeaked, and lifted onto his back legs. I scooped him up. The tiny rat seemed to like me. Zinnia watched as I placed him on my shoulder, and he tucked himself in close, but she didn't comment.

"Okay... well, this one here is licorice. I use it in a few of my healing tinctures. The root is good for an upset stomach, for example," she said and pointed to the one beside it. "This one, on the other hand, will give you an upset stomach if used... irresponsibly." She smirked. "So watch yourself, my lord, or you may find yourself making frequent and urgent visits to the bathroom."

"Are you threatening me with diarrhea, little witch?" I said and fought a grin.

"Possibly."

"Threatening your consort is never a good idea, especially when he's a god." I tilted my head to the side, studying her pretty lips. "Do you require more correction, do you think?"

Her face flushed, and my body heated with hers. "That would be a no, thank you. *Correction* doesn't work on me. I have my own mind, and no amount of spanking from you will change it."

"Apparently not." I took a step closer. "It will make you come very hard, though, won't it, Zinnia?"

She grinned wider. "Tell me, my lord, exactly how blue are your balls? Still planning on holding out to teach me a lesson, or have I been punished enough?"

She enjoyed mocking me, playing, teasing, and I liked that as well, even if I feared she didn't take the reason behind my actions seriously. "My balls are fine, thank you, love. I have my hand and images of you riding my cock locked away in here." I tapped the side of my head. "So I'll survive just fine." It was a lie. I was suffering so goddamn badly. "But if you're struggling, a quick blood oath will put this all behind us, and I'll happily spend the next few days in bed curling your very pretty toes."

Her smile slipped. "I'm not doing that."

I wanted to fucking snarl, to demand she do it, to drop to my knees and fucking beg her to let me keep her safe. "Why?"

"You really don't get it?"

"I really don't," I said and had to fight back the growl in my voice.

She planted her hands on her hips. "Because I'm your consort, Mors, we're supposed to be partners... even if the power dynamic is so unbalanced, it's ridiculous. And even if my time with you here is most likely limited, I will not be bound by oaths and forced to obey you like a prisoner, not anymore. Why can't you understand that?"

I understood it, but history told me not to believe in good intentions or promises from those I loved. When someone cared for you in return, risking their lives for you was nothing. It didn't matter that I was a god and she was mortal. She'd already shown me she was prepared to walk into an unknown, dangerous situation when she thought I needed her. Things had progressed. She felt my emotions when they were elevated or I was distressed—something she'd already proven—which was why a blood oath was more important than ever.

The look on her face, though, was one I recognized well. She would not back down, not yet, and if we carried on with this conversation, she would only end up even more angry with me, and I didn't want that. I wanted her smiles and her teasing. I wanted her blushes and her soft looks. So fool that I was, I chose to change the subject back to her garden. "I will attempt to," I said, lying through my teeth. "This garden, it's really important to you, isn't it?"

She stared up at me for several moments, knowing exactly what I was doing and deciding if she wanted to call me out on it or let the subject drop. She blew out a frustrated breath but went with the change of subject. "Creating a garden is the first thing a witch does when she moves to a new home, especially when she's mated or married," Zinnia said. "On our mating or wedding day, we're given a small pot with a vervain plant in it to start our new garden."

"Why that herb in particular?"

"The leaves of the vervain and its tiny purple flowers can be used to protect against evil spells and negative energy. It can also be used to purify our homes and has many medicinal uses. Vervain represents home and family—love." She tucked her hair behind her ear. "When a witch takes it out of the pot and plants it in her garden, though, is the most significant."

"Explain," I said, searching her face, struggling to read the look in her eyes and hating that I didn't know what she was thinking.

"We only plant the vervain in our new gardens when it feels like home. That one herb provides us with nearly everything we need to take care of and protect our families... so we only plant them when we're sure that's where we are, with family. When we're with the people we choose to love."

I looked down at the plants flourishing in her garden. "Which one is vervain?" I asked.

She was silent. I looked back up.

Her gaze held mine. "I don't have one."

I swallowed abruptly. Of course not. Of course she didn't have one. Words escaped me as she stared up at me.

"We didn't have a mating ceremony, Mors, and my family didn't send me off with my new husband holding a tiny pot of vervain after an epic party. That's not what this is... This is no love story for the ages."

My heart physically ached at her words.

You have no idea, little witch.

The answer to all of this was mixed up in those words. She had the answer to how this ended, how it could end, but she just had to surrender to it, to let me in.

She just had to choose me.

Chapter Twenty

THERE WAS a soft knock at the bedroom door. "My lord."

Death jolted beside me, waking instantly. "What is it?"

He'd been restless in sleep the last few hours, and I'd been lying here awake, frustrated and contemplating my situation.

"We've had another breach," Egon said in a hushed, urgent voice.

Death stilled completely. "Fuck."

I felt his eyes on me, and I kept mine closed. Whatever this was, he didn't want me to know. I felt it. The tension was a dense wall between us. The way he eased off the bed, trying not to jostle me, told me I was right.

Death wanted my trust while he kept so many things from me. He quickly dressed and slipped out of the room.

I could just lay here and do nothing, stay in the dark and blindly do as he instructed, or I could do what I always had and protect my soul and my heart and choose the truth—whatever it was.

I'd rather be faced with all the horrors and ugly parts of a person, see all their scars on full display, than live in ignorance for my own comfort. Pushing back the covers, I quickly dressed, shoving my feet in my boots. Hemlock scurried across the bed, squeaking at me. "You have to stay here, okay? It's too dangerous." He hissed, then turned his back to me and wriggled under the covers, showing me he was not happy.

Better that than something happening to him.

I slipped out into the hall. At night, the whispers of the souls here were louder, as if the darkness amplified their thoughts and feelings. Ice slid down my spine as I rushed along the hallway. It felt as if they were right behind me, their mouths to my ear, telling me their secrets, their regrets—the darkest marks on their souls.

When I reached the bottom of the stairs, I stuck close to the wall. Death was talking with Egon. The demon nodded at whatever his lord said, then strode away, and Death spun and walked out. With the coast clear, I rushed across the room and eased the door open, slipping out.

Death was striding down the skull path, shrouded in shadow. I hung back, following at a distance, using all the magic I had to try and conceal myself from him. It wouldn't last. I could only summon a thin and fragile barrier that would wear thin, then dissolve completely from the strength of his power, but that was okay. It just needed to hold long enough for me to learn what the hell was going on.

He lifted his hand, and a path appeared through the trees, one I'd never seen before. We were close to where I'd been attacked by Alga. Where I'd seen Death remove her head, then carry her wriggling corpse away in a sack moments later.

An awful shriek came from up ahead—the same awful sound I'd heard from the undead female while she'd circled me, swiping at me, clawing me.

The shadows thickened before his cloak swirled around him, his staff appearing in his hand a moment later. He didn't pause but kept walking as the shriek came again. We carried on for a little longer, and then Death stopped. I quickly stepped off the path and pressed my back against one of the large trees. Leaving the path was risky, but I had no choice. I didn't want him seeing me, not before I knew what this was. Sliding my knife free, I hung back and watched.

Death turned to his right and said something, his voice low, rough, and then he held out his hand. Bony fingers appeared first before one of the undead stepped awkwardly from the forest beside the path, its movements jerky and disturbing. Its clothes were hanging off bones draped in old skin and tendons. She took Death's hand.

"Come now," I heard him say. "You know you're not supposed to wander."

As they passed a tree with sparse foliage, light from the faux moon shone down on her. She had her skeletal face upturned, looking at Death, and from what I could see of her hair, it had once been black and wavy.

Death didn't remove her head or shove her in a sack like the last one we encountered; no, he was talking to her, his low voice drifting back while she said the odd, garbled words and walked jerkily at his side. As if they were going on a midnight stroll together.

What the fuck was this?

They carried on for several yards, and I followed, keeping a good distance between me and them. Then they stopped, and I realized the path had ended. Death cupped her skeletal face—then pressed a sweet, soft kiss to her bony cheek before he straightened, lifted his staff, now glowing with power, and iron gates appeared. Shrieks filled the night, moans, garbled voices calling for him. As if he had some undead army behind that gate that worshipped him.

Had I been right? Had Death amassed some fucked-up undead

horde? With his evil bitch of a mother and her army of demons right next door, I guessed it made sense for him to amass his own, but no matter how you looked at it, this was wrong. It was twisted and cruel. If he had done this, then he wasn't the male I thought he was... hoped he was, not at all.

Nausea gripped my stomach as he opened the gate and the undead female stepped through. As soon as she had, he pulled it shut, and the gate vanished.

Death turned then, and I had two choices, either hide and run through the forest, hoping I'd beat him home or—

I dropped the gossamer thin barrier of my magic that remained and stepped out of my hiding place and onto the path. I wasn't the kind of female to hide or run, not when the danger concerned someone I cared about, consequences be damned.

Death went still.

"Who's your friend?" I asked, legs braced, waiting for the impact of his anger.

He started toward me, his cloak flaring out behind him as he walked, his staff gripped tight in one hand. The volatile emotions rolling off him were *intense*, and it took everything in me not to step back as he strode right up to me, towering over me.

"Your new girlfriend?" I asked, refusing to cower under that ferocious glare. "I guess it makes sense that Death would be up for some necrophilia."

His nostrils flared. "Go back to the castle, Zinnia."

"You're not going to tell me who that was?"

His blue eyes glowed down at me. "No."

I ground my teeth. "Mors—"

"Do not speak."

What I felt coming off him was wild, unstable—goddess, a raging storm. My knees almost buckled under the weight of all that was pouring off him. I didn't understand it, what caused him to feel this way, but it was horrible.

"Talk to me. What's going on—"

"Go." He said it softly, but it was as if he'd roared it.

I flinched and backed up when the storm grew more violent. Pushing him right now would be a serious mistake, so I said nothing more and walked away.

He said he wanted me as his consort, he said he loved me, even if I hadn't actually believed it, but he constantly shut me out. I understood his trepidation, and I knew he couldn't tell me anything, but living with so many secrets between us wasn't going to work. His expectations were too high. He wanted too much from me without any of the trust and without giving me even a glimpse of the payoff. He couldn't even promise me a life.

The foundation I thought we'd been building, the closeness we'd slowly developed, had already been on shaky ground after his demand that I obey him. Now, after tonight, it was crumbling, slipping away beneath my feet.

Because it was built on nothing.

I glanced back over my shoulder. He hadn't moved, his dark gaze following me as I strode away. I got another wave of all he was feeling, and my knees almost gave out beneath me a second time. The anger inside him was breathtaking, and it was aimed at only one person—me.

Death didn't come back to bed after that. I'd lain awake, waiting, but he never came. He wasn't at breakfast the next morning either. I checked Somnus's room but found only the slumbering god.

"Where's Death?" I asked Egon when I walked into the kitchen.

He glanced up from the silver he was polishing. "He's busy with an urgent matter."

"What urgent matter would that be?" I leaned on the table.

"My lord has a lot of responsibility in his realm. Sometimes his attention is required away from the castle," Egon said and started polishing again.

"His army of the dead? Is that what has his attention?"

Egon stilled for a split second, then continued polishing. "I'm afraid I don't know what you're talking about, my lady."

"You do, because you came and got Death last night when one of them escaped."

He kept his head down, polishing the silver jug in his hand like his life depended on it.

"I followed him, Egon... I saw one of them. She's the second I've seen." I planted my hands on the table. "Please tell me what the hell's going on here."

Egon blew out a breath and placed the jug on the table. "You know I can't tell you, Zinnia," he said, using my name for the first time. "I wish I could tell you all you need to know, I truly do." His fingers curled tight around the rag he was holding. "You have no idea how much, but I can't. For many reasons—reasons I pray to the gods you learn, and soon."

I ground my teeth. "Death tells me I have to work it out for myself, yet I'm not allowed to wander around on my own or ask anyone else questions. How the hell am I supposed to figure out whatever it is he wants me to figure out when I'm being hobbled at every turn? I go back home in three days, Egon. That's another month away, and another month closer to my sister's birthday. I'm going to be trapped here with a god who is so angry with me, for reasons he won't share, that I'm starting to feel dread when I'm around him." I planted my hands on my hips. "What the hell does he want from me?"

"The answer is a simple one," Egon said, holding my gaze, beseeching me to read his damn mind.

"Only it's not," I said. "Nothing about this situation is simple."

I spent the rest of the day in my garden with my herbs. It made me feel closer to Jasmine, to my cousins and aunts, to my coven.

And I needed them now more than ever.

Death wasn't at dinner that night, and he didn't come to bed. He was absent at breakfast for a second day as well. Egon said nothing, but he seemed stressed.

I, on the other hand, was pissed.

After I'd watered my garden, I went up to Death's room and gathered Hemy's and my things and moved them back to my room. If he was staying away to avoid me, I'd make it easy for him.

When dinnertime finally came around, I left Hemy napping by the fire and headed down to the dining room. No Death. I sat and thanked Egon when he filled my glass with wine. Like the last three meals Death had missed, his place was set, which made it clear he wasn't communicating with Egon either.

I was hungry. I'd barely eaten the last two days, but thanks to my anger, my appetite was back.

The sound of the main doors opening and closing echoed through the castle.

I turned to the door, and a moment later, Death appeared. His gaze sliced to me as he strode toward the table.

My heart leaped in my chest. *Do not give him the satisfaction.* Forcing myself to freaking move, I scooped up some mashed potatoes and shoved them in my mouth.

"I hope you didn't rush back on my account," I said and stabbed some beans with my fork and shoved them in my mouth as well, then grinned to piss him off when he took his seat opposite me.

"I've had things to do," he said as he dished himself a plate of food.

"Oh, me too. While you've been gone, I've been super busy taking all my things out of your room and packing for my trip home."

He said nothing, didn't even look up as he started eating.

"So are you going to tell me where you've been?"

"No."

"Awesome." I took a sip of my wine and sat back. "Question time, big guy. Tell me, why are you angry with me? What have I ever done to you? I think I deserve to know that, don't you?"

He chewed his mouthful. "You already know."

I snorted. "The fuck I do."

He lowered his knife and fork. "Maybe if you stopped talking and started fucking thinking, you'd work it out."

I stared across the table, confused and hurt and pretty sure my anger was close to matching his. "I can't read your mind, Death. You're going to have to help me out a little."

He slammed his fist on the table. "I can't."

It was as if he was reverting back to the Death he was when I came here. So full of darkness and rage. "Why do you even want me to? The anger I feel inside you now, it's almost as if... as if you hate me," I said, as an awful, gripping feeling in my stomach tore through me.

His nostrils flared. "Think," he said with quiet violence rolling from him and ignoring what I'd said completely. "Fucking think," he roared and slammed his fists on the table again, this time knocking over his wine.

I blinked across the table at him. For the first time in a very long time, I was filled with fear and dread. The full force of the god he was, was reflected in his face and his voice. It wasn't him I was scared of, but the thoughts and feelings he was capable of evoking in others. I'd stopped feeling it, the horror and woe, the soul-gripping fear and heartbreak that Death was capable of making others feel, but I did now, and humiliatingly, tears filled my eyes. The feelings he was summoning in me were so strong and awful, I wanted to curl into a ball and weep. "This isn't going to work," I forced out past trembling lips.

He glowered at me. "What?"

"Release me," I said, shaking so hard that he had to see it. I hated that as well.

"Never," he snarled.

"I found a way to hide from you before," I choked out. "I can do it again."

His gaze swept my face. "You will not. You try it, and I will drag you back here and never let you leave."

"Isn't that what you have planned already? Never letting me leave? Trapping me here in this hell with you until I die brutally?" I shook my head. "I'm not going to accept that. I'm not yours. I don't belong to you, and the fates can go and fuck themselves. I've given up enough because of you. I won't give up my life as well."

He sat forward. "You think you know what it is to suffer? You know nothing of loss."

I didn't know this version of him. This wasn't just anger; this was cruelty. He was trying to hurt me. To push me away even while he desperately tried to hold on. "No, you're right. I don't know the loss you have. How could I? I'm a mere mortal, not a god with an eternity of living behind him. But I do know loss, I know fear, and I know heartbreak."

He sneered. "What have you lost? Enlighten me."

My heart was racing, and I was trembling so hard now, my voice shook. "When I was fifteen years old, still just a child, a powerful god invaded my dreams and told me I was his—"

"I already know this story, little witch. Don't waste your breath," he bit out, a nasty smirk curling his lips.

"I was so scared," I said, pushing on, "that I took dangerous amounts of forbidden potions and elixirs to make sure I stayed awake. I didn't want the terrifying god to come back. I was afraid he'd hurt me, but most of all, that he'd hurt my sister, so I searched for help, and eventually, I found it." Death was staring at me, his eyes black, no blue left; not even the night sky was reflected in them, just pure blackness, but he didn't interrupt this time, and I had no intention of stopping. "I wasn't thinking clearly with the potions and the lack of sleep. I was delirious, confused, afraid. I heard of a demon named Fluke who could help, so I went to his cottage."

Death snarled and sat forward. "What did he do, Zinnia?"

"He got me to lay down. He drugged me and shoved his hand in my stomach. The pain was so bad, I lost consciousness. I don't know exactly what happened when I was out... not good things, I know that much. My entire body hurt when I woke with the markings on my arm." I ran my hand over the scar where I cut the mark out so Death could find me. I glanced back up at him. "I'm pretty sure he took more than my womb that day as trade." Death shot to his feet with a roar, his chair flying back and crashing against the floor. I stood as well. "So yes, Mors, I know loss."

"Fluke belongs to Nox," he said as he grabbed the end of the huge wooden table and flipped it, tossing it halfway across the room. "I will kill him. I will make him scream. I'll find a way to destroy my mother. I will make her wish for death."

Of course Nox, that twisted bitch, had a hand in what happened to me. She'd seen me coming. She'd found me when Death had. I could rage about the unjustness of it all, like Death was, but it was too late. It was done. One truth remained, though. "We're not good for each other," I said.

He was breathing hard. "You're not leaving me."

No denial—he knew I was right. "I've been here for a lunar month. I leave first thing in the morning. While I'm gone, I want you to decide if this"—I motioned between us—"really is what you want. If all this pain and anger you're feeling is really worth it to trap me here, when it's obvious neither of us want this. You don't love me, Mors. You don't. What you're feeling is a lie, a manipulation, a byproduct of the fates' meddling. Love isn't forcing someone to be with you... not when you've made it clear you despise me more than you truly want me."

"You're wrong," he choked out. "You don't understand—"

"Then make me understand. Give me something... give me anything."

He stared across at me, mouth gritted shut, eyes burning into me, but he said nothing.

His hands were tied.

Still, disappointment filled me as I turned away and strode from the room.

Chapter Twenty-One

Zinnia

I GLANCED at my bags by the door as I got into bed. Hemlock was curled up in my carpetbag under one of my scarves. He was ready to go home and see everyone. He missed them as much as I did when we were gone.

Death had to see how toxic this situation was. Yes, he'd let down his guard with me and shown me another side of him, but on the turn of a dime, he'd snap. Something about me called the darkness in him, and the anger always crept back. Even when he didn't outwardly show it, I felt it.

He had to see ending this was for the best.

The only times we were good together were when we were naked, and he'd taken that off the table in an attempt to control me—a seriously destructive move, especially if he was trying to build some kind of real relationship with me. But he wasn't. I got the feeling he was waiting for the inevitable—my demise, just like the rest of them.

There was so much I didn't understand about this place, about his motives. He said I needed to work it out for myself but then blocked me at every turn. I promised him I'd try, but I was getting nowhere. Jazzy's twenty-first birthday was fast approaching, and if I couldn't convince him to release me, I'd be trapped here, trapped in his anger and loathing until whatever killed his previous consorts killed me too.

I pulled the covers higher and stared at the ceiling, trying to calm my racing heart. I knew all these things, but goddess, I missed him. I missed those small calm moments when he looked at me in a way that curled my toes, and I missed his grin, and that laugh, and the way he touched me, kissed me. No one had ever made me feel as wonderful or as fucking awful as he could.

My eyes grew heavy, and I let them drift closed, allowing the darkness to pull me under for maybe the last time in this room.

The sky outside the castle window was dark and heavy. She pressed her hand to the glass, a sob falling from her lips. The weight of her pain was unbearable. She was scared and lonely, so incredibly lonely. Hand trembling, she picked up a knife and, holding it tight, brought it to her throat....

The room spun, and a female walked outside. She was running, running through the forest. Running with nowhere to go. She fell, but she didn't get up. She lay in the dirt and prayed her heart would stop, that it would just stop.

I woke with my heart pounding. Two different females this time, and their agony was like an ache in my bones, my soul. Their pain and loneliness were my own.

A dark, intoxicating scent reached me, and I knew I wasn't in my room alone anymore. Shoving myself up to my elbows, I blinked into the darkness. Death stood at the end of my bed in only a pair of dark trousers. His hairless, tattooed chest almost glowed under the muted light coming through the window.

His head was dipped like he was praying, his hands at his sides, fingers curled into fists. I sat up, but he said nothing, and neither did I for the longest time.

Finally, I wrapped my arms around my knees. "They killed themselves, didn't they? Your consorts ended their own lives?"

He lifted his head and sucked in a breath when his bright blue eyes locked on me. No shadows, no darkness, just clear, vibrant blue. "All but one, yes."

The one at the cliff. She hadn't jumped; she'd been pushed. "Why?"

"Because they were never meant to be here."

"I don't understand."

"You need to try."

I wanted to scream in frustration. "Will that happen to me? Eventually, will I...?"

"No," he said, voice breaking.

"Why not me? Why am I different?"

"Because it was always you... because it had to be you," he rasped.

I didn't understand. I didn't understand any of this. "Death —"

"I need you," he choked out. "I need my consort. I need you, Zinnia."

He'd said all he could. He could tell me no more. I had two choices: I could push for something he couldn't give me, or I could let it go, at least for tonight. I didn't know what the future held for me, for us, but however you looked at it, it wasn't good. In this moment, he needed me, and I could admit that right then, I needed him as well. What I'd seen had shaken me; those females, they'd pulled me down into the depths of their pain. I didn't know what it meant, and I couldn't think, not when Death was the only one who could drive the ache from my bones and the loneliness from my soul.

I tossed back the covers. "Then take me," I said softly into the heavy silence surrounding us.

His chest expanded sharply. "You still want me?"

Grabbing the bottom of the shirt I wore, I pulled it up and off, tossing it aside, leaving me in only my underwear. "Yes."

He took an abrupt step forward, and then he was striding around the bed. Leaning in, he hooked me around the waist and tugged me down on the mattress before covering me.

He stared at me, looking deeply into my eyes. "You have no idea just how precious you are to me, none," he rasped. "Trying to protect you, to force you to bend to my will by punishing you, was a greater punishment for me. I have not slept for days, my body aches constantly, my hands itch to touch you, and my heart feels as if it's being impaled by poisonous spikes whenever I see you. So much of the anger you feel when you're with me is directed at myself."

"But even more is directed at me," I whispered.

"Yes."

"And you won't tell me why?"

He shook his head. "I can't, but I need you to know that you're not to blame. That the anger I feel doesn't diminish how much I worship you, and that it is born from frustration over a situation that you have no control over. That's all I can tell you."

"What if I never work any of this out? What if I never learn the truth on my own?"

His Adam's apple slid up and down his throat. "I have to believe you will."

For the sake of his own sanity, he was deep in denial, and I felt the pressure of that, of saving him, of saving us both, immensely. I cupped the side of his face. "If you truly love me, Mors, then you need to let me go. Release me... it's the only way to save me from the same fate as the females that came before me."

His breathing was erratic, heavy. "Saving you, protecting you, is my greatest desire, but what you ask... I can't. I can't do it, love."

If we kept talking, we'd end up arguing. I didn't understand any of this, and he couldn't tell me. So instead of begging him to make me understand—something I knew he couldn't do—I brushed my thumb along his lower lip. "Then kiss me."

He slid the tips of his fingers down the side of my face, the roughened skin bringing every one of my nerve endings alive. "I am yours to command, my queen," he said, and then he covered my mouth with his and kissed me achingly slow and with a reverence that made my heart ache and my head spin.

He slid his hands along my side, over my waist, his fingers digging into flesh and muscle, massaging, worshipping. I wrapped my arms around him, running my hands over the smooth, muscled skin of his back, and tangled my legs with his, holding him close. The kiss deepened, and my world narrowed to him, to this. Fire built inside me, so hot that I was afraid I'd burn to ash and float away if Death didn't hold me down.

When I couldn't take it any longer, I wrapped my legs around his hips, desperate to feel him against me. Desperate for the sweet relief only he could give me. "Mors, I need you," I pleaded against his lips as my hands slid around his waist.

He lifted his hips away from me, giving me room, and I quickly undid his pants, shoving them down. His kiss became more urgent, a fierceness of need that more than matched my own. He wore nothing underneath, and his cock, hot and heavy and impossibly hard, fell into my hand. I squeezed him, stroked him, and he growled against my lips.

Gripping my underwear, he tore them from my body, his hand sliding up until his fingers were gliding through my slick folds, pressing against my opening. "Are you ready for me, love? Because I can't wait."

"So ready." I took his length in my hand and led him to me, pressing the head of his cock to my opening; then I lifted my hips, taking the tip inside me.

He groaned. "You so easily erase all traces of my control," he said roughly and grabbed my wrists, lifting them over my head. "Infuriating, irresistible, brave little witch." He pressed sucking kisses along my throat. "You terrify me. You beguile me." He kissed along my jaw and looked down at me. "You fucking own me."

Then he slid inside me, a slow, steady glide that had my mouth falling open as a needy, raw sound left me. He kept that pace, sliding out just as slow, then filling me, stretching me to my limits, and the whole time, he watched me, watched the play of my features as he made me feel things I didn't know I was capable of feeling.

His expression was set, determined, while his big body trembled above me, his muscles jumping, his veins and tendons standing out. I clung to him when he thrust inside me and stayed there, rocking against me, hitting me deep. I whimpered when the first orgasm rushed forward, crying out when I started coming around him so hard, all I could do was hold on.

"I'm going to fuck you all night, so when you leave me tomorrow, you'll feel me with you. I need you to feel me with you," he rasped.

He thrust faster, deeper. "Mors—"

"Will you think of me, my love? Will you think of me while you're gone?"

There was no missing the desperation in his voice. "Yes," I said, telling him the truth.

He thrust faster still. "I'll be counting down the minutes until you return," he said, his eyes flashing, the shadows swirling. "Without you, I am only darkness. Without you, I am a starless sky. I am nothing."

Tears burned my eyes. The things he said... I could love this male, this version of Death, and I could believe that he loved me—but it never lasted.

Sliding his hand between us, he rubbed my clit as he fucked me harder, kissing me, breathing my air and sharing his. Our hearts slammed together as if they were one, our bodies caught in a violent rhythm, an animalistic dance that came so naturally, as if we'd been doing this dance our entire lives, an eternity, not just weeks.

Arching against him, I cried out as I came again. Death hissed, grabbing my thigh and holding it high, the other hand cupping my face. "You are my beginning and my end, my everything, my sweet Stella," he groaned and came, pulsing fiercely inside me, grinding against me, filling me over and over until we were both spent.

And this time when he called me Stella, it didn't feel wrong—it felt so right.

Wrapping his arms around me, he rolled to his side. We stayed like that, me locked in Death's arms while we caught our breath. He pressed his lips to my forehead. "Rest while you can. The night has only just begun."

~

Death was gone when I woke, and I wouldn't lie, I was disappointed.

My feelings for him were complex, but there was no denying that I did have feelings for him, strong ones. But we'd said all that needed to be said last night, all that could be said. He'd taken me all night, only letting me take short naps before he reached for me again, and I gave myself over to him willingly.

My body still ached, and my skin felt branded by his hands, his mouth, and he was right, I felt him. With every step I took, I felt him inside me. I quickly showered and dressed, then braided my hair. I was about to leave, but something stopped me. There was something I felt compelled to do first. Rummaging around in my pack, I found the small wooden box that I'd made when I was a kid. I used to keep my earrings in. I took them out, zipping them in the side pocket of my pack, then grabbing a piece of paper from the small desk in the corner, I quickly wrote a note, folded it, put it inside the box, and placed it beside the bed. Then I slid on my pack, and Hemlock scurried up my arm and climbed inside; he'd be asleep before we made it out of the castle. I looked around my room a final time and took in all the other little things that sat on shelves and on the dresser, the pictures and the keepsakes, and then my own now here for eternity with the rest. I didn't know what was going to happen, what the future held, but this place, this room—the females that came before me—were now part of my story, and I wanted to be remembered along with them.

I picked up the rest of my things and headed downstairs. I said my goodbyes to Egon and Lyle, then walked out the wide front doors—and pulled up short.

Death stood outside, waiting.

He said nothing, just held out his hand. I took it, and we headed down the stairs and started down the skull path that led to the gateway. He'd never walked me to the gate. He always left the castle before I did, moody and quiet. I glanced up at him now. He kept his eyes trained forward, a look on his face I couldn't read, but his hand gripped mine tighter.

"Will you be seeing the hounds while you're away?" he asked, still not looking down at me.

"Probably. Why?"

His jaw tightened. "Hounds are unpredictable. But then so are wolf shifters... and crows. Just make sure you're careful."

"None of them would ever hurt me," I said. "You have nothing to worry about."

He didn't reply. Was he jealous?

"Death?"

"Mors," he said.

That was the first time he'd ever asked me to call him that. "Mors?"

"Yes."

"I'm not going to sleep with anyone while I'm gone. You have no reason to be jealous."

He stopped, forcing me to do the same. "While you're away, I am sick with jealousy, not just of other males, but of everyone who gets to be in your presence, Zinnia, when I can't be."

He was trapped here, unable to move through the mortal world, at least not in his corporal form. He could use Somnus to visit dreams, and his soul could leave here when he recruited a reaper, like he had with Magnolia, but otherwise, he was stuck. "I'm sorry," I said lamely; there was nothing else I could say or do to make that easier on him.

He started walking again.

The gateway loomed ahead, and I had a rush of adrenaline. I was going to see my sister again. My heart filled with happiness, and there was no hiding it, but there was no denying how much I would miss Death while I was gone or how much I'd grown to care for him—more than I'd allowed myself to admit. But that still didn't mean we were right for each other.

His hand still gripped mine as the gateway opened, holding me close to him, not wanting to let me go.

Jasmine was on the other side, Ren with her. I could see them, but they couldn't see me yet; we weren't close enough.

"Zinnia," Death said, bringing my attention back to him. "You've seen a side of me that I'm not proud of, but know that I want you here with me more than anything—I need you to know that." He smiled, and there was pain in his eyes. "And when the lunar month is over, I want you to return to me. Promise you'll do that, love. Will you promise me that?"

I searched his eyes, the darkness swirling in the blue, as if he was barely holding the shadows at bay. "You know I will. We have a bargain."

"You said if I truly loved you, I should let you go, that releasing you was the only way to save you," he said, his thumb sliding over my cheek as he looked at me. "If that's what I must do to prove it to you, then... Zinnia Thornheart, I release you from your bargain."

My legs went weak. "You're releasing me?" It was what I'd

wanted for so long, what I'd asked for, but still, his words were like a dagger to my heart.

"After your month away, whether you return to me or not, the choice is yours, little witch." The shadows swallowed more of his bright blue eyes. "But I'm begging you… choose me over everything and everyone, over a life with them, over the possibility of death here with me." He pressed a soft kiss to my lips. "Choose me," he said roughly, then released my hand and strode away.

I watched him go, unable to look away.

His cloak swirled around him, covering him as he walked, as his staff appeared in his hand, thumping on the ground with each step he took away from me, as he disappeared around the bend in the path.

It was harder than it should be to turn away. I looked at my sister, and goddess, my heart felt as if it were being torn in two.

Go. Leave. I snatched up my bags before I did something stupid, like go after him, and stepped through the gate and into Jazzy's arms.

My sister squeezed me tight. "I'm so glad you're home."

I watched the gate close behind her, locking me out of Limbo, and the ache in my chest returned more painful than ever before.

What the hell was I going to do?

Chapter Twenty-Two

Zinnia

Home: Week One

As soon as I walked into the clubhouse, I was handed a drink. A moment later, the music was turned up, and my cousins swooped in, pulling me in for a round of tight hugs while Hemy got pats and treats and kisses.

My cousins had made sure I was walking into a party when I stepped into the room with Jazzy and Ren, and I needed that—anything to help me stop thinking about Death and what he'd said to me.

To stop me from focusing on the awful feeling of dread inside me that I couldn't shake.

Everyone was here—all my cousins and their mates, Asher and a few more wolves from Draven's pack, and all Bram's brothers—and just for tonight, I was choosing oblivion with people I cared about. I'd think about the choice I had to make tomorrow or the next day. I had four weeks to think about it, four weeks away from Death and the choice he'd thrown at me before I left.

A full lunar month without his mood swings and demands, his unpredictable rages and unexplainable, hurtful anger.

Twenty-eight days without his growls or his kisses, without the feel of his arms around me or the devastating, swoony, and heart-stopping things he said to me, taking me by surprise.

I was jostled from the thoughts flying about my head by a pair of massive arms coming around me and lifting me off my feet before I was engulfed in the kind of hug that had the power to take all your worries away, at least for a little while. "Fucking good to see you, Zinny," Relic said against my ear, holding me tight.

His heat seeped through me, and I hugged him back just as fiercely. "You too, my friend."

He finally put me down, and I looked up into his handsome face. "You wanna get shit-faced?"

He grinned, flashing those white teeth and fangs. "I don't get shit-faced, babe. Male as big as me, packing this much muscle, impossible." He flexed and winked, and I burst out laughing. "But more than happy to drink you under the table, lightweight."

"We'll see who the lightweight is." I gave him a shove toward one of the standing tables where Magnolia and Bram had wandered over to.

I curled my arm around Mags's neck when I reached her and planted a kiss on her cheek. "You wanna try my new potion?" she said, sliding over a shot glass full of something purple.

"How fast will it get me wasted?"

She winked. "Let's start with this one and see how we go."

I downed the sweet-tasting potion, and a moment later, I was hit with a wave of euphoria. Whatever was in Mags's potion had my serotonin levels shooting through the roof. "Another!" I cried.

Then Jazzy was there, and Rose and Willow and Iris, and we were dancing—well, Iris was more swaying with how heavily pregnant she was. Relic took my hand, spinning me around, and we were all laughing and singing. I sank into it, letting Mags's potion do its thing—letting it take me out of my own head, just for a little while.

~

I let my head slide across the back of the couch and land on Relic's shoulder. "I think I'm all partied out."

"Like I said, lightweight," he muttered and wrapped his arm around me. "You have a good night, babe?"

The party was still going, but it'd thinned out. Wills had gone downstairs to be with Warrick and Vi. Rose and Ronan and Iris and Draven had left a little while ago, and Mags and Bram were sitting on the opposite couch talking in that way couples obsessed with each other did, as if there were no one else in the room, while Jazzy was on Ren's knee on a chair beside us, making out.

"I had a great night. Being with all my favorite people, it's hard not to." I rested my hand on his stomach and tilted my head back to look at him. "Thanks for hanging with me tonight," I said and yawned. I was still feeling the effects of the potion and the beers, and my eyelids drooped.

Blue eyes filled my mind, wild and glowing, and I jolted awake.

Relic frowned. "Okay?"

I blinked up at him. "I think I drifted off for a second."

He grinned, flashing his killer dimples. "I'll be your pillow anytime."

"You're too charming for your own good, and the biggest flirt I've ever met." I huffed out a laugh.

"It's a skill I've perfected over the multiple centuries of my existence. It's a gift," he said, dropping his voice so it was low and growly.

"Relic, you seriously are a handsome devil, but that growly, dirty thing you're doing, as hot as it is, won't work on me," I said with a smirk. He wasn't being serious; he just was the flirtiest bastard I'd ever met.

"Baby, I gotta try. I've been angling for a feisty little witch of my own for a few years now, but I'm starting to think I've lost my touch 'cause every one of your cousins, your sister, and now you have flat-out rejected me," he said, that handsome-as-sin grin still on his face.

"You have no trouble picking up females."

"This is true, but I did think, just for a moment there, when we hung out in my room that time, that you might have actually considered taking me up on my offer of a night you'd never forget," he said, looking cocky as hell.

He was right. Who wouldn't consider it? A sound like a roar filled my head, and I jolted, sucking in a sharp breath. What the hell was that?

I shook it off and gave Relic a little shove. "Possibly," I said and rolled my eyes. "Just for a moment."

It was after my first month with Death; he'd ignored me, except for when he watched me, freaking me the hell out.

Before Death's bargain, I'd been working, using my powers to help people by speaking with their loved ones who'd crossed over, helping lost souls move on, or vanquishing evil ones. I'd felt lost while I was away that first month, disconnected from who I was, confused. Relic had been there, just doing what he did, being the truly awesome male that he was.

"I knew it." He winked. "If you ever change your mind, baby, you know where to find me."

I chuckled and shook my head. He'd offered me an escape from the pain I was feeling. No bullshit or pretense that it would be more than a good time. He'd offered me a night of orgasms and, because it was Relic, no doubt some laughter as well. I'd wanted to go to his room with him when he'd asked, and I had, but we'd ended up talking, and I'd fallen asleep on his bed. I'd woken in the night, Relic beside me. He'd been awake, chest bare and hard as hell behind his worn jeans. I'd been about to roll toward him, but a voice in my head, Death's voice calling me his, roaring it in my mind, had stopped me.

It was like Death had been there.

And a moment ago, he'd been here as well, hadn't he? He'd been in my head, looking through my eyes right at Relic. He had to be with Somnus, and as soon as I'd drifted off, even though it was just for a split second, he'd had an opening.

"You okay, Zinny?" Relic asked, tucking my hair behind my ear.

I sat up straighter, shaking off the tiredness. "Ah... yeah. All good." Relic didn't want me, and I didn't want him, not now. That night in his room, I thought he must have been feeling as lost as me. "She's out there, you know? I know she is. She's waiting, Relic. You just have to find her."

His cocky grin slipped, the look in his eyes flattening. I had no idea how much he felt. Lucifer created the hounds and gave them the ability to feel lust, anger, and loyalty, but the rest didn't come easy. Relic was second-gen, though, still hundreds of years old, but not as old as Warrick and not directly created by Lucifer. I'd never asked, and he'd never said what his emotional range was. Some of the others faked it, but I didn't think that's what Relic was doing. He felt more than them; I was sure of it. Maybe not as much as us mortals, but definitely more.

"You know I love making a female feel good, babe, but sometimes, all I'm fucking after is a simple touch, a hug, you know? That's all. As for a mate, I'm good. I have brothers who've been waiting a fuck of a lot longer than me. They should be first," he said, and it was as serious as I'd ever heard him. "It wouldn't be right."

Hounds were extremely tactile, craved touch, and loved hugs, and what he'd just said broke my heart a little. "That's not how this works, and if you need a hug, I'm here... well, when I am here. But if she's out there, you'll find each other. Whose turn it is or if we're ready has nothing to do with it. The fates do whatever the hell they like." I knew that better than most. I gave his big, rough-skinned hand a squeeze and stood.

"The fates are evil bitches," he said and took a sip of his beer.

Or maybe they were the only ones who actually knew what was good for us, and we needed to just stop fighting it and give in.

It was late when we got back to Jazzy and Ren's place. They'd gone straight to bed, and I'd popped earplugs in when sounds started drifting down the hall that I sure as hell did not want to hear.

I'd also had plenty of opportunities to tell Jazzy or one of my cousins what Death had said to me before I'd left Limbo, but I hadn't.

"But I'm begging you... choose me over everything and everyone, over a life with them, over the possibility of death here with me."

"Choose me."

I squeezed my eyes closed and curled my fingers into fists. Why the hell had he said that? We could have carried on as we were for just a little longer. Now he was going to force my hand. He was going to make me choose. I wasn't in love with him—but I felt something. There was this pull inside me, distant but strong. Incredibly strong. Not love—it couldn't be—but something... something else. And even if what I felt for him did run deeper, even if I was falling for him, how could I choose him? How could I leave behind my sister? My family? I couldn't. Goddess, this hurt. I hated him for doing this to me, and I hated myself for even feeling the slightest bit conflicted about this. The answer should be easy. He forced me into a bargain I didn't want. He'd taken me away from everyone I loved.

This should be easy.

Then why the hell wasn't it?

Chapter Twenty-Three

Zinnia

The wind blew outside the castle. As she numbly sat on the couch in front of the fire, she stared down at the small vial gripped in her shaky, paint-stained fingers. It was full of something dark and noxious smelling. She was so cold, empty, broken. A tear slid down her cheek as she pulled out the cork and poured it into her mouth. Pain burned her throat and gut, scorched through her veins. Blood coming from her nose and eyes dripped from her chin onto her hands. She screamed, but not from the pain—from the relief.

The room spun away to another place, looking through another female's eyes—no, this time, I was looking through my eyes.

Death stood among the trees, his cloak covering him. Snarls and growls came from beneath his hood.

Rage.

He slammed his staff down on the ground, and the earth shook beneath my feet.

"Mors," I called, running toward him, but he was moving

farther and farther away from me. I called his name again, trying to reach him.

The world around me froze, and so did I.

Death tilted his head back and roared.

I gasped, shoving back the covers as I sat bolt upright. Then I was frozen, trying to find purchase. I was caught between the horror of the first vision and the desperate fear of the second.

Gods, I didn't know if my brain had conjured the vision of me and Death, or... or if that really had been him and something was terribly wrong.

Rubbing my face, I tried to wake myself up as I slid my feet into the slippers Jazzy had waiting for me and dragged on my favorite oversized cardigan that Else had knitted me years ago, which reached my knees. Hemy scurried across the mattress, and I held out my hand so he could run up and perch on my shoulder. He burrowed under my hair. "Morning, my sweet boy."

I walked out and found Jaz was at the kitchen counter. She was smearing butter on toast and had a butterfly of some variety on top of her head. "You have a good sleep?" she asked, lighting up when she saw me.

I pulled my earplugs out and held them up. "Thanks to these, yes." I popped them in my pocket. "Listening to my sister enthusiastically bone her mate isn't something I ever want to hear again."

She flushed. "Oh shit, sorry."

I shrugged. "It was gross, but it also made me happy that you're so happy and apparently getting laid really well."

She snorted and shook her head. "Yes, I most definitely am, but let's never mention that again." She held up her toast. "Want some?"

"Deal." I rounded the counter and popped two pieces in the toaster. "Ren home?"

"Nope, he had to go to work." She poured me a coffee and slid it over. "How's the head?"

"I mainly stuck to Mags's potion, so not bad at all. Our cousin has a gift," I said and took a sip.

"She really does." Her gaze held mine for a moment, and I saw the questions there, so many, but she took a bite out of her toast instead.

Now would be the perfect time to tell Jazzy everything that had happened. She was dying to ask me how my time in Limbo had been, but everyone tiptoed around the subject now, though. They waited for me to bring it up first, because I'd made it clear that's what I wanted. I opened my mouth to tell her what was happening, but the words wouldn't come out. I didn't know where to start or how to make her understand the way I was feeling. Everything was so messy and confusing, I just wanted to keep it to myself for a while longer.

You're keeping it to yourself because you haven't decided what you're going to do, and that would hurt your baby sister.

"So Else and Aunt Daisy are having a dinner tonight, just the family. You'll be there, right?" Jazzy said and sipped her coffee.

"Absolutely. I have a few things I need to do today, but I'll meet you there later. Can I borrow your car?" I said as nerves filled me.

"Or course. Anything I can help you with?"

My nerves shot higher. "No, not this time. Thanks, though."

"Do you have any white snakeroot?" I asked Wills, who was working at her store, The Cauldron, today, and pressed a kiss to Violet's peachy-colored hair. She was strapped to her mother's front, fast asleep. Hemy poked his head out of my bag, saw that Vi was asleep, and, disappointed, disappeared again.

Wills chuckled and broke off a piece of bread from her sandwich sitting on the counter. "We're all out, and our next delivery's not for a couple weeks. The council are being hard-asses on certain ingredients, and snakeroot's on the restricted list." She rested her hip on the counter. "What are you using it for?" She held the bread, and Hemy's nose appeared, twitching; then he took it and vanished again. "Something important? Anything to do with your bargain?"

I shook my head. "I have a job," I said, lying through my teeth. "An old soul, like really old. I'm thinking I'll need a little more juice to make contact."

"I hope..." Her green eyes held mine. "I hope you haven't given up, Zin, because we haven't. Jazzy hasn't stopped trying to find a way to free you from Death—none of us have."

Guilt filled me. I should have told my sister this morning what was going on, but I didn't know how. Everything was so complicated. "I appreciate it, I do, but whatever happens, I'll be okay," I said and gripped the edge of the counter when another wave of guilt washed through me.

She nodded, not looking convinced. "As for the snakeroot, I know of a place that has a steady supply, but it's in the demon part of town. Yeah, they mostly follow the rules there—Rune runs a pretty tight ship—but still, going alone, no matter who you are or how capable you are, wouldn't be a good idea," she said, changing the subject back. She knew when not to push, and I loved that about her.

"Cool, where do I need to go?"

"There's a store—Malicious Brew. Give me a few hours, and then War can take Vi, and I'll come with."

If I hung out with Willow all day, there would eventually be questions, questions I wasn't ready to answer, that I didn't know how to answer. "Thanks, Wills, but I told my clients I'd get back to them this morning. I'll call Relic to keep me company."

My cousin looked disappointed, which just made me feel even more guilty. "I'll see you tonight, though? At your mom's for dinner."

"I guess I can let you off the hook this time then, but I want some one-on-one hang time and soon, okay?" she said, studying me way too closely. Out of all my cousins, Wills and I were the most alike, in appearance and personality, and she always seemed to know when I was hiding something.

"Absolutely."

I texted Relic as I headed out and asked if he could meet me. Relic being Relic, he immediately agreed. Traffic was heavy, and by the time I could park and let him know where I was, he was already close.

I found him a street over, standing by his bike, tall, in worn jeans and his leather vest, tapping away at his phone. The hound grinned when he saw me. "Just couldn't stay away from me?"

Hemlock poked his head out of my bag to see where we were and who we were with, and Relic gave his head a scratch. I snorted. "You wish."

"You have no idea. But since sex is off the cards, I'm happy to display my superior fighting abilities and protect a damsel in distress."

"I'm not a damsel."

He planted one of his massive hands on top of my head and mussed my hair. "Whatever you say, princess."

"You've been going to Willow's movie nights, huh?"

He chuckled, low and rough. "Of course, can't you see how evolved I've become? My emotional education is coming along nicely. I'm almost like a *real boy.*"

"Jesus."

He winked. "So what are we doing here?"

This street was kind of a no-man's-land. Humans avoided it because, even though they didn't know demons existed, their flight instincts kept them away; they sensed there were predators nearby and avoided this part of the city all on their own, but as soon as we rounded the corner, we were in demon central. These demons could pass as human, though—that was one of the main prerequisites to live here. You also needed to know how to follow rules and not hurt humans. The forest-dwelling demons had none of those things. "I need some ingredients for a job I'm doing today."

The demons looked our way as we passed, but as soon as they saw Relic, they averted their eyes. Demons were naturally afraid of hellhounds. Lucifer used them to control the demons in Hell, and the fear was built into their DNA.

"Yeah? You found that job quick," he said, his gaze sliding to me. "Must be some kind of a record."

He knew I was up to something, or he at least suspected it. That's what you get for hanging out with a hound. "My client made the booking before I went to Limbo," I said, adding another lie to the list that day.

"Right," he said, making it obvious he didn't believe a word.

"Just up here," I said, relieved when I saw a sign with *Malicious Brew* scrawled on it swinging above the door.

I pushed open the door and walked in. I'd never smelled anything like it—not bad, just... busy. So many scents of herbs, plants, elixirs that I wasn't used to.

Relic looked around, tilted back his head, and sniffed the air. "This shit is burning my fucking nostrils." He scowled. "I don't like this, Zinny. It's too much. I can't smell anything else. No nose, no idea what the fuck's coming..."

The beads hanging in front of a door at the back of the room made a musical sound as they were drawn back, and a small female walked out. The demon was short and curvy and had bloodred hair that hung down her back in waves. Her face was humanoid and utterly stunning. She had a slightly upturned nose and full pink lips. She took several steps out, then slammed on the brakes, her unusual peridot eyes widening when she saw Relic. Her gaze sliced to the patch on his leather vest and the Devil Dogs MC emblem.

"I didn't do anything," she said. "Whatever they told you, I'm innocent." She lifted her hands and backed up a step like she was going to bolt. "I didn't do anything. Don't take me back... please... don't..."

"Not here to take you back to Hell, demon," Relic said. "So slow your roll and take a fucking breath."

She blinked up at him several times. "You're not?"

"Nope."

"He's just keeping me company," I said quickly because she still looked ready to turn and run. "I'm here for a couple of ingredients, that's all."

She kind of slumped in relief, then scowled. "What the fuck is wrong with you, witch? You brought a freaking hellhound into my shop? I almost pissed myself." She turned her scowl on Relic. "And you should know better." She shook her head. "Hounds, man. Meatheads, the lot of you."

Relic's head jerked back. "What did you call me, demon?"

"You heard me." She straightened her spine. "Lucifer didn't send you for me. You can't do shit, so save the intimidation bullshit for the next demon you drag back to Hell."

"Well, this has gotten off to a great start," I said as Relic strode past me and up to the little female.

She tried to step back, but he grabbed her arm and held her still while she squirmed to get away. He dipped lower, sniffing her head.

"What the hell do you think you're doing, mutt?" she yelled, and I saw she had fangs, short but sharp. "Let me the hell go."

"You're not just demon."

Her fight stopped instantly, and she blinked up at him. "How do you know that?"

"I can smell it." He smirked down at her. "Can't quite make out what else you are, but looking at you, I'd say a gremlin or maybe a troll."

She shrieked and slammed her knee up, aiming for Relic's nuts but only managing to get him midthigh. She was far too short to reach, but I doubted many beings could reach a hound's nuts that way, honestly. I respected her for trying, though. He deserved it.

"Okay, back up," I said to Relic.

He ignored me, wholly focused on the little demon in his grip.

"Meathead," she muttered again and started tapping her fingers against the side of her thigh, one after the other, over and over again.

"You couldn't handle my meathead, gremlin," he said and flashed her his fangs.

Okay, we were straying into some other weird freaking territory here that I did not want to be a part of. "So do you have any white snakeroot?" I asked.

"You do realize that gremlins don't actually exist? They're a myth." She pressed her hand to his chest and shoved, but he didn't move. "It's pretty cringe that you don't know that."

She shoved a second time, and again, Relic didn't budge; he did release her this time, though. He tilted his head to the side. "You have a very smart mouth for someone so small and annoying."

"And you have a giant head and ridiculous... muscles." She flushed. "You look like a deformed Sasquatch."

"Now I'm embarrassed for you, Gremmy, if we're talking about things that don't exist."

"Don't call me Gremmy," she gritted out, her fingers tapping against her thigh again.

"But it suits you"—Relic flashed her that thousand-watt grin —"Gremmy."

He was enjoying himself.

She crossed her arms tight over her chest. She was pissed, but I also saw the way she trembled. She was scared and doing her best to hide it. She was still a demon, and he was a huge hellhound invading her space. It was like a giant cat toying with an injured mouse. I wasn't sure Relic noticed.

"Leave," she said.

"I don't think so," he said back, definitely enjoying himself.

She looked down, her lids blinking rapidly, and then she sucked in a breath, teeth clenched, and looked back up. "I want you to leave, you giant pain in the ass. I want you to leave my shop now." Her voice was raised, pitched high. No, not scared—terrified. She was still desperately trying to be brave in the face of the huge male towering over her, and Relic missed it completely. Honestly, I was surprised.

"If I were in your ass, Gremmy, I promise it would only hurt for a minute, and then I'd make it feel real good."

She hissed.

"Okay," I said, stepping forward. "If you could just get the ingredients I need, we'll leave. Right, Relic?"

He winked down at her. "Sure."

She spun away, strode down one of the aisles crowded with ingredients, snatched something off the end, then stomped up to me and shoved it in my hands. "Now leave."

I slid my hand in my pocket for money. "I need to pay you."

"I don't care. Just leave."

I quickly pulled out some cash, more than what it was worth, but after what I'd just witnessed, she deserved a tip. I dropped the money on the counter, then grabbed Relic's arm and shoved him from the store.

He let me, but not without a little resistance.

The sound of the bolt being thrown behind us came as soon as we walked out. I spun around as the demon flipped the Open sign to Closed, then disappeared out of view, but not before I got a glimpse of exactly how rattled she looked.

"What the hell *was that*?" I asked Relic when we started walking.

"What?" He was still grinning.

"You terrified that female, then sexually harassed her," I said, because looking at him right now, the hound was clueless.

He stopped in his tracks. "No, I didn't... That's not what happened."

"I've never heard you speak to a female that way." Hounds were protective of females, worshipped them in a lot of ways—they did not harass or scare them.

Relic frowned down at me, glanced back at the shop, then back at me. "No... she wasn't afraid. She was—"

"She was shaking. You're a hellhound, and she's a demon. She was trying to hide it, but she was terrified. I thought she was actually going to cry for a moment." I wasn't trying to make him feel like shit, but he needed to be aware of what just happened back there.

"Cry?" he said, his voice so rough, it lifted goose bumps all over me. "No..." He looked back at the shop again. "No," he repeated.

"Yes."

"Fuck." He started back toward the shop, and I grabbed his arm.

"What are you doing?"

"I don't make females cry. I don't scare them, and I don't... sexually harass them." He actually looked nauseous.

"Going back there now will only make it worse. She wants you gone, and you need to respect that."

He stopped, looking confused and shaken. "Fuck," he said again and let me tug him back the way we were going.

He didn't say much after that, and he was distracted when he gave me a hug before he left for his shift at the Hell Fire, the hellhounds' bar. I watched him leave and then headed for home and our cemetery.

It was early afternoon by the time I got there. Sometimes I found it easier to call on spirits at our cemetery. It was a place of great power, and without any real information to go on, I needed all the help I could get.

The cemetery was quiet when I arrived, no Aunt Daisy or

Arthur here today, thankfully. Daisy was probably in the kitchen getting ready for tonight. She went all out when she had us all under one roof. Closing the wide iron gates behind me, I ran my fingers over headstones, saying their names as I walked by, telling my loved ones, my ancestors, how much I missed and loved them, finally stopping beside my grandmother's grave.

"Hey, Gran," I said and sat on the ground. Daisy and Art had planted chamomile all over the grounds. It had spread everywhere, which was what they'd wanted. When Art cut the grass now, it smelled amazing.

"I need your help to find some people," I whispered as I slipped my bag over my head and set it beside me. Hemy scurried out and trotted to the herb garden to nibble on the basil. "I know you're resting, and I hate to disturb you, but I'm not sure I can do this alone. You see, Gran, I need to make a decision, one that should be simple, but now... now it's not." Death said he loved me, and I wasn't sure what I felt, but I felt... something. Something unexplainable. It was wide and deep and so incredibly strong, but also it felt... distant. I didn't understand it, and I needed to understand it.

Opening my bag, I pulled out the thimble, the book, and the small pot of dried paint I'd taken from my bedroom back in Limbo and placed them in front of me. I'd never met any of these females, besides Aster. I didn't know their names. I didn't know anything about them. All I had that told me anything of who they were, were my visions and these items. Worn and well-used items they'd taken the time to bring with them when they'd made their own journey to Limbo, however that came about. Items that had been left behind, survived when they hadn't.

Females Death had cared for, possibly loved.

And as much as I didn't want to consider it, there was this unsettling feeling inside me. Death was prone to bouts of rage and jealousy, of unreasonable and controlling behavior. The cloak was darkness, and sometimes, it pulled him into the shadows.

He said if I left him, he'd let the cloak take him, that he'd let the shadows and the darkness take hold. Death had remained covered, preferring the shadows, when I first went to Limbo, and I'd believed him capable of anything. I didn't know how easy it was for him to slip back into that place, but if he had when he was with his consorts, if he'd let his anger take hold, perhaps he'd done something, something terrible, when he was lost to the shadows. Something that had pushed them to do what they had, to hurt themselves.

Even thinking it made me feel sick with guilt, but I had to be sure.

Taking a tiny piece of snakeroot from my bag, I placed it in a small square of soft leather. Then I added one verbena leaf, three drops of agarwood oil, and two of juniper oil and placed it on the ground. Then I took a ball of string from my bag and cut a length off. Making a slice in my palm, I let my blood pool, then smeared it on the string before gathering up the leather square into a small pouch and tying it closed with the blood-soaked string.

Rubbing the pouch between my hands, I mixed everything together, warming it until its fragrance reached me and the oil soaked the leather through. I swiped the oily pouch over the items I'd taken from my room in Limbo, and then I squeezed my sliced palm and dripped some blood on Gran's grave as an offering before dropping more blood in a circle around everything.

Slipping off my shoes, I pressed my feet into the soft chamomile lawn that had grown over Gran's grave, digging my toes in, pulling power straight from the source. I let the magic that still flowed through Gran's bones reach out to me and latched on to it.

I gasped as it filled me, twisting around my own magic and lifting it higher and higher. Closing my eyes, I let the spell wrap around me, let the words come, let them form and build to call on Death's consorts, to ask them to show me the way, until they finally spilled from my lips. "Thank you, Mother, for the gifts you have given me, for the love you have bestowed upon me. I call on you, my sisters, sisters who came before, who loved and laughed and hoped for a life of peace and warmth, my sisters who were taken too soon. I call on you to come forward, to show me who you were and how you were taken. I ask for your help, dear sisters, to guide me, to lead me to the right path." I squeezed my hand tighter, and warm blood trickled over my hand and into the small circle. "Show me, sisters."

The world spun around me—but there were no souls to be found, only a suffocating darkness, a void, and it was cold and incredibly lonely.

Tears slid down my face. I felt so much, so much pain and fear as if it were my own.

A sob burst from me as I searched, but they weren't there. It was as if they were nothing.

As if they had ceased to exist.

Chapter Twenty-Four

THE TABLE WAS laden with food; Daisy and Else had outdone themselves. Everyone I loved was in the same place, sitting around the table laughing and talking, and I tried to let it fill me so I could shake the awful empty feeling inside me, but what happened at the cemetery lingered, clinging to me like a cold hand around the back of my neck, not letting go.

I rubbed my arms and smiled when Vi gave Hemy another wide grin. He was besotted with her, performing for my tiny cousin, running down my arm and up Willow's, then peeking at Violet through Willow's hair. He did it again, and Violet giggled uncontrollably. Hemy spun around, triumphant.

"You little show-off," I said and scratched his head when he ran back to me.

"I need a Hemy," Wills said. "Imagine everything I'd get done with him keeping my little drama queen busy when I'm trying to make dinner or pee or just take a shower." She turned to Ren, who was sitting beside War. "I have asked my loyal familiar to go fox and entertain his niece, but he won't do it."

"Because I want her to love me for me, and not because I'm a fuzzy, cute woodland animal," he said with a smirk. "And thanks to Jaz's mural, she's now obsessed with them."

Jazzy chuckled. "I can't help it if I'm just that talented."

"Would you go crow and flap around to entertain babies and small children?" Ren asked Bram.

He shrugged. "Depends. If they were my own kids, then yeah, but then they'll probably have their own wings, so I'm not sure I'll need to."

Mags spun to face him. "And then I'll be left standing there while you all fly off and leave me behind." Her lips turned down. "I'm jealous already, and we don't even have kids yet."

"I'll carry you, babe," Bram said and kissed the top of her head.

"There's always the broom," Else said at her spot beside Daisy.

"What broom?" Iris asked, her hand dropping from her massive belly and grabbing the edge of the table. She was due in a few months, but with twins, she looked ready to have them now.

"Don't even think about it," Draven said to his mate, who still thought she could do everything she used to.

"What broom?" Mags asked, impatient.

Daisy frowned at Else. "Hey, we made a pact never to bring that up."

"Oopsie," Else said. Stan, Else's devoted and deceased familiar, stood behind her, chuckling, amused by her as always. Only Jaz and I could see him and knew he was there. He'd asked us not to tell her.

"When I asked if we had a family broom, you said we didn't," Rose said from her spot on Ronan's lap.

"We lied," Else said. "None of you could be trusted not to do something crazy with it." She shrugged. "But your daughter's mated to a crow, Daisy, so I think she should have it." She sipped her wine. "There's a hat as well."

"Else!" Aunt Daisy said. "What has gotten into you?"

"A hat like *a hat*, the pointy kind that most families have, but you said we didn't," Wills said.

"It doesn't do anything," Daisy said. "And if you knew about the hat, then you'd know there was a broom."

"Because it hasn't found its new owner. Jaz and Zinny haven't tried it on for size yet. Maybe it belongs to one of them," Else said.

Brooms, pointed hats, cauldrons—they were the things that humans associated with witches, but there was a reason for that. All covens supposedly had those things, items of power. They were tangible, things you could see and touch, unlike actual magic, and during the witch trials, the connection between the witches tried and those particular items had been noted, hence the association to this day.

Else stood slowly, then shuffled from the room. Stan followed her. He was always with her; the only time he left her side was when she was asleep, but he never went far.

"I can't believe you never told us we had them," Mags said.

"We tried the hat on each of you when you were babies. It didn't claim any of you, so we put it away," Daisy said, looking guilty. "Honestly, I was kind of scared of it. It's old and powerful. Who knows what it can do when it finds its owner?"

Else shuffled back in carrying both. Mags jumped up, and Else handed her the broom. "Fly, my pretty," she said and cackled.

Bram frowned, looking it over. "If you use that thing, you have to wear a helmet."

Mags looked disgusted. "A *helmet*. No way. None of my ancestors would have worn one."

"And I bet there were a whole lot of witches walking around with concussions." He gave it another once-over. "I don't know about this. You could break your damn neck."

"No, I won't," Mags said, running her hand over it.

Else placed the hat on Jazzy's head. "It won't toss her off, and she won't fall. Once you're in the air, you're stuck on it until you land." The hat was worn rich brown leather. Soft, the point at the top not super tall, not like in fairy stories. It was too big for Jazzy, though, and covered her eyes.

"See, nothing to worry about," Mags said to her mate, eyes shining with glee.

Else plucked the hat off Jasmine's head. "Nope, not yours. It might be destined for one of the babies," she said. "Could be Vi's or one of the twins." She moved behind me and put it on my head.

The moment she did, something happened. The room spun, the world shifting around me, followed by a massive surge of power flowing through my body. It was meant for me. I felt it. The hat had been waiting for me, and I knew instantly that if I was wearing it, any spell I used would be boosted.

"Whoa," Rose said. "It shrunk down to fit."

"How does it feel, Zinny?" Wills asked.

I had to take several breaths while the power surge settled. "Yeah, it feels... right. Good." That was the only way I knew how to describe it.

Else took it off my head and set it on the kitchen counter. "Then it's yours, my girl. It belongs to you now."

"Looks good too," Mags said.

"Thanks, Else." I took her hand.

She smiled, so much love in her eyes and warmth on her weathered face. "I had a feeling that the time was right," she said, then grabbed for the chair, stumbling.

"Else!" Daisy shot to her feet, but Warrick was there first, scooping her up.

Else went limp in his arms.

Else looked so small in her bed, covers pulled up to her chin, her long silver hair, wavy and soft, spread out on her pillow. Stan lay on the bed behind her, his arm around her.

They were the loves of each other's lives, but then they'd been torn from each other when Stan was murdered. He'd only been twenty-one years old.

He looked up at me now and shook his head.

Else wasn't coming back from whatever this was. Jasmine was standing behind me, and she rushed from the room, trying not to let anyone else see that she was about to cry. Stan had made us keep our promise, and we had; we never told our aunt or anyone else that he was with her. He'd wanted her to move on, to at least try and have a full life without him, and he knew she wouldn't be able to if she knew he was there.

She never really had, though. There was Connor, the sweet old guy she was kind of dating, but they'd never really been more than good friends. She'd never gotten over Stan, and she hadn't really tried because she didn't want to get over him. He was it for her.

Mags was kneeling on the floor beside her. "Else?"

She opened her eyes slowly. "Don't you yell at me," she said to Magnolia. "I didn't tell you because worrying gives a body ulcers. I've seen other healers, the best, and there's nothing anyone can do. My time's up, pumpkin," she said, her usually strong voice sounding weak.

Daisy brushed her hair back. "I won't give up, Else. There has to be something—"

"It's my heart, Daisy… and nothing can be done." She wrapped her fingers around Daisy's hand. "I'm ready to go. I'm… I'm so goddamn ready to see my Stan."

Chapter Twenty-Five

Home: Week Two

DEATH CALLED MY NAME, *his voice echoing through the trees. His roars and unhinged growls should terrify me, but they didn't. I needed to find him. "Mors!"*

But the faster I ran toward him, the farther he got from me. I sobbed, tripping over tree roots and sliding in the mud. Blood dripped from my grazed palms, and each step grew more difficult than the last.

"Zinnia!" he roared.

I sat up with a gasp, my heart thundering in my chest. Hemlock was curled in close, sensing my distress even in sleep. "I'm okay, my sweet boy." It was a lie, and I wasn't fooling him or myself.

The dreams had been constant. Every night the last two weeks since I'd been home. I'd dreamed of Death calling for me, and every night I tried to find him in that forest, and I couldn't. It felt so real, but he was always out of reach. He needed me, but I couldn't get close to him. If Somnus was helping him, he'd be able to come to me, though. He'd be able to talk to me, like he had when I was fifteen.

But he hadn't done that. Maybe it was just a dream? It had to be because he'd talk to me if he was really there. He would.

There was a tap at my bedroom door before it opened. Jasmine walked in carrying a mug of coffee. "You sleep okay?"

"Yeah," I lied and took the mug, sitting up. "Any news?"

"She's still the same."

Else had deteriorated, but she was hanging on. I shoved back the covers. "Let me quickly get dressed, and we can head back."

We walked into Aunt Daisy's house a short time later. Wills was at the kitchen table, Rose beside her. They both looked exhausted.

"How is she?" Jaz asked.

"She's comfortable, but she's getting weaker," Rose said, her eyes filled with pain.

~

Home: Week Three

I was surrounded by stars. I was alone and so scared. The stars spun past, faster and faster, darkness flashing to light—

I hit the ground so hard, I cried out.

I blinked up at the sky, then looked down at myself. I was naked, lying on the grass.

A giggle fell from my lips as I wiggled my toes.

"Stella?" a rough voice called.

I woke with a jolt, my gaze slicing to Else. She was still asleep.

"You okay?" Jaz asked from her seat beside me.

Another week had passed of nightly dreams or visions—I still didn't know what. Every night, I felt Death close and was never able to reach him, and I saw those females, their lives and their deaths, feeling their fear and not understanding any of it... All while sitting with my cousins at Else's bedside watching her get weaker and frailer by the day.

Right now, though, it was just me and Jazzy in here with Else.

"Nightmare?" Jaz asked.

"I'm... I'm not sure."

She studied me. "You look exhausted."

I was. Every time I fell asleep, another vision or dream came to me, and now this, this weird vision of the night sky, of Death, but in the past, of him calling out her name, calling Stella. I felt as if I were losing my damn mind.

"I'll go get us a coffee," she said.

"Thanks."

She walked out, and I looked back at Else. She was watching me. "Hey," I said and took her hand.

"Spill," she rasped. "I've been watching you the last few weeks. I may be on my death bed, but I'm not blind."

My mouth went dry. "There's nothing to tell."

"Now you're gonna lie? Right to your dying aunt's face?"

Her body may be weak, but her mind was still just as sharp. "So much has happened, Else. I'm not sure where to start—"

"Then give me the highlights." And for a moment there, she sounded like her old bossy self.

"Right, the highlights." I leaned forward, resting my elbows on my knees, and gave her hand a light squeeze before I let it all go, everything I'd been holding inside. "I'm not the only consort Death's had. He's had... well, I'm not sure of the actual number, but all have died horribly. I've tried to contact them, but I can't, and he won't tell me anything. Apparently, I have to work it all out myself. His brother, Somnus, lives in the Dream Realm protecting their younger sister from their mother, Nox. Her name's Marigold, and she's in a temple Death created as a child in the Night Realm. She's been locked in stasis for some reason since she was three, but I have no idea how old she truly is. Up until last month, Death never touched me. Now... things have, ah... well, progressed. He says he loves me, Else, that he'll release me from our bargain, but he wants me to choose him, even if that means death... for me. Even if that means leaving everyone I love and only being with him for as long as I survive. And those females, the one's that came before me, I... I feel them, but I can't reach them. There's nothing, just... goddess, there's just an empty void. And I have these visions, or maybe they're just dreams, I don't know, but in them, Death comes to me, but I can't reach him. I also have visions of the past, of those females, of their lives, their deaths, but that's all they can give me, and I have no idea what any of it means."

Else blinked up at me. "Boy, you weren't kidding. And that was just the highlights?"

I chuckled and wiped away the stray tear that had fallen without me realizing it. "I had a full-on month in Limbo."

"You can say that again, Zinny girl." She squeezed my hand back. "Did you know the mother and Nox hate each other?"

"They do? Why?"

"Not sure, but they fell out over something a very long time ago. It's mentioned in a few history books."

"I had no idea."

She shrugged a narrow shoulder. "Gods are touchy, and they get bent out of shape easily." Her eyes cleared and locked on me. "As for Death... well, nothing is ever as it seems. Do you love him?"

"Things have been far from smooth sailing. I... I care about him, deeply. There's this connection, a magnetism pulling me toward him that's so strong, sometimes I feel like I'm being torn in two, but love...."

"Okay, let me put it this way, pumpkin. If you dropped that brick wall you've built around yourself, if you forget the other consorts and the visions and the brother and Nox and the kid in stasis and all the other things, if you shove that all aside, and it's just you and him, do you think you could love him?"

My heart thumped in my chest, and my palms grew sweaty. I was on the verge of hyperventilating. "I... I..."

She gave my hand another squeeze. "I'll take that as a yes."

Fuck.

"I just, I don't know what any of it means, what the visions are trying to tell me."

She studied my face, her eyes bright with life even though her body was failing her. "What if they're not just visions? What if they're something else?"

I stilled. "Like what? An alternate realm? Another timeline? Nox beaming a lie into my brain? I'm due to go back in less than a week, and I still have no idea what I'm going to do."

She shrugged a frail shoulder. "I wish I had the answers for you, but what I do know is it never hurts to look at something from a different angle. To wipe the slate clean when you're having no luck and try again."

~

Home: Week Four

Death stood behind me, his hands on my rounded belly. "Are you afraid?" he asked.

I shook my head. "How can I be afraid when I have you by my side? How can I be afraid when we're about to meet our child?"

"Aster," he rasped against my ear. "My star, my love, my light."

I woke with my hands on my flat stomach. I was in my room at Jasmine's house. No round belly. No baby. No Death. Loss washed through me with such force, I had to bite back a sob. I wanted the vision back; I wanted it all back.

Aster, the first of Death's consorts. She'd given him a child.

The visions were becoming more intense, more real. More brutal on my frail emotions. I was raw from my days with Else and my nights in the past—Death's past.

I shoved back the covers and quickly got dressed. My time was up. I was supposed to go back tomorrow, or not, a decision that, on paper, should be easy. Life or death? Who wouldn't choose life?

But either way, I wasn't going to leave my family, not yet, not while they still needed me.

Snatching my phone off the bedside table, I checked for missed calls or texts. Nothing, thank the goddess. Else was still here, still with us.

Shoving on my boots, I scooped up Hemlock, put him on my shoulder, and walked out. Jazzy and Ren were already gone. I didn't bother with breakfast; my stomach was too knotted and filled with nerves, and the sadness from that dream still hovered around me like a dark cloud. My hands fell to my stomach. For a moment, I'd felt what it would be like to be pregnant, something I would never experience for myself, and I wanted it back; I wanted to be back in that dream with Death.

Stop.

You're losing your damn mind.

Shoving my hands in my pockets, I walked through the field where Ren had built my sister her dream house and headed down the road to Daisy's house. Mags and Bram had been staying in Bram's tree house in the backyard every night instead of heading to the crow village like they did a few nights a week. Good thing since I needed to talk to her, like now.

It was still pretty early, so instead of heading inside the house, I walked around the side to the backyard. The light was on in the kitchen; Daisy and Art were in there with Rose. I needed to speak with Mags before anyone saw me. They'd known what date it was, even if no one had said anything to me, because this situation was already hard enough. Jazzy had been avoiding me the last few days, and I got it. She was already hurting enough. Knowing her sister was about to leave while Else was like this, it was too much for her, for everyone.

I climbed the ladder to the tree house and knocked on the door.

Bram opened it a few seconds later. "Zinny, hey." He frowned. "Everything okay?"

His black hair was tied back, the sides freshly shaven. He had a few new markers tattooed on the right side of his head since my last visit, and going by the massive knife strapped to his thigh and the frustration in his eyes, he was about to leave on a job. My cousin's mate was an assassin, and he and his brothers frequently had to vanish for days on end to do what needed to be done. "How long will you be gone?" I asked him.

"I'll be back by morning, all going to plan." He pushed the door wide, letting me in.

Mags was standing at the kitchen counter, sipping a coffee. "Hey, Zinny. Hey, Hemy."

Bram strode over to her, pulled her into his arms, and kissed her. When the kiss ended, he rested his forehead against hers and said something low for her ears only. Then he kissed her again, gave me a chin lift, and walked out. A moment later, he dove off the small balcony, his wings exploding from his back and catching the air, and then he was gone.

I turned back to Mags. "Okay?"

She leaned on the counter. "Yeah, I mean, I hate it when he goes, but I'm usually fine. It's just now, with Else..." She shook her head. "I just want everyone close, you know?" Her eyes lifted to me, and she bit her lip. "Sorry."

Yeah, no one had forgotten that I was supposed to leave tomorrow. "That's kind of why I'm here. I need your help, Mags."

She straightened. "What do you need?"

I wanted to hug her right then. She'd do anything for me; they all would.

"Do you think you could get a message to Death?" My baby cousin was one of Death's reapers due to a whole shitty situation that happened when she and Bram got together. I knew she went to Limbo frequently, but I never saw her, and she couldn't reach me. When she delivered a soul, she went straight to that soul's "individual Limbo," and she hadn't found a way to veer off the path and find me, but surely there was a way for her to reach Death. There had to be.

She studied me closely. "What kind of message?"

"I'm not leaving, not yet, not while I can still be with Else, and not when my family needs me. I don't know if it's possible, but do you think you can find a way to get a message to him for me and tell him that?"

She put down her mug and rounded the counter. "I have no direct line to Death. He doesn't communicate with me at all. I feel the call to collect a soul, and I deliver it—that's it."

"Can you try anyway?"

"I'm... I'm not sure how." She looked as frustrated as I felt.

My only other option was to go to the gateway and wait, hope he came, and try to explain, but that would take most of the day, and I didn't want to be away from Else that long. "Sorry to ask. I just... I didn't know what else to do."

She chewed her lip again. "Let me try, okay? I'll see what I can do." She walked to her shelf and pulled down an old book of spells and a wooden bowl. "I think I have an idea, but I'll need to really focus."

I needed this to work.

"Call me if there's any change with Else," she said and took a small vial from the shelf as well. "If this is going to work, I'll know pretty quickly. I'll come find you when it's done."

Else was sleeping more than she was awake now. This was agony.

Connor, her friend, sat beside her. He was holding her hand, talking to her softly, telling her how much he cared about her, how much he was going to miss her. Rose and Iris sat beside me, and we were all struggling to hold back our tears. One slipped down my cheek, and I quickly dashed it away.

Stan, as always, was her constant, even if she didn't know it, though I wondered if she felt him now. There was a peace in her eyes when she was awake that was impossible to miss, as if she knew he was waiting for her.

Mags opened the door and walked in. I'd left her place two hours ago. Her gaze went from Else to me before she made her way to my side and took the seat beside me. She looked exhausted, dark rings under her eyes and fresh bandages on one of her arms. Whatever she'd done had taken a lot of blood, and she'd drained her power.

"I found my way there," she said quietly. "Not to Death, but there was a demon, Lyle. He said he'd pass on your message."

I sagged in relief and grabbed her hand. "Thank you."

She gave it a squeeze. "Anytime."

A weird pressure built in my chest as I sat there, as if I felt the hours, the minutes and seconds ticking down.

I wasn't leaving in the morning, and I honestly didn't know if I'd ever walk through that gateway ever again.

Chapter Twenty-Six

Zinnia

THE LAST TWO days had been brutal.

I shoved my hand under my pillow and stared out the window. Clouds had gathered throughout the day, and the darkness of the night sky was almost oppressive.

Else wasn't eating, was barely drinking; she'd given up. She was ready to go, but Mags especially was having trouble accepting it. She'd been poring over the healing volumes in the library. Aunt Daisy was constantly baking and cooking, deep in denial, and the rest of us were just trying to squeeze in whatever time we had left with Else, one of the most amazing, stubborn, brilliant, loving females we'd ever met.

I was feeling so many things—guilt, sadness, and, yeah, confusion. I missed Death. Admitting that to myself hadn't been easy. Allowing myself to admit that I had feelings for a god who had a room full of things, treasured possessions from his previous, deceased consorts, felt like a kind of self-harm. What kind of idiot falls for a male who couldn't promise them anything at all, not even life?

What kind of idiot contemplated going back to that?

How could I do it knowing my family was already suffering, knowing they were about to lose Else? Considering leaving, with the possibly of never making it back, was selfish.

Letting myself fall in love with Death was so goddamn selfish.

I clung to my pillow tighter and let my eyes drift closed. I needed him, was desperate to see him, and sleep was the only way, even if it was painful. My lids grew heavy almost immediately; it'd been a long day. I sank into it and invited the darkness in.

The ground was cold, damp against my bare feet, and I shivered. The skull path stretched ahead of me, leading to the castle. Whispers, cries, and screams echoed through the forest. It was dark, and the feeling of dread that surrounded me had me gasping for breath.

I looked down at myself. I was wearing the dress, the black dress Nox had made me wear, the one Death had torn off me. Lifting the skirts, I ran as fast as I could. I rounded the bend, and the castle loomed ahead. A single candle was glowing in a window on the upper level. Death's room.

I ran up the castle stairs and pushed open the entrance doors. Silence greeted me. A stillness filled the massive stone building as if it had been submerged, as if it now sat at the bottom of the Night Sea.

"Mors!" I called his name as I stepped inside.

The floor was cracked by big, jagged fissures that went from one side to the other. Shards of shattered glass and broken furniture littered the ground. No one walked out—no Egon, no Lyle. They were gone; everyone was gone.

Gathering up my dress again, I rushed up the stairs and down the hall to Death's bedroom door. It was closed. I didn't know if the heavy wood was keeping everyone out or keeping him in because I felt a dark energy through it. Dark and filled with fury. I pressed my hand to it. "Mors?"

Nothing, not a sound came from inside.

Hand shaking, I turned the handle and pushed open the door.

I searched the dark room, but I couldn't see him—until my gaze slid to the bed. A shadowy figure lay there, unmoving. "Mors?" Nothing. I stepped closer. "It's me." I reached down and touched his shoulder. "Mors?"

He spun to face me with a feral snarl.

"I'm here," I whispered.

One moment, he was on the bed; the next, he was in front of me, looming over me, backing me up. Light flared, the fire on the other side of the room igniting. He was in his cloak, the hood obscuring half of his face. "You didn't come," he growled. "I waited and you didn't come."

I opened my mouth, but it slammed shut. I tried, but I couldn't open it; I couldn't speak.

Death shook his head. "No more lies from those lips, consort. No more."

My gaze slid over him. His shoulders heaved with his fury. His cloak hung open, revealing a strip of his naked body beneath. His chest and stomach were tight, his cock impossibly hard. I pressed my hand to his chest, over the intricate stars tattooed there, and pleaded with my eyes for him to understand.

He gathered up the front of my dress. "If you won't stay with me, I'll have you here in your dreams. I'll own you here, little witch," he snarled.

I wanted to tell him he could have me. That no matter where I was, I was his and he was mine, but he wouldn't let me speak, too lost in his rage to see, to see me. I let him hook his arm around my waist and pin me to the wall. I wrapped my arms around his neck and hung on tight when he tore my underwear from my body.

"I hate you," he said roughly, "for doing this to me." He nipped my earlobe. "Why did you do this to me?" His voice was a desperate plea. He swung my leg around his hip, and I lifted the other one, hanging on. "Why?" he growled and slammed inside me.

I tried to cry out, but no sound came; all I could do was hold on as he took me, pouring all his pain and rage into me.

"You break me and break me, and I let you." He made a sobbing, gasping sound. "I let you destroy me." He fucked me harder, fisting my hair and tilting my head back. "I won't do this again." He shook his head. "I won't do it."

He thrust into me over and over, nipping, sucking on my skin, my mouth, while he made sounds like a wounded animal, while he fed me his hate and anger and lust and gave me no choice but to take it, not letting me give him anything at all.

I wrapped my arms around him tighter, hanging on, clawing at his back. The darkness surrounded us, and his face shifted, transforming as the shadows gathered, turning him into the God of Death, my god. He slammed into me until there was no holding it back, and I tried, I tried so hard, because I had an awful feeling that when this ended, nothing would be the same again.

He sank his teeth into the side of my throat, and I screamed silently, still unable to make a sound, coming hard around him. My body jarred against the wall, and he thrust into me two more times and came as well, grinding into me until we were both spent.

Finally, he lifted his head, looking down at me, his face nothing but a skull, the blue of his eyes gone, obscured by shadow. "No more," he rasped, and then he stepped back.

My body stayed suspended against the wall, and Death lifted his hands.

"No more," he roared like a wounded beast, then jerked his hands to the side.

My world spun—

I slammed against the mattress, waking with a cry.

I gripped my stomach, my chest, my head. I felt as if I were being torn apart. Tears soaked my cheeks, and I realized my pain wasn't physical. No, what I was feeling was my heart breaking. Everything was a mess; something was happening to Death. That wasn't a dream; it was real, what had happened between us. He was in pain, and I'd caused it.

Someone knocked on my door. "Zinny, it's Else. Quickly, get dressed."

～

We were all in Else's small room. Not everyone that loved her was here—it would be impossible to fit them all in this house—but the people who knew her best, who had been lucky enough to know what it was to be loved, really loved, by her, cared for by her, and fiercely protected by her, were gathered in this room.

The small space was overflowing with so many emotions; there was sadness, of course, but mostly there was love.

Magnolia held one of Else's hands, and Daisy, the other. Stan looked at me, his gaze sliding between me and Jasmine, and he smiled. "*Thank you,*" he said.

We'd been the only people he'd been able to communicate with for so very long, and now he and Else would finally be together again.

I took Jasmine's hand, and we walked forward. I crouched beside the bed, and Jazzy kept hold of my hand. "You know we love you, Else. So much. You were there for us when our own mother couldn't be, so when I tell you this, you have to promise not to be mad at us... or Stanley."

Else took a ragged breath. "Spill."

I brushed my hand over the back of hers, so frail now when she'd always been such strength for us, for all of us. "He made us promise not to tell you, but he's been here, right here, by your side since he died. He's been a friend to me and to Jazzy, a confidant, and an example of what true love looks like, because, goddess... he loves you, so very much. It's so big, Else, so beautiful. He's standing right there"—I motioned to where he stood just in front of us—"and he's been standing there, at your side, for over fifty years. Laughing at your jokes, making eyes at you as if the sun and the moon rose and fell with you, and waiting. Waiting until you could finally be together again."

Jaz came down beside me and gently touched her soft hair. "You have nothing to fear, Else. Not one thing. Stanley will be there to greet you with open arms. You'll be together forever."

A tear slid down her wrinkled cheek. "He's... there?" She looked to the spot beside her.

I nodded.

Another tear slid down her face. "I thought... I-I t-thought he'd gone... but then I felt him. I-I've been..."

Her breathing became more labored, and Jaz and I stepped back to make room for our cousins. Mags climbed onto the bed beside her. Everyone surrounded her. Daisy started the chant, and then, one by one, we all joined in. We were saying words of love, of faith, calling on the mother to usher her safely into the arms of her loved ones. As the words overlapped, they became more a melody than a chant—a song so sweet and so filled with warmth, Else smiled, her gaze moving around the room to everyone here.

Stan stepped forward. "See you on the flip side," he said to me and Jazzy, and then he held out his hand to Else.

Chapter Twenty-Seven

ELSWYTH BEATRIX THORNHEART died at 2:48 a.m., surrounded by her loved ones on a crisp and cloudy winter's night.

Jasmine and I watched her soul rise from her body, and when Stanley greeted her, pulling her into his arms and holding her tight, she transformed, becoming the bold, stunningly beautiful young witch she had once been. Her hair, long and black, hung down her back as she smiled at him.

"She's with Stanley," I said to my aunt and cousins. "She's young again and so incredibly beautiful."

"They're walking away holding hands," Jasmine added with a shaky smile.

We'd spent the rest of the night preparing her body for the burial. We didn't like to wait to return our dead to the earth, to the mother. Everyone that could, made it to the funeral the following day. Nearly all our coven was there, and Connor arrived with a van full of witches from the Coven Elders' Assembly. Numerous council members and nearly everyone from Draven's pack as well as Bram's brothers and their aunt attended. The hounds arrived on their bikes, all dressed in black, and Ren's parents came too. Our cemetery was usually warded, but for today, we'd dropped it to allow everyone in to pay their respects. It was crowded, and the hounds and wolves had offered to make sure no one who shouldn't be there got in or took anything that they shouldn't.

People were still assholes, and the Thornheart cemetery was still one of the most coveted cemeteries in the city and farther afield.

Now, it was late evening, and everyone was gathered in the backyard at Daisy's house. There was a fire, and we were all eating, drinking, and sharing our memories of Else. It was hard to believe she was actually gone. It still didn't feel real.

And I felt so incredibly guilty because I couldn't stop thinking about Death and what happened in my dream just before Else died. Something was terribly wrong. That was no dream. It was him; he'd been with me.

But when I'd finally fallen back into bed in the early hours of the morning, he hadn't come back. I'd wanted to see him again, to talk to him, if he'd let me, but I hadn't dreamed at all. I had this sick, awful feeling inside me that I might never see him again—and I realized that wasn't something I could abide.

I didn't want to give him up, to never see him again, but I didn't want to leave my family either, especially now—and yeah, I sure as hell didn't want to die.

I glanced around the yard, and suddenly I found it hard to breathe. I needed to be alone, to think. I should say goodbye, but instead, I slipped away, down the side of the house, and broke into a run as soon as I reached the street, desperate to release the pressure building inside me, to burn off the awful feeling that wouldn't go away, screaming at me that something was wrong, that Death needed me, that I was making a mistake.

I made it back to Jasmine and Ren's place, but I couldn't bring myself to go inside. The house was empty, but I thought I'd lose my mind if I walked in there, if I went to my room and pretended that this was my life now, that I was fine and that never returning to Limbo was what I wanted. Instead, I sat beneath Jasmine's favorite tree. She loved this spot and sat here all the time. I rested my head against the rough trunk, listening to the insects and the rustle of the spruce trees.

My chest was hollow, so incredibly empty, as if some fundamental part of me had been scooped out, and the only way to feel whole again was to go back—to him. How could that be? How could I actually be considering giving it all up, every part of me, possibly my life, just to be with him again? I shoved my fingers in my hair.

"Do you love him?" Else's words filtered through my mind. *"Okay, let me put it this way, pumpkin, if you dropped that brick wall you've built around yourself, if you forget the other consorts and the visions and the brother and Nox and the kid in stasis and all the other things, if you shove that all aside, and it's just you and him, do you think you could love him?"*

I hadn't been able to answer her then, but it was obvious, wasn't it? Why else would I be torn over this? Why else would the pull to return to him be so strong?

Because I loved him.

So much that I was considering giving up everything—my life —to be with him again.

All of a sudden, holding myself up was too much. My body ached from crying the last two days, and emotionally I was drained. I lay on my side, my hand to the soft grass, and let the vibrations from the earth, from the mother, fill me, trying to let them restore me. Hemlock crawled out of his bag and curled up under my chin, and I closed my eyes, willing the darkness to come, to take me under as I let the exhaustion weigh down my limbs, my head, my stomach and chest, until I felt as if I were becoming one with the earth. I let it surround me in its familiar embrace and soothe the pain.

My eyes drifted closed.

I screamed as pain tore through me.

"That's it, love, push," Death said against my damp hair. "She's nearly here."

I bared down, squeezing his hand, and pushed again as another contraction gripped my rounded belly.

Death grinned, his eyes glistening as he reached between my legs. "One more, Aster."

I pushed hard, delivering our tiny daughter into the protection of her father's hands.

"She's here," he said, wrapping her in the blanket I'd made for her.

He lifted her, placing her on my chest, and I held her carefully as tears of happiness, of contentment and love, filled me. "You're finally here." I kissed her. "Hello, Marigold."

I jolted awake, blinking into the darkness. I didn't move, barely breathed.

"What if they're not visions? What if they're something else?"

Again, Else's words filled my head, and the truth filled my heart.

They weren't visions—they were memories. When I dreamed of them, of the others, I was watching, but now when I dreamed of Aster, I wasn't just looking through her eyes; I *was* her.

As soon as the realization hit me, waves of energy crashed through my body. I cried out as my back arched, bowing against the strength of it.

"Zinnia!"

Jasmine's voice was muffled, drowned out as it all came back. Right from the beginning. In the night sky beside Death, Nox taking him away from me, turning him into flesh and blood. Missing him so much, my light began to dim. Finally being plucked from the sky, Nox standing over me, blood rushing through newly created veins.

Being reunited with Death. I'd been wearing the black gown, the fabric like fine cobwebs and made from night and shadows—the one Death ripped from me when he saw it. Nox had used it to hurt him, to taunt him. And it had, because my soul was connected to his, was created to be at his side.

I saw it all. Me, Death, and Marigold, how happy the three of us were together—but then something happened to me after her birth. I'd been afraid all the time, so very fragile. Nox reached out to me; she was in my ear, in my head, twisting my fragile mind, making me believe Death would hurt our daughter, hurt me.

I'd taken Marigold, and I'd run. Nox's demons had promised to take me to her, but it was only Marigold that Nox wanted. She'd been there the day at the cliffs. She ordered her demons to snatch Marigold from my back. She ordered them to push me over.

Oh goddess, I'd left him. Nox had somehow poisoned my mind, and I'd run from him.

I'd left Death.

I'd taken his daughter, and we'd left him all alone.

Death had raged at me, had been so full of anger toward me, because I'd left him in my first life, and he'd been protective to the point of controlling because he was terrified Nox and her demons would get to me again.

And he was furious because I didn't remember any of it—because I didn't remember him.

My soul had come back, over and over and over—but Death had never opened himself up again. My mind continued to feed me visions, so many all at once. I was staring through their eyes, the females that came after, the females I'd seen in my visions, their lives—their deaths.

In all of them, Death was in his cloak, drowning in darkness and rage, and in all the visions, the females housing my soul cringed away from him.

He never let me back into his heart or his bed—not until now. Not until he found me.

Because Death was mine.

This time, it wasn't just reincarnation; this was rebirth. I'd been given another chance to get it all back, to get the love of my life back, to get my daughter back. Oh goddess, I wanted them back.

Death had been mine almost since the beginning of time. He looked at me, touched me, spoke to me like he knew me, because he did. He'd shown me the cave, the tree house, places we'd spent time loving each other, because he wanted me to remember. He raged at me, sometimes hated me, because I looked at him like a monster, like a stranger, the way I had after I'd given birth to Marigold, after Nox had poisoned my mind, when we'd been everything to each other. Everything.

The world around me rushed back into focus. I was in my room, and Ren was laying me on my bed. Jasmine was leaning over me, eyes wide with fear.

"I'm not hurt," I said and pushed myself up. My heart ached, the feeling of loss unbearable. I missed my consort; I ached for him, and I ached for my child, locked in Death's temple, frozen in time. No, I hadn't birthed her—Aster had—*but I was Aster*. I was his Stella. We were one and the same. I flew out of bed.

"Zinnia? What's going on?"

I loved my sister, and she loved me, but she didn't need me, not anymore. She had Ren now, and as much as leaving her killed me, Death needed me; our daughter needed me. I forced myself to slow down, and I took her face in my hands. "There is so much I want to tell you, but it's... so big, too big. I don't know how. All I can say is, Death loves me so much, Jazzy, and I love him. We belong together. I have to go, and I don't know what happens next, but I might not be able to—"

"Don't say it." She gripped me tight. "I don't want you to leave." Tears welled in her eyes.

I swiped them away. "You're so strong, Jaz. You don't need me anymore." I glanced up at Ren. "You have your own family now."

"I'll always need you," she choked.

"And I'll always need you, and I promise, I'll find a way to reach you. I promise, but my family is waiting for me, and I have to go."

She wrapped her arms around me tight, and I clung to her, pouring a lifetime of love into my baby sister—a lifetime that I might have to miss. "Love you, Jazzy."

"Love you too, Zinny."

I looked at Ren again over her shoulder, and he nodded. He had this. He had her. I didn't need to worry; he would always have her back.

I pressed a kiss to the top of her head. "I need to pack."

"Okay." She smiled shakily. "But before you leave, I have something for you. Something you need to take home with you."

Half an hour later, I was watching Jasmine's car drive away and walking into Oldwood Forest. "Stay hidden," I said to Hemy.

I wasn't sure if Death's protection would still work, so I gripped my knife tight. I heard demons, saw several, but they didn't see me. Either he was expecting me, or he was hoping I'd come. I let that fill me with hope; I needed it, especially after our last encounter in my dreams.

When I walked into the clearing, a demon was sitting there, leaning against a tree near the pile of rocks and boulders that would form the gateway to Limbo. He was playing with his phone, snickering at whatever he was doing.

He didn't look up, didn't see me. With Death's protection surrounding me still, I should be able to walk right up, open it, and walk through, and he wouldn't be any the wiser. I'd seen demons here before—this wasn't unusual—but still I approached cautiously, watching him closely.

The demon, apart from the greenish tinge to his skin, looked fairly humanoid. He tapped something out on his phone with a grin. Still, he gave no sign that he saw me at all. He couldn't; Death had made sure of it. I don't know why I was feeling so anxious. Maybe because I was so close to being back with Death and Marigold that I was terrified something would go wrong.

I made a slice in my palm and lifted my hand to drip my blood onto the rocks and boulders that would form the gateway.

One moment, the demon was by the tree; the next, he'd grabbed my wrist and shoved something cold and hard onto one of my fingers. My blood hit the boulders a moment later, and I yelled the words to open the gate as I swiped my blade at him.

He released my wrist and shoved my hand away, backing up with a smirk. "A gift from Nox."

The gateway opened behind me as I looked down at the tarnished gold band now on my hand and watched in horror as it turned liquid and swirled around my finger, sinking into my flesh, into bone. I screamed as pain shot up my arm.

"Have fun," the demon said before he slammed his foot into my stomach, pushing me through the gateway.

I fell through, hitting the path hard. Cold immediately seeped into me, through me. I lay there, looking around. Something wasn't right. The forest smelled dank, like decay; the air was heavy with it. Mossy strands hung from the trees, and the feeling of dread and sorrow was so thick, it took everything in me not to curl in a ball and give in to it, to sob from the hopelessness that sank deeper inside me. This was what I felt when I first met Death; this was what radiated from him and twisted inside me when I'd first come here. For months, I'd felt this—but somehow, it was worse now, so much worse.

Get up. He needs you.

It physically hurt to move, but somehow, I pulled myself off the ground and got to my feet. Scanning the area, I realized this wasn't the path I usually walked along. This wasn't the way back to Death. I was somewhere else. In Limbo, but somewhere I'd never been before.

My finger throbbed, blood oozing from around the dull gold embedded in my flesh. Shaking out my hand, I grabbed my hunting knife from the ground beside me. Nox, the evil bitch, was the reason I died the first time. She'd stolen our daughter, and then her demons had killed me on her order. I forced myself to walk. Whatever she had in store for me, I would not let her win, not this time. The path ahead seemed endless, and I walked faster, faster, then broke into a run.

I ran and ran for so long, my legs were close to giving out, but I never got anywhere. The same trees, the same path—it all remained the same. I was getting nowhere. Panting, I stopped, looking around me.

Death always warned me to stay on the skull path. Nox wanted me to stray from it. She wasn't giving me any other choice. The goddess was dangerous, especially when she felt threatened, which meant I was close. I was close to breaking whatever curse she had on Death, and she wanted me gone for good.

Well, she wasn't going to win. I would not die, not this time, and I wouldn't abandon Death, not ever again.

Gripping my knife tight, I did the only thing I could. I stepped off the path—

And into a cottage.

The forest was gone, and I was in a room... filled with dolls.

Stumbling back, I knocked one off the shelf. What the actual fuck was this? Everything was pink and frilly, and there were dolls, weird leather-looking dolls, in different colored, lacy dresses covering every surface. Hemy wriggled against me through the bag. "Don't move. Stay where you are until I tell you to come out," I whispered.

He stilled immediately, doing as I said.

The door opened, and a man walked in. He was huge, dressed

in dirty jeans and a grungy navy-and-black flannel shirt like a lumberjack. His gaze sliced to me, eyes widening.

I held up my hands. "I'm sorry. I'm not sure how I got here—"

"Who are you? Why are you with my babies?" he said, eyeing me suspiciously. "You can't have them," he yelled. "You can't have them!"

Chapter Twenty-Eight

Death

I'D WAITED at the gateway for fucking hours, feet rooted to the ground, willing it to open, for Zinnia to walk through.

But she hadn't come.

Gripping the edge of the window, I took in the forest below the castle. The decay was setting in, my despair turning Limbo back into the desolate, cold, and joyless nothing it had been before I finally found her and brought her home.

As I'd stood at the gateway, I'd told myself that maybe she got the days mixed up or the date, maybe she was hurt and couldn't make it. Night had turned to day, then back to night as the shadows swirled thicker around me, calling me back to darkness.

I'd finally forced myself to walk away, to come back to the castle, and I'd done the only thing I could, something I'd done more than once since she left this time, something I hated doing—I'd used Somnus to find her.

Zinnia hadn't been hurt—she just hadn't chosen me.

In my despair, I'd lain there, willing her to come, to me, to join me in the Dream Realm, and she had. She'd come to the castle, come to my room, and I'd taken her like a fucking monster, taking everything I could from her one last time. I hadn't let her talk, and I'd fed off her warmth, the feel of her skin, the smell of her hair, like a fucking leech. I'd absorbed it all—and then I'd released her.

I didn't want to hear her apologies or her regrets. I didn't want to hear the reasons she wouldn't be returning, so I hadn't given her the option.

Never again.

I couldn't do this again.

My Stella's soul was always meant to be with me, but only someone powerful and loyal and prepared to sacrifice it all to be with me could draw me from the cloak. Someone without fear. I thought Zinnia was that female; I believed it with everything in me. I still did, but that didn't matter if she didn't want me. I knew what would happen next if I'd kept her here. I knew what happened next because I'd seen it. I'd held the limp, bleeding, poisoned bodies in my hands. I'd buried them.

Still, before the darkness took me completely, before I let her go forever and my world went back to the cold and empty void it was before I brought Zinnia here, I had to be close to her just one more time. Just once more.

Striding down the hall, I walked into Somnus's room. My brother lay there peacefully. He let me use his power to reach her; he had for centuries. I was the only being he allowed near him while he slumbered after all he'd been through. I didn't want to use him again this way, but this would be the last time. The very last.

Lying on the bed beside my brother, I wrapped my hand around his, closed my eyes, and let the dreaming in.

Darkness swam around me, a whirlpool of images and sounds flashing past. I knew where to find Zinnia. As soon as Somnus told me she existed, finding her here had been as easy as breathing.

But this time, I was met with an empty void. Nothingness. As if she didn't exist anymore.

I knew this feeling from when she'd concealed herself from me the first time.

She'd done it again. She'd locked me out.

I roared into the void, the last tendrils of hope sinking to the bottom of the ocean of dreams around me, into the darkest depths, and vanishing without a trace. I sank with them, swallowed by the dark, unforgiving waves, letting the cold soak into my bones.

Mors sucked in his last gasping breath, filling his lungs with putrid water, until only Death remained.

Zinnia

"I don't want your, ah... babies," I said as the shock and alarm in his eyes turned to something else, something that made me try to step back once more, only to hit the shelf of dolls behind me again.

"Who sent you? You can't have them. They're mine. *They're mine!*" He swung wildly, taking me by surprise. His fist connected with the side of my head, and my legs gave out.

Everything went dark.

I woke tied to a chair in only my underwear, with odd shapes drawn all over me in permanent marker. I pulled at the ropes biting into my wrists and ankles, but they were too tight. This was his Limbo. This room or house of dolls and horror was the lumberjack's Limbo, and somehow, I'd just walked into it.

The chair scraped as I tried to fight my way out of my ropes while I frantically searched the room for Hemy. I couldn't get free. Panting, I looked down at one of the shapes, this one drawn on my thigh, the rest all butting up against one another as if he was trying to fit in as many of them on my available skin as possible. It kind of reminded me of when Daisy would sew. She'd lay out her piece of fabric and pin the pattern onto it, moving the thin tissue around to fit each piece as best as she could, so as not to waste any of her fabric. My gaze sliced around the room, and I took a better look at the dolls.

Oh fuck. They weren't made of leather—they were made of skin.

They were all made of *skin*.

This was some fucked-up *Silence of the Lambs* shit, and Nox had offered me up to the lumberjack so he could add to his doll collection. *Fucking bitch.* Hemy tore out from under my clothes in a pile on the floor, running to me. Thank the goddess he was okay.

Humming came from the next room, and so did footsteps moving around on a hardwood floor. He was about to come back in here and carve me up. I fought harder, trying to wriggle my hands out of the rope strapping them to the arms of the chair. I couldn't get free. "Fuck this. Stay back," I said to Hemy. My feet were on the floor, and I rocked forward, standing at a weird bent-over angle then, and ran back, crashing hard against the wall. One of the legs snapped. I slammed into the wall a second time as the door opened. More of the chair broke away. The lumberjack stormed in, carrying a massive knife.

"No!" he yelled, running at me.

I spun around as he reached me, slamming the broken chair into him with all my strength. He fell, and I crashed down on top of him. The chair collapsed completely, what was left of it breaking apart. I quickly rolled away and jumped to my feet, shaking off the now-loose ropes and broken wood.

The big male rolled to his hands and knees to get up.

"Hemy!" I called, spun, and ran from the room. Hemy darted ahead, leading me through the house, where more skin dolls filled every available space, to the dining room and down a long hall.

The lumberjack pounded after me, the knife still in his hand. "Come back," he yelled. "Come back."

Like fuck. Hemy led me into a kitchen.

A door.

The lumberjack exploded into the room behind me, and I dove for the door, twisting the handle, and threw myself out—

And hit a stone floor.

I was dressed again, and Hemlock was back in his bag. I tugged up my sleeve. The patterns on my skin were gone. I turned slowly, taking in the room. A TV was going on the opposite side, big couches were scattered around, and there was a pool table.

I was in the hellhounds' den, belowground in the common room. It looked a little different, but that's exactly where I was.

Scrambling off the floor, I gripped my knife. This was supposed to throw me off, make me drop my guard, but that wasn't happening.

"Who the fuck are you?" a deep, rough voice growled.

I spun around. A huge male with long hair and a scruffy beard stood there. Most definitely a hellhound.

His head tilted to the side, eyes narrowing. "Willow?"

I shook my head. "Her cousin. Zinnia." I gripped my knife tighter. "And who the fuck are you?"

He grinned, flashing white teeth and fangs. "Axton, a good friend of your cousin, and the alpha's right hand."

Chapter Twenty-Nine

THE MASSIVE HOUND was watching me closely.

I had no idea how long he'd been in Limbo, but I'd never heard anyone talk about him. The hounds spoke of the brothers they'd lost, but no one had ever mentioned a male named Axton. Because they were created by Lucifer; once their bodies were burned, their life force should automatically go back to Hell. At least, that was the way it was supposed to work.

"Why are you here?" I asked him.

Nox had sent me here, to this hound, for a reason. Most likely to disarm me, maybe get me to drop my guard. Hellhounds were protective of females; they always said themselves that they worshipped them, which was why I'd been so surprised by the way Relic had treated that demon. It was so far out of character for him, for any hellhound.

His jaw worked. "I lost my head, sweetheart," he said, voice deep. "But none of my brothers were around to burn my body, so my life force was trapped here instead of going home." His shoulders kind of slumped. "Now I'm stuck here, walking around this fucking replica of our den alone."

Not only was that awful, it made logical sense as to why he was here. "I'm sorry," I said and meant it. Maybe Nox thought I'd feel so sorry for the hellhound, it would stop me in my tracks, or the comfort of the familiar would slow me down. She was wrong. Nothing would stop me. "I'm so sorry that happened to you, and if you tell me where your body is, maybe I'll be able to get a message back to War when I get out of here. They can find it, burn it. Free you from this place."

A smile transformed his handsome face. "You'd do that for me?" Like all the hounds, there was something compelling about him. They were all handsome in their own way.

"Of course. War's family, and that makes you family."

A roar came from behind him, followed by cheers and howls.

I lifted my knife. "What the hell is that? I thought you were here alone?"

His fingers curled into fists. "I am. But I can still hear them. Death taunts me. He lets me hear my brothers, but I can never find them."

That was torture. "I'll talk to Death. I'll ask him to make this more bearable for you until I can get my message to War."

"You have Death's ear?"

"I did... hopefully, I still do." Hopefully, he hadn't given up on me completely. I just needed to get to him. "I'm sorry you're stuck here like this, but I have to leave."

He shoved his fingers through his hair. "I get it... can you just... will you stay for a little while? I'm... I'm so lonely, Zinnia. So fucking lonely."

This male was War and Relic's brother; they loved him, no doubt missed him terribly. Maybe they didn't know he was dead? Maybe they just thought he'd left or was in Hell, serving Lucifer. The hounds all took turns controlling the demons there, spending time between Hell and Roxburgh. Whatever had happened, my heart ached for him. "Maybe... just for a little while."

His expression lightened, his smile returning.

"I can't stay long, though."

He nodded. "Of course." His gaze slid to the couch. "Can we just sit on the couch? I'm not trying to be a creep. I just want to feel someone close. I haven't been touched by another being in... in so long. Not trying to cop a feel, Zinnia. I just want a hug, yeah?"

Everything he'd told me was plausible, and with what I knew of the hounds, their feelings about females and their unwavering loyalty, I truly didn't think he wanted to hurt me. Hounds were devoid of certain emotions, but they were extremely tactile; they liked touch, needed it. It would've been torture for Axton without it and without his brothers. Yes, Nox was trying to slow me down, and staying here with Axton was playing right into her hands, but I could spare him ten minutes before I left. "Okay then."

He took a shuddery breath. "Thank you," he said, the sincerity in his voice clear. He walked to the couch, looking awkward, and it pulled at my heart strings.

So I sat and waved him forward. He closed the space between us and sat beside me; then he slid down, resting his head on my lap, and wrapped his arms around my middle with a sigh.

"Better?" I rubbed his back, and light glinted off the gold wrapped around my finger. It'd stopped bleeding, but it hurt like hell. It wasn't hard to work out that whatever it was had me trapped in this limbo loop. I just needed some time—time not being chased by insane lumberjacks or emotionally propping up lonely hellhounds—to figure out how to get it off.

"Fuck, this is... I needed this, thank you," he rasped.

"No problem." I gasped a little when he tightened his arms around me.

"Sorry," he muttered. "So have you spent much time at the clubhouse?"

"Yeah, when I'm in Roxburgh. Willow and War have a

daughter now, and Wills has these movie nights for the hounds and anyone who wants to come along."

"Yeah?"

"Yeah, and Relic is a really good friend."

He snorted.

"What?"

"Relic's a piece of shit."

I blinked down at him, confused. The hounds didn't do that; they didn't talk shit about one another. They had disagreements, sure, but I'd never heard them say shit about each other, not like that. "You didn't get along?"

"Relic, like the others, thinks the sun shines out of the alpha's ass."

"You and War didn't get on? I thought you were his right hand?"

He shrugged. "Maybe I exaggerated. I should've been alpha."

Unease slid through me.

Axton's eyes drifted shut, and he breathed deep. He made a low groan, then breathed in again.

He was scenting me.

I glanced down, and my unease increased. His dick was straining against the zipper of his jeans. *Fuck.* Something was seriously wrong here. He was lying to me. If the hounds lost one of their own, if he was damaged beyond the possibility of healing, they'd find him and burn him and send him home. They were the best trackers around. I was an idiot. Why didn't I think of that? I'd looked at him, and I'd seen Relic and War and the other males I cared about; I imagined what it would have been like for one of them. If the hounds wanted to send him back to Hell, they wouldn't have stopped looking for him until they found him.

"Haven't been with a female in a long time, Zinnia. You know we need it. Making a hound go without fucking for as long as I have is the worst kind of torture. You'll let me fuck you, won't you? You'll be my bitch and get on all fours, won't you, witch?"

Fear sliced through me, but I made myself breathe easy. I had to play this carefully. "I'm Death's consort. He wouldn't like it if I was with anyone else."

He chuckled. "If you're his, then why are you here? Why hasn't he come for you? Nah, that's not it. You afraid of how big I am? A lot of females are. You'll only cry for a little while, but then I'll stretch you out, and you'll be fine."

I wanted to vomit. Now I knew why he was here. War had sent him here. "I have to admit, I've always wanted to sleep with a hound. Do you promise to be careful? At least to start with?"

He reached down and squeezed his hard-on. "Sure. I'll go easy if you let me call you Willow. You look like her with all that red hair. Been wanting to fist that hair for a long fucking time."

Fuck. Warrick most definitely sent him here on purpose.

"A bit weird for me, but sure, whatever floats your boat," I said. "Do you mind if I take a shower first? I've been traveling, so I feel pretty gross."

"I like you all dirty," he said roughly.

"I'll be quick."

He sat up, his fingers wrapping around my throat. "You try anything, and you'll pay, understand, Willow?"

"I understand, Ax—"

"War. You call me War or Warrick from now on."

Fuck. Fuck. Fuck. "Okay, War."

He smiled. "You know where my quarters are?"

I nodded.

"Shower, then get in bed on all fours and wait for me."

I nodded again.

He released me, and I got off the couch and forced myself not to run for the door.

"In case you were wondering, the stairs that lead out of the den aren't there," he said and grinned before I could walk through it. "Just in case you were wondering."

I shrugged. "Nope." What the fuck was I going to do? As I

rushed down the hall, howls and cheers echoed around me, as if more hounds were here. It sounded so real. I broke into a run. Hemy poked his head out of the bag, a little hiss leaving him, sensing the danger.

"I'll get us out of here. I will," I said to him.

There had to be another way out. I didn't know why, but I ran toward those howls, the familiar sounds of the hounds I knew and loved. They led me to a pit. Willow had told me about it—a place where they trained, blew off steam, or settled any disagreements.

My feet paused at the door as a scene played out before me. Warrick and Axton were in the pit, and it was surrounded by hounds. Ren was there, and Willow as well. They looked so real, but when I tried to touch one of them, my hand went right through.

Warrick advanced, fisted Axton's hair, and dragged him to the edge of the pit, smashing his face into the charred packed-earth wall. Axton dropped to his hands, and War yanked his head back again.

The bravado had dropped from Axton's face, and he shook his head. "No... please, Alpha..."

"Fucking coward," Lothar said to Willow.

"I'll leave... I'll never come back," Axton said.

Warrick stared down at him. "You attacked my female, you made her bleed, and then you dared to challenge me. The former alone is enough for me to put you to death, and the latter you walked into willingly, knowing exactly what the consequences of defeat were."

"No... please..."

War snapped the other male's neck, then pulled a knife from his boot and hacked off his head.

"Jesus," Willow said.

"If he doesn't take his head, he could survive. We heal from most injuries," Jagger said to her.

The hounds gathered around the pit and lifted their hands

palms up. Flames danced across their skin, licking over their thick fingers.

Warrick shook his head, and silence filled the room.

The hounds lowered their gazes as they curled their fingers into fists, extinguishing their fires. "What's going on?" Willow asked Jagger.

"Burning him would send him back to Hell. Leaving his body to rot means he will be in eternal limbo."

"I didn't think you had souls?"

"We don't, it's more our... life force, our essence, for want of a better term."

War met his brothers' eyes, one by one, rage rolling off him. "You lay your hands on my female, you dare touch what's mine, and I will fucking end you. You challenge me for head of this pack, you enter the pit prepared to fight to the death. You'll get no mercy here."

Growls and grunts of approval echoed around them.

Axton had attacked Willow and challenged War. If it were the challenge alone, he wouldn't be here, but attacking Willow had been his fatal mistake.

The scene flickered, and it started all over again, the cheers and howls filling the room.

I ran back the way I came, searching my mind, trying to remember everything Willow had said about the den. There would be another way out of here; there had to be.

Then I remembered something. When Wills was telling me about how she and War first got together, she told me about a door in Warrick's room that led up to the clubhouse that females would knock on, trying to get him to let them in. It had to be the way out.

Axton would be coming for me soon, so I had to be quick. I sprinted to War's quarters and shut myself in, throwing the bolt after me. It was heavy, strong, made to give a hellhound pause, but it wouldn't hold for long. Spinning back, I took in the room. This was how it was before War renovated, before he opened it up, combining several rooms for him, Wills, and Violet. Which meant less for me to search, thank fuck. I scanned every inch of exposed wall, but there was no door. Had all the doors been taken? Was that the real reason Nox had sent me here, because there was no way out?

There was a tall dresser against the wall; it looked built-in, but it was definitely big enough to cover a door. I rushed over, running my hands around the edge. Not built-in. I tried to shift it.

The door handle rattled. "Let me in, Willow," Axton said.

"Just a minute... War. I want everything perfect for you," I called back and threw my back into it. The dresser scraped against the floor. Hemlock hissed again, scurrying out of my bag and onto my shoulder.

"What are you doing in there?" he called.

Yes! A door. Thank fuck. "I'm making it nice. Now be patient," I called back, doing my best impersonation of Willow.

I shoved again, and it scraped forward some more.

"Open the fucking door. Now, Willow!" he roared and smashed against the heavy wood.

I dragged the dresser forward a bit more, enough for me to squeeze in behind. He crashed against the charred wood again, trying to break in. I tried the handle, but the door was locked. Cursing, I pulled out my knife and worked on the hinges while Axton roared and continued to slam against the door. Thank fuck it was made by hounds; any other door would have buckled instantly.

I got the first hinge out, and then the second came easily, but the last was wedged tight. I dug my blade in and smacked my palm against the handle of my knife over and over.

The door crashed open behind me as the last hinge gave. Hemy shrieked and hissed, and I slammed my shoulder into the door, and it dropped as the dresser went flying.

Axton roared and reached for me as I fell through—

My hands landed on damp grass. It was night, a false moon

lighting the area enough that I could still see everything clearly. I was in a small clearing, surrounded by trees. Hemlock was on the grass beside me, and I scooped him up. "It's okay," I said and stood —bumping against something behind me. An iron gate. One that I'd seen before.

A shriek echoed through the trees, and then another one. The same sounds I'd heard when I'd seen Death with the undead.

Only this time, I was on the wrong side of the gate.

I slid my knife free, gripping it tight as more shrieks filled the night. There was movement in the shadows, slow, awkward movement. They were coming. Then, one by one, they shuffled forward. There were three of them, and as they got closer and I got a better look at them, flashes of memory assaulted me.

I knew them from my visions. They'd each housed my soul at some point—the females who had cringed away from Death when he'd brought them to the castle. He'd sensed my soul, but it hadn't been enough. For some reason, they hadn't been enough to draw him from the cloak.

They'd all suffered, never content, never complete, sad, alone, confused, always pining for something, for someone, and not knowing what it was. It was Death. He was the missing piece, but they never saw him, they never got to see beneath the cloak, and without him, they'd ended their own lives full of despair, and Death's hope had been shattered over and over again. He blamed himself, his guilt unbearable.

"Whether you return to me or not, the choice is yours, little witch. But I'm begging you... choose me over everything and everyone, over a life with them, over the possibility of death here with me."

"Choose me."

Death didn't see the shell, not really; he saw my soul, the only thing that could make him whole again, make us both whole again. I'd been with him since almost the dawn of time, taken from him over and over again. Then when he'd finally found me and I'd drawn him from the cloak, from the shadows, and he'd allowed himself to hope—I hadn't recognized him. I hadn't remembered the love we shared.

He'd been waiting, hoping I'd remember, but I hadn't.

Until now.

I looked up at the females around me. Empty shells somehow still here, trapped, probably until I broke Nox's curse.

This was torture.

I remembered every tragic life these females had led—that *I* had led.

There was only one way to end this, for them and me. I had to get to Death.

"It's time to set you free," I choked, pressing my hand into the grass and placing the tip of my blade to the base of my gold-wrapped finger. Gritting my teeth, I thrust the knife down on it with force—slicing my finger off with a cry.

Everything paused; the females blinked at me, not moving. Hemy squeaked, and then the world around me shifted—

I was back on the skull path, just inside the gateway.

Quickly grabbing a shirt from my pack, I tore it into strips and wrapped the bleeding stump where my finger had been; then I started down the path. This was the way home, finally. I recognized the forest, but it looked as dark and desolate as it had when I first arrived, and it felt the same as well. The horror and pain, the despair, it was all I could do to keep walking.

Hemy emerged from my pack, then scurried back in, feeling what I did.

We rounded the bend, and the castle came into view. It was like I was living out the dream I'd had. I walked quicker, breaking into a run, taking the steps to the main doors two at a time, shoving them open.

The air was punched from my lungs. It was dark and cold, a mess of broken furniture—and the floor was cracked from one side to the other.

Movement caught my eye. Egon. He lifted his head from

where he sat in the shadows. He stared at me as if I were a hallucination.

"Egon?"

He jolted and shot to his feet. "My lady?"

"Where is he?"

"You've been gone... so very long." He shook his head. "It's too late. He's... my lord is not the male you left."

An awful feeling crawled through me. "How long? How long have I been gone?"

"In human time?"

I stilled. "Yes."

Sympathy filled his eyes. "Twelve months."

I rocked back, grabbing onto the broken table so I didn't fall down. "Twelve months? I've been gone a full year?" I choked, shaking my head. "I was here."

Egon twisted his fingers in front of himself. "He couldn't feel you... you were gone. He thought..." His gaze dropped to my forearm, where my scar was, where the tattoo the demon had given me to hide from Death had once been.

He thought I'd hidden from him? *Oh goddess, no.* "Is he in his room?" I choked.

The demon glanced up to the second floor. "It's too dangerous."

I took off, running up the stairs, ignoring Egon calling after me, and moved along the shadowed hall to his door. A year? How could that be? Flinging the door open, I rushed inside. It was dark, the air stale. It smelled like actual death. Like a corpse had been left to rot away to nothing, and now only bones and dust remained.

"Mors?" I rasped, walking deeper into the room, using his name that he'd forbidden me to use for so long because it hurt, it hurt to hear it from me when I didn't remember who he was.

Nothing.

I didn't need to search the room; I knew exactly where he was. He was on the bed, draped in his cloak, unmoving.

Biting my lip, I moved to his side. "I'm here. I've come back to you," I choked out.

Nothing.

"Mors."

His cloak swirled.

"Please, look at me."

Slowly, he lifted his head, then turned to me.

His hood slipped back, and I swallowed down a cry of agony. His face was skin stretched over bone. There was barely anything left of him.

Then he opened his mouth and roared.

Chapter Thirty

Zinnia

THE FORCE of his rage had me cowering, his roar so loud, the windows rattled. The sounds of the forest went silent.

He stared blindly ahead, not seeing me, so lost in his despair and rage, he saw nothing else.

"It's me, Zinnia... your Stella," I choked out. "Mors, it's me."

He blinked, his gaze clearing just for a moment.

I cupped his skeletal face. "I came back."

One of his hands snapped out, and he caught me by the throat, his face contorting. "You left," he said, his voice rolling through the room like thunder, lifting the hair on the back of my neck.

I shook my head. "I'm right here. Your beloved. Look at me, please. I'm right here."

He snarled, his head moving in an odd way before he lurched forward, yanked me onto the bed, and shoved me down. I lay still while he loomed over me, searching my face, his features contorted in rage. "Stupid little witch," he said in a voice that sent ice down my spine. "You should never have come back here, because I will never let you leave. Whatever deal we had is void." There was nothing but rage in his voice.

He had completely reverted to the male he was when I first came here—I felt it—but worse. He was so hollow, like a husk of himself. Mors was buried deep beneath the surface, and Death was fully in the driver seat.

I reached up to touch his face again. "Mors—"

"Do not call me that," he snarled. "I am the God of Death."

"And I am your consort," I said softy. "Yours."

He shook his head. "You never came back."

"I did. I'm right here. You have to believe me. I came back, but—"

One moment, he was looming over me; the next, he was up, hauling me off the bed. He slammed open the door, dragged me down the hall and into my old room. "Stay out of my way." He shoved me inside and walked away, leaving me to be forgotten like the others, so deep in the cloak, so deep in denial.

I wasn't giving up; I would bring him back. He said he'd let the cloak take him if I left, but the darkness and shadows couldn't have him. He was mine.

I grabbed the dresser to hold myself up, a rush of dizziness making my limbs weak.

"My lady?"

Egon stood at the door, his face etched in concern. I held up my hand. "I've lost some blood. How good are you with a needle and thread?"

Color drained from his face. "You're injured. Sit. I'll return momentarily."

Sitting heavily on the bed, I rubbed my hand over my face. I needed rest for the fight ahead. I would bring him back one battle at a time until I won the war. I had to; anything else was unacceptable.

Egon rushed back in with his basket of healing supplies, and I carefully unwrapped my hand.

The demon gasped. "What happened?"

"I cut it off. It was the only way to get back to him," I said, pain radiating up my entire arm. "There's some balm in my pack. Use it after you sew it up."

Egon nodded, mixing a tincture with a sedative and antibiotic herbs to prevent infection. He handed it to me, and I gulped it back, then lay down and gave in to the tiredness. I was back. I'd made it back to him.

I woke in the early hours of the morning drenched in sweat and shivering. The tincture hadn't worked. Egon had sewn me up and used the balm, but my hand was tight, obviously swollen. Infection had set in, and I had a fever. I struggled to regain consciousness, but it was impossible.

"My lady?" Egon was sitting beside the bed. He quickly got up and lifted my head, spooning a tonic into my mouth. I felt him unwrap my hand, checking it; then the scent of Else's healing balm reached me, and I instantly missed her again. Tears welled in my eyes before the tiredness took over again.

Death

Noises were coming from downstairs. Banging and crashing and talking. Shoving myself up off the bed, I strode to the door and flung it open. Whoever the fuck was disturbing my peace would pay with their head.

I reached the bottom of the stairs and stopped, surprised at what I saw.

Egon had ignored my order to leave the castle as it was and to remove himself and leave me here alone to rot.

Instead, he'd allowed more people into my home, and they were cleaning the destruction I'd caused in the main room and, by the sounds of it, in several other parts of the castle as well. "Egon," I roared.

Egon rushed by, ignoring me, carrying a bowl full of something strong smelling.

I grabbed his shoulder, stopping him, fighting back the savage rage that lived inside me now, that had returned stronger than ever before. "What the fuck are you still doing here? And why are all these people in my home? I want everyone gone." I wanted to be left alone.

He looked up at me stubbornly. The demon had been with me for centuries, and never once in all that time had he given me so much as a look of defiance, but that was what I was looking at now. "Do not test me, demon. You will do as you are told."

Egon squared his shoulders. "I will not. Her ladyship is unwell. I won't leave her in that state, and I will not allow her to live in squalor."

Every muscle in my body seized, razor blades eviscerating my insides. *Her ladyship?* A snarl was torn from me. "Do not mention her in my presence again. She made her choice. You are delusional. That female is never returning, now leave."

Egon blinked up at me several times. "Are you so deep in darkness that you do not know a dream from reality? She has returned. She returned last night." He rushed past. "Come and see for yourself if you don't believe me."

He was wrong. It was only a dream. She came home in my dreams, in my fucking nightmares. I had them every night. I shook my head, trying to clear it. Was I still asleep? Was this some sick trick of my warped mind? I shook my head again, forcefully, but I didn't wake, because I already was. And even though I tried to resist because what he said wasn't true, it couldn't be true, I stormed after Egon, up the stairs and to her old room—where I'd thrown her last night, *in a fucking dream.*

The door was open, and Egon was murmuring softly. "Please swallow, my lady. You need to drink this."

I rounded the door—and an invisible fist slammed into my chest. "No... it was a dream," I choked. "I'm still dreaming."

"It is not," Egon said. "Now help me. She's fighting an infection, and she's far too hot. I need you to hold her up so I can feed her some of my tonic."

I grabbed for the door as my legs buckled beneath me. She was here. She was in her bed, in my castle.

I didn't trust this. How could I trust this? "What the fuck is this? Why is she here now?"

"You will have to ask her that yourself, but if you don't help me now, she may die. She's strong, but we could still lose her. So either stand there and stare and let her die, or get over here and help me."

I lurched forward, and my throat grew so fucking tight, I was struggling to breathe. "Where is she hurt?"

Egon motioned her bandaged hand. "She lost a finger," he said as I carefully lifted her head for Egon to spoon some of his tonic into her mouth.

"How?"

"She cut it off herself with an unwashed blade. She said she did it to get back to you."

I stared down at her, desperately trying to swallow. A snarl curled my lip in disbelief even as my heart thumped hard in my chest. "This is a lie."

Egon growled, surprising me again. "She is right there, my lord. In your arms. You have lost her so many times—I was here with you, and I know what that did to you—but, my lord, this time, she has returned. She came back..." He swallowed audibly. "She chose you."

∼

Zinnia

I blinked up into Death's emaciated face. My sight swam, and my body ached. He stared at me, gaze hard. He took my wounded hand in his and lifted it. I tried to speak, to say something, but I was too damn weak. Then my eyelids were too heavy, and I let them slide shut.

When I woke again, a scream pierced the room. It went on and on. I wanted it to stop, but then I realized the scream was coming from me. Stabbing pain radiated through my body, and my limbs were so heavy, and I was so hot, so incredibly hot. I kicked at the covers. The T-shirt I was wearing was soaked, plastered to my skin. Egon was there; he held a straw to my lips, and I drank the cool water before my vision went dark and I was submerged again.

The next time I woke, I was so cold, my teeth chattered. I was in water. There was something hot against my back, surrounding me. The cold water stung so badly, I sobbed and begged for it to stop. A deep voice rolled over me. It was comforting, insistent, but the cold remained. They held me in the water until I thought I might die.

My eyes blinked open again. It was dark, the fire crackling and flickering across the room, bathing it in a muted orange glow. I was in my room at the castle. Lifting my hand, I looked at the bandages and wriggled the fingers I still had. The swelling had gone down. I'd beaten the infection.

"How do you feel?"

My head twisted to the chair beside me. I couldn't see him, but Death sat there, watching me from the shadows. "A lot better."

"Any pain?"

"Nothing I can't handle." The stabbing pain through my body was still there—no, not as sharp as before, but still very much there. I wasn't going to tell Death that, though, not yet. To him, I'd been gone a year. He felt betrayed, abandoned. I didn't want him to hold back or hide what he was feeling because he was concerned for me or thought me still in the throes of a fever and confused.

"Why are you here?" he asked coldly.

I pushed myself up. It was hard, but again, I refused to show him any weakness in this moment. "I'm here because this is where I belong, with my consort."

He went utterly still. "You expect me to believe you suddenly woke up one morning and decided you wanted to be with me?"

His voice was deep and broken and chilled me to the bone. I shifted under the covers so I was facing him, even though I still couldn't see his face. "To you, I've been gone a year. For me, only a month and eight days have passed since I left here."

"Is that right?"

He didn't believe me. "Yes." I slid my legs out from under the covers and pressed my feet to the cool stone floor. "I sent you a message that I'd be late. Magnolia said she got through to Lyle."

"I received no message, witch."

"Else was dying. I couldn't leave her or my family, so I stayed until she passed." I slid to the edge of the bed. "The night of her funeral... I finally learned the truth."

"What truth?" he said harshly.

"I lay in a field after her burial, and I slept." I eased off the bed. "I had visions of you... of us..." I swallowed, emotion clogging my throat. "All the things you wanted to tell me but couldn't. That you desperately wanted me to remember—"

"Lies," he snarled.

I ignored him and kept talking. "I was in the night sky... but then you left me all alone, and I missed you so much. Nox created me. She gifted me to you. We were so happy. I saw my belly swollen with our daughter, saw you take her in your arms when I gave birth to her." I stepped closer. "I remember, Mors. I remember everything. Every single life I had without you after that because I didn't know, because I didn't remember that you and Marigold are *everything* to me." I closed the space between us and reached into the shadows of his cloak, cupping his hollow face. "Every time I didn't choose you." I moved in between his legs. "But I know now, I remember, and I choose you, my love—"

He snarled and snatched my hand away from his face. Gripping my wrist, he stood. He backed me up until we stood in front of the fire. I didn't fight as he gripped my jaw and stared deep into my eyes. No, I wanted him to see the truth, to see me. His hand curled around the back of my head and his face went to my throat. I held still as he pressed his nose to my skin and dragged it up, breathing deep.

My pulse raced wildly. "Death..."

He pulled away suddenly, flinching, and a look transformed his face, like he'd been sucker-punched—pain, sharp and fierce filled his eyes, followed by brutal disappointment—then rage. "You are a liar, an imposter." He bared his teeth. "When I look into your hollow eyes, now that I finally can, I see nothing. I feel nothing. You don't even smell like Zinnia." His mouth twisted. "It's a good likeness, I'll give you that. You almost had me fooled there for a moment. Nox outdid herself this time, but you have no soul, creature. You're an imposter—"

"I'm not an imposter. I have a soul... It's me—"

"Zinnia has been gone an entire year. She left, she concealed herself from me, and she ran."

"I was trapped going from one damned soul to the next, trapped in the worlds you created for them. I couldn't get out—"

"Lies," he roared again. "You are one of Nox's creatures sent to torment me."

He searched my eyes again, and hatred flashed down at me. He truly didn't see me; something was stopping him from *seeing me.*

"Egon," Death yelled.

The demon open the door. "My lord?"

"Choose four demons to escort Nox's creature back to her. I won't have her here."

"But, my lord—"

"Do as I say."

"I won't do it," he said.

Death snarled and flung his hand out, slamming the door and shutting Egon out. I stared up at Death, begging him to see me. "How do I know everything I just told you? How can I know those things if I'm something Nox created?"

"Nox knows exactly what happened, and she has spies everywhere, as you well know," he bit out.

"You're wrong," I said, trying to pull from his hold. "Look at me."

He shook me brutally. "All I see when I look at you is a lie. Be thankful I don't just end you here and now. The only reason I'm letting you live is so you can deliver a message."

"What message?"

"She will never win." Then he dragged me to the door, flung it open, towed me along the hall and down the stairs. There was a group of demons sweeping the floor, and Death ordered them to come to him.

Four of them rushed over, and Death shoved me at them. "Take her to the Night Realm and deliver her to Nox. I want her gone tonight."

They instantly obeyed, towing me from the main room in only a T-shirt and underwear, my feet bare and fresh blood oozing from my bandage.

I called for Mors, but he did nothing, he said nothing.

He let them take me.

The demons dragged me from the castle and into the night.

Chapter Thirty-One

Death

I STOOD OUTSIDE, listening to the sounds of the night. There had been no light here for a year, only darkness. My realm was part of me, and I felt as black and cold inside as it was out here.

Nox lived to cause me pain. How could you despise your children so much? I would give anything to have Marigold with me, to end the curse my twisted bitch of a mother put on me and have her back. Sometimes, just the thought of my daughter shattered me into a million pieces. If it weren't for Somnus taking care of her, I would have lost my mind long ago.

But that wasn't enough for Nox; no, she wanted to destroy me in every way possible. Her curse had blocked Zinnia's soul from remembering me, from remembering us and our life together, and had bound Magnolia to her realm.

Surrounded by her demons, Nox sat in her temple plotting ways to fuck with me. She'd even gone as far as creating a soulless creature to impersonate the only female I had ever wanted—the

278

mother of my child—and make me think the end of the curse was near, that I could have my family back with me like we'd once been.

Another god more malicious and evil didn't exist.

I strode back inside, and even though I told myself not to, I stopped at Zinnia's bedroom door. My Zinnia. When I first saw her when she was only fifteen years old, something had reached through the shadows and tugged sharply. Her soul had been back many times before. Somnus would find her, would take me to her, and I'd bring them back to the castle. But none of them had been able to reach me; they'd cringed away in fear, in horror. And I'd stayed in the shadows, trapped in darkness.

Zinnia wasn't just a vessel for her soul; she and Aster were one and the same. Zinnia hadn't been second best or a replacement for the female I'd lost; she *was* my beloved. And somehow, I loved her more now than I ever had. My soul had ached for hers. We were meant to walk side by side, but again, she'd run from me. Nox had cursed me to be alone, which meant she would always run from me. I would always lose her.

On our journey to the Outer Realm, I'd taken her to the cave we'd lived in together so very long ago, then to the tree house where we'd spent countless hours in each other's arms, but nothing had worked, not the castle, or the bedroom she'd slept in when she first came here, not Egon, and not me, nothing had made her remember.

All she had to do was *fucking remember*, and the curse would be broken. Just remember she loved me, choose to be with me of her own free will, and we'd be together again and our daughter would finally be released from Nox's grip.

My hand lifted, curling around the door handle to her room. The demons had dragged that creature from my castle the day before, and I was still shaken. For a moment, I'd truly believed she was back, that she wanted me. I realized now that was an impossibility.

Walk away.

My feet wouldn't move, wouldn't carry me away to my own room, where I would lie back down and let myself waste away for eternity. I stared at the door. I shouldn't go in there; it would do no good to surround myself with her things, with the shadows of her existence here with me. But I couldn't stop myself. I turned the handle and shoved the door open.

Something darted across the room—something white. It flew toward me, trying to escape. I scooped it up, lifting it higher to get a good look at the rodent.

Nox had actually gone as far as creating a familiar for her creature? It squeaked and wriggled in my hand frantically, trying to get away.

I gritted my teeth, and tightened my grip, about to squeeze, about to tear it to pieces and have this be over with, but it stilled suddenly, staring at me, its little nose twitching. Bringing it closer, I stared into its tiny black eyes, reaching inside the soulless creature—

I froze. "How do you have a soul?"

He squeaked again.

"Hemlock?" I choked.

He squeaked again and started wriggling frantically. I loosened my grip, and he scurried up my arm and down my side, then ran to the pack sitting on the ground. He scrambled inside... and then something was tossed out. I picked it up. A finger—Zinnia's finger—and it was wrapped in enchanted gold. Fuck, embedded in the flesh. Only the gods had access to this; it would poison whoever it touched, conceal them—shroud their soul.

No.

I spun around, and my gaze landed on a small pot sitting on the dresser. A plant of some kind. I strode over to it. No, an herb covered with tiny purple flowers. *Vervain.* I remembered the way Zinnia had described it when I was with her in her garden. She'd brought it with her. She'd brought it here because she wanted to make this her home—because she'd chosen me.

A tiny wooden box sat beside the bed, I'd seen it before, after she'd left, but thought nothing of it. She'd touched it; I felt her. Picking it up now, I opened it. There was a piece of paper inside. I unfolded it.

If you're reading this, you're one of the lucky ones. Fate chose you to be his. I know it doesn't feel that way now, and I know you're scared, but take my advice—don't waste time being afraid. Instead, make the most of whatever time you have with him. Love him.

Zinnia, consort to Mors, the God of Death.

"Zinnia," I choked out. She'd come back for me, and I'd sent her away.

Scooping up Hemlock and Zinnia's things, I ran from the room and pounded down the stairs.

"My lord?" Egon said.

"I'm going after Zinnia."

"Thank the gods."

I rushed out of the castle and whistled loudly. A moment later, Raze and Zuri ran from the trees. Egon was already at my side with the girth straps and bridles we'd need, and Lyle rushed out with provisions and strapped them to Zuri while I swung up onto Raze. Lyle was shaking, and there were tears in his eyes.

Then I remembered what Zinnia said. "Look at me, Lyle."

He trembled harder but did as he was told. "You were approached by one of my reapers, given a message, weren't you?"

He nodded, and tears spilled down his cheeks.

Fuck. "Why didn't you tell me? Why would you keep it from me?"

"Nox," he choked out. "One of her demons threatened to hurt my mate and my son. He said he was always watching. He saw the reaper, he knew what the message was, and he said I wasn't to tell you, or he'd kill them."

Egon growled. "You betrayed his lordship? What were you thinking?"

"Where is the demon now?" I asked.

"H-he lives in the forest."

"I'll take care of the demon," Egon said, fury in his eyes.

"And you," I said to Lyle, "you will not leave the castle until I return, and you better pray that her ladyship is alive." Because if she wasn't, I would tear Limbo apart. I would destroy it, balance be damned. I would throw the universe into chaos until I found her again.

He spun and ran inside.

"I'll make sure he doesn't leave," Egon said and straightened his shoulders, fighting back his own emotions.

I gave the older demon a nod and nudged Raze. He took off, Zuri right behind him.

They had a day's head start. I wasn't stopping until I reached my consort.

Zinnia

We'd spent the night out in the forest. The demons had placed some kind of icons around our camp to prevent anything from attacking us. It'd worked, but the farther away from the castle we got, the creepier they seemed to get, and I realized it wasn't what skulked in the forest that I really needed to be worried about.

The four of them watched me now, and one of them actually wiped drool from the corner of his mouth while he did it.

"Why does Death send you to his mother?" he asked. "Why does his lordship want you banished from his realm?"

"We should get going," I said and winced as I stood. My feet were all cut up, and I was frozen to the bone. Moving meant they were distracted. Moving meant they had other things to focus on than me. I needed them to get me through this forest, and then I could figure out what to do next. I was a sitting duck on my own, and the pain from the fever still had me weakened and struggling. Add in the cold, and my magic was seriously weakened as well. I wasn't going to fight these assholes until we were close to the tree house Death had taken me to, if it was still there. I was counting on it still being there. I was pretty sure I knew where it was. I'd be able to rest up there, get warm, then work out my next step before I made my way back to the castle.

I would make Death listen to me.

The pain in my limbs intensified, and my core temperature changed so suddenly, my heart jumped in my chest. I wasn't shivering anymore; I was sweating. When the demons around me spoke, I could see their breath on the cold air. The last thing I should be was hot.

My fever was coming back. "We need to move," I said, because it was only a matter of time before my magic was completely gone and I was delirious, possibly unconscious, and utterly at the mercy of these demons, who didn't know the meaning of the word.

"We'll move when we're good and ready, female," another demon said.

"Your master told you to deliver me to Nox. Perhaps you should do as you're told," I said, trying to insert authority into my voice—not easy when I was standing in only a T-shirt with sweat dripping down my face.

"He's not here, though, is he? He won't give you a second thought now that he knows you're an imposter. He and his mother don't exactly talk, so how will he know if you make it to the Night Realm or not?"

"Death knows everything, and you'd be fools to cross him." I tried to keep the fear from my voice while I called on my weakened magic, letting it build and swirl inside me. They weren't going to leave me any other choice but to fight them here. *Shit.*

"Death has forgotten you exist. There's only one female he

wants, and you're not her. The moment we left with you, he forgot all about you." The demon stood and cracked his neck. "I'm not really in the mood to journey all the way to the Night Realm. What about you?" he asked his friend.

The drooling one stood, swiping his nose with the back of his hand. "Nah, I'd rather stay here."

Grunting their agreement, the others stood as well.

I lifted my hands and called on the anger burning in my gut. "You want to know what I am?" I said as flames appeared, dancing above my palms. "A witch. A witch who has killed more than her fair share of demons. Come any closer, and I will incinerate you." Maybe I could brazen this out, make them believe I was at full power and send them running.

A wave of pain washed through me, and I stumbled to the right. The drooler lunged, and I sent a bolt of fire at him, setting his feet on fire. *Shit.*

He stomped and cursed while his buddies laughed it up.

I was trying to set the asshole on fire, not just singe his shoe leather. I was screwed.

"Is that all you got, witch?" one of the demons said, chuckling.

"No, that was just a warning. Now back the fuck up, or I'll burn you to a crisp," I said through clenched teeth, fighting to stay conscious.

He grabbed the demon closest to him by the back of the shirt and threw him toward me.

With a cry, I fired my power at him. His shirt ignited, and he yanked it off and stomped it out. They all laughed again and rushed me. Screaming, I called on every bit of magic I had left and let it rush from me with force. The demons were knocked back, but they jumped back up. If I'd been at full power, I would have blown them yards way. If I'd been at full power, I would have set them all on fire and removed their heads one at a time.

As it was, I could barely stand.

They came running back, and I tried to fight. I swung and

kicked and bit and scratched, but there were four of them. They overpowered me, slamming me into the ground. The air was knocked from my lungs, and I fought for breath as they pinned me down.

One minute, one of the demons was looming over me, trying to shove his disgusting body between my legs; the next, the ground was shaking and the demon was flying through the air. The earth cracked and branches snapped. I rolled, pushing myself up so I was sitting. The demons were screaming, suspended five feet in the air, backs bowed, heads tilted up, arms and legs thrust back. Death sat on the back of Raze, his hand lifted and aimed at them, rage contorting his emaciated face.

He climbed off Raze and walked over to them. His hand was black and he reached up and grabbed the first demon by the throat. The demon screamed as blood poured from his mouth, brain matter slid from his ears, and then he disintegrated, turning to ash. The others screamed in terror as he gave them all the same treatment one by one.

Then, finally, when nothing but ash remained, his gaze slid to me.

I couldn't read his expression. I didn't know what he was thinking or feeling.

Unsteadily, I climbed to my feet.

Death started walking, his cloak opening, flowing behind him, and in only a pair of trousers, I saw just how much damage he'd done to himself. He was skin and bone. He didn't stop until he was standing in front of me. So incredibly tall, he towered over me. I tilted my head back. "Mors...."

He lifted his blackened hand and held it in front of my face. I tried to jerk back, but he grabbed me with the other one, holding me in place. Power flowed into me from his palm, and I felt it tug on something, something foreign, something that shouldn't be there. My mouth opened on a cry as it was drawn out, as Death manipulated it in midair, then flung it on the ground. A golden liquid. I watched as it ran together, forming a mass that hardened into solid gold.

"What was that?" I gasped, looking up at Death.

"Enchanted gold. It's poisonous unless you're a god," he said, staring into my eyes, searching.

"Mors?"

He flinched, then dropped to his knees. Trembling, he wrapped his thin body around me. "Forgive me," he choked out. "Forgive me, my love."

My heart pounded in my chest as I slid my hands under his hood and slipped it off. It dropped, and I tilted his head back, exposing his drawn face and the agony shining from his blue eyes. "You see me?" I asked.

"I see the past and the future. I see my heart in your eyes and my soul sitting in the palm of your hand." He stared deeper into my eyes. "I see you, my perfect, feisty, incredibly powerful witch, and I see your soul, a soul that is more familiar to me than the stars in the sky. I see the life we shared together, the loss, the heartache, and the joy. You have been mine since the dawn of creation. I see you, my love, and finally..." His throat worked, and a tear slid down his sunken-in cheek. "You see me too."

Tears welled in my eyes, and I leaned down, pressing my lips to his. They were cool, not hot like they usually were. "How can I help you?" I rasped.

"Kiss me again," he choked out. "The more I'm in your presence—the more you look at me like that, talk to me, touch me— the more I will be pulled from the shadows."

When I first came to Limbo, he'd stayed concealed because, under his cloak, he'd wasted away. That was why he'd finally been able to go without it, because I'd been with him long enough that he'd been restored. I lowered myself to the ground in front of him and pressed my body to his.

"Are you hurt, love? Did they hurt you?" he said in a pained voice.

I shook my head. "I'm not hurt."

His mouth slid down the side of my cheek, seeking my mouth, and I turned toward him, offering it to him. He kissed me again, deeper, more urgently. I shivered, and he surrounded us with his cloak, in his dark, rich, smooth scent. Warmth washed over me, the world around us disappearing. We were no longer in the forest; we were in the night sky, stars blinking above. Death lowered me to the ground, and it was like I was lying on the softest mattress.

"I need you," I whispered against his lips.

"You have me, my beautiful consort, for an eternity."

"Eternity?"

"Not even death can reach you now. You will forever be by my side."

Finally, I got my forever with the love of my life. "When they tore our daughter from my back and I fell to my death, I vowed to return to you." My hands trembled as I touched his face. "I'm sorry it's taken me so long."

He made an agonized sound. "No one will ever take you from me again."

I ran my hands up his back, my fingers sliding over his cool skin, feeling every rib, every bone on his skeletal form. I held him closer, running my hands over him, touching him, whispering to him, doing whatever I needed to heal him, to bring every part of him back to me.

I kissed him more fiercely. "I love you," I said as tears slid down my cheeks. "I've missed you." A sob left me. "I didn't know how much, but now I do, and it hurts so much that I've been parted from you for so long."

He groaned. "Time was stolen from us, but our love transcends all. What we share will survive even the end of times."

He slid my shirt up and off, his cold, trembling hands moving over my breasts. I reached between us and shoved down my underwear, kicking them aside, then quickly undid his pants and took him in my hand. His narrow hips moved between mine as I led him to me, wrapping my legs around his waist.

"My love," he groaned as he slid inside me, filling me.

We moved together under the shadows and stars of his cloak, and with every glide of my hand down his back, I felt him transform. My beautiful Death. He was perfect to me no matter how he looked. When he stared into my eyes, he saw the soul beneath, and I did as well. But when he thrust into me next, the sharpness of his bones under skin had been replaced by flesh and muscle. He wasn't cold anymore; he was so incredibly warm.

He moved faster, and I rocked with him, lifting my hips, crying out when he hit me so deep. He moaned my name against my ear, and I clung to him as he claimed me, as we were reunited again, just two more stars in the sky.

I came with a sob, shaking and clinging to him as he groaned, coming with me.

Panting, we lay in each other's arms.

He rose up, staring down at me, sliding the tip of his finger along my hairline and down the side of my face. "This was destined. You made it so," he said roughly, and then his hand went to his chest, right over the three stars tattooed there. "I've been waiting so long to have you back, my little witch, my Zinnia... and our Marigold."

He'd carried us on his chest, me and Marigold, a part of him, surrounded by him, and now I knew what the constant ache in mine was. It was them. "Let's go and get our daughter."

Chapter Thirty-Two

Zinnia

THE PASS over the Night Sea had been rough as hell. Thankfully, things had calmed, and I breathed in the ocean air as Mors gently held my wrist while he carefully worked the glove he'd made me over my hand. I'd slathered the wound with numbing balm and padded it. It was still raw and hurt like hell more often than not, but the balm was helping. I'd work on healing it properly when we got back to the castle. For now, I needed to be ready for whatever waited for us. I needed to be able to hold my knife and use my magic. I had to be ready to fight.

"How does that feel?" he asked.

I wriggled my remaining fingers and thumb, then pulled out my knife, gripping it. "Feels good."

"Your goal when we hit land is to stay alive at all costs, understand?" he said roughly. "You get yourself killed again, and I'll be seriously pissed off."

He said it lightly, but the depth of fear in his eyes told the

"

truth. "I'm not going to die." I didn't want to hurt him, but I had to ask, "What will happen to the others, the undead?"

"They rose when you came to Limbo. They felt it, your soul, and were drawn to it. It was part of Nox's twisted curse. They will finally be at peace now that it's broken." He shook his head, pain in his eyes. "I failed them," he choked out. "They suffered, and I didn't know how to help them."

Which was why Alga had screamed "give it back" at me. She'd wanted her soul back, her life back. "None of this is your fault. Nox is responsible for all of it."

"I was so desperate to have you back that when Somnus found your soul, I couldn't resist it. I was deep in the cloak, lost in the dark, and three times, I took innocent females from their worlds and brought them to the castle, only thinking of my own pain, desperate to get you and Marigold back... but it was never right, and because of that, none of them were able to draw me from the cloak. So I stayed in darkness. I ignored them, neglected them. I didn't protect them like I should have. None of those females were strong enough to house such a powerful soul—a soul they never should have been given—and they were driven to madness by it. They ended their own lives."

"So you stopped looking."

He nodded. "Somnus found your soul again and again, and I refused to bring them to the castle only to watch them suffer the same." Pain filled his eyes. "Feeling you so close but not being able to reach you, hurting innocent females over and over again... I couldn't do it anymore. Then Som found you, and something was... different. For the first time in centuries, I let him take me to you, and as soon as I felt your presence, as soon as I saw you, I knew you were the one, that this time was different. But you vanished completely, and I didn't know what the fuck to do. Then I sensed some kind of connection to you in your cousin and I thought you had somehow disguised yourself... or fuck, I don't know, but I was drawn to her soul because of you, desperate for you, and when you finally revealed yourself to me, it was the happiest and most terrifying day of my long existence." His gaze stayed steady on me. "So I need you to promise me that you won't leave me again."

"I promise. You have nothing to worry about. My magic is at full power. I feel strong, strong enough to keep both myself and our daughter alive if it comes to that."

Those magnetic blue eyes met mine, and there was no missing the concern. "It can't be easy navigating the female you once were with the one you are now. If this starts to feel like too much, if you're struggling to cope with all that's changed or you get scared and feel the urge to run from me—"

I pressed my hand to his chest. "I'm not going anywhere. Yes, I'm Aster, the female you loved, the female who gave birth to our daughter, and everything she was—her thoughts and feelings— they're mine now. But I'm also Zinnia, a powerful witch, a Thornheart, and Jasmine's big sister. I don't know how to explain it other than for the first time in my entire life, and that includes my very first life, I feel whole, as if a missing piece of me has been returned. Like this was how it was always meant to be." I slid my hand up to the side of his throat. "I'm stronger now in every way. Stronger than I've ever been. This life has made me stronger. Before, I was born fully grown. I was naïve, I trusted too easily, and didn't understand the world I'd been thrust into. Nox could never get in my head now like she did back then, and I will never, ever willingly leave you, understand?"

His fingers delved into my hair, and he pressed a kiss to my forehead. "Okay."

"Okay," I said.

He released a rough breath. "As strong as you are, you leave Nox to me. Don't engage with her. Don't let her goad you into an attack. She lost. The curse was broken when you came back to me of your own free will. She has to let us get Marigold and leave." He tucked my hair behind my ear and slid his thumb along my jaw.

"But she won't," I said. "That's what's supposed to happen when the curse is broken, but it won't be that easy."

"No, it won't. My mother hates to lose. She has nothing left, nothing to amuse herself but hurting others. She lost her humanity a long time ago, and to her, this is a game. Entertainment." He shook his head. "Until she realizes she's lost, and then things will get really dangerous."

I squared my shoulders. "I won't let her tear us apart again. I won't let her do it."

Shadows swirled around him. "Neither will I."

I turned, looking toward land. Nox's temple stood in the distance, glinting under the moon. "Do you think she knows we're coming?"

He wrapped his arms around me. "Count on it."

When we were close enough, we dropped anchor and climbed into the dinghy. Fog had moved in, making it impossible to see anything, and the oars creaked as we made our way to shore as silently as we could. Hemlock was in a hard case strapped around my waist that Death had made for him. It was like an iron bum bag with little bars on either end. He hadn't protested when I put him inside. It was a trade-off—the cage or he had to go back to the castle. My familiar knew my moods and understood that shit was about to go down. He hadn't made a peep since we left the ship.

I scanned the shore. "I can't see anything moving out there."

"Me either," he said, "but they're there."

Ice slid down my spine.

"Okay?" he asked, not missing a thing.

"I'm fine. A little fear's healthy."

"If we get separated—"

"If we get separated, we carry on with the plan. You distract Nox, and I'll get Marigold, and then we'll meet you back here," I said and closed my eyes for a moment, visualizing it, manifesting the moment we got on the boat and sailed away. All of us safe, together. Then I whispered a spell, calling on the mother for her help. It wasn't the first time I'd tried to call on her, to reach her, but I wasn't sure she heard me or that it was even possible here. Still, I tried because we needed all the help we could get.

The dinghy scraped against the beach, and I opened my eyes. Quickly and quietly, I stepped out, slipping on my pack and sliding my knife from its sheath.

Mors grabbed my other hand and draped us in his cloak so we blended with the shadows. We headed away from the path that led to Nox's temple. No point taking the most obvious route and making it easy for them.

We headed up the side of the cliff; it was steep and slippery, dangerous, but it not only avoided Nox, it was a more direct route. I looked up the cliff face to the sharp edge high above and shuddered.

"What is it?"

My mouth had gone dry, my palms sweaty. "Marigold was taken from me... just up there." My gaze locked on the edge. "That's where they pushed me over." I turned to him. "The vow I made that day, to come back, to get my revenge, to make them pay... that's why I kept coming back, no matter how hopeless it felt, because I wanted my family back, and to make Nox pay for what she did to us." A vow made in death is one of the strongest there was.

"I want her to pay as well. I've wanted to make her suffer, to torture her until she ended the curse, to watch her blood drain from her evil body until she was gray and lifeless, but the night needs its goddess despite how heartless and insane she is. Like Hell needs Lucifer, the Dream Realm needs Somnus, and Limbo needs Death." He stopped me, turning me to face him. He looked stricken. "I felt them take you from me that day. I felt it, and I heard your vow. That's why I searched, why Somnus searched. I knew you were coming back to me." His hand was trembling when he cupped the side of my face. "I knew balance between the realms had to be maintained, but still I fought Nox. We battled for so very long. Blood was spilled, but no one won—no one could win. There was only one way to win, and that was to break her curse. I had to walk away from our baby girl because Nox bound her to her realm. I was forced to take her to my temple and put her in stasis to keep her safe. There was no way I'd let Nox have our child. I refused to let her near Mari. It nearly fucking killed me, losing you both."

His thumb swiped my cheek. "But that incredible—fuck, *magnificent* rage you unleashed is what brought you back to me. Nox never counted on that. You're right. Without that vow, you wouldn't be standing in front of me now. I would have lost you and Marigold both forever. There would have been no hope." He shook his head. "But that rage, it's what could get you killed now. I can feel it, Zinnia. It's stronger now than it ever was before. I can't die. My soul can't be taken from me. But I won't risk you. You are immortal now, yes, but not if she takes your head. So until we get Marigold, until we're back at the castle, you are still vulnerable. Only then will you be able to walk by my side for eternity, finally safe. I can't lose you again. I can't wait century after century and hope you come back or that you'll remember us. I can't fucking do it, Zinnia. You are strong and powerful—that's why I know you can bring our daughter home—but where Nox is concerned, let it be my rage that fights for us, let it be me."

As much as I wanted to destroy Nox, he was right. I wasn't strong enough. My rage alone wasn't enough to defeat her. But taking the power back from her would cut her at the knees. "I won't do anything stupid. I won't risk our happily ever after."

He smiled, and my knees went weak; then he kissed me.

A branch snapped, and we froze. I smelled them before I saw them. Demons, all three of them in Nox's colors. "They can't be far ahead," one of them said, tilting his head back and scenting the air.

They couldn't see us under his cloak.

But then he stilled and sniffed again.

Death nodded. We needed to make a move, use our element of surprise. I nodded back. Ready. Death thrust his hand out through the cloak, grabbed a demon by the throat, then tore off his head, turning him to ash. I exploded from our cover, slashing the throat of one with my knife, then threw another back with a burst of magic. The demon grabbed his throat with a gurgled cry, and I dug my blade into his chest and dragged it down, spilling his innards, before wrenching his head back and hacking his head off while Death dispatched the other one.

My consort tilted his head to the side, listening, his blue eyes glowing. "There are more, but they're farther away. Let's go."

We scrambled up the steep track. Once we got to the top, we'd be more exposed, and we'd have to make a run for it. My thigh muscles burned, and my chest ached with a rage so intense, I had to grit my teeth. The darkness was oppressive when we reached the top; Nox was trying to make it as hard as possible for us, but it only helped our cover. If she thought the dark would stop us from finding our way back to Death and Somnus's temple, she was so wrong.

My child was close. I felt her. I felt that little girl's beating heart right beside mine. Nothing would stop me from getting to her.

As we neared the top, voices drifted down. Death dropped his cloak around us once more. There were at least four demons up there, waiting. They were scanning the cliff's edge. Death grabbed up a rock and tossed it halfway across the clearing. It cracked against a tree at the edge, and the demons spun that way, running toward the forest.

We quickly scrambled over the edge and ran toward the tree line on the opposite side of the wide clearing.

We burst into the trees, and Death wrapped an arm around me, holding us still so he could listen again.

"Let's go," he said when he heard nothing.

We walked for a while without any sign of demons, but they'd be at the temple waiting. If they didn't manage to stop us on the way, they'd be waiting for us there. The whole time we walked, I inwardly focused on building my power, on harnessing my magic. I slipped my finger through Hemy's cage, checking on him, and he gave my finger a little nibble to tell me he was okay.

The distant *hoot* of Nox's owl came from somewhere above us.

Death stilled, tilting his head to the side as the sound of movement filled the forest around us. He cursed. "Demons."

"We can fight."

"There's too many." He held my gaze. "When I throw off the cloak, I want you to make yourself as small as possible and stay under it, understand?"

"No, we can—"

"They'll want to take me to Nox. I'm going to let them. When it's clear, go and get Marigold."

"Mors, hang on—"

"We knew this might happen. I won't risk you getting hurt." The look in his eyes said it wasn't up for debate. "I know you can fight," he said, knowing I'd try to anyway, "but I'm counting on you to get to Mari, to get our daughter. Just do what I said, and the temple will let you in."

I nodded. I hated it, but he was right. "You can trust me," I said. "I won't leave without her."

"I know you won't," he said. "Just stay under the cloak and stick to the shadows."

"But the cloak, it doesn't know me."

"It knows you." He brushed the backs of his fingers down the side of my cheek. "It's made of the night sky, love. It remembers you, missed you, and it wants to protect you."

We'd talked about this happening. We had a plan. I knew what to do. "I'll meet you at the beach."

"I'll see you there," he said before he shoved off the cloak.

I dropped to the dark, overgrown forest floor, and the cloak settled over me like a dark shadow.

"Where is she?" one of the demons demanded.

Death roared like a wounded lion. "You killed her. You took her from me."

Good plan. They'd think I was dead. I wasn't sure how long they'd buy it, but it'd give me a head start.

The sound of a fist hitting flesh came next, of demons screaming and snarling. The sound of their fighting grew more distant as he led them away from me. Silence slowly surrounded me until all I could hear were my own shallow breaths, and still, I didn't move, not yet.

Finally, when I was sure I was alone, I slowly, so slowly, pushed back the hood and looked around.

Standing, I turned, taking in my surroundings—

A male leaned against a tree.

I snatched up my knife and lifted my hand, my magic swirling.

He held up his hands. "Don't shoot. I'm not one of them. Well, they think I am, but my loyalties lie elsewhere."

He had humanoid features and the pointed ears of the fae. "Who are you loyal to?"

"Somnus," he said, holding my gaze.

"I don't believe you, and I don't have time for you." My magic grew higher.

"He was right—you are powerful." He stepped away from the tree, his hands still up. "I'm not going to hurt you, Zinnia. I want to help you get Marigold back. That's the plan, right? Death distracts the demons while you go for your daughter. I can help you."

My alarm bells weren't ringing, but I wasn't going to just lower my hand and believe him. "Who are you to Somnus?"

"The love of his life. He and I met in my dreams a very long time ago." He took a step forward. "I'll help you, and you'll take me to him."

There was genuine pain in his eyes, but my daughter's life was at stake. "Prove it."

"He said you'd be a tough nut to crack." The male smiled. "He said you have an herb garden outside the kitchen, and he enjoyed your dinner together, that you're strong and threw him off-balance. You reprimanded him when he not so subtly tried to convince you that your place was with his brother. You asked him when he'd last done something for himself and told him that he wasn't practicing what he preached."

No one else could know that. How could they?

I took him in. He was a lithe male, with larger blades strapped to his thighs and smaller ones strapped to his chest. You didn't arm yourself like that unless you knew how to use them.

"Grab her," a demon yelled, charging through the forest toward us with three others right behind him.

I backed up, gripping my knife tighter.

The male claiming to be Somnus's lover moved so fast, he was nothing but a blur. Steel flashed as knives flew, taking all four demons down. The male strode forward, and pulling one of his larger knives free, he relieved them of their heads. He slid his knife back in its sheath, brushed the ash from his sleeves, and glanced back at me. "Believe me now?" he said with a cocky grin.

I wasn't sure I could trust him, but he could have let those demons take me. He was also obviously skilled with a blade and could have incapacitated me easily by now, but he hadn't. The sound of more demons coming echoed through the trees.

"If anything happens to me or our daughter, Death will hunt you down and torture you until you pray for death, understand?"

He inclined his head. "As he should." He glanced over his shoulder as the demons grew closer.

"What's your name?" I asked.

"Pascal. Shall we get the fuck out of here, then?"

I nodded, spun, and sprinted toward the temple.

Chapter Thirty-Three

Zinnia

IT WAS QUIET, way too freaking quiet.

"How are you getting in there?" Pascal asked.

There were several yards between us and the temple. So far, we hadn't seen any demons scouting the place, but they had to be there. I slid the vial from my pack. "Death's blood."

"Are you sure it'll work?"

"No, but Death said it would. It's our only hope right now." I still wasn't sure if this male could be trusted, though every instinct I had said he could be. I tucked the blood safely back in my pocket and slid out my small knife. I made a slice in my palm and then whispered a magic-boosting spell.

"What the hell are you doing?" Pascal asked, sounding horrified.

My power instantly shot higher. "I'm a witch. My coven uses blood to spell and for a power boost. If we get attacked, I'm going to need my magic at full strength."

His head jerked back. "You're a witch?"

"Yes, why?" I said, narrowing my eyes at him.

He shook his head, but a small smile teased his lips. "No reason."

I didn't have time for whatever that was. "You ready?"

He nodded. "If the demons come, leave them to me. Your priority is to get the door open. They can't follow us in, so you get the door open, and we're safe."

Pascal had a nice face. The guy was handsome, charming, and Somnus had mentioned him by name at our dinner. He'd said he'd trust him with his life, with Marigold's life. "If you are who you say you are, Somnus will be pretty pissed if I let you get hacked into tiny pieces by a bunch of demons."

He chuckled. "You think they'll get the chance? You've seen what I can do."

This was true; the male was skilled.

I turned back to the temple. Marigold was just inside. I almost had her in my arms. I just had to get through that door, and I'd have had my baby back. I'd have my daughter.

Lightning flashed in the distance, cracking through the sky right over Nox's tower.

"They're fighting," Pascal said. "Last time they fought like this, it felt as if the world were ending."

The first time Nox killed me, they'd battled. I hadn't asked Death how. "Death's powers are weakened here."

Pascal shrugged. "They don't seem weakened anymore."

He'd better be okay. "We need to make a move."

He nodded, jaw tightening with determination. "Just get to Marigold, and leave the rest to me."

"If you betray me, if you turn on me—"

"I won't."

"If you do, if my daughter gets hurt because of you, I will hex you. I'll make you wish you were dead," I said, meaning every word of it, the words coming from my gut, an oath wrapped in power.

He dipped his chin. "And I'd deserve it." He slipped one of his blades from his chest holder, sliced his palm with a wince, and grabbed mine. "I will never betray you, Zinnia, or anyone you love." Our blood mingled, binding his words in a blood oath.

Okay, I was definitely starting to like this guy. "Glad we're on the same page."

He grinned. "Me too. I sure as hell wouldn't want to be your enemy."

"Wise." Death's cloak was like a stormy sky gathering around me. It sensed the temple as well.

I dug one of Mags's potions from my pack and handed it to him. "Wait until the demons are close, then throw it. The glass needs to smash, but get the hell out of the way fast."

His brow lifted as he slid it in his pocket. "What does it do?"

"Melts faces off."

His eyes widened, and then he grinned again. "Excellent."

Taking the vial of Death's blood from my pocket, I poured some on my palm, and the shadows slid along my arm, around my hand. I turned to Pascal. He stood beside me, a wicked curved knife in each hand, twirling them slowly as he scanned the area around us. "Ready?"

He flashed another grin. "Let's do it."

"In three, we run."

He dipped his chin.

I held up three fingers. *Three. Two. One.*

We both exploded out of the trees and made a run for the temple door. The demons hiding, guarding the place, hadn't been expecting us. They'd obviously bought Death's lie. We made it to the door, and I copied the symbol Death had done when we first came here, drawing it in his blood while Pascal guarded my back.

Demons swarmed us, closing in.

The shadows gathered thicker around my hand, and the door rumbled; then slowly, shuddering, it finally swung open. "Come on!" I called to Pascal.

"I'm right behind you," he said, fending off the demons, using those knives, moving with a kind of grace, a dance, like nothing I'd ever seen before.

I ran in, my heart slamming against the back of my ribs. Every muscle in my body trembled, adrenaline pounding through me as I slowed and walked weak-kneed down the hall toward my daughter. She'd been in stasis so long, so very long. There was no way she could know who I was. When she went to sleep, I was someone else. My heart knew her, though, and my memories were so vivid. Her birth, the weight of her in my arms, the way she smelled, the sound of her voice—it was all there, so real, as if it were this body, this life, that had experienced all of it.

Taking a deep breath, I pressed my hand, still stained with Death's blood, to the door in front of me and whispered the words he'd given me to gain access.

The last barrier between me and my daughter. The door swung open and I walked into the room.

She lay there, so small, her eyes closed, her little cheeks pink, her hair spread out on the pillow. I'd chosen Death, and the curse was broken, but I had no idea how to wake her up.

Goddess, my heart ached looking at her. Her father was a god, and I really didn't know what made up the other half of Marigold. I'd been a star made mortal—but if this was what the fates had planned, then the female I was now was what she needed, and I was where I was supposed to be. I had to go with my gut. I was a witch, and that meant using magic, the blood of my coven, and my gifts from the mother.

It was all I had, and I prayed it was all I'd need.

Dropping my pack on the ground, I slid my spelling knife from my pocket and pricked the tip of my finger. There was blood still on her forehead, Death's, and I let instinct guide me, pressing mine to it. "Wake up, Marigold," I whispered. Power slid down my arm, but it was wrong, not strong enough. I needed something, something more. Panic filled me, my heart pounding faster. What the hell was I supposed to do? Death was counting on me; Marigold was counting on me.

I tried it again, but again nothing.

I sucked in a breath.

Magic.

I felt magic around me—not mine, but magic I recognized. So familiar it was as if I were home with my family, but no, it wasn't mine—it was Marigold's.

She was a witch, and somehow, her ancient bloodline was connected to mine.

I shook as I held Marigold's tiny hand. "Wake up, baby girl."

She didn't move.

Something caught the corner of my eye. My pack. Something had slipped out made of worn brown leather. The hat that Else had given me. Picking it up, I moved it around, studying it. My hands tingled. It was vibrating, a low hum of power running through it like it did when I was in Aunt Daisy's kitchen. Lifting it higher, I placed it on my head.

It was hard to describe, but there was this... this knowing as soon as I put it on. The hat was guiding me, so I closed my eyes and followed. The world seemed to expand, open up. The magic pulsing through it transcended space, reaching out. I felt home, I felt Roxburgh, and I felt my sister and cousins, my aunt.

I needed them. I needed their help.

I reached out.

Rose

My hairbrush slipped from my fingers, clattering to the counter. A vision filled my mind, fuzzy but growing clearer—no, it was more than that.

"Rose?"

Ronan walked in behind me, and I felt him move in close, his front to my back, his arms sliding around my waist when he realized what was happening, supporting me as I let whatever this was reach me.

The picture finally cleared.

Zinnia.

My legs went weak, and if it weren't for Ronan, I would have hit the floor. *Oh, thank you, goddess.* She'd been gone for a year, no word, no idea if she was okay—if she was even alive.

Zinny was in a room, a small child beside her. I gasped in a breath, because in that moment, I knew the things my cousin did, I knew everything, and I gasped from the enormity of it. The child was hers, and she needed us to help wake her up.

Zinnia was reaching for me, for us. She needed us.

I gasped out another breath, the vision dissipating until I was back in my bathroom with my mate. "I need to gather everyone at the cemetery."

Twenty minutes later, I stood in a circle in the middle of the cemetery with Mom, Jazzy, Mags, Iris, and Willow. We clasped hands, power flowing through us, building, twisting.

I closed my eyes and invited Zinnia back in.

"I can feel her," I called over the wind now whipping around us. "On the count of three, send her everything you've got."

"We got you, Zinny," Jazzy said, tears sliding down her face, her eyes bright with joy, with relief that her big sister was alive. "Let's give her all the power she needs."

"One, two... three." Power surged through me, and I cried out, holding on, holding it inside me. I wouldn't let go until the right moment.

I closed my eyes, and a vision of Zinnia standing over the child filled my mind once more. Her red hair flew around her face. "Now," she yelled, calling out to us.

"Now," I called back and released it, sending every bit of magic we had through the connection between us.

Zinnia

I pressed my finger to the blood on Marigold's forehead, mixing my blood with Death's as power surged through me and into my daughter's tiny body. She jolted, her mouth opening on a small cry.

I yanked my hand away, and the connection between Rose and me fell away. *Oh goddess.*

"Marigold?" I brushed her hair back from her face. She had to be okay. "Wake up for Mommy."

Her eyelids quivered.

"Marigold?"

She blinked once, twice—then stared up at me with wide blue eyes.

My heart felt as if it exploded in my chest, and my hand shook as I brushed her hair back again. "Hello, baby," I whispered.

She sat up, and her hair, long and soft and as black as night, fell around her shoulders.

We stared at each other, those wide blue eyes identical to Death's searching mine.

Then finally, she reached up, her hand touching my jaw, still blinking as if she was trying to clear her vision, and then she tilted her head to the side like Death often did and smiled. "Mommy."

She felt it. Oh goddess, she felt the connection between us the same way I did. A tear streaked down my cheek as I scooped her up and held her to me.

She wrapped her little arms around me tight. "I've been waiting for you," she said in her sweet little voice.

"I'm so sorry. I'm so sorry I took so long, baby." I stood, carrying her from the room as Pascal burst through the doors, covered in blood and ash. He was scratched and bruised, but thankfully, nothing life-threatening.

"Pascal!" Marigold cried, her eyes lighting up.

He dipped into a bow and grinned at her. "Lady Marigold, princess of Limbo, queen of all witches, as always, I am at your service."

She giggled.

"We spent a lot of time together in the Dream Realm, didn't we, Mari, with Uncle Somnus."

She nodded, then rested her head on my shoulder.

"Queen of witches?" I'd definitely felt her magic. I'd been right; the other half of Marigold's DNA was witch, and somehow, her bloodline was connected to my coven.

"You know your soul was once a star, yes?" Pascal said.

It seemed impossible, but it was true. "Yes."

"Well, you had sisters, and when you were pulled from the sky, they fell with you, but they were scattered to different realms. You and your sisters were the very first witches. No, they didn't practice magic like you do, but the magic was there."

"How do you know this?"

"I've been around a very long time, Zinnia, in the Night Realm and a part of Nox's court." His mouth twisted, hatred filling his eyes. "She truly is an evil bit—" His gaze slid to Marigold.

"But that doesn't explain how my and Mari's bloodlines are connected now."

"One of your sisters fell to earth, and your family descends from her. That's why it worked this time, why the fates chose you to break the curse and wake Marigold…" He smiled gently. "It was always going to be you. It had to be you."

My heart pounded in my chest. I'd been a witch in my first life as well. That's why my dying vow wasn't in vain—it was wrapped in magic.

"Love the hat, by the way," Pascal said, looking me over.

"So do I, you have no idea how much," I said and pressed my nose to Marigold's head, breathing her in.

"Can we go home now?" she said sleepily.

Pascal read my instant concern. "She'll be sleepy for a little while, until she gets used to being awake."

I tilted my head to the doors and raised a brow in question.

Pascal nodded. "I made good use of your potion."

I tucked Mari in close. "Yeah, baby, we can go home now."

The forest was quiet when we left. We had to hide a few times from demon scouts, but we made it back to the beach without too much trouble. When we reached the dinghy, three demons were waiting for us. Pascal's hands were a blur as he took them out easily with his knives.

Now we just had to wait for Death.

But the lightning and thunder hadn't slowed; it intensified, and I was getting seriously worried.

Death was a part of me now, and his rage was bigger than I'd ever felt it, and the more time that passed, the more lost to it he became. He was buried so deep in his hatred, in his need to hurt Nox for all she'd done to him and his brother and to me and Marigold, he couldn't get back out.

I knew if I didn't do something, he'd lose all sense of time and place; he'd be trapped in that rage and struggle to find a way back out.

I had to do something, and I had to do it now.

"You need to go with Uncle Pascal, okay, Marigold? Mommy will be back soon."

Pascal turned to me, alarm on his face. "What are you doing?"

I looked up at the sky as lightning forked through it, and a moment later, a boom rumbled so loud, the ground shook. "I need to go and get him."

"It's too dangerous," he said, shaking his head.

"I don't have a choice." I handed my daughter to Pascal, and he took her, holding her in a way that let me know he'd done it before in her dreams. "Take her to the ship and wait there. If I'm not back by morning, go without us."

Pascal jerked back. "What? No."

"The only thing that matters is keeping Marigold safe. If we're not back by morning, get her to the castle, to Somnus."

"Zinnia—"

"Promise me," I said.

"Hang on a minute—"

"*Promise me.*"

His jaw tightened. "I promise."

"Thank you. Now get in the boat." I kissed Marigold's soft cheek. "I'll see you soon."

"No," she whimpered. "No, Mommy."

"It's going to be okay." I opened the cage strapped to my waist, and Hemy scurried out. "This is Hemlock, my familiar. He's going to be sad without me. Can you look after him for me until I come back?"

Her eyes lit up as she gently stroked his back, nodding.

"Good girl. He likes lots of cuddles and treats. Do you think you can do that?"

She nodded again as I handed him to her. I kissed his furry little head. "Look after her," I said to him.

He squeaked that he would, a fierce look on his sweet face.

I gave Marigold one more kiss, then started back the way we'd come.

The kind of power Death and Nox had wasn't something I understood, but that went both ways. They didn't understand magic. We worked on different frequencies; we drew our powers from different places, in different ways. That was my advantage, my only advantage. Still, I needed more than magic; I needed the power of a goddess.

This time, when I called for the mother, I did it with the magic of my family behind it, amplifying it. This time, I had the hat. The mother was volatile, and she hated being disturbed. But our coven had worshipped her faithfully for generations. We gave and we gave, and it was time she gave back.

Breathing deep, I let my soul call out her name, her true name.

Terra.

Chapter Thirty-Four

Death

"YOU TOOK EVERYTHING FROM ME," Nox screamed. "I created you and your brother. He was *mine*, and you snatched him away." Lightning danced across her fingers before she fired it at me.

I fired back, knocking it away easily. She screamed again, her fury cracking thunder above us. Nox was far older, and because of that, she had always been stronger than me, but she'd only stayed that way from the gifts she'd received from other gods—gifts she'd received from selling Somnus to whoever wanted to use him and his powers.

She didn't have Somnus now, though, and she hadn't for a very long time, and the gifts she'd been given had all been used up. She was weaker than me now. Fury burned in her eyes but also fear, because she knew it as well. Her skin and hair were singed from my lightning, and she was panting hard from the exertion.

The last time I'd been able to break through the block she had on my power was after she'd murdered my consort and stolen my

309

child. Sheer rage had done it. She'd been stronger than she was now, and the curse had prevented me from taking Marigold from the Night Realm. I'd only been able to take her to my temple, so at least Nox couldn't get near her.

Breaking the curse had been a massive drain on my mother, and once I got to her temple, I'd easily shattered the bind she had on me. My powers throbbed through me now, wild and unstoppable.

She swiped away the sweat that poured down her face with shaking hands and held them out in front of her.

I almost had her, and I would not leave until her body lay charred and broken on the ground, until I'd heard her scream in agony and not just fury. I couldn't kill her, but I could break her. I could break her so badly that she would take centuries to recover.

My vision burned red as I slammed my staff on the ground and another bolt of lightning shot from the top of it. Dark laughter fell from me when it hit its mark, knocking her back. "You can't win. You can barely stand," I snarled and hit her with another bolt.

She flew back, slamming into a marble column, then hit the ground. I stalked toward her, towering over her, holding up my staff, that glowed bright with power.

A smirk curled her lips. "I murdered your consort once, and I will do it again. No matter how long it takes, I will take her from you."

"You won't get near her."

"You know I can." Triumph lit her eyes. "I already got to her once. I gave Fluke my blood to mark her so you couldn't find her." Her eyes flashed. "You love to punish me, you took you and your brother from me. So if I can't be with my children, then neither can you. Marigold is mine, and you will never have another." She smiled, and it was pure evil. "Fluke took her womb so if you ever did find her, she would never be able to give you another child. Now what do you say?"

"I say you are poison, and I will not stop until you are broken and alone," I snarled with all the hatred in my heart.

She actually frowned in confusion. "Did you not hear me? She is barren."

Nox truly thought I would reject Zinnia over her inability to bare children. "I already know the evil you did."

"Then why are we fighting? What use is she to you now?"

Unconditional love wasn't something she had ever understood. Loving someone with your whole heart and not asking for or wanting anything in return was foreign to her. "Use? I love her. She is all I need. All I will ever need."

"I don't believe you." Nox shook her head, eyes wild. "Give me Somnus, and you can have Marigold."

She didn't get it. She was also in no position to make any deals, and she knew it as well. She knew she was losing.

"I already have Marigold."

I spun around at the sound of Zinnia's voice. She strode toward us, dressed in all leather, my cloak flowing around her, her wild red hair spilling out from under a pointed leather hat. She was beautiful and fearless, and she shouldn't fucking be here. "Stay back," I growled.

She shook her head. "This needs to end, now." Her gaze sliced to my mother. "Sorry the whole 'I took your consort's womb' thing wasn't the gotcha moment you were hoping for. You thought it was the ace up your sleeve, that you'd tell him, and he'd leave me?" She shook her head. "You really don't understand how love works, huh?"

"You will not win," Nox shrieked, getting to her feet.

Zinnia's lips moved, but she wasn't talking; she was spelling under her breath, chanting as she strode closer. Ignoring Nox, her green eyes came to me. "It's time to go now, Mors," she said gently. "You need to stop fighting. Marigold's waiting for us."

I looked between her and Nox. "Not yet. Not until she's

bleeding and broken." I tried to pull her behind me, but power sparked off her, throwing my hand away.

Nox straightened, triumph on her face. "I created him, and now you can watch as I destroy him."

I stepped in front of Zinnia and lifted my staff—

She touched my arm and shook her head as she moved back around me. "No, my child," she said in a voice that wasn't her own, not anymore. Her eyes, now black, glowed with otherworldly power—with godly power. "Your mother and I have a few things to discuss."

Nox flinched, stumbling back in shock. "Terra?"

Terra? Mother Nature, the Great Goddess, the creatress of all life, or the mother, as the witches who worshipped her called her. I felt her now, dark and light magic, her incredible power flowing through Zinnia's body.

"You created him, did you?" Terra said.

Nox flinched.

"Who is the creatress of all life, Nox?" She shook her head. "You played but a small part in the creation of your sons, and you know it. Without me helping you, they would not exist, and neither would Aster and her sisters. You begged me for help, and what did you do after I gave you what you wanted? You abused them. You used and bartered with my creations to increase your own power, and then you hid here from me in the Night Realm." She laughed. "You cannot hide anymore. Zinnia Thornheart has made it possible for me to reach you anytime I like. Make no mistake, you may not harm my creations, and now Zinnia has been possessed by a goddess, you cannot harm her either."

Nox shrieked. "You do not come to my realm and tell me what I can and cannot do—"

Zinnia's hands flew up, the power of a goddess flowing from her, and she slammed Nox back down before she lifted her off the ground and held her against the column behind her. "I can and I have. I am older than you, stronger than you, and you will do as I say, or I will tear you apart piece by piece." Terra strode up to her. "Do we understand each other?"

She shook, fighting it, but Terra was right—her power was far stronger. "Fine," Nox bit out. "Now release me and leave my realm. Leave!" she shrieked.

Zinnia's head tilted back, her body jolting, and I felt the goddess leave her. Zinnia stepped back as Nox hit the ground. I grabbed my consort around the waist and pulled her back. Zinnia shook in my arms but not from fear, from fury.

"You fuck with me or my consort, you come near Marigold or Somnus or Pascal..." Her hands curled into fists. "If you try and hurt any of my family again, I will call Terra back. I will let her have me, and she will tear you apart, because she wants to. I felt it, her hatred of you. All she needs is a reason, and if I give her one, she will destroy you. She's already proven she can create gods. She can replace you."

Nox stared at her, full of fury that she couldn't unleash.

Zinnia dismissed her, then turned to me, taking my hand. "Our daughter is waiting for us."

I didn't dare fight her on it; I didn't want to. No, I let my exquisite, strong, beautiful, fierce consort lead me from Nox's temple.

"Thank you for what you did for Zinnia and for protecting my daughter," I said to Pascal. "Anything you need or want, please ask. I owe you a debt, and I won't ever forget it."

The male turned from the ocean to me. "You owe me nothing. It was my honor, my lord. I've spent a lot of time with Marigold in the Dream Realm." He smiled. "I'm extremely fond of her and your brother."

"He'll be awake when we return," I said.

Pascal's chest expanded on a sharp indrawn breath. "I know."

"Will this be the first time you've seen each other out of the dreaming?"

"Yes."

I could feel how much he cared for Som, and I could feel the goodness inside him. "All will be well," I said, not sure how to reassure him. But I knew my brother. If he'd allowed Pascal around Marigold, he trusted and cared for him.

Leaving Pascal to contemplate his reunion with Somnus, I headed below to the cabin. When I opened the door and slipped inside, I stilled. Zinnia lay on her side, Marigold tucked in close. Her little arm was wrapped around her mother's neck, her fingers in Zinnia's hair. Hemy was curled up behind Mari, tucked in close. Pulling off my shirt, I climbed on the bed behind my consort and wrapped my arms around all of them.

"Hey," Zinnia said softly.

"Did I wake you?"

"No, I couldn't sleep." I heard her swallow. "All my life, I've had this feeling that something was missing, that there was this hole in my chest, that I'd been born with a fundamental part of me missing. I don't feel that way anymore."

I lifted up and looked down at her. "You don't?"

A tear slid down her cheek, and she shook her head. "How could I when I have everything I've ever wanted right here in this bed? The male I love more than life itself, who owns my soul, and a daughter who is my entire heart."

"And you own me, heart and soul, my precious consort." I leaned in and pressed a soft kiss to her lips. "Thank you, Zinnia, for choosing me, for pulling me from the shadows and loving me. Now, we have an eternity to look forward to, and I promise you that nothing will ever part us again." I wrapped them both tighter in my arms, holding them safe.

"Nothing," she said softly.

Epilogue

Zinnia

Four years later

MARIGOLD SKIPPED AROUND THE HEADSTONES, Hemlock on her shoulder, Violet's hand gripped in hers, while the rest of her cousins followed in a disorderly line. "Keep up, Kai," she called.

Rose and Ronan's baby, Kai, had his father's dark hair and his mother's blue eyes. He was holding Torin's hand, and they were babbling away to each other like they were speaking their own language. Torin was big for his age, but according to Warrick, all hellhounds were. They were both fourteen months old, and Rose and Willow had given birth only two weeks apart.

Mari loved spending time with her cousins; she also loved that she was the oldest and could be in charge. Her black hair was in a long braid down her back, swishing from side to side as she glanced back and rolled her eyes at Tate and Raff, Iris and Draven's twins. Tate had gone wolf, and Raff was hanging on to his tail, cracking up every time he tugged on it and made his brother yelp, while

Iris's familiar, Nia, bounded along beside them, barking with excitement.

"Not long now, and there'll be two more mini monsters in the coven," I said to Jaz and Mags, who were gathering rosemary beside me, Iris, Rose, and Wills, who were currently filling our jars with cemetery dirt.

Jazzy chuckled, butterflies dancing around her head as she snipped off another sprig of rosemary. "Thank the goddess we have Mari. We won't have to lift a finger."

Mags straightened with a groan. "I'm thinking sooner rather than later for me. This little girl wants to come early. I'm sure of it."

They were due three months apart, both having girls, but Mags was positive her baby was going to make an appearance earlier than she should.

"It'll be fine," Wills said. "Mom's brewing you an elixir that'll keep that little girl where she needs to be for a little while longer."

"It works," Rose said, sitting on the picnic blanket under the oak tree. "I used it for Kai."

Iris poured a glass of lemonade. "Anyone want one?"

"None for me. We need to get going," I said and shielded my eyes, looking over at my daughter. "Time to go, Mari."

She hugged her cousins and ran over to the picnic blanket. There wasn't much left over from lunch, but Marigold had put a cupcake aside for her father. She carefully wrapped it in a napkin and cradled it gently in her hands, then turned to me. "All ready."

"Hang on a minute. I think you're forgetting something," Mags said.

Marigold giggled, then made the rounds, hugging everyone else and laughing harder when they gave her big smacking kisses on her cheeks.

Jazzy gave me a hug. "You'll be here for the ceremony next week?"

"I wouldn't miss it." It was something we did every year to honor the loved ones we'd lost. All our coven would gather here.

After another round of goodbyes, Mari and I headed off.

Twenty minutes later, we were pulling up at the entrance to Oldwood Forest. I parked the car and Mari watched me closely as I did the spell to conceal it until we needed it again. She was already doing simple spells at seven. She was a natural. My baby would be a powerful witch one day. I felt the magic inside her growing every day.

I took her hand, and we walked into the forest. Night was falling, and moonlight filtered through the trees. Like her father, Marigold loved the dark.

"When do you think my familiar will come, Mommy?" she asked as we walked.

"I wish I could give you an answer, baby, but a familiar finds you when the time is right and not before."

Her eyes lit up. "What do you think they'll be?"

"I don't know, but whatever they are, they'll be perfect for you." Hemy squeaked his agreement from my shoulder.

We were free to move between Limbo and Roxburgh now. Though Death still worried while we were gone, he didn't try to stop us. We had an eternity ahead of us, the three of us, and he'd finally allowed himself to believe it.

Marigold ran across the clearing when we reached it, and I laughed and ran after her. She jumped up and down with excitement while I made a small slice in my hand to open the gateway.

The stones rumbled, rolling and reshaping, and a moment later, it was open.

We stepped through onto the skull path, and the gate closed behind us.

"Daddy!" Mari cried and took off.

I looked up as Mors rounded the corner, tall and broad and utterly gorgeous. He grinned wide when he saw us, scooping his daughter up as soon as she reached him.

"Did you have fun with your cousins?" he asked.

"We played in the cemetery, and had a picnic, and I brought you a cupcake." She thrust it out, and he took it.

He leaned in and pressed a kiss to my lips. "I'm glad you're back."

I grinned up at him. "Me too."

"Tell me, Daddy!" Marigold said.

He looked down at her. "Again?"

"Yes, again," she said excitedly.

"Your wish is my command, princess," he said in his beautiful voice.

She tilted her head back in anticipation, looking at the night sky, a sky Death had created, replicated, when he built this realm from the ground up. "Which one was Mommy?"

"See the small cluster of stars above us? They were your mommy and her sisters."

"And they landed in different realms when Mommy came to Earth," Mari said, jumping ahead because she'd heard this more times than I could count.

"That's right," he said. "See the two bright stars to the left—"

"That was you and Uncle Somnus."

"Right, again, and the cute little star twinkling closest to me, the brightest one in the cluster, that's your mommy."

She blinked up at the sky. "And you loved her even then."

"I did," he said in a low, rough voice.

She sighed. "I love that story."

Yes, she did. She had her father point out those stars almost every night. He curled his arm around my shoulders and pulled me in close. "I missed you both."

We'd only been gone half the day, but we didn't like being away from each other for very long. I wrapped my arm around his waist. "We missed you too."

We rounded the bend, and the castle came into view. Lyle's son, Ryker, stood on the steps waiting, a son I had no idea existed until we brought Mari home. Death's castle hadn't exactly been a very welcoming place, and neither had Death before Marigold and I moved in and changed things. Now, Lyle's mate helped around the castle as well, and Ryker was there all the time. He and Mari had fast become best friends. As soon as Mari saw him, she called his name. Death put her down, and she took off to play, Hemlock bounding after her.

"Follow me," my consort said and led us away from the castle. "Somnus and Pascal are watching Mari tonight."

I looked at him. "Oh?"

He waved his hand, and a path appeared in front of us. "Did you think I'd forget our anniversary?"

The anniversary of the curse being broken, of us finally being together the way we were always meant to be. As we walked, Death's cloak swirled around him, and my clothes evaporated, replaced by a black dress made of night that looked like fine cobwebs. It was no longer torn and old, like it had been in Nox's temple. It had been restored to how it once was when the mother created it and me, like Death's cloak had been for him. A clearing opened up ahead of us. It glowed with soft lighting from the stars, from the moon. A table was to one side, and when he waved his hand, food, candles, and wine appeared. Then he clicked his fingers, and the sound of his piano playing echoed around us.

I gazed up at him. "This is... it's beautiful."

He smiled, his cloak swirling, his eyes glowing blue and utterly gorgeous. "Anything for my perfect consort, my wife, my precious guiding star."

Then we swayed to the music, dressed in nothing but the night sky and wrapped in each other's arms.

Also by Sherilee Gray

Hell On Wheels:

Bad Demon

Blood Moon Brides:

Blood Moon Bound

The Thornheart Trials:

A Curse in Darkness

A Vow of Ruin

A Trial by Blood

An Oath at Midnight

A Promise of Ashes

A Bond in Flames

Knights of Hell:

Knight's Seduction

Knight's Redemption

Knight's Salvation

Demon's Temptation

Knight's Dominion

Knight's Absolution

Knight's Retribution

Rocktown Ink:

Beg For You

Sin For You

Meant For you

Bad For You

All For You

Just for You

The Smith Brothers:

Mountain Man

Wild Man

Solitary Man

Lawless Kings:

Shattered King

Broken Rebel

Beautiful Killer

Ruthless Protector

Glorious Sinner

Merciless King

Boosted Hearts:

Swerve

Spin

Slide

Spark

Axle Alley Vipers:

Crashed

Revved

Wrecked

Black Hills Pack:

Lone Wolf's Captive

A Wolf's Deception

Stand Alone Novels:

Breaking Him

While You Sleep

Sherilee Gray is a kiwi girl and lives in beautiful New Zealand with her husband and their two children. When she isn't writing sexy contemporary or paranormal romance, searching for her next alpha hero on Pinterest, or fueling her voracious book addiction, she can be found dreaming of far off places with a mug of tea in one hand and a bar of chocolate in the other.